Justice for Baby B

Justice for Baby B

MerriLea Kyllo

gatekeeper press

Columbus, Ohio

This book is a work of fiction. The names, characters and events in this book are the products of the author's imagination or are used fictitiously. Any similarity to real persons living or dead is coincidental and not intended by the author.

Justice for Baby B

Published by Gatekeeper Press
2167 Stringtown Rd, Suite 109
Columbus, OH 43123-2989
www.GatekeeperPress.com

The cover design, interior formatting, typesetting, and editorial work for this book are entirely the product of the author. Gatekeeper Press did not participate in and is not responsible for any aspect of these elements.

ISBN (paperback): 9781642379839
eISBN: 9781642379846

Library of Congress Control Number: 2020941671

Writing a book can be daunting and frightening as you are opening up your creative ideas to scrutiny and criticism. I have several people to thank for their support while I created this project.

To my loving husband, Barry, and daughters, Rachel and Karlea, your love and support during my journey helped bring my dream into reality. You will always be my treasures!

Julie Olson (whose love for my story did not prevent her from doing what she does best – edit and critique!) I will forever be grateful!

I would like to thank many friends who took the time to listen, read, and give feedback to me during this journey. A special thank you to my book club Sheila Jilek, Kathy Kiehkaefer, Kelli Machemehl, LuAnn Weisenburger, Jackie Ziermann, Kim Radtke, and Lisa Gustafson for listening to the first chapter in Kathy's kitchen and giving me unconditional support and encouragement! Kristi Schmidt your unrelenting optimism kept me going when I lost the faith (your upbeat and awesome messages were read many times)!

Finally, to my kids from other countries: Julia, Tina, Anna, Tomas, Lucas, and Jacob (as well as my nephew, Brad). You taught me how to love children I did not carry inside myself. Tomas (my Joe), I will always appreciate your love and unconditional support.

CHAPTER 1

Carolyn jumped, startled by the lightning flashes from the storm, the burst of light illuminating photos lining the walls of her treasured family home. She gently brushed her finger across a slightly askew photo of a smiling Joe with his front tooth missing, straightening the memento taken at a Mother's Day school celebration with a loving finger. He was so proud handing her the pansy he planted himself – a gift for her. The memory brought a knot to her stomach and a lone tear tracing a path down her cheek. Every flashing light from the storm illuminating another precious memory, as if reminding her how much she could lose. Disturbing dreams came more frequently, and with more intensity. The cries of babies haunting her in the night. She was grateful to the storm for waking her, allowing her to change her damp nightgown which now lay in a heap next to her bed.

A scratching sound came from near the kitchen drawing Carolyn from her thoughts. Quietly she crept through the house knowing just which floorboards to avoid. The light snoring drifting down from upstairs reassured her that Tom, her husband, was still sleeping peacefully. The scraping sound came again louder as she drew closer. Flicking on the light, she saw the culprit, a tree limb scraping the window next to the table. That can wait until morning she quickly decided as she flicked the light back off to go upstairs.

In the shadowy darkness she saw the light from under the door of the basement. She must have left it on when she brought the canned pumpkin upstairs yesterday. The moment appeared to freeze and without thinking, she felt the cold metal of the door knob turning in her hand. The knot in her stomach grew and a taste of bile burned in her mouth. She was unable to resist, not after the dream - it was too real, too fresh. Every wooden step groaned with her weight. Bare bulbs illuminated the forgotten treasures of her family's life. Absentmindedly, her finger grazed a kindergarten noodle necklace, one of Cassie's creations. A small Mother's Day flower pot with "I love you Mom" scrawled in Joe's first-grade handwriting, now sat empty on a shelf. She picked it up and clutched it to her chest.

Moving closer, she set the pot down amongst old coats, on a box scrawled in Tom's writing, "Christmas ornaments," next to the worn rocker. As she sat in the chair, her lap felt empty after years of rocking babies, she slowly reached her arm back behind a suitcase. Her fingers found the familiar shape. She gave a gentle tug and the tattered box fell into her arms. The familiar musty smell from the box wafted toward her as she closed her eyes for a moment, her fingers running along the rectangular edges feeling the rough circle around the hole where the oxygen tubing once blew air. The "baby B" smudge barely legible on top. "B" stood for boy, to remind them what to write on the death certificate without having to see the small lifeless body. Slowly she lifted the lid to find the still-familiar blue and pink blankets that she had used to wipe off his newborn blood and vernix. The blankets now looked more like rags, but still held the smudges from his newborn body. Raising the blankets to her nose she inhaled their musty smell, triggering memories of that fateful day, this time without the sleep to cloud her memory.

1969…. Joe's birth…the sterile delivery room….the bright lights….the tape….the box.

"Get the box." Dr. Jefferson's quiet command was said with such authority it prompted immediate action.

I looked down at the baby still covered with a mix of newborn vernix and his mother's blood. Though his breathing was labored the doctor didn't reach for the suction bulb or baby blankets to dry him off. There was no impatient resuscitation, just a foreboding calm I didn't understand. This was only my fifth time filling in as a float nurse during a delivery. I felt much more at home in the Emergency Room or Intensive Care Department. Seeing adults struggling for survival was much easier to watch and understand. My son had been stillborn less than a year ago after a normal pregnancy. I had avoided this area of nursing as much as possible ever since, as the ache was still real and the void still fresh.

I raced out of the room and grabbed the incubator outside the door and started to wheel it in, certain the box he requested was the life-saving box that struggling infants were put in to warm them up and allow oxygen to flow. As I wheeled it into the delivery room the doctor's head snapped up and he growled, "Not that. The box!"

His eyes turned to meet the eyes of the older, seasoned nurse, Eve, who was in her thirties and quite beautiful. She hesitated, then left the room, her crisp white shoes noiseless on the white tile floor. I followed, wheeling the incubator back out, unsure as to what I had done wrong.

I watched Eve go down the hall to the equipment supply closet, which was always in perfect order. Eve had never married, and there was speculation that she was having an affair with one of the doctors. Eve had worked OB for at least seven years and knew everything. I watched as she reached above the diapers and bottles of new formula to a shelf that held three or four boxes slightly bigger than a shoebox. Eve stood on her toes, grabbed one, and quickly turned back toward the delivery room. I looked at her quizzically as she walked past me, unable to meet my gaze. I followed not saying a word, but something inside squeezed my stomach.

This was not protocol. This was not taught in nursing school.

Eve handed the box to Dr. Jefferson. He placed a piece of medical tape over the baby's mouth. I felt overwhelming suffocation as he picked up the baby boy and placed it in the box. As he did so I saw the bulge on the baby's lower back. The baby had been born with spina bifida, a birth defect which meant that this child would, in all probability, never walk.

The mother was under anesthesia and could not see what was happening to her son.

"What are you doing?" I asked breathless and horrified.

Dr. Jefferson glanced up briefly from his task, irked that a nurse would question his actions. "I am saving this mother a lifetime of grief having to care for a child who can never be normal, never walk, in constant need of care. It is better she think the child never made it through delivery."

I looked to Eve. She had more years of experience and seniority, surely she would speak out to save this innocent. Eve's eyes were on the infant. Was it pain I read in her eyes? But yet she remained silent.

This couldn't be happening. The pain of losing my son was still raw and now a baby was being murdered before my eyes.

Dr. Jefferson handed the box with the now silent, but still breathing, infant to Eve. "You know what to do." His eyes met hers briefly, almost daring her to disobey.

"Yes sir." she whispered, lowering her eyes. I could tell she didn't agree with what she had been told to do but we'd been taught not to question a doctor. In our world doctors were gods.

I had always thought of nurses as angels of mercy in our white starched uniforms and nursing hats. But this . . . this is an angel of death.

I tried to follow Eve out of the room but Dr. Jefferson snapped, "You, Stay." It was not a request. "Take vitals while I repair the episiotomy."

Securing the blood pressure cuff with shaking hands, I stole a glance at the mother's face. She looked peaceful, fully expecting to wake up to the cries of her new child. But she would hear no cries. Dr. Jefferson had silenced them.

It was common to anesthetize mothers so they didn't feel the pain, especially when there was a forceps delivery. I had also been under anesthesia when my son was born, and I remembered the inconsolable pain of being told he died at birth. That memory haunted me. My eyes burned but I would not cry here, not in front of this doctor.

The mother was soon stable and we wheeled her out of the hospital's one delivery room and into her regular hospital room. The post-partum nurses would take over. We slid her over onto the crisply sheeted bed as she woke up. Her first words were "Where's my baby? Did I have a boy?" Margaret had said when being admitted that her husband desperately wanted a son. My heart ached to tell her that yes, she had her son.

The nurses looked up at me and I back at them. No one wanted to give her the news. I didn't know what to say. "Your baby is being murdered by your doctor," is what my head screamed, but I couldn't say it. Nurses were not allowed to give medical information to the patient and certainly not relay wrongdoing by a doctor. All I could muster was, "Margaret, your doctor will be in soon. Rest."

I ran out of the room. I had to find Eve.

Eve was just shutting the closet door.

"What did you do with the box?" My voice was low and much calmer then I felt.

"In the closet." Her eyes and the slight tilt of her head indicated the equipment closet where she had retrieved the awful box earlier. "We keep it here until the doctor returns to pronounce then we take the body to the morgue."

Her monotone voice betrayed no emotion, although I saw a slight tremor in her hand as she smoothed her hair under her white nurses' cap.

"Then this has happened before?" I dreaded the answer.

"Yes." Her eyes darting around, avoiding my shocked look of horror.

"When? How many?" My voice pitch higher as my mouth dried up. I grabbed her arm, my nails digging desperately into her skin.

I needed to know.

"Many," Eve answered, looking at my hand, my knuckles turning white. She slowly continued, choosing her words very carefully, "If Dr. Jefferson delivers a baby with a defect he feels he is sparing the parents years of pain by telling them the baby was a stillbirth."

The world lurched upside down. I felt for the wall to steady myself, my hands trembling. Anger erupted in me, "Who is he to play God??" I thought about my own son. The lights of the hallway dimmed and my legs began to give way, but I refused to give in to the nausea and weakness.

"He is the doctor," she answered quietly. She removed my hand gently from her arm and walked away soundlessly.

Before I realized it, I was inside the supply closet. The box rested innocently beside the incubator; one box for saving a life, the other for taking it.

I quietly lifted the lid. The baby's chest retracted with every breath. He was fighting to live. I quickly peeled off the tape and reached for a blanket from within the incubator and started to wipe off the baby, my nursing instincts taking over.

He was beautiful. His tiny fingers and toes fanned out as if reaching towards me, beckoning me to pick him up. I felt the hot streaks down my face as the tears I had held back finally fell on this tiny baby that wanted to live even though he had been deemed unworthy by his mother's doctor. I leaned over and grabbed oxygen tubing already in place on the tank, always ready for emergencies. I turned the tank on and held the tubing close to his nose. I took a suction bulb from the supplies on the incubator, and started to withdraw the mucous that made it hard for him to breathe. His color pinkened up immediately and he stopped retracting with every breath. I wrapped him up in a blue blanket and held him in my arms with the oxygen tube next to his nose. His slight weight seemed to fit perfectly in the crook of my arm. I stared at the beautiful features of his face. His eyes opened to meet my gaze, mesmerizing me.

In that moment I knew I was meant to save him.

Minutes ticked by and with each passing moment this baby became mine. I traced his nose and cheeks with my finger as all new mothers do. He was a beautiful baby with a full shock of slightly curly black hair. He felt my touch and immediately turned his head towards my hand, rooting for food. We were connected somehow, a bond that neither one of us had chosen but could not deny.

The door opened suddenly and in the burst of light I saw Eve's outline in the doorway. I held my breath. Our eyes met and I knew she understood my intentions. She didn't say a word but turned away quickly, quietly the door closed. I waited for several minutes, my heart beating so hard I could feel it through my chest, but no one came.

While cutting a hole in the box to feed the oxygen tubing inside, the jagged edges nicked my finger. My blood mixed with the blood on the blankets. I wrapped him in a warm blanket and placed him back in the death box. It took great willpower to put the top back on the box but I could not bring myself to replace the tape across his mouth.

Quietly I eased myself out of the closet with supplies under my uniform top for my hurried plan. Leaving them in the stairwell, I went back to the nurses' station. I told my co-workers I was hungry, as it was 2pm and I had missed lunch. I headed for the hospital cafeteria willing myself to walk at a normal pace even though I felt the urgency in every fiber of my body. As soon as I made the stairwell I grabbed the supplies and ran down the two flights and headed down the basement hallway to the morgue. It was a room I hated. It felt like death but today it might give my baby life.

I cracked open the door to the morgue; it was dark and empty. Good. I went to the drawers holding corpses and saw there was a box much like the box that held a live baby upstairs. I didn't have time to wonder at the nature of this baby's death, whether it was a natural death or death by doctor. I carefully put this baby in the box I had placed in the stairwell prior to going to the nurses' station and put packing material in the other box, sealing it with tape. I was working without thinking, almost in a state of shock. I was determined to save my baby.

Today he would not die.

I put the box on a cart and covered it with a sheet as if I was carrying supplies to the closet. Riding up in the elevator I felt my heart beating what seemed like a thousand times a minute. Blood rushed to my brain. What was I doing? I couldn't answer; I kept hearing a whisper: "Save this baby." It was as if my actions were being dictated by someone else.

When I came off of the elevator, I saw Dr. Jefferson leave Margaret's room with Eve at his side. Sobs could be heard from inside the room. "Please don't let him go to the closet, not yet," I prayed. Down the hall another nurse beckoned urgently and they headed that way. Relief flooded my body as I reached the closet and slid inside. I exhaled as the door closed, realizing I had held my breath since the elevator doors opened to the floor.

I willed myself to calm down, even though every nerve ending in my body seemed to be on high alert. I heard noises from within the box and smiled. He was ok. I tugged off the lid, grabbed a pack of Similac infant formula from another shelf, and put a nipple on a pre-made bottle. He'd soiled the blanket so I diapered him, realizing I would need some things to tide us over. I stuck a couple of diapers and another bottle in the box.

He started to cry so I placed one of my fingers in his mouth to quiet him. Instinctively he started to suck, hard. I picked him up, snuggling him close while I nudged the nipple of the bottle into his mouth. At first he didn't seem to care for it, but I coaxed him to take it and finally he did. After about an ounce he fell asleep in my arms.

I am taking you home, I decided. I placed the box I had brought up from the morgue in place of my son's.

The box from the morgue should buy us some time. With luck they would not realize what I had done for several days, and by then they would have to remain silent or their misdeeds would also come to light.

Because really, what had I done? I had saved a baby that had been declared dead by a doctor. If they accused me of kidnapping, they would have to answer why he had signed a death certificate on a live baby. Legally, I had kidnapped a corpse.

It was easy to leave the hospital. No extra nurses loitered in the hallway. I punched out, changed out of my scrubs, wrapped the box in an extra lab coat, and walked out looking straight ahead. Only guilty people looked from side to side.

I had saved my son! But no one must ever know…not Tom… Not Anyone……

1998

Tom's voice at the top of the stairs startled her awake. "Carolyn, are you down here?"

She quickly sat up, shaking off the vestiges of memory-filled sleep. The box lay open in her lap, the blankets scrunched up beside her. "Yes, I'll be right up." Carolyn called, trying to keep her voice level. "Please start the coffee." She threw the blankets back in the box and shoved it on top of the Christmas decorations sitting on the floor next to her feet. She would have to put it back in its hiding place later. Glancing around the room for an excuse to explain her early morning basement escapade, she spotted the turkey roaster from a nearby shelf and grabbed it on her way up the stairs.

"Climbing these stairs is getting harder and harder," she joked as she set the roaster on the table.

"What were you doing down there so early?" Tom asked as he handed her a hot cup of coffee and kissed her forehead before sitting down at the kitchen table. Smiling, she took her usual chair next to his.

"I was just looking for the turkey roaster. I can't believe Thanksgiving is next week. But I got caught up looking at the kids' homemade projects and lost track of time." She answered with just a hint of a waiver in her voice, her eyes darting to the roaster.

"It's going to be great to have all the kids home!" Tom said glancing at the morning paper. Joe lived 20 minutes away and made a point to come to dinner at least once a week, because he claimed nobody cooked like Mom. Tom knew Joe was especially close to Carolyn. She had been his motivator, his cheerleader, his physical therapist, his nurse, his EVERYTHING growing up. She took Dr. Paul's prediction of their son's limitations as a challenge to discover their boy's possibilities. She researched new treatments and exercises and worked tirelessly in her pursuit of equality for him.

Joe had learned to walk after all, though he still needed braces and a metal crutch to assist him. Tom and Carolyn stood with pride and cheered when he'd walked across the graduation stage, collecting his high school graduation diploma, and then again in college and law school. He'd given the valedictorian speech at all three assemblies. His mother had personally seen to it that no one would keep Joe from realizing his potential, first fighting to make the school accessible for him and arranging alternative scheduling for physical education. She lobbied the school board to count his physical therapy toward his physical education credits and then the college to allow a motorized scooter to assist Joe in getting across campus without wasting so much time and energy on travel.

Cassandra, their first daughter, became a physical therapist. The hours she spent watching her mom do physical therapy on Joe's legs prompted her to ask if she could do it herself. Their youngest, Jessica, was in her first year at the University of Minnesota Medical School. Dr. Paul, their family pediatrician, suggested and encouraged Jessica to pursue her dream of becoming a pediatrician. All of the children would be home and seated around the table on Thanksgiving and that meant the world to both Tom and Carolyn.

"When is Jessica's last class this week?" Tom asked, barely able to contain his excitement at the prospect of her coming home. Jessica had been away since September and they were always happy when she could come back to their little hobby farm. The house was more animated with her in it.

"Wednesday morning, and she's heading home right after," Carolyn answered, "and she's bringing a friend. A BOY friend."

Tom's eyebrows raised in surprise. "When did that happen?" Jessica was their rambunctious daughter, full of energy and life. Boys seldom fit into her plans, though that certainly didn't stop them from trying. She tolerated them, but most weren't around long enough to make it to a family event.

"He's in her Gross Anatomy class and also her study group." Tom's protectiveness regarding his daughters was a well-established fact. She knew this young man would have many questions to answer come Thursday, from both Tom and Joe. "Cassie and Jacob can't make it until Thursday morning but they will be staying until Sunday." Cassie had taken a physical therapy position in Rochester at the Mayo Clinic after completing her schooling and met Jacob Schultz, a new internal medicine doctor just out of residency. He asked her to marry him last summer. "Perhaps this weekend we can pin them down on some wedding details. These young kids don't know how long it takes to plan a wedding."

"Or how much they cost..." Tom added mournfully as he scanned the headlines of the morning paper.

"Don't start that again. You knew when you had kids that one day there would be weddings. I just wish Joe could find someone. He works too much."

"Don't try to marry off our son, too," Tom laughed. "One wedding at a time."

"Okay, okay. I have a list of chores for you to do in the next two days," Carolyn pointed at the piece of paper on the counter, "Oh, one more thing, there's a tree branch scraping the window, please cut it off." Carolyn stated, remembering her late-night discovery. "Don't worry. I have a list of my own that's even longer," she told him as Tom feigned a pained look. The next two days would be a whirlwind of activity but would be worth every second.

Sammy alerted them to a car approaching the yard and Jessica came bounding down the stairs two at a time, "Joe's home!" She exclaimed, throwing open the porch door with Sammy, the family dog, at her heels.

Jessica ran down the ramp, tackling Joe as he stood next to his car scratching Sammy's head, both were official greeters of the Steffan family.

"Hey baby sis, when did you get home?" Joe asked holding his little sister tightly. He missed her terribly the past few months, but tried not to show it.

"This afternoon. I've been waiting for you, as always." Jessica teased.

"I got here as quickly as I could. You know work, that four letter word. I had a case that I thought they would have the good sense to settle, which they didn't, so I had to show them the error of their ways. Did mom make a roast?" Joe asked nonchalantly as he reached in the car for the metal crutch he still used to help him walk.

"Yes, and biscuits, and baby red potatoes, your favorites!" Jessica said rolling her eyes and running her fingers through Joe's beautiful dark curls. She had always wanted curls but unfortunately ended up with straight strawberry blonde hair.

"Like they're not your favorites, too!" Joe said smiling. He loved his mom's cooking. He would be hard pressed to say anything she made wasn't his favorite. "Hey get the wine in the back seat, please?" He said throwing his backpack over one shoulder. He hated that he still had to walk with one metal crutch which made it difficult to carry things, and the braces on his legs sometimes scratched his skin, but he loved the fact that he could walk when so many who had spina bifida couldn't.

"Sure, now that I'm legal, I'd be happy to carry in the alcohol." Jessica said smiling. "What's with the back pack? Are you staying at home tonight?" She asked hopefully.

"I thought I would. Give us a chance to have a late-night chess game. Gotta remind you once in a while that I'm the smarter one."

"Bring it on, big brother." Her ponytail swung as she swaggered up the walk.

Carolyn was standing at the door watching the exchange between her children. Heavens, she had missed this. "Hi Joe." She gave him a tight hug. "How was work?"

"Busy, but productive." He relished his mom's hugs. She smelled of biscuits and pies and all things motherly. "Smells great in here!"

"Joe, you work too hard. You need to take some time off!" She couldn't help but worry about him. He was too much of a loner, too wrapped up in work to take time to have a social life. When he had been a child, he would immerse himself in books, because in fantasy he was normal and could run and jump and play just like the other kids. His siblings were his greatest playmates. They understood his physical limitations and played games he was physically capable of doing. They loved playing with the orphan animals their mother always seemed to be caring for and on rainy days board games occupied their time. Joe loved Scrabble; Jessica, Monopoly; and Cassie, The Farming Game.

The boys his age wanted to play physical sports: football, basketball, baseball. To become more accepted, he learned all he could about the sports so he could at least talk the talk. He spent hours watching football and basketball on television and knew all the rules, plays, and stats. He was teased about being 'weak' when he was young because he wasn't able to run like the other boys, so he asked his dad to get him some arm weights. Eventually he was able to do some weight-lifting with his legs, but would never be able to walk steadily without the braces.

"Hey, Joe I need some sampling help in here" Tom called from the kitchen. Joe was always known to sample the raw stuffing and give his 'stamp of approval'.

"Coming Dad" Joe said smiling. He would never get tired of coming home.

"Tom, finish up with that so we can eat supper. The roast is finished and we are all hungry." Carolyn said trying to speed her family along. "Honestly, trying to get you all to sit down can be like herding kittens."

Supper was delicious as usual and Joe and Carolyn did the dishes. She enjoyed the closeness she had with her eldest. It was quiet time. Sometimes they talked, but sometimes just enjoyed the moment of quiet togetherness.

Jessica joined her dad in feeding the menagerie of animals they had on their little hobby farm. She missed the animals while she was at school and was anxious to see how big Mopsy, the orphan lamb they had been nursing since spring, had grown.

When Tom and Jessica returned, Carolyn declared exhaustion and since she was getting up at 5am to put a 25 pound turkey in the oven, she was going to bed. Tom agreed and they retired, leaving the kids to enjoy some time catching up with each other's lives.

Joe got out the chess board and set it up while Jessica poured each another glass of wine.

"Now that you're of age you are getting quite sophisticated in your drinking habits." Joe teased.

Jessica wrinkled up her nose at him, "Well beer makes me belch. Which do you prefer I drink?"

"Knowing that fact, I'm glad you picked the wine." He said, smiling at their sibling banter. He had missed this.

"So big brother, any new romances I should know about?" she asked, already knowing the answer.

"No, but I hear you have one brewing. Where is he? I was hoping to do an interrogation this weekend."

"He is Brian and the interrogation will have to wait," Jessica replied. "His family demanded he make a family Thanksgiving trip home."

"Oh, that's too bad." Joe said feigning disappointment, but actually was pleased with some alone time with his baby sister. He knew that as their lives went separate ways, time alone would become very precious. "Why didn't you go with him?"

"Not ready for that yet." Jessica answered. But the fact was that she desperately wanted to see her family and wasn't ready to sacrifice this time to meet strangers.

Joe became serious, "All kidding aside, I'm glad you're home."

"I am too." Jessica answered with a special smile for her big brother. "Now I'm going to whoop your butt at this game!" She said lightening the mood.

CHAPTER 2

"Cassie and Jacob just pulled in the driveway. Get up sleepy head." Jessica said doing a full body dive on the bed and on top of Joe.

"This I did not miss," Joe said, pulling the covers over his head.

"Oh, come on, you know you love me," Jessica said flashing her eyelashes and brilliant smile.

"All right, all right, I'm up." he said pulling the covers of his childhood bed off his head.

"Please tell me someone has made coffee." Joe said wiping the sleep out of his eyes.

"Joe, hellllooo, where are you?? It's home. Of course there's coffee made. But I'm going to drink it all if you aren't out in five minutes." She said making a mad scramble for the door.

Jessica just about knocked Cassie off her feet as she came around the door. "Hey sis," Jessica said giving a big hug before heading off to the kitchen.

"Well good morning to you!" Cassie yelled after her then turned her attention to her sleepy brother, "Who was that ball of energy?"

Joe answered with one eye open," You always knew she was a morning person! I swear it's why there's only three of us. Mom and

17

Dad needed to expend so much energy on controlling their ball of energy they probably didn't have sex for a decade."

"Let's not put Mom and Dad in the same sentence as sex shall we. I just have a hard time picturing it or more to the point, I don't want to picture it!!" Cassie answered scrunching her face.

"Okay, on the condition that you close the door so I can get up and put on some clothes. I need that coffee Jessica was talking about." Joe said sliding his legs off the bed.

"Joe, I've seen you in boxers before." Cassie said as she exited, closing the door softly.

It wasn't his state of undress that he didn't want her to see. As he grew older, he was more self-conscious than ever about his metal braces. At least with his pants on they were covered and no one but he would be reminded of his disability.

The kitchen was the hub of activity. Carolyn was as good as her word, rising at 5am to put the bird in the oven. It already smelled divine! She was up to her elbows in peeling potatoes when Joe came in the kitchen. She reached for a mug and poured him a cup of coffee. Smiling, he gave her a morning hug before taking the mug to the table where Jessica was already reading the local weekly paper.

"Catching up on the local news?" Joe stated.

"Yes, trying to see if I missed something." Jessica stated without looking up. "Mom, did you know that one of the doctors at your hospital was given a Humanitarian of the Year Award?"

"Oh really, which one?" Carolyn answered concentrating on the pile of potatoes in front of her.

"It says a Dr. Clayton Jefferson." Jessica answered.

The potato Carolyn was peeling slipped out of her hands onto the floor and the knife she was using nicked her finger. Joe jumped up to grab some paper towels as he saw a stream of blood running down Carolyn's arm. Jessica grabbed the slippery potato from the floor. "Mom, what's wrong," Joe asked, looking into her eyes. Her face had gone noticeably pale. He was very perceptive with people and knew something deeper was wrong.

"Nothing, just slipped out of my hands. Can you get me a bandage from the cupboard." Carolyn said holding pressure on the finger.

"Sit down, Mom. I'll get it." Joe said, then turning to Jessica," Why don't you finish up the peeling. Mom looks tired."

"That's not necessary," Carolyn said trying to smile, "I'm almost done".

Jessica saw the look on Joe's face and when he takes command of a situation you don't argue. She started peeling the last couple of potatoes and Joe administered the required first aid. Joe noted his mother's trembling hands trying to push her hair back and the paleness of her face as she stared out the window.

"Mom, do you know this Dr. Jefferson?" he asked quietly, carefully watching the look on her face as he finished putting the bandage on her finger.

She suddenly turned and looked at Joe. He saw fire in her eyes, "Yes, I do, and believe me, he's no humanitarian."

She stood suddenly and went to the oven to baste the turkey. Her body language invited no further discussion on the subject. Jessica looked quizzically at Joe and he answered with a shrug. There was definitely something there, but he knew when to pull back. If his mom needed to talk later, she would. But if Joe knew one thing, Dr. Jefferson had crossed her path and not in a good way.

Cassie joined them in the kitchen holding a picture of a house she and Jacob were contemplating buying. "Mom, what do you think? Isn't it the cutest with the red brick and the white front porch?"

Jacob was right behind her and slipped his arm behind her back adding, "It's only 15 minutes from the hospital and in a great neighborhood with good schools."

Carolyn smiled watching the two of them. Young love with their whole lives in front of them. "It looks lovely. How many bedrooms?"

Jacob answered smiling, "Four, plenty of space for you to visit and spend the night."

"I was thinking more about filling it with grandchildren." Carolyn smiled only half kidding.

Cassie pinkened a little but smiled back at Jacob. Thinking that was also their plan.

"Well then, don't you think we should be getting this wedding planned?" Carolyn asked.

"How does April or early May sound?" Jacob offered. "Not too large."

"Wet, but we can work around that!" Carolyn answered. "Why don't we put some ideas on paper after Thanksgiving dinner. Gramma Jo will be here soon and she may have some good ideas."

"Speaking of Gramma Jo, she's just pulling up into the yard," Tom said stepping into the kitchen. "Jessica why don't you help me carry in her pies and salad."

Everyone moved into the living room and prepared to meet the whirlwind known as Gramma Jo. If anyone wondered where Jessica got her energy from, as soon as they met her Gramma Jo, they were given their answer!

"Happy Thanksgiving everyone!!" Gramma Jo greeted as soon as she walked in the door, showering everyone with kisses and hugs. Giving her namesake an extra squeeze as she made her rounds. "I just love holidays when I get to see all my grandbabies together!! Grampa John would have loved this." Grampa John was Carolyn's father and he had passed away when Joe was entering Law School.

Gramma Jo had inherited her father's sizeable estate and was insistent on setting aside a good amount for each grandchild to help them with their education expenses. Joe had received several scholarships along the way and had hardly touched his fund so Gramma Jo suggested he use it to help him build his dream house. Cassie also had at least half her fund left which Jacob and she were using as a down-payment on their first home.

Jacob loved Cassie's fun-loving family. Tom and Carolyn's home was filled with such love and laughter that he really looked forward to their visits back to this hobby farm. His own family was quite the opposite.

"Okay everyone, there's wine to open, potatoes to mash, and turkey to carve." Carolyn directed, quickly connecting people with jobs and getting them to the table before the hot food got cold.

Gramma Jo loved watching Carolyn take charge of her kitchen. She enjoyed sitting back sipping wine watching the coordinated chaos around her. She had done her job well raising that girl!

As they all sat around the table saying grace and eating the fruits of Carolyn's labor, Gramma Jo caught up on the three grandchildren's busy lives. "Jessica, I want to meet that boy you were supposedly bringing home."

"Get in line," Joe joked.

"I'm beginning to think he dodged a bullet." Jessica muttered as she gave her brother's ribs a nudge.

The conversation soon diverted to wedding plans and football scores as the Thanksgiving feast was enjoyed.

Toward evening Gramma Jo was wearing out and said her good byes. This was the time that the kids had always loved, bringing up the Christmas tree and ornaments to start decorating for the Christmas holiday. Jacob, Cassie, and Jessica headed down the basement stairs to bring up the boxes. Tom and Joe shuffled furniture to make room for the tree in its traditional spot while Carolyn headed into the kitchen to bring out the homemade eggnog spiked with a little rum. The room was alive with laughter and Carolyn's heart was full when suddenly there was an eerie hush sending a slight chill up her spine as she walked through the hallway. Entering the room, she felt all eyes on her. Questioning frowns turned towards her. Her glance went from face to face, the laughter had left their eyes.

Joe – her Joe, her perfect Joe – was in the old brown recliner beside the fireplace, the tattered box resting open in his lap.

"No! Oh, my God, no!" The tray shook, cups clanging together. Her legs froze in place.

"Mom, what is this?" Moving aside a pile of cloth, he held up a folded piece of tape that had at one time been white but was now a dirty grey. "These look like old dirty baby blankets, and a piece of old medical tape?" He frowned. "These blankets are stamped with your hospital's logo. The box has 'Baby B' scribbled on top?" He dropped the fragment back into the box. "You said I was dropped off at your door in a laundry basket?" His eyes searched her face. She could read his dawning comprehension, the horror of it. But it was only part of the story. "Mom, did you take me from your hospital?? Did you steal me?"

Carolyn looked around the room. Her family, her precious family, that she'd fought so hard for and loved so much. Tom had a look of shock on his face. The girls and Jacob, eyes wide with stunned disbelief, waiting for an explanation. Her tongue was glued to the roof of her mouth. *How? Why? Now?*

Carolyn's mind was racing: how to tell him, would he believe her, God, would she lose him now?

"Joe, I...I.." The words stuck in her throat.

Her silence was more damning than words could ever be.

Joe's voice was louder now, harsher. *"Did you steal me?"*

Tears trickled down Carolyn's face. She had to make him understand. "I loved you," she said softly, desperately. "I saved you."

"Saved?" He made a slashing, dismissive motion, the movement jerky in a way that reminded her of his first brutal, painful steps, so many years ago. "You always told me I was abandoned. But you stole me? You took me from . . . my mother?"

Pain sliced through her. So that's what it felt like, she thought, when your heart breaks in two. "Joe, no, I'm your mother. I saved you," she repeated, reaching for her son, as if her touch would convey the truth to him.

Joe pulled back. He couldn't think if she was touching him. She had been a good mother, no... great mother . . . but she was *not his mother*. She'd taken him from his mother. He shoved himself to his feet, started his damned awkward gait toward the door, longing, in a way he hadn't for years, that he was fast and whole and could sprint free. He needed distance. Distance from her, distance from this, distance from home.

"Joe, stay... I will tell you everything... don't go... don't gggoo..." Her voice caught on a sob and she lunged toward Joe, falling to her knees instead, the Christmas ceramic mugs crashing to the floor. Eggnog spilled everywhere, mixed with sharp shards of glass. Carolyn scrambled for the pieces, trying to salvage them, her vision blurred from the tears, the shards cutting her palms and fingers. Her blood mixed with the ruined eggnog, swirls of pink in the liquid on the floor.

But he was gone. She stayed kneeling on the floor, her heart...her world...lay in pieces just like the shattered cups, her shoulders shaking from her sobs. She tried to balance her life and her secret, holding each tenuously, always dreading the moment the two would clash. Tom made the first step toward her wrapping his arms around her quaking body.

"Come. Come now." He carefully extricated her from the mess surrounding her and grabbed a Christmas towel from one of the open Christmas boxes to temporarily wrap around her shredded hands. Carolyn wiped her face with her arm, smearing the tears rather than wiping them off. The only sounds in the room were Carolyn's sobs and Joe's car tires crunching on the fresh coat of snow covering the driveway.

The sound of his tires on the new ice grew distant and with each passing mile Carolyn felt him slip farther away. Her worst fear made real, her nightmare coming to life.

"He's gone," Carolyn whispered.

CHAPTER 3

Carolyn's world was in pieces, as irreparable as the cups she'd bought their first Christmas, planning for the family holidays to come. The warmth of a familiar arm wrapped around her, Tom's voice trying to soothe her. "Carolyn, I'm here. It's going to be all right. Joe will be back."

Carolyn's legs wobbled as Tom helped her to the chair in the living room. The day she dreaded for thirty years had come. All she could think about was that Joe hadn't given her a chance to explain.

Jacob and Jessica bent over her hands, ensuring no shards were stuck in the fresh cuts. Cassie carried in a basin of soapy water and the first aid kit. They worked quietly with barely a whisper spoken. After Carolyn's palms were bandaged, Jessica cleaned her face while Cassie and Jacob picked up the pieces of glass and wiped up the spilled eggnog. Numb with shock, Carolyn stared into the fire. The offending box sat on the coffee table in front of her, daring her to speak.

She was barely aware of her husband as he knelt next to her, gently holding her wounded hands. "Carolyn, what is this? What does it have to do with Joe?"

Carolyn finally found her voice, but it was soft and strange and didn't sound like hers. "It was supposed to be his coffin." She heard gasps from her girls and a sharp intake of air from Tom. She couldn't look at them. She would lose her nerve.

Silence, except for the snap from the fire as a log popped. The merry smell of nutmeg and cinnamon spice filled the air from the spilled eggnog, nearly making her ill. "He was right. I took him… but I took him so he could live."

Her hands tightened in her husband's. It should hurt, she thought vaguely. Shouldn't it hurt? "I couldn't bear to let him die. The doctor who delivered him, Dr. Jefferson, believed that imperfect babies weren't . . . good enough. That *Joe* wasn't good enough. They kept the boxes in the equipment closet. When a baby was born with a defect or disability, the doctor would put a piece of medical tape over its mouth so no one could hear its cries." Carolyn picked up the old piece of tape and held it out in her bandaged palm for her family to see, her hand slightly shaking. "This was placed over Joe's mouth by Dr. Jefferson." Carolyn took a ragged breath, surprised her lungs still worked. "Then the doctor would have a nurse go to the closet and retrieve one of the boxes. I didn't even know they were in there." Carolyn rubbed her face, smearing her tears, choking back a sob, "He put the baby in the box and the box would be placed back in the equipment closet with the baby in it….to die."

Even now, the terror could catch her unaware, that raw panic, as if it had happened but a moment ago. "I couldn't let that happen to Joe. I had to save him. I *had* to." Carolyn finally looked up at her family and saw the disbelief and horror in their eyes. It wasn't that they didn't want to believe her but it was so far out of their experience, the good people they were, to believe a doctor would actually kill innocent babies just because they were flawed. Carolyn started from the beginning, the words she'd held inside for so many years tumbling out, the whole story of Joe's delivery, up until she walked out carrying Joe and then the words ran out, leaving her drained but relieved.

Jessica paced, as if the room wasn't big enough for her, or the anger. "I hope," she said, "that doctor rots in hell."

Carolyn nearly choked on a bubble of laughter, leaving her family to wonder if she was starting to lose it. "He was just given an award for 'Humanitarian of the Year.' Ironic, isn't it?" She nodded towards the coffee table where the paper lay, his smiling picture staring back at them.

Cassie, who had been silent up until now, reached over and tore the paper into vicious bits. "This is wrong. Just wrong."

"How did you keep it from everyone?" Troubled, Jacob frowned. "You didn't know any of this, Tom?"

Tom shook his head slowly, trying to remember that day. He'd been so damn happy, she'd been so damn happy – a baby, a live baby, their son at last, to fill the void of the one they had lost. It seemed fated, somehow. Maybe he'd been too afraid to question it too much. "Not a clue."

"Mom?" Jessica asked. "How? How did you keep this a secret from everyone?"

Carolyn was brought back to that car ride home in 1969…. She began again explaining the lie she had concocted to legitimize Joe's adoption.

1969

The ride home from the hospital seemed short although it was 35 minutes. When I started to look for nursing jobs three years ago the Memorial County Hospital was the only one hiring the shifts I wanted, so I took the job even though I drove by a closer hospital during my commute. Today I am relieved to have that distance.

As I pulled up into our driveway, I was thankful for our rural life. Our next door neighbor was at least a half-mile down the road and there was a copse of trees between us. The small barn Tom had fixed up for our menagerie of animals was quiet now. Tom's truck wasn't in the driveway and no one had unexpectedly stopped for a cup of coffee. Thank God; I didn't want prying eyes on me as I carried my new bundle into our home. Tom owned his own lumber supply store in Prairie Meadows, a growing, bustling community 15 minutes away. The store was doing well and the mortgage had been paid off by my grandfather as a wedding present. Grampa Henry had raised my mother, Josephine, with a good work ethic and a strong moral compass, something she'd instilled in me, her only daughter.

Stealing a baby would have been the last thing I could imagine doing. But leaving him to die was not an option.

I had taken the top off the box after I was in the car and a safe distance away. My son was now peacefully asleep, his little mouth puckering from time to time. He was a beautiful baby with black hair and arched eyebrows. I knew he was going to need medical attention due to the spina bifida diagnosis and had already formed a plan by the time I passed the Prairie View Hospital sign.

Once I was inside the house, I carefully picked up the baby from the box and spread a couple of baby blankets in the laundry basket nearby. I took the box of death and carried it to the basement of our farmhouse, tucked it under an old record player and covered it with a tarp. I couldn't bring myself to burn it; something inside of me told me to keep it.

When I came back upstairs, I scribbled a note that read: "I had a baby at home, but can't take care of it. I know you are a nurse. Please help." My fingers shook as I dialed the sheriff's office. I never broke the law, never even drove more than two miles over the speed limit. But there was no turning back now. I gripped the phone with renewed resolve. When someone answered I reported that a baby had been found in a laundry basket on my front step. I told the dispatcher that I was a nurse and stated it looked to be a newborn needing medical attention. The sheriff asked if I could bring it to the closest hospital *and he would meet me there. I, of course, agreed. I hung up the phone and smiled a real smile for the first time today. I called my husband and gave him a quick synopsis, telling him I was taking the baby to Prairie View Hospital and asking him to meet me there.*

Tom was a wonderful husband. We had been childhood sweethearts. He would be a great father to my son. He would want me to be happy... us to be happy...to be a family.

I carefully drove my son to the hospital. The laundry basket sat on the seat next to me, Joseph wrapped up in blankets to keep warm. I had some baby outfits that had never been worn by my first son, stillborn a year ago, but I did not want to take the time to dress him. Nor did I want the authorities to think this was planned in any way. It was the truth, really, because in all honesty I wasn't thinking more than one step ahead this whole day. I silently said a prayer for strength to get me through this night and giving thanks for the son I now carried in my car.

I turned into the parking lot of the hospital I had driven by almost on a daily basis. I hoped there would be compassionate doctors and nurses here that would see past the birth defect and into my new son's beautiful face and see the possibilities his life could hold.

When I carried him into the Emergency Department I felt a flutter of nerves in my belly but I willed them away. The receptionist peered into the blankets in the laundry basket and smiled. She asked, "What is the nature of the visit?"

"I...I ... called the sheriff's department and they said to bring him here. I found him on my doorstep when I came home from work. I'm a nurse ... there was a note..." I handed her the note, belatedly hoping I'd disguised my handwriting well enough. "The sheriff said to bring him here. The baby has a birth defect and needs medical attention."

Just then my husband, Tom, came through the door, his denim work shirt proudly embroidered with his business logo: 'Steffan

Lumber Company.' Tom was handsome, his dark brown hair mussed just the right way; even in his work clothes he exuded masculinity. He didn't need to jog or work out; his business and our farm kept him active enough to stay in great shape. We had been in love since we were juniors in high school and courted all through college. We had always been a great couple, but losing our first son had put our marriage in a precarious place.

I could see Tom was relieved to see me, but he had a look of apprehension on his face as he peeked into the basket. "He looks so little. He must have just been born." I saw doubt in the lines on his face. I was sure he was reliving the pain we had gone through this past year and probably hoping this didn't dredge up those horrible memories for me, for the loss of our son had nearly broken me. I was still sometimes awfully close to sliding back into a dark and terrible place. Daily I walk past the still empty nursery with its empty crib and sometimes think I hear a baby cry, a cry I couldn't answer.

Following shortly behind Tom was the much older sheriff. 'Griff' is what we called him. He had been sheriff since before we were born and our quiet country community apparently did not offer enough crime to keep Griff in shape as his girth slid over the top of his pants. "Hi, Tom. Carolyn. What do we have here?"

"It's a boy... he appears to be a newborn." I stated clearly and factually just as if I was giving shift report. "His umbilical cord is still attached. I checked him out at my house before coming. It seems he has a birth defect called spina bifida. He will need surgery to secure the protrusion from the defect on his back. I put a dressing over it before heading over."

Griff nodded. He didn't question my nursing assessment. "How did you find him?" He took a look in the basket, smiling at the baby; who wouldn't smile at such a beautiful baby? And suddenly I was furious again, at the doctor who'd looked at him and judged him unworthy. Careful, I told myself, too much emotion could give me away. "I came home from work, a day shift. He was on my doorstep. This note was in the basket with him." I took the note from the receptionist and handed it to Griff.

The receptionist looked expectantly at the sheriff. "Under what name shall I register him?"

"Well, I guess Baby Boy A will have to do for now," Sheriff answered. "I'll have to have a social worker come out to give more information. I guess if we can't find his parents he'll be a ward of the state. Would you mind if we came out and took a look around your house? Maybe there's some clues left behind."

Tom answered quickly, "No, no problem. Help yourself Griff. We don't have anything to hide."

Carolyn gripped the basket rim a little tighter but smiled outwardly and nodded her agreement.

"I don't anticipate finding anything," Griff stated matter of factly. "Most of the time in these cases the mother is hard to find. Probably a teenage mother who was hiding her pregnancy. When she saw the protrusion on his back she probably got scared. Glad you found him before something terrible happened."

An emergency room nurse came out to get my precious basket. "Do you mind if I come with? I'm a nurse, too, and I don't want the baby to be alone."

She glanced at the sheriff and when he smiled his acknowledgement, she nodded her approval. Tom trailed us into the emergency room.

The pediatrician who had been called by the emergency room doctor to check on Joe was a young man, looked to be just out of residency. He introduced himself as Dr. Bruce Paul. His smile was gratifying and put me more at ease. He had gentle hands. Joe was hungry again and was rooting around for food so Dr. Paul called to the nurse to bring a bottle of Similac. Without a second's hesitation he handed the baby to me to feed. "Well, except for the Spina Bifida, he seems to be in pretty good health. Sure is a beautiful boy."

Tom reached over with his finger, which Joe grabbed with gusto. Tom broke out in a wide toothy grin. "So about this spina bifida, Doc. Is it serious?"

But I was the one who answered. "It means he will probably never walk."

"That used to be the case," Dr. Paul corrected. "But new plans of care and research are showing that it depends on the severity of the defect, things like where it's located along the spinal column and how much the nerves are affected. New physical therapy treatments are having some success. He may be able to walk with braces. Hydrocephallus - water on the brain - is a bigger worry, possibly causing intellectual disability. But at this time I don't see any signs of that. He'll have to be watched carefully so that if he does get those symptoms a shunt can be put in right away, before there's any damage" Dr. Paul tucked his stethoscope back in his lab coat pocket. He took a deep breath and went on, "I was told you aren't his birth parents. That he was found on your doorstep."

"Yeah, that's right," Tom answered. Carolyn couldn't tear her gaze from Joe. She already felt as if Joe were her son. Birth parent or not, she wasn't going anywhere. "What's going to happen to him, do you think?"

"Children with disabilities are often very difficult to place in foster families, let alone adoptive homes." Dr. Paul answered making notations on the chart he was holding.

My eyes shot to Tom's to see his reaction. He knew me well enough to see the longing in them, just as I sensed his hesitation. Our marriage had been rocky since our son's loss. We grieved in very different ways, very much alone in our isolation and pain. Tom tapped his index finger against his jean-covered thigh, something he did whenever he contemplated making a big decision.

Dr. Paul studied us for a moment before his gaze dropped back to the infant in my arms. "This baby will need to be placed with a parent who has a medical background to give him the best chance to reach his full potential." He let the words lie between us.

Tom had struggled to make sense of our own baby's death, to, if not find purpose in it, to at least make something hopeful out of it, a way to give his life meaning again. "Dr. Paul, we lost our own son to stillbirth this past year," he said carefully. "We wanted that boy so much .." A hitch caught in Tom's voice. He rubbed his jeans with his hands, trying to deal with his pain and put it aside. He looked into my eyes, trying to read my thoughts. "Perhaps this baby was sent to help us . . . heal. As far as I can see he's a perfect little baby." Tom reached over and patted Joe's diapered bottom.

"Well, you can think about it overnight, make sure this is something you want to take on. And, of course, social services will have to approve. There will be challenges to overcome. I'm admitting the baby. We'll do surgery in the morning to reduce the spinal defect." He nodded to himself. "Dr. Thompson, our surgical neurologist, has an opening at 9am on his schedule, and we'll do more tests to ensure I am correct about the hydrocephalus. Let me know how you feel tomorrow. If you want to proceed to foster the baby, I will make my recommendation to social services." He reached over to shake our hands.

"You . . . would do that for us?" I couldn't help thinking that he had been placed here for us, that this all was no accident, a sign I took as approval for what I had done.

My mind was spinning. Just this morning I'd woken up with empty arms. Tonight, I was a mother. "Thank you, doctor," I said with sincerity. "Do you think it would be ok if I stayed with the baby through the night? I know how staffing is and I would want someone here for him."

"Of course," he replied smiling, I could tell he was pretty sure what answer he was going to get tomorrow. "I'd better go write the orders." He glanced back over his shoulder as he left. "You're going to have to decide on a name for him, Baby A just doesn't do it for me."

Tom looked at me with all seriousness now. "Are you sure you want to take this on?" Now that, I thought, didn't even deserve an answer.

"Okay," he said, with that slow, wondrous smile of his I hadn't seen for a year. "What are we going to name him?"

"Joseph. Joe for short." He'd finished his bottle and blinked up at me. A very appropriate name. My Mother, Josephine, had instilled a strong love of all creatures in me. She'd cared for all the orphan animals on our farm, and the surrounding farms besides. She felt all deserved a chance at life, and she'd loved them all.

So, Joe he would be.

The next morning Tom walked into Joe's hospital room carrying a small suitcase with some clothes and make-up. "How was the night?" He asked noticing that oxygen was now running to the baby.

"Joe had a small mucous plug about three this morning. It was good I was here. I cleared the plug and called the nurse on duty. We got oxygen going as a precaution. Dr. Paul had left standing orders just in case," I explained.

Just as I finished filling Tom in on the night, Dr. Paul arrived with the anesthesiologist and a pre-surgical nurse.

Dr. Paul didn't seem surprised at all to find Tom there at such an early hour. "Sounds like you had an eventful night. Thank you for staying with the baby."

"It's Joseph now, Joe for short," I said.

"Works for me." He nodded. "We'll be taking Joe to surgery now. Dr. Thompson is already scrubbing, and I'll be assisting. It won't take long for the procedure. You can wait here and I'll come as soon as we wheel him into recovery."

I reached over the hospital bed where they were already working on gaining access to Joe's tiny veins. I placed a mother's kiss on his head and patted his back. I knew he'd be back soon.

I took a couple of minutes to clean up after they wheeled him to surgery. As I looked in the mirror, I no longer saw the pain etched in my features; it had been replaced by a mother's determination.

Not only was Joe going to live, he was going to thrive. I would make sure of it.

I went to the bathroom to change into the clothes Tom had packed for me and noticed that he'd also put in a couple of outfits for Joe and a very soft blue blanket with monkeys and elephants on it. I brought it to my face and rubbed the soft texture on my cheeks. Now, finally, this blanket would be wrapped around a child, be dragged everywhere by a toddler, be tucked away by a teenager who couldn't quite let it go. I felt happy for perhaps the first time in a year, truly happy and whole. I came out of the bathroom holding the blanket and went to wrap my arms around my husband. Our kiss was sweet and loving and full of promise of the future.

I knew Tom still had misgivings about becoming Joe's foster parents. Joe's health and future were uncertain. He also knew that losing our baby almost crippled our marriage and if anything happened to this child, too, it would certainly be more than we could survive. But perhaps this is was the one thing that could bring us back together.

The morning dragged. As we took a moment to eat some of the food they sent to the room for breakfast, I tried to reassure Tom that this was going to be okay. "Tom, I know you're worried about this.... about taking him home."

"It's just all happening so fast." *He looked at the piece of half-burned toast halfway to his mouth, as if he couldn't quite figure out how it had gotten there, and dropped it to the plate without taking a bite.* "Seems like we should think about it a little, maybe, for his sake." *And yours; he might as well have said it out loud.*

"I know it's fast." *Somehow, I had to make him understand. This wasn't a choice anymore. It was meant to be* "But...I don't feel empty anymore. God, Tom, I've been so empty! Joe needs us and frankly, I think we need him." I clutched his hand. "I feel us moving closer together now, instead of drawing apart. Don't you feel it, too?" He had to see it, to feel it. He had to.

Tom slowly smiled and nodded his head, "I do feel it." He swallowed hard. "I do."

When he hugged me, so hard I lost my breath, I knew, at just that moment, we'd become a family of three.

The morning crawled by and I was just about to scrub up and bust into the O.R. myself because I couldn't take the waiting anymore when Dr. Paul returned, still in his surgical scrubs, followed by a young woman in a yellow dress with bright red flowers and red heels.

My heart lodged up in my throat.

"The surgery went very well," he said. "Joe will be in Recovery for at least an hour but then he'll come back here. If there are no complications he could be discharged in the next couple of days."

Tom and I couldn't contain our happiness. We smiled at each other as if we had been told we'd won a lottery.

I'd almost forgotten the young woman was there until she spoke. "Hello, I'm Mary, the county social worker. The sheriff told me about our little newborn. You must be Carolyn and Tom. First of all, thank you for caring for the baby. Dr. Paul has told me that you may be interested in becoming his foster parents. Is that correct?"

"Yes," I stated firmly. "Tom and I agree that we would love to take care of Joe. Joseph, that's the name that we came up with last night. If that's ok?" It hadn't occurred to me until then that I might not have the right to name him. He'd seemed like mine all along.

"Sure beats Baby A!" Dr. Paul said.

Mary smiled. "Yes, that's fine. But there will be paperwork and a background check to complete."

"This baby needs foster parents where at least one of them has a medical background. I won't sign discharge papers unless this condition is met. Do you have another set of parents that could meet this qualification?" Like most physicians, Dr. Paul could be very emphatic when he wanted to be. I could tell Mary was a bit intimidated; she was very young, and I wondered if she'd just gotten the job.

"No, not off hand."

"Then I guess we're lucky you have one right here."

She hesitated only briefly. "Well, I guess I had better get going on the paperwork then," she said. "I will need to see your house and have papers for you both to sign. Could we meet this afternoon?"

I looked at Tom and he back at me. "I took today off already, so I'm free. Carolyn, do you feel like you could leave the hospital for a couple of hours?" I was surprised that he had taken the day off, but happy that he felt that this was important.

"Don't worry," Dr. Paul said. "We have good nurses here, too."

Just then the door opened and Carolyn's mother peeked in, "Am I disturbing?"

"Mom, how did you know where we were?"

"I called Tom this morning and he told me all about the little one. If I'm a new grandmother I sure wasn't staying away!" Mom had been heartbroken when we'd lost our son. I knew how hard it had been to watch me suffer and not be able to do anything about it. If she thought this baby would help me heal, Gramma Jo would do everything in her power to help.

"Dr. Paul, Mary, this is my mother, Josephine." I smiled at my mother, who always seemed to be in the right place at the right time. "She's a retired elementary teacher."

Mary lit up. "I know you, you taught my brother, Calvin and myself in third grade! Oh, we both loved you! You were our favorite teacher!"

My mother got that a lot. "What was your last name, dear?"

"Anderson."

"Why yes, I remember you both. Your parents were Ella and George."

Mary was clearly delighted to be remembered. "Yes, that's right." There was now approval in her expression when she glanced back at me. "Carolyn's your daughter?" My mother smiled and nodded. My worry over Mary's approval eased; my mother just put the stamp of approval on my forehead!

"Well, the paperwork can be expedited, I'm sure," Mary said. "We'll still need to meet at the house today, just as a formality. But I doubt it will be difficult to get things done by the time Dr. Paul plans to discharge."

"Did I hear that you need someone to sit with Joe while you get the paperwork started? I'm here and I'm available," Mom said. I leaned over to give her a hug, whispering a quick thank you for her ears alone.

The social worker's paperwork seemed endless but the home visit went fine. She was surprised to see the ready-made nursery, the yellow curtains over the window, the elephant and monkey bedding on the crib, diapers neatly stacked in the corner. Tom told her about the child we'd lost. There was definitely a softening in Mary's demeanor and new energy as she flew through the rest of the paperwork. Her questions were gentler, as if she realized that this was the right placement for Joe.

Just before Mary left she added, almost as an afterthought, "We will have to try to locate Joe's biological mother, of course. But if we don't have any luck you two will have first opportunity to adopt, assuming everything continues to go well."

My breath caught in my throat. I hadn't thought about that. They would attempt to locate the biological parents. It felt like a kick in my stomach and I gripped the chair arms tightly to try to not react. "Of course we want to adopt him," I forced out. "We understand the legalities, but we already feel like he is ours."

Tom walked her out to the car as I started to make dinner, my hands automatically going through the motions as my head spun with plans. What was I going to do about my job? The hospital? And worst of all, the doctor who needed to be stopped?

I had already called the nursing supervisor and explained that we had a family emergency and I would need a couple of weeks off. She was understanding and didn't request a lot of details. I was on the schedule only part-time, anyway, so it wasn't many shifts to fill. I was cleaning vegetables at the sink when I felt Tom's arms around me. I turned into his embrace and let myself enjoy being cherished. It had been so long, so very long. He was opening his heart. We were healing each other from the pain we had held separately. But this, here, with him, was where I belonged.

Tom took my hand and led me up to our room. It was the first time in months that we found solace in each other's embrace. Afterwards we held each other close. There were no words to say. We were lost in our thoughts and hopes for our future together.

The time off work flew by, and Joe came home. He was the perfect baby, crying only when hungry and in need of a diaper change. The new disposable diapers, Pampers, created a rash on his bottom so I had to use cloth. That meant a load of diapers every day and I hung them out to dry so they would smell fresh like the flowers and grass. I didn't mind at all. It was all for my baby Joe.

We found a routine, a wonderful routine I cherished as we became a family. I got up with Joe for the 2 AM feeding. Since Tom woke up for work around 5AM he took that feeding. Sometimes I would sneak out of bed just to watch the two of them together, Joe reaching up for Tom's face and Tom running his finger along Joe's cheek. It was precious.

Eventually I had to go in to the hospital to sign the leave papers and get my schedule. I was dreading driving up to that building. How was I going to have the strength to go inside? I had formulated a plan, one that I hoped would stop Dr. Jefferson from ever using one of those boxes again.

The hospital looked old and grey today. As I walked through the doors the strong antiseptic smell stung my nostrils. I had been away a few weeks and now when I walked through the hospital I didn't smell bleach like I once had – the smell of cleanliness and protection from germs. I smelled death, dirtiness that no amount of bleach was ever going to wash away.

I forced a smile on my face and told myself to go one foot in front of the other. Move like an innocent person and they will think you are. Even though I felt vindication for my actions in saving Joe, I did feel a sense of guilt that I knew I would have to learn to live with in the coming years. My actions in taking Joe did deprive his birth parents of their right to raise my son, but I could not take the chance that they would have agreed with Dr. Jefferson in letting Joe die. Nor could I allow him to be placed in one of the institutions parents of disabled children were often encouraged to send their imperfect children, to live out their life never knowing the love of a family. No, it is better I learn to live with my guilt. I would be the best parent anyone has ever seen, so no one will ever be able to say Joe would have been better somewhere else.

Mary Mason was the Director of Nursing and her office was on the main floor. I needed to sign my leave papers and to put in place the first part of my plan. Her office was empty except for piles of papers on her desk. By the looks of her office, she was very unorganized. That was one of the reasons they were looking for an Assistant Director of Nursing. The job had grown beyond what one person could do. The last health inspection had given them a borderline acceptable rating and the administrators knew they needed to improve or risk a substandard grade. It wasn't necessarily Mary's fault, but she needed help and I needed to know what was in those piles.

"Carolyn, thanks for coming." Mary breezed into the office in her classic dark suit and pantyhose. Mary's hair was graying and several strands liked to escape from the tight bun she wore. She had a pencil behind her ear and another pile of folders in her arms. "I just need your signature on a couple of forms so you will be paid for your time off," she said absentmindedly as she started looking through a pile for the correct form.

"No problem, Mary. I was also hoping to discuss something with you."

Mary looked up from her pile, a frown starting to form, forehead wrinkling ever so slightly. "Yes . . ." I figured she was afraid that she was about to lose a well-trained nurse. So many nurses left when they became mothers and she had heard through the grapevine that we'd become foster parents to a disabled baby.

"I saw on the job posting board that you are looking for an Assistant Director of Nursing. With the new baby we are fostering there will be extra costs associated with his, uh, special needs." I couldn't bring myself to say 'disability' as I was bound and determined to think of Joe's possibilities rather than his disabilities. "I was thinking that perhaps I would be a good candidate for that position. I'm very well organized. I know the hospital and current policies as well as the staff and providers." The last word held just a hint of venom that Mary didn't discern. I didn't really need the extra income but I was determined to get into a position that I could oversee the obstetric department.

Mary sat down in her chair and mulled over this proposition. "You're young," she said.

"But I believe I'm well thought of in the department. I learn quickly, and I can promise you, no one will work harder than me. I really need this job." I had to have this job.

Maybe my conviction convinced her. "I do believe you would be an excellent candidate. I'm looking at making a decision within the next day or so. I will highly consider you. You do know that the position would be 4 days a week, correct?"

"Yes, I know. That's what I'm looking for. Thank you."

I got up to leave but instead of turning to leave I reached across the desk to shake Mary's hand and make direct eye contact. I wanted her to know I meant business.

Walking out of the office I felt very good about the meeting. As if on cue, when I turned into the hallway, I felt a large hand grab my arm and pull me into a conference room. I almost screamed, biting down hard on my lip to stop it. I knew who it was before I even turned.

Dr. Jefferson. I yanked my arm away, not even caring that it hurt.

"What are you doing here? What did you talk to Mrs. Mason about?" His handsome face contorting in anger, he glanced nervously at the door.

My knees shook so I grasped a leather chair to ensure I didn't fall to the floor. This doctor was not someone with whom the nurses felt comfortable chatting with over the charts at the desk during a quiet shift, coffee cup in hand. He was extremely handsome, but arrogant. His sense of superiority over the staff was obvious.

I reached up to nervously push my hair off my forehead. "What do you want?"

"I want to know what you were discussing?" Dr. Jefferson asked again, this time taking a step towards me.

"No, you want to know if I told her what a monster you are." I replied calmly with a hint of venom, taking a slight step back putting a chair in between us.

"Listen, you have just as much to answer for as I. You kidnapped someone else's baby. You could go away for a very long time." His face was an angry dark red, and his hands were in tight fists at his side, his knuckles a pale white.

"You signed a death certificate. I saved that child from a monster." Fear and anger kept me upright. I wanted to run; I wanted to hit him.

"Really? You want to risk that in court? It's your word against mine." His voice was softer now, and somehow that was more frightening than the anger.

"I have a witness." Eve had been there, too. Surely she wouldn't lie for him in court, not about something so horrible.

"Eve? Didn't you hear? She's gone." He watched Carolyn's face for any sign that she knew about this.

A gasp escaped. *"Gone where? What do you mean gone?"* Eve wouldn't have left of her own volition; she loved the hospital. In fact, I'd figured she was my biggest competition for the Assistant Director of Nursing position.

"Gone as in vanished. So you see, it is your word against mine. You know who will lose." He kept his voice flat with no intonation.

I had to think fast. Eve's disappearance created a wrinkle I hadn't foreseen; but then I wasn't sure whose side she was on anyway. *"I'll keep my mouth shut about you being a murderer if you say nothing about my son."* There was nothing I wanted more than to expose him. But he was right; how could I prove it. And in truth, there was one thing I cared about more, and that was my family.

Stalemate. I wished he didn't look so relieved; I hated having him think he was getting exactly what he wanted: my silence. But it wasn't going to be quite that simple. *"One more thing."* I met his eyes fully, hoping he would believe what I was about to say. There was nothing I could do to save the babies he'd already killed; but I couldn't live with him doing so again. He had to be stopped, or we'd both lose everything. *"No more baby boxes. Not ever. I'll be watching, and if you do it again, I'll shout it from the rooftop. It won't matter if I can prove it. Everybody will always look at you and wonder."* I took a deep breath. *"And you will give me your strongest recommendation for the position of Assistant Director of Nursing, by tomorrow."* This was unconditional. It would be difficult enough to resume working in this hospital with the memories of that day constantly haunting me. His *presence needed to be a nonissue. "I'll be here to keep an eye on you, make sure you keep up your end of the agreement."*

He slowly nodded his head, a grim look on his face. He didn't like being held accountable, especially to a woman. He took a threatening step forward. "Ok, I agree. But if you ever break this agreement, I will take you down so far you will have to look up to see Hell." He didn't wait for my reply.

The instant he charged out of the room I slumped into one of the leather conference chairs, too tired to take a step. I just made a deal with the devil. It felt dirty, but it would save my family and countless other babies who might have ended up in boxes. I didn't want to share any secrets with this man, but now I shared one that could ruin us both. I wanted to hold him responsible for all that he had done, so many lives lost by his playing God, unfortunately, that would come at a price too dear for me to pay right now.

My gaze turned toward the window at the fall flowers growing in the window boxes, such pretty decorations for hell. . .

The faces of her family swam around her; she numbly searched for . . . what? Acceptance? Condemnation? Understanding? All emotion drained from her, the secret finally shared with those she loved.

The silence was deafening. The terrible box still rested in her lap, her bandaged hands covering her face. She felt like she was naked. There was nothing left to hide. She felt a warm arm around her back and strong fingers around her wrists bringing her hands down to her lap.

Tom was beside her. "Why didn't you tell me?"

"I didn't want to involve you in the lies. You didn't need to carry this burden. It was my decision. I was guilty, not you." She brushed her fingers over Tom's cheek, feeling the stubble, before gently tucking his slightly greying hair behind his ears. "I need to trim your hair," she murmured absently.

"Why didn't you go to the authorities?" Jacob asked quietly, not meaning to prod but wanting to understand.

"Because it would have been my word against his and he was the doctor. My primary focus was Joe. I was just so focused on saving Joe. He needed medical care – which Dr. Jefferson was not going to give. You don't know what it was like in those days. Doctors were gods, they could do no wrong. For goodness sakes, a nurse had to stand when a doctor entered the room!" She'd asked herself this question a hundred times, a thousand times. She knew if she had to do it again, she would, but she still wasn't completely sure it was the right thing. There was always nagging guilt in the back of Carolyn's mind that by taking Joe she had filled her own void, assuaged the deep pain of her own loss, but for her family's sake she needed to believe she was right. "If I had gone to the parents there was a strong possibility they might agree with Dr. Jefferson. How was I going to save him then? Maybe it would be my word against three, and I would have been fired on the spot. By the time I could get anyone else there it would have been too late. Joe would have been dead. I couldn't chance it. I *couldn't*." Carolyn stated emphatically her voice raising an octave with the last word.

"There had to be someone else. Someone who knew what he did." Jacob asked quietly and without judgement knowing that there were many hidden medical practices that in the current day would be judged as barbaric.

"He had been getting away with it for a long time," Carolyn said shaking her head. She knew it sounded inconceivable, but it had all happened so fast, and she'd been so scared, and really, the only thing that had mattered to her until it was too late to do anything else had been Joe. "Nobody had dared to stand up to him before, and Eve, the other nurse who attended the birth, disappeared suddenly right afterward. She was gone before I came back to work." She swallowed hard; the painful lump in her throat stayed right where it was. "It really was a standoff between Dr. Jefferson and me. I told him I would keep silent about his immoral medical practices and he was to keep silent about my taking Joe. I also made him agree to stop putting babies in boxes to die. That's why I took the job as Assistant Director of Nursing. No more him handpicking the nurses he wanted to work with. I assigned the ones I trusted, and I investigated every still-birth when he was on duty, just to make sure." Carolyn fought down nausea at the thought of other babies in boxes. "I *hated* staying at that hospital after that day. It felt like purgatory, but I had to stop him somehow, and I didn't know what else to do."

Jessica was still pale with shock. "Did Eve ever come back?"

"No, never." Carolyn had asked a few questions about that, trying not to be too obvious, but it was as if the woman vanished off the face of the earth.

Tom saw the torment in Carolyn's eyes, the pain that comes from keeping a horrible secret far too long. "Honey, you did what you had to do for Joe's sake. You did nothing wrong as far as I'm concerned. In fact, I'm damn proud of you! Nothing you said changes the fact that Joe is our son and belongs in this family. If anything, it shows me to what great lengths you will go to protect your family. We love and support you." Tom looked directly at each daughter and future son-in-law, conveying to them the need for their affirmation of his statement. They all nodded their agreement. Tom leaned over and kissed Carolyn's forehead and then stood up and headed for the door.

"Where are you going?" Carolyn asked.

"I'm going to find our son and bring him home." Tom answered.

CHAPTER 4

It had started lightly snowing when Tom left home. He was pretty sure Joe had headed back to his own house about 15 minutes away. Tom just needed to get him home. He needed to hear the truth from Carolyn. Tom had always joked that she was Joe's guardian angel and he now believed it more than ever. Carolyn was known to be a fierce protector of her family but especially of Joe. Tom thought back to when he had stupidly made an introduction of his family to a new worker at their business. Joe was about three and Cassie was almost two. He had said Joe was their 'adopted son' and Cassie was their daughter. When he got home, Carolyn had hit him right between the eyes so to speak. She was so angry fire came out of her eyes. She told him she never wanted to hear him refer to Joe as their 'adopted' son again. He was their son, period! Tom said he didn't know there was a distinction, but Carolyn felt Tom was setting Joe apart from his sister. She never wanted him to feel less loved or wanted just because he didn't share their genes. She was so adamant she said if Tom felt there was a difference their family was a sham and she would leave and take both their children. It took a good week for Tom to get out of the dog house and from that moment forward Carolyn set the tone for the family. If Carolyn had a fault it was that she was a mother who had unrealistic expectations for herself. She sometimes drove herself to exhaustion trying to meet each of her children's needs.

Pulling up into Joe's driveway Tom could see a light on in the front room and a shadow passing by the window. Tom had spent many hours working on this house for Joe, a labor of love. The house had all the latest devices to assist someone with a disability without seeming to be handicapped accessible. The ramp to the front door even had decorative stone that Tom painstakingly laid by hand to ensure placement was exact for Joe's gait. Tom knocked on the door but no one answered. "Joe, I know you are home. Answer the door."

"I don't feel like talking," came the reply from the other side.

"Then don't talk, just listen. But let me in, I don't like talking to a door and it's damn cold out here!" Tom said a bit louder and more forceful than before as he rubbed his hands together feeling the bite of the cold Minnesota night against the skin of his gloveless hands. Every breath and word that came out of Tom's mouth showed a plume of frost in the air.

The lock turned and the door slowly opened. Joe was standing there with his metal crutch in one hand and a drink in the other. Tom could see the anger in Joe's frame, his shoulders slightly pushed back, his jaw tensing and releasing. Joe stepped back allowing Tom to brush by him.

"Joe, I want you to come home. You left without giving your mother a chance to tell you the whole story." Tom explained cautiously.

"What's there to tell? She stole me." Joe said angrily, his words cutting like the edge of a serrated knife, emotions flying in the face of Joe's usual methodical analytics.

Tom grimaced, suddenly glad to have this conversation in private as Joe's words would have cut Carolyn to the core. "There's a lot more to it than that," Tom said. "You know your mother."

"She's not my mother." Joe said emphatically interrupting Tom.

Tom's fist clenched at his side. He had never laid a hand on his kids and he wasn't going to start today, but his voice rang out in anger, "She IS your mother, and I am your father. She has devoted herself to her family and deserves your respect. That woman would throw herself in front of a train for any one of us. You know that she has never deliberately hurt anyone and must have had a damn good reason to do what she did. You need to give her the respect of at least hearing what she has to say. You are a lawyer, but you left without all the facts in evidence. You were prosecutor, judge, and jury without even allowing her the courtesy you give your criminals."

Joe stared at his drinking glass. His dad made a strong point he had to grudgingly admit. His emotions got in the way of logic. As much as he didn't like to be wrong, he was in this instance. "You're right." Joe said quietly nodding. "I'll come tomorrow morning." He knew he had too much alcohol to drive tonight.

"You'll come now. Neither of you will sleep until you hear what she has to say," Tom said emphatically. He saw the drink in Joe's hand and added, "I'll drive you."

Joe hesitated, what if he didn't like what she had to say. What if he still felt the need for distance.

As if reading his mind, Tom said, "If you don't want to stay after hearing her out, I'll bring you back home." He added in his mind, 'but you'll want to stay.'

As the SUV turned into the driveway Joe could hear the cracking of the frozen ice under the tires. Minnesota's weather was always a concern during the winter season but as a native you learned to look past it. The cold outside was a stark contrast to the warmth of the homes inside, especially the one in which he grew up.

This hobby farm, this house, his family had been his sanctuary. School had been difficult in the beginning. Always being seen as different he felt like an outsider until his sisters were there with him. Both of them became fierce protectors of their big brother, but in different ways. Jessica used her words, some of which could become very harsh when warranted, Cassie her athleticism. When boys on the playground would make fun of his inability to run, or push out his crutches from under him, his sister would always be nearby. Cassie often would challenge the offending boy to a race of some sort and she would be her brother's legs. She would always be victorious. Her victory stipulation would be that if the boy so much as said a bad whisper about her brother she would let it be known throughout the school that he lost to a girl, a younger one at that. It took only a couple of races for the boys to realize that Joe was off-limits for bullying. Not only did it stop, but the boys actually started to stick up for him if any new kid made the mistake of thinking he was an easy target. He loved getting off the school bus though and walking up this road with his sisters at his side. They patiently slowed their gait to match his slower pace, always saying words of encouragement. Their mother often stood watching from a distance. He couldn't wait for her welcoming hug.

Tonight, he could see the warmth through the windows. While he was gone his siblings had set the tree upright and strung the Christmas tree lights. It stood waiting for the ornaments to adorn its branches. The living room was quiet and peaceful, just the snap of the fire which had gone down to a slight glow. His siblings and Jacob must have gone upstairs to bed, wisely assuming he would like some privacy with their mother. He could see Carolyn's legs covered by her favorite throw on the ottoman facing the fireplace. She had stayed up. He knew she would. She always was the last one to go to bed when one of her kids was out. The mother hen needing to know her chicks were all safe inside before retiring herself.

Joe, you go on inside. I'm going to park in the garage and check on the animals in the barn." Tom wanted Joe and Carolyn to have time to work through this privately.

Joe got out and carefully made his way up the ramp Tom had built when Joe was quite young. The fresh snow was beautiful, but made walking hazardous. The door creaked as Joe entered but Carolyn's head didn't turn. He slowly picked a path through the boxes on the floor labeled 'Christmas decorations'. Standing next to the chair he could see Carolyn had drifted asleep with a picture in her bandaged hand. He caught a glimpse of his sisters and him in Christmas finery taken when he was about 12 years old. He reached down to gently touch her bandaged hands feeling a pang of guilt over her injury. Years of mothering sick children and listening for bad dreams had made her a very light sleeper. Instantly her eyes fluttered open. She instinctively reached for his hand, needing to hold on to him to keep him from running again.

"Dad said I left without hearing all the facts. He is very persuasive. Perhaps he should have been the lawyer." Joe said slowly withdrawing his hand from Carolyn's and removing a box marked 'ornaments' from the couch. His eye drawn once again to the box on the coffee table whose presence had opened this 'can of worms'. "I'm willing to listen now. I need to listen. I need to know the truth. Was I in this box?" Joe's hand reached out to the box, his index finger touching the top gingerly.

"Yes." Carolyn answered. Her eyes now fixed on the box as well. "Yes, I took you, but not with the intention to steal you. I wanted to save you. This box was meant to be your coffin." She spoke slowly and softly, determined not to cry just to make him understand.

Joe's startled eyes jumped to her face. She looked pained. He saw the reluctance in her eyes. She was telling him the truth, but he could see it was something that she hadn't wanted to share, ever.

"What do you mean, coffin?" Joe said incredulously, his finger pulling back as if it had been burned.

"I was in the delivery room when you were born. The doctor who delivered you saw that you had a bulge on your back. He knew that you were born with spina bifida and that it was a disabling diagnosis. Back then a few doctors thought they could play god. He wasn't going to try to save you. He called for a 'box'. I thought he meant the incubator, but I was wrong." Carolyn's voice became a whisper. She closed her eyes trying to shut out the horror she was forced to finally share with her son. "Another nurse, Eve, knew what he wanted. They kept these boxes on a top shelf in the equipment room. I never even knew they were there. Back in the 1960s some of the doctors felt if a baby was born with a disabling disability the doctor had a right to allow that baby to die, to play god. Dr. Jefferson put a piece of tape over the baby's mouth and placed the baby in a box like this…. and waited for it to die."

She stopped for a few minutes letting the silence calm her then continued, "The box was put back in the equipment room until…. the doctor came back to pronounce. It was then taken to the morgue."

Joe saw the piece of old, yellowed tape lying next to the box and instinctively touched his mouth. He felt like he could vomit.

His mouth dried up, but he had to ask, "Was I placed in the equipment room…to die?"

Carolyn slowly nodded her head, "Yes, until I could get in there. I couldn't leave you to die. When I realized that was their intention, I slipped into the equipment room and opened the box. You were fighting to breathe. I grabbed some blankets and cleaned you off and wrapped you up. I cleared your airway with a suction bulb and held oxygen to your face. You pinkened right up in my arms. You were a beautiful baby, perfect to me. I fell in love with you in my arms." She reached for Joe's hand and this time he reached back toward her. When their hands met Carolyn knew he understood. "I cut a hole in the box with my bandage scissors and stuck the oxygen tubing through it and figured out a plan to get you out of there. I almost got caught. Eve, the other nurse, opened the door and saw me holding you. But she never told. I think she wanted you to live as well."

Joe sat back on the couch, reeling with this information. After a bit he put his face in his hands, ashamed that he thought his mother was anything less than an angel.

Carolyn knew Joe was hurting. Finding out that you were unwanted and meant to be tossed out as trash had to be devastating and was one of the reasons she had never wanted him to learn his birth story. Carolyn knelt next to him, her arms instinctively held him to her trying to shield him from his past and to once again be his protector.

"Mom, I'm sorry for leaving. Can you forgive me?" he asked his voice hoarse with emotion.

Carolyn's arms tightened around him, "There's nothing to forgive. You became my child the moment I held you and you always will be." Their tears mingled as they let the silence bond them once again.

Tom came in finding them sitting on the couch together. He knew they had both shed tears from their red streaked faces. Joe had stoked the fire and had his arm around his mother.

"I think it's time for some of my special eggnog, don't you?" Tom asked, already heading towards the kitchen.

"I think that's a great idea, Tom." Carolyn answered. "There might be a few cups still unbroken in there." She stated wryly.

"I could go for some leftover pumpkin pie, Dad." Joe added.

They reminisced about holidays past, enjoying the tree and fire and time with their oldest child. Carolyn felt her burden finally lift. The secret was out and now was in the past or so she thought.

CHAPTER 5

Joe woke up the next morning with both his sisters next to his bed staring at him, Jessica with a cup of coffee in hand extended toward him.

Cassie spoke first, "Joe, we're so glad you came back last night. Mom told us what happened." Before Joe could sit up he found both his sisters' arms wrapped around him like a vice. He always felt loved by these two, but this was almost smothering.

"Hey, you two, it's ok. Mom and I talked. I know she not so much stole me but rather saved my butt. But you two are about to smother me. Let me up for air." He said trying to lighten the mood. "That coffee for me??"

Jessica, the consummate emotionalist, already in tears, started to laugh. "Yes, we thought if we were going to wake you, we should bring a peace offering. Now get up. We helped Mom make a great breakfast and we still have to finish the tree this morning."

"Okay. Okay. I'm up." Joe said smiling, reaching for the coffee cup. "Now leave, please, and close the door on your way out."

Joe came out of his room feeling refreshed and rejuvenated from last night's childhood revelations. "Smells wonderful, Mom." He said coming into the kitchen.

"Morning Jacob. I suppose pretty soon I'll have you in my bedroom as well when I wake up!" Joe joked while picking up a crispy piece of bacon.

"No way. I prefer you dressed and upright." Jacob joked back, glad for the light-hearted morning after the revelations of last night.

Joe went to his mom and wrapped his arms around her. Planting a warm kiss on her cheek he asked. "Sleep well?"

"Yes, wonderfully." She said smiling and she meant it. It seemed for the first time in years she didn't fear closing her eyes. Joe now knew his past. It was all behind them; or so she thought.

Tom came in from the morning chores. "We have some baby kittens outside that are itching to have some time with you later."

"Not before that tree gets finished and the boxes are out of my living room." Carolyn said. "Everyone, sit down and eat, before it gets cold."

The light-hearted revelry continued into the living room as the individual tree decorations came out and everyone grabbed their favorites to hang in a place of honor. Jacob was happy to sit back and watch the three siblings as they joked around and kidded each other, reminiscing about a homemade ornament that had been made with loving hands. At the time the ornaments had seemed perfect to them as they presented their prizes to their mother, but now, years later, had become a bit disheveled. Carolyn still loved each and every one and wouldn't hear of throwing even one away.

"Mom, do you remember when we made these popsicle ornaments with pictures? Was I six or seven?" Cassie asked as she examined the ornament for a date.

"You were six." Carolyn answered matter of fact. Her memory regarding her children was sharp as a tack.

"Don't you think it's time to retire some of these ornaments and buy some new ones to replace them?" Cassie stated, already knowing the answer.

"I will never replace these ornaments. They were gifts from my children. No purchased ornament could replace their memories." Carolyn said adamantly.

When the ornaments had all found a place on the tree and they began carrying boxes back downstairs, Cassie picked up the box that had carried the secret upstairs. "Can this trouble-maker be tossed? Why did you keep it all these years, Mom?"

"It was part of my evidence should my actions that day ever be questioned. Dr. Jefferson was right that if it came down to my word against his, he would be the winner. I had hoped this hard evidence would support my side of the story if needed." Carolyn said stoically. "I lived in fear for years that the events surrounding Joe's birth would come out. Now I can sleep in peace at night. It was time the secret was told, the past few months I had nightmares replaying that day. I would hear the soft cry of a baby in the distance waking me, but I couldn't get there to answer the cries."

"Well, can we throw it out now?" Cassie persisted, wanting to put aside the pain of last night for them all.

"No," Joe said, walking in the room from the kitchen holding another cup of eggnog.

They all turned towards Joe, surprised by his interruption.

"That's evidence. And it's going to help my case." Joe answered flatly.

Carolyn's face turned white and she slowly sat down, her back rigid. "Evidence for what? Do you intend to prosecute me?"

Joe sat next to her and took her hands in his. "Mom, no one is going to ever prosecute you for saving me. I would never let that happen. But Dr. Clayton Jefferson is going to pay for what he did to me and to other babies that didn't have you protecting them."

"But... how?? It is my word against his and even with this box.. the evidence??" Carolyn stuttered.

Mom, you said there was another nurse in the delivery room. I believe you said her name was Eve."

Carolyn nodded her head to confirm, but couldn't find her voice.

"I'm going to find Eve and together we are going to build a case against this murdering doctor." Joe stated emphatically. "This box goes with me and I am going to punish the man who put me in it."

Joe solemnly picked up the tattered box, its secrets now revealed, and brought it to his room for safe keeping. His sisters, parents, and Jacob watched him in bewilderment. How was Joe going to make a case for crimes committed almost 30 years ago?

This wasn't over...... not by a long shot..... Carolyn's fears returned and with great cause.

Chapter 6

Saying good bye to her kids was always difficult for Carolyn and as the girls left to return to their daily lives (Jessica to the University, Cassie to Rochester with her soon to be husband, Jacob) she gave extra hugs partly for herself, putting off as long as possible the inevitable good bye. She had talked Joe into staying for supper so she would have him for a few more hours.

Walking into the living room with Joe she saw a blank yellow pad of paper and pen on the table, a sense of unease came over her. The warmth from the fire could not warm her hands.

"Mom, I need to ask you a couple of questions." Joe stated seriously as he slowly picked up the yellow pad with the pen poised to write down her recollections. Memories she had tried desperately to forget, but that haunted her dreams for years.

"I'm keeping no more secrets. Whatever I can tell you, I will." She answered quietly settling in to the oversized chair looking at the fire, hoping to feel its warmth as she put the throw blanket over her lap. Her fingers mindlessly picking at the stitching of the blanket.

"Can you remember Eve's last name?" Joe asked poised with his pen ready to jot down notes.

Carolyn took a second and sat back thinking, "I think it was Crenshaw. But she was single back then so it may have changed."

"I'm counting on it. If she married or divorced there would be legal records. My investigators can track those. If she is living and willing to testify, there certainly could be a case against Dr. Jefferson." Joe stated flatly.

"The next question I'm going to ask may be difficult and I want you to know it is not my intention to seek them out but rather to understand how you were able to get me out of the hospital." Joe said quietly, but with his big brown eyes fixing his gaze on her.

Carolyn nodded with resignation, not surprised this was coming. She was actually surprised he hadn't asked it Thursday night.

"Why didn't my birthparents question what went on at my birth?" Joe asked without emotion.

Carolyn shook her head slowly, "I don't know. Perhaps because they were told it was a stillbirth. That's what Dr. Jefferson told parents when he did this. He said he was 'saving the parents years of misery'. There was no birth certificate issued, only a death certificate." Carolyn didn't want to tell Joe these things. She never wanted him to feel he was an unwanted child because of a physical defect, but she promised herself after the revelations of Thursday that she would never withhold any information from him again – if he asked.

"Your birth mother was sedated. She wasn't told about your birth until she was back in her room. Your birth father was in the waiting room. I saw Dr. Jefferson talking with him as I slipped into the equipment room that day." Carolyn was becoming agitated as she retold parts of the story again. She rubbed her sweaty palms against the striped blanket. She wouldn't withhold the facts but Carolyn had her suspicions. Thirty years ago, raising a family wasn't easy, especially a child with special needs. She hadn't gone to Joe's biological father to plead for the child's life because she feared he wouldn't want him. She could have lost her job if she crossed that line and Joe still would have died.

"Had you seen Dr. Jefferson do this before?" Joe asked, his gaze never leaving her face.

"Never. I didn't regularly work OB. When I questioned Eve afterward, she said it had happened many times. She seemed very sad when she said it. She probably felt as helpless as I did that day."

Joe could tell that Carolyn was agitated and he needed to stop for now. Standing with the help of his metal crutch he reached down to put the pad and pen in his brief case. He slowly walked over next to Carolyn and leaned down quietly asking, "Could you come to my office Monday morning? I need to present this to the DA and I need you to tell what happened first hand."

Carolyn looked at the floor. This was going to get worse. Everyone was going to know, but she owed it to Joe to see it through if this is what he wanted. She slowly nodded. "If this is something you feel you need to do, I will do whatever I can to help." Lifting her blue eyes to meet his brown, "Just know that if you pursue this there won't be any way to go back. Things could get ugly, hurtful. I have spent my life protecting you, but I can't protect you any longer." She reached her hand up to touch his face, remembering the first time she touched his face as a baby. He was a beautiful baby grown into a handsome man. "Just remember that we love you and you are our son. Please don't let anyone hurt you."

"I know, Mom. And I won't let them hurt you either." Joe promised reaching over to hug his mom, not realizing what a huge promise he was making and one which couldn't be kept.

Chapter 7

Monday was a cold blustery November day. Carolyn arrived at Joe's office precisely at 9am. She had been there many times before, often with cookies or cake to share with his co-workers but not today. She knew today was all business. She felt like she should have brought something if for no other reason than to give her hands something to hold as she sat wringing them over and over.

Tom decided to come with her when she told him what Joe was asking. At first Tom adamantly stated Joe needed to drop this, after all, what good would come from digging up the past? But Carolyn stood her ground. She had promised Joe that she would come. She owed him this after keeping the story of his birth from him all these years. Tom finally acquiesced when he saw how resolved Carolyn was to see this through.

Usually Carolyn and Tom would go right into Joe's office. Today they took a seat in the waiting area and alerted the receptionist to their arrival. Carolyn had taken great care with selecting her attire this morning and had decided on a nice blue suit with the ruby broach Joe had surprised her with on her 50th birthday. Tom had dressed up a bit as well, with a pair of black dress pants and a warm maroon sweater.

Tom saw Carolyn fidgeting with her hands and reached over to hold one to help calm her. She smiled gratefully, intertwining her cold fingers with his warm weathered hand. The phone buzzed causing Carolyn to jump. The receptionist smiled and directed them to go down the hall to the conference room. As they entered, Joe and the District Attorney, James Kiehl, stood up.

James smiled with familiarity at both Tom and Carolyn. They had met several times over the past couple of years. He reached out his hand to both of them, "Tom, Carolyn nice to see you both. Joe has told me a little bit about what went on over Thanksgiving at your house, so much for a quiet holiday." James nodded towards the empty chairs at the table and continued, "He has asked me to listen to your story myself to see if there is any way to pursue charges against Dr. Jefferson. Please sit down and make yourself comfortable. There is water and coffee on the table. Help yourselves."

Before Joe sat down, he withdrew a piece of paper from a file in front of him.

"James, I'm going to ask you to do me a favor." The three of them looked at Joe wondering where this was going. "I promised my mother that no one would ever prosecute her for saving my life. Sometimes a person has to do something wrong to do what's morally right." He slid the sheet across the table to James and continued. "I'm going to ask you to trust me on this and sign this release acknowledging that my mother will never be prosecuted for anything relating to what she is about to divulge."

Carolyn and Tom were shocked. Carolyn remembered Joe's promise that no one would ever prosecute her for saving him, but she didn't expect that James would have ever done so. Joe just wanted to emphatically make a point that he was protecting her best interest.

James hesitated a moment. "Joe, you know it is highly irregular to sign a waiver without even hearing the evidence."

Joe nodded. The only sound in the room was the click of the pen, then he slowly slid the pen across the table. Joe held James' gaze, neither blinking. When Joe didn't waiver, James slowly signed his name.

"Well, now that's out of the way." James said sliding the paper back to Joe. "What is this all about?" Carolyn began to relate the story once again. It had become easier to tell now that her family knew. Tom held her hand throughout the re-telling of the story. James took copious notes as did Joe. Their yellow tablets now had pages of jotted down facts. After she finished recalling the events James and Joe took turns asking questions.

"Why didn't you go to the authorities then?" James asked.

"You didn't question doctors back then. Besides, it was my word against his. I didn't know which side of the fence Eve would back and still, we were only two nurses." Carolyn answered. "They were...they were like... gods...rulers of the medical world. We were trained to take orders and do as instructed. We were even taught to stand up when a doctor entered the room." Carolyn lamented. "Times have thankfully changed a bit, but there is still very much a hierarchy in the medical world. It's the same in the legal field. Can you question a judge when you are in their court?"

James's eyebrows raised. He was appreciative of her insight and she brought with it a great example. "I understand." He stated flatly.

Carolyn continued, "When I found out Eve had left, vanished, I didn't know what to think. But I knew I had to keep silent after that. At least I was able to keep Dr. Jefferson from doing any more harm."

James studied his notes and made a few more notations. "Unless we have some corroborating witnesses, we still have one person's word against another, with, of course, the box as evidence. Joe, if you want to pursue this further you will need to find Eve, if she's still alive. You cannot even think of charging him without her. Even with her it is still a bit of a long shot unless you can unearth some hard evidence."

Joe nodded his head in agreement. Carolyn and Tom had seen Joe's determination in action. He was just given the challenge, and he would rise to meet it.

The meeting was coming to a conclusion. Carolyn and Tom stood to leave gathering their winter coats when James extended his hand to Carolyn and then to Tom, "Joe is lucky to have you both, and Carolyn, I wish all children had an angel like you looking out for them." Carolyn managed a small smile for him. She was physically drained by the meeting and facing the demons that continued to haunt her. She knew from the determined look on Joe's face that he was not going to be satisfied until Dr. Jefferson was made to stand trial for his gruesome acts. This was far from over.

Chapter 8

The Christmas holiday came and went without any further word on where Joe was on the case. Carolyn tried not bringing up the topic, hoping that Joe would lose interest or gradually feel it unnecessary or unable to pursue. Joe didn't bring up the subject, but there was an unease she could see in quiet moments. Perhaps her demons had infected his subconscious as they had spent years in hers. Carolyn was sleeping better, but still woke at times during the night to the soft cry of a baby in her dreams. Perhaps this haunting will never go away.

Cassie brought home many wedding dress designs and had Gramma Jo sewing away through the months of January and February (the months all good Minnesotans spent curled up at home with some inside project or a good book).

Cassie was home doing a dress fitting with Gramma Jo and Carolyn when Joe's car came speeding up the driveway. Carolyn was concerned he would end up in the ditch as the snow was starting to melt making slick spots. She ran to the door to check on Joe as something was definitely abnormal.

"Joe, what are you trying to do? You could have ended up in the ditch or a snow bank??" She yelled concerned for his welfare.

"Mom, I found her," Joe yelled back through his car window, the words illiciting puffs of fog. He fumbling impatiently with the metal cane as he got out of the car. Though needed, at times it complicated his mobility as much as it assisted him.

Carolyn could feel the blood drain from her face. She knew, even without him telling her that, her, meant Eve. She gripped the railing on the porch. The added time that it took Joe to climb the ramp gave her a few extra minutes to come to terms with this revelation.

When Joe got to the porch he said, "Eve, we found Eve." His enthusiasm told her that this was something that would never be dropped. This is something he was determined to see through to the end. Her stomach flipped again just as it did the fateful day that sent them on this journey.

"Where?" she asked, trying to sound upbeat, but it came out more ambivalent than anything.

"I don't have all the logistics, but from what's been reported she moved from here to Illinois to be with family. She was pregnant. After her daughter was born she met and married a man named Albert Stockwell. They moved back to southern Minnesota in 1975 where he farmed and she worked as a nurse in the local hospital. They never had any more kids – just the one daughter she had prior to her marriage which her husband adopted."

Pregnant. That's why she left. But why leave? Joe was continuing to talk but, Carolyn's mind was going in many different directions. She wrapped the sweater around her trying to keep the early March winds at bay. She felt cold but the cold was coming from within.

"Mom, I'm driving down to talk with Eve. She's living with her daughter now. Her husband passed away three years ago and she moved in with her daughter last year. She's fighting breast cancer. We have to move on this or Eve may not be able to tell us what she knows." Joe was very serious and talking very quickly. She could tell his mind was racing trying to put all the pieces together. That's why he liked the law. He liked putting the pieces of a case together, to solve the mystery. She understood, right now he needed to solve the case of his own attempted murder. It was personal.

"How far a drive is it?" Carolyn asked.

"Just to Rochester. Her daughter is a nurse at the Mayo down there and that's where Eve is getting her treatments I assume." Joe answered.

"Will you be back in time for supper?" Carolyn asked, anxious now to find out what information Joe will uncover.

"I don't know Mom, could be late." Joe answered. He knew his mother would be troubled by what he may learn and knew he would be the only person who could alleviate her anxiety. "How about I come by afterwards, but don't wait supper on me."

She nodded with a small smile. He knew that there would be a plate in the warmer for him when he got back. He turned to leave, but suddenly turned back and gave Carolyn a warm reassuring hug. He softly whispered in her ear, "I love you, Mom." Her arms tightened in response, feeling reassured before he turned to leave to continue his quest for answers.

The drive down to Rochester was uneventful. When he arrived at the house, he noted the quaint rambler was well kept. The white picket fence now covered in snow from the shoveled pathway was a nice touch. He had knocked on many doors in his profession, following up on leads from investigators but none of his past investigations had such familial ties. He found himself nervous as he rang the doorbell.

A beautiful strawberry-blonde woman in nursing scrubs answered the door. As he handed her his Assistant DA card he felt a quick moment of electricity pass between them.

"Hello, I'm Joseph Steffan. I'm an Assistant District Attorney with Meeker County. I understand Eve Stockwell lives here. I'd like to ask her a few questions about an investigation I'm conducting.

"Please come in." She said studying his card. "My name is Anne Stockwell. My mother is Eve Stockwell. She's resting right now. Please sit down. What is this in regards to?" She asked frowning slightly.

"Your mother was a staff nurse at Memorial County Hospital in 1969. There was an incident which we are investigating and would like some information." Joe stated evasively. He didn't want to tip his hand until he actually saw Eve.

"So long ago, why the sudden interest in something that happened almost 30 years ago?" she asked glancing at his card for his name, "Mr. Steffan is it?" Anne had felt the attraction as well. It had been two years since her broken engagement and she had avoided relationship involvements. The last year her mother's health had deteriorated and it was necessary she focus on her.

"Just following up on information that has recently come to my attention." Joe answered evasively.

There was a brief moment of awkward silence before a weak voice called from the hall. "Who do we have here?" a voice said entering the room. A frail looking older woman using a cane entered the room. Her head was covered with a kerchief presumably covering the effects of chemotherapy treatments. Her skin looked paper thin and had many bruised areas. Joe correctly presumed this woman was the Eve he had been searching for these past few months. His math had her at about 65 years old but this woman looked much older.

Joe stood up and extended his hand. Eve motioned for him to be seated. "You'll forgive me if I don't shake your hand. I've been told to keep my contact with others at a minimum due to the cancer treatments."

Joe nodded. "I'm Joseph Steffan, Assistant District Attorney for Meeker County."

"Yes, I heard. I presume you've met my daughter, Anne." Eve stated, nodding towards Anne as she took a seat on the sofa.

"Yes." Joe answered nodding with a smile toward Anne, wishing this was more of a social call. "I've been hoping to talk with you about your work at Memorial County Hospital in 1969." Joe stated becoming once again the consummate professional, somewhat taken aback that Eve appeared not to be surprised by his visit.

Eve leaned back on the couch and pulled a crocheted shawl around her shoulders exposing very thin fingers as she grasped the yarn. She didn't say anything for a few moments and then addressed her daughter. "Anne, you best get going or you will be late for your shift. I'm fine here with Mr. Steffan. Could you hand me a cup of coffee before leaving, dear." Then addressing Joe, "Would you care for a cup?"

"No, thank you," Joe answered, anxious to get to his questions but realizing that perhaps Eve was waiting until they were alone.

Anne brought over the coffee and whispered in her mother's ear.

Eve waved her off, "I'll be fine. You go to work."

Anne kissed the top of her mother's head as she cast a questioning gaze towards Joe, wishing she could stay, wondering what this 30 year old investigation was about, but knowing she had to leave to be on time for her shift.

She nodded politely to Joe, "Nice to meet you. I trust that this won't take long. She tires very easily."

"I understand, Miss Stockwell. I'll be as brief as possible." Joe answered sincerely. He realized that he needed Eve's testimony to move forward with the case, but that her condition is tenuous and he would have to be careful not to overtax her strength.

When they heard the garage door close and the crunch of Anne's tires on the hardened snow, Eve turned her attention to the matter of Joe's visit. "Now, Mr. Steffan what can I do for you?"

"In September of 1969 you attended the birth of a baby boy with spina bifida delivered by Dr. Jefferson at Memorial County Hospital. Do you remember that day?" Joe asked.

"Mr. Steffan, I'm a nurse and I have attended the births of hundreds of babies in my career. What makes you think I remember one in particular?" Eve answered evasively without making eye contact.

"Because instead of resuscitating the infant Dr. Jefferson ordered you to get a box from the equipment closet which you did, he then placed the infant boy in the box with tape over its mouth and ordered you to put the box with the infant back into the equipment closet presumably to let it die." Joe answered matter of fact, trying to keep his emotions in check, always referring to the baby in the third person. But Eve had already noticed the metal cane and came to her own correct conclusion.

There were a few minutes of complete silence while Eve tried to calculate her next move. Does she tell him everything she knows? But then Anne would find out the correct circumstances of her birth and that was a secret Eve willingly planned to take to her grave.

"Mr. Steffan, I am an old, sick woman with breast cancer. The doctors say I probably have a year left to live, if that. I'm trying to get my personal affairs in order. Why would I want to spend any of my remaining time on something that happened nearly 30 years ago? Why are you trying to dredge up the past? I've moved on from that time and made a good life for myself and my daughter. I married a good man and we raised a wonderful daughter together. There are some things that are better left buried, don't you think?" Eve said putting her cup on the table.

Joe could tell she was bothered by this because her hand shook when she placed it back in her lap.

"Mrs. Stockwell, I'm not planning to prosecute you for any crimes committed that day. I'm trying to hold Dr. Clayton Jefferson responsible for his actions." Joe noticed that when he said Dr. Jefferson's name Eve looked out the window and put her frail hand to her face, something more was going on here. "Did you know that they just presented him with the "Humanitarian of the Year Award"?

Eve's face turned quickly to Joe and a small smile crossed her lips, "I'm not surprised. Everyone in that hospital thought he walked on water. Even I had succumbed to his handsome features and intellect. But believe me, he was no Humanitarian."

"Yes, I heard much the same message from my mother." Joe said.

Eve finally asked the obvious, "You are Carolyn Steffan's son, correct?"

"Yes."

"How is she?" Eve asked with obvious interest.

"She is well."

"How many children did Carolyn have?"

"Three. I have two sisters." Joe answered, fidgeting slightly, anxious to get back to his questions, the ultimate reason for his visit.

"You are her only son."

"Yes."

"I bet she was a great mother."

"The best." Joe answered, not totally understanding the reasoning for this topic but felt that if Eve became more familiar with him, she may trust him with her hidden secrets.

"I knew she would be. She was a good nurse compassionate, empathetic, and smart. She went through a lot when she lost her first baby." Eve stated calmly, leaning back into the pillows. Eve always held Carolyn in high esteem and saw how devastated she was when told her first baby didn't make it.

"Mrs. Stockwell," Joe interjected trying to get her back to the subject he had come to research.

"Oh, please, call me Eve. The formality is unnecessary and frankly cumbersome."

"Eve, what does this have to do with my original question? You seem to remember plenty about my mother, but you evade telling me what you know about the birth." Joe said, trying to bring her back to the original line of questioning.

"Yes, I remember the birth, YOUR birth. If we are going to be honest let's be honest. Your mother finally told you about the circumstances obviously and now you are bitter. Yes, Dr. Jefferson was a monster by today's standards, but back then it was a different time. Doctors were given certain latitudes if you will. If you proceed down this path to uncover truths, people will get hurt. You, your mother, your family, me, my family, and yes, Dr. Jefferson and who knows how many others. There's a slippery slope. You don't know the half of what you think you know. I'm an old frail woman who would rather die at peace with the secrets I must bear and the sins which I will soon have to answer for." Eve's secrets went far beyond what Joe had been told. She was the answer to cracking this case and yet it was evident she didn't want to help.

"Why do you refuse to discuss that event? Is it because of your daughter? I know you left Memorial County Hospital shortly after my birth. My investigators followed your trail to Illinois and then back here to Minnesota. You were pregnant when you left." Joe shared his information waiting to see if knowing how much he already knew would prod her into sharing the rest of the story.

Eve's face turned to stone, "My daughter knows little about my life prior to meeting her father. I plan to keep it that way.

She knows that she was born prior to our marriage. She believes her father was a Vietnam War Veteran that I met and secretly married. She was told he died during his next tour over there. My husband adored Anne, adopted her as his own. She was our only child and our sun rose and set on her. End of story. I will not tear down my life's story and hurt my daughter by opening wounds best left forgotten. I will not! Dr. Jefferson be damned!" Eve's voice came to a crescendo with the end of her tirade.

The silence between them became deafening. Joe knew this discussion was at an impasse and slowly rose to leave. "I'm sorry you feel this way. I thought I was giving you an opportunity to make things right, to uncover hidden truths. The hiding of which, allowed this man to continue to be revered in his community. How many babies died at his hands, babies that didn't have a guardian angel like my mother to save them, all because they had the unfortunate circumstance of being born visibly imperfect. We may have disabilities that can be seen on the outside, but truth be told, Dr. Jefferson, and you, have imperfections on the inside. You may choose to continue to hide the truth of the past; but I choose to hold Dr. Jefferson accountable for playing god." Joe stopped for a moment frustrated by the seemingly lack of concern with what Joe had come to think of as a holocaust of the disabled. Joe slowly turned toward Eve while putting on his overcoat and suddenly stopped, "What if I had been your daughter, Anne? Would you have loved her any less? Would you have wanted her to die in an equipment closet with tape over her mouth, smothering her cries?" Joe's voice cracked with his last statement and he turned to pick up his metal cane. Without turning around he said, "Good day to you Mrs. Stockwell. Sleep well."

CHAPTER 9

The flash of Joe's headlights coming up the driveway alerted Carolyn to start his plate warming.

Tom met Joe at the door with a warm hug. "Long drive? How were the roads?" A typical Minnesotan winter question, always worried about road conditions.

"Yes, long, but the roads were good." Joe answered with exhaustion creeping into his voice. Joe's slow movements indicated that he was reaching the end of his endurance today. Due to his special challenges it takes twice the energy for Joe to walk and sit and drive than people without challenges.

"Mom's getting your plate warm." Tom answered reaching down to pet Sammy who had nosed her way between them. "I think Sammy misses you. You've been pretty scarce the past couple of weeks."

"I know dad. Work." Joe answered, but the truth was this case was keeping him up nights and he didn't want them worrying about him. He wanted his questions answered and he felt the questions were creating a wedge in their relationship. Things wouldn't be right until he finished the journey that started the day he saw the box.

Carolyn came in carrying a plate heaping full of pork chops, mashed potatoes, corn and a warm biscuit. "I knew you'd be hungry, so I saved plenty." She said putting the plate on the dining room table.

"Looks fantastic, Mom! I sure have missed your cooking!" Joe said smiling. His mouth watered just looking at the food.

Carolyn poured the three of them a glass of wine as Joe started eating the mound of food set before him. He voraciously ate the delicious plate of food while his parents exchanged unvoiced concerns about Joe's appearance. He appeared to have lost some weight and was notably exhausted.

Carolyn tentatively approached the subject of his visit with Eve. "Did you meet Eve?"

"Yes, and her daughter, Anne – briefly, quite a beautiful woman," Joe answered between mouthfuls.

"How did it go?" Carolyn questioned. Her antennae raised.

"Not very well I'm afraid." Joe answered keeping his eyes on his food. "Eve is going through chemotherapy for breast cancer. She probably has a year, at best, to live and doesn't want to spoil the charade she's concocted for her daughter to believe about her past. She believes that if she tells the truth about her past it would change all of it. I'm not exactly sure as to why she lied to her daughter in the first place. Is it that important to save face just because she was an unwed mother?"

Carolyn was thoughtful for a moment. Her finger absentmindedly tracing the pattern in the table cloth before offering, "I thought about this while you were gone. I made a couple of phone calls myself. There were rumors going around the hospital back around the time of your birth that Dr. Jefferson was having an affair with one of the nurses."

Carolyn looked at Joe and found he was very attentive to her every word at this moment.

"I called a couple of the nurses that worked at the hospital back when Eve was there. One nurse, Mary Clark, is now retired, but she remembered finding Eve and Dr. Jefferson in the delivery room on a quiet night shift. She walked in to deliver some supplies and flipped on the light. They were on the table in a very compromising position. Mary kept quiet because Dr. Jefferson was on the hospital board and she wanted to keep her job." She paused before announcing, "I think Anne is Dr. Jefferson's baby." Carolyn quietly finished her revelation.

Joe's fork hit his now empty plate.

"Of course," he whispered more to himself than anyone else.

"Joe, you're going to stay here tonight." Tom stated. It wasn't a request.

Carolyn placed her hand over Joe's. "We've missed you and you look exhausted. No more driving tonight. There are fresh linens on your bed and towels in the bathroom. You need a good night sleep and I need to feed you another meal!"

Joe smiled and nodded his agreement. He loved these two. No matter where this case leads, that will never change. "In that case how about dessert?" He asked, knowing his mom had whipped up something just for him. "Pie? Cookies?" He suggested hopefully.

"Blueberry pie, your favorite." Carolyn said getting up to serve it.

"Ala Mode?" both Tom and Joe said together and started laughing.

The next morning Joe's eyes fluttered open, his hand on something soft and furry. He lifted his head to find Sammy lying next to him on the bed. "Well, at least you didn't wake me up like my sisters. But they brought me coffee." He said scratching Sammy behind the ears. Sammy inched forward to lick Joe's face lovingly.

"Yah, I missed you too." Joe said trying to extricate himself from the pup's expression of adoration.

Joe walked in to the kitchen to the smell of pancakes and bacon cooking. Tom was at the table reading the paper and Carolyn flipping cakes on the stove. "Dad, do you wake up to this kind of breakfast every day? I may just have to move home!" Joe said taking a seat next to his father.

Tom smiled as he lowered the paper, "No, son. If I did, I would be about 300 pounds. Your mom is worried that you're losing weight. Needs to fatten you up I guess."

"Hush now," Carolyn said to Tom, putting a plate with fresh cakes and bacon in front of him and Joe. "You get plenty of good cooking even when the kids aren't home. But Joe, you are losing weight. Please remember to eat. You and your father are cut from the same cloth. When you are immersed in a project you ignore your stomachs."

"That's because when I cook it doesn't taste nearly as good as yours!" Joe said delving into the stack of cakes in front of him.

Carolyn smiled at the compliment and, sitting down, poured coffee for the three of them. "So, where do you go from here. You made it sound like Eve isn't going to help. Can you force her?"

"I can subpoena her, if that's what you mean." Joe said taking a bite of bacon. "That's generally not a great idea if you don't know what information they will divulge." Joe sat back thinking for a moment. "I guess I will give her a week or so and maybe go back and hope she's changed her mind. I can't table this for long, Eve's health may deteriorate further and the court process can be long. The other side can draw it out even longer. If she dies her secrets die with her and that bastard gets away scot free."

Carolyn nodded. She understood how important this was to Joe. He needed to see it through even though she had wished he would drop it when it began. She now needed to stand by her son and help him as much as she could. Perhaps a visit mother to mother would make a difference to Eve.

Carolyn stood outside the small house in Rochester. It was very quaint, a cottage style house that had decorative scrolling on the porch outside. The white shutters had cut outs of hearts on them and the icicles that now melted from the eaves made it look like a story book home. This was Anne's home. Eve had moved in with her when her chemotherapy started. Joe had told her that Anne was also a nurse. It is uncanny how many nurses have daughters that followed in their footsteps.

Carolyn had called information to get Eve's number. She had wanted to surprise her as she could easily choose to avoid her visit, but good Minnesota manners and concern for Eve's health dictated that she call ahead. Eve seemed surprised to hear her voice on the other end when she called. Carolyn had been persistent about needing to talk "about old times" with her and Eve acquiesced. When Carolyn said she could come when Anne wasn't at home or she could surprise them when she was, and fill Anne in on what this was really all about, the choice was Eve's. She chose to meet Carolyn on a day when Anne would be tied up at work for a 12 hour shift.

When Carolyn rang the doorbell Eve immediately opened the door even before the ringing stopped.

"Carolyn, you're looking well." Eve said, "Come in."

"Thank you for seeing me, Eve. It's been a long time. I'm sorry to hear you are ill. I brought some homemade cookies." Carolyn said removing her winter trappings. Carolyn could tell that Joe's description of Eve was accurate. The chemotherapy treatments were taking their toll on Eve's body. She was very thin. Gone was the beautiful blonde hair Carolyn remembered. Eve had tried to put make up over the discolored blotches of skin on her face, but the blueness was still showing.

Eve cozied herself under a blanket and shawl on the couch and pointed to the coffee and cups on the table in front of her. "Please share a cup with me." Even though Eve wasn't happy initially about the visit, she had liked Carolyn when they worked together and wanted the visit to be on cordial terms.

Carolyn poured the cups of coffee for both of them, setting a cookie beside Eve's cup before settling back into the wingback chair. "This is a nice cozy home." Carolyn offered wanting to break the silence. The house was small but beautifully furnished and immaculate.

"Yes, I moved in with my daughter about a year and a half ago. I just was too weak to continue to maintain my house with my husband gone. It is convenient to the hospital for both Anne and I." Eve stated with pride looking around at the home her daughter was so proud to purchase.

"I heard your daughter also became a nurse. How nice for you." Carolyn stated smiling. She noticed a photograph of Anne on the table in front of her. "She's beautiful." From the photograph Carolyn could see a remarkable resemblance to Dr. Jefferson. He was quite a handsome doctor so it would only make sense that his daughter be beautiful.

"Yes, it has been helpful. How about your daughters?" Eve asked, taking Carolyn by surprise. Joe must have told her about Cassie and Jessica.

"No, no nurses. My oldest daughter lives here in Rochester and is a physical therapist. She's engaged to an internal medicine doctor. Perhaps you've heard of him, Jacob Schmidt. My youngest is in medical school at the University of Minnesota, and of course, you met my son."

"Yes, quite a handsome young man. He's done very well. His disability doesn't seem to hamper him at all." Eve answered.

Carolyn's back stiffened at the mention of Joe's disability. She spent hundreds of hours working with him on exercises and poured through medical journals reading the latest research, and sitting by Joe's bedside through his numerous surgeries. "I choose to think of that as his special challenge not a disability."

"He sure is lucky you chose to become his mother." Eve answered.

"You mean rather than letting him die? Yes, I suppose that is lucky." Carolyn bristled.

"Carolyn, let's cut to the chase. I accept what happened 30 years ago. Joe lived. Isn't that enough? Why do you want to open old wounds? You know it won't help you either – you'll come off looking like a kidnapper. You deprived Joe's parents of raising their son. There's a good chance that Joe may learn things that may change his feelings about you."

Carolyn set her cup down and nervously rubbed her hands on her pants. "It's not my decision any longer – it's his. He wants to hold Dr. Jefferson accountable for his actions. I didn't kidnap him. I saved him from dying. Something you weren't willing to do."

"I couldn't. You don't understand. This went deeper than you know." Eve spat out.

"I know. You were pregnant....with Dr. Jefferson's child." Carolyn said triumphantly.

Eve's face went ashen and she gripped the couch with her hand. "You know?"

"Not at first but yes, I now know, and now so does Joe."

"Then you should understand why I can't help him. I don't want Anne to know the monster that her biological father was. I didn't totally see it until I saw the courage you exhibited by saving Joe and then raising him as your own. I realized then I needed to leave town to save my own child." Eve said rubbing her forehead with her fingers.

"To save your child? Was she in danger?" Carolyn questioned, not understanding this piece of the puzzle.

"Yes, Clayton,.. Dr. Jefferson found out that I was with child. He was trying to get me to abort her. He said if word got out that he fathered an illegitimate child it would hurt his family and his practice. He said he could perform the abortion and no one would ever know. That's when I knew what a monster he was. He wanted to kill his own child to save his precious reputation, his standing in the community." Eve said angrily, her eyes getting damp with unshed tears. She remembered begging him to divorce his wife and marry her so they could raise their child together. He had laughed at the thought of divorce. He was Catholic and had several children with his wife. He wasn't about to uproot his life for her and her bastard child.

"I left knowing that without my presence the incident with Joe's birth would be buried. He would be safe in your arms." Eve put down her coffee and looked out the window at the water dripping from the icicles making small rivers on the pane. "I heard several years later that Dr. Jefferson suddenly stopped the practice of putting disabled babies in boxes right after I left. I knew deep down it was you who stopped him. I was very thankful for that. You are a good person Carolyn."

Eve took a deep breath as though making a long-awaited confession, "I've made many mistakes in my life. Many I regret, but I don't regret having Anne. That being said, I don't want her to know about the past. Is it so bad to keep things buried? We have so much to lose." Eve implored. Her gaze fixed on Carolyn. Eve was hoping for absolution or consolation, Carolyn didn't know which.

Carolyn's hands gripped each other in her lap, but her gaze was squarely on Eve's face, "I promised Joe after he found the box that he had been placed in after his birth, the box that he was suppose to die in, that I would never keep anything from him again. It's his past also, and he has a right to feel the way he does. Dr. Jefferson and you were willing to throw his life away. Is that right? Does it make it okay because he lived? You told me that day that Dr. Jefferson had put many babies in boxes to die. Call it what it truly was – murder. He murdered those babies. They were alive when they were born. They were human beings at their most vulnerable and helpless. What about them? What about their parents. Those children need us to speak up finally, to make their lives matter. It is our duty as nurses, as human beings."

Carolyn could see the doubt cross Eve's face so she quickly added. "If your daughter is a nurse, she will understand this, too. Eve, we finally have a chance to do what's right." Carolyn suddenly stood up and went to the window looking out at the dirty snow-covered streets. "As for Joe's feelings about me, I will have to take that chance. I love him. I couldn't love him more if he had come out of my own body. It's because of that love that I have to allow him to follow this through to the end."

"Carolyn, I will think about it. But if we open this up just know that things could get messy. It is not my intention that you or your family get hurt, but if I talk, I will hold nothing back. There's much that will be uncovered." Eve warned.

Carolyn was taken aback by Eve's statement. She didn't fully understand why she was warning her, but all she could do was nod her acceptance.

"I will be in touch." Eve said cutting the visit short. She had much to think about and her energy was sapped.

Due to the shortened visit Carolyn thought she had time to drop by Cassie's and Jacob's new house for a tour. Cassie begged her to stay for supper so she called Tom to tell him he was a bachelor for the evening. It felt good to look at paint swatches and carpet samples and forget for a moment the past lies and cover up. Jacob had to return to the hospital for a quick consult leaving Carolyn to spend some time with her daughter.

By the time she got back to the hobby farm that night the road was covered with new snow. It was falling hard making driving slow and difficult. Pulling up next to the house she recognized Joe's car next to Tom's truck. Both were covered with the new snow so she knew they had been home for quite a while.

The snow fell from her cap and coat as she entered the front door. Her boots made a puddle on the freshly washed floor.

"We were really getting worried about you," Tom said coming over to take her coat and give her a warm hug. "You feel cold. Wasn't your car warm?"

"I think the heater is acting up again. We may have to break down and trade that car in one of these days." She answered, glad to be home and warm again.

"Joe, I hope you plan on spending the night. The roads are getting nasty. You know how March snow storms can get." Carolyn stated out of concern for her son.

"Dad invited me over for his famous chili and to watch the high school basketball playoff games on TV. The time got away from us. By the time I noticed the heavier snow I made the decision to stay and make sure you got home ok." Joe answered. "I didn't know you were planning on making a drive to see Cassie today."

"Well, I didn't go down just to see her." Carolyn answered, sitting in a chair next to the fire and wrapping one of her favorite throws around her legs. "In fact, I didn't plan on seeing her at all. I went down to talk with Eve." Carolyn's eyes darted to a guilty looking Tom as he knew Carolyn's plans, but felt it was up to her if she wanted to share them with Joe.

Joe's gaze quickly turned to his mother's face, but he waited for her to continue before uttering a sound.

"When you came home after your trip to Rochester, you seemed disappointed with the outcome. I thought perhaps, mother to mother, I could be more persuasive." Carolyn explained.

"I'm surprised, Mom. You haven't really seemed happy that I'm pursuing this, so why the change of heart? Why try to persuade Eve to come forward and help with the investigation?" Joe asked taking another sip of his beer.

"I guess it's true that I haven't been excited to dig up the past, but I see it's important to you and you are my son. I owe this to you, to see this through. Perhaps we were meant to do this. People should know this happened." Carolyn explained.

"Those who forget history are doomed to repeat it." Joe quietly said more to himself than anyone else.

Carolyn nodded.

"So, were you able to persuade Eve to share what she knows?" Joe asked hopefully.

"I don't know. Time will tell. I think she has to come to terms with it herself and perhaps share some things with her daughter. That will be difficult, but the Eve that I knew 30 years ago would come forward. She has your number, right?"

Joe nodded.

Subject was closed.

"Now, after that terrible drive I'm hungry for some chili. Any left?" Carolyn asked smiling at Tom.

"Yes, of course, you know I make enough for an army." Tom answered heading into the kitchen. "Did you enjoy your evening with Cassie?"

"The house is beautiful and we went through paint swatches and carpet swatches. I'm hoping for some nursery swatches soon after the wedding." Carolyn joked. "Say, I'd take a hot chocolate since you're in there."

"Yes, m'lady." Tom joked back.

It felt good to be home. Carolyn watched the flames of the fireplace dance and her mind drifted to her conversation with Eve. She will have some difficult decisions to make. It isn't easy dismantling walls of the charade she had built. Will her daughter understand?

CHAPTER 10

The house was dark when Anne drove up. She saw a flicker of light from what looked like a cigarette through the front window. Why wasn't her mother in bed resting?

As Anne came through the garage into the kitchen, she turned on the lights. Eve was sitting next to the window putting out a cigarette with the light to her back. Why was her mother sitting in the dark? Why was she smoking? She had quit years ago.

"Mom?" Anne said questioningly, "Everything okay? Why are you up and sitting in the dark?" She wasn't going to even ask about the cigarette as Eve's face obviously had worry etched across her brow.

"Anne, I was waiting for you, a little worried about the snowy roads." Eve answered. The truth was that Eve was more than a little worried about what she needed to finally tell her. After Carolyn left, Eve tried to rest, but every time she closed her eyes her mind would race back to the days she had tried to leave behind her. Why did Carolyn have to bring the past to her doorstep? Why couldn't they leave the past buried? But now that she uncovered the past, she knew her memories couldn't be put to rest until she faced them, whatever the outcome.

"I'm fine, Mom. Let's get you to bed." Anne answered, knowing there was something more that was bothering her mother.

"Anne, come and sit with me. I need to share some things with you." Eve nodded towards the couch.

The tone in her mother's voice told Anne this is serious.

"Honey, I need to tell you about your father, your biological father." Eve began. "He wasn't a war hero that died in Vietnam. I made that up to protect you from my past." Eve paused for courage then moved forward, "He was a doctor that I had a long-standing affair with back before I moved to Illinois. He's alive and lives in Meeker County."

Eve watched Anne's face for signs of disapproval or anger but all she saw was one of acceptance. "You don't seem surprised?" Eve stated taking a sip of the drink she had made to give her courage.

"No, I'm not surprised." Anne said. "You've never wanted to talk about him or give me information – even his name. Several years ago, I had many questions so I went up to the attic and looked in the basement for anything that might give me answers." Anne slowly got up and went to her beautiful oak desk in the study off the living room. She came back into the living room and turned on a light next to Eve's chair, and handed her a few pictures. One of them was the only picture she had of her and Dr. Jefferson together. Anne noticed she had his eyes and presumed correctly, that he was her father. The other picture was of Eve's nursing school graduation photo. She was very beautiful and wore a distinctive angel necklace in the photograph. "Is this the man who was my biological father?"

"Yes, Dr. Clayton Jefferson," Eve whispered staring at the photo. It transported her back in time. Clayton Jefferson was very handsome and charismatic as a young doctor. When he started to show her attention a couple of years after she started working at Memorial County Hospital she was flattered. It started out innocently with flirtatious gazes, then small notes slid through charts, brief kisses in linen closets or empty patient rooms. The sexual tension grew between them until it couldn't be contained. The first time he touched her under her clothes he left a hot trail of kisses that seemed to burn into her skin. She knew he was married but he wanted her, not his wife. He whispered how it drove him crazy just being in the same room with her. He planned a weekend getaway. He told his family he was 'hunting' and took her to a cabin in the woods. They were in bed all weekend. They couldn't get enough of each other's body. After that weekend she was his to take wherever and whenever the mood struck him. She fell deeply in love with him and he with her, or so she thought. When she first suspected she was pregnant she was thrilled thinking this would be their chance to be a family. She was so sure he would choose her and their child, for it truly was their love child. But when she told him she was pregnant with Anne, he became cold. He still wanted her body, he desired her, but he didn't love her, at least not enough to give up the façade of a happy, respectable family man.

Eve dropped the photo on the floor, just holding it now burned her fingertips. The years she wasted waiting for that man to choose her, to love her, to marry her. Wasted time she could never get back. But he did give her Anne, beautiful Anne. She had his eyes and his smile. She was all the best of him, but with a heart of gold.

Anne hugged Eve as tears of regret slowly slid down Eve's face. "It's okay, Mom. I love you no matter who my biological father was. You gave me a great dad when you married Pops. He was my father."

"You are right. You had a great dad." Eve affirmed. "I wish I had been the wife he deserved."

Anne looked at her with surprise. She always knew her parents weren't very demonstrative of their love for each other. They were kind to one another but she saw no stolen kisses, no affectionate touching with each other, but both doted on her and showered her with kisses and hugs. "Don't get me wrong. I loved your father, but I was not 'in love with him'. I thought he was a good man and would be a good father to you which he was. But we didn't have passion, that spark that ignited sensations throughout your body. I had given that to your biological father and regretted the wasted years. I married your father for security and we did make a good life. We had mutual respect. I hope one day you can have both, preferably in the same man."

"Why are you telling me this now?" Anne asked softly, wondering what precipitated her need to divulge this now when she had avoided this question so fiercely in the past.

"I needed to tell you this because there will be a court case against your biological father shortly and I will be a witness against him." Eve took a breath and leaned back in her chair, silently wondering what it will be like to look into his blue eyes again.

Anne's eyes were big and her face was ashen. In one statement her mother had just unloaded a lifetime of truth. But what was more shocking was the statement about a court case.

"What kind of court case?" Anne asked in a whisper.

Her mother whispered back, "Murder".

Chapter 11

Two days later Joe was up to his elbows in documents when he received the call from Eve's daughter, Anne. Could he come down to meet with her mother in their home rather than Eve coming to his office due to Eve's health issues. He arranged for the District Attorney to come along. They would tape the interview for future review.

When they reached Anne and Eve's residence the D.A. took on his professional overture. This was serious business and he would treat it as such. Although this was personal for Joe, James needed to look at this logically and even more objectively to ensure they were looking at all the possibilities. Dr. Jefferson was a notable figure in the county. Accusing him of attempted murder should not be taken lightly or without much preparation and forethought.

They gathered in the living room. Eve sat surrounded by pillows and warm throw blankets at one end of the sofa. Anne sat next to her, holding her hand. James and Joe sat in the facing wingback chairs with yellow notepads on their laps and a tape recorder on the coffee table in front of them.

Joe had done the introductions and since he was the most familiar with the case, Joe would be taking the lead on the interview.

Joe knew Eve's hesitancy with sharing things with her daughter present so he broached the subject delicately, "Eve, we are going to be recording this interview so we can review it when needed. It will not replace your testimony, however. I will be asking questions that may be difficult for you. Are you sure you want your daughter to be present for the entirety of this interview?"

"Mr. Steffan, I, like your mother, have promised my daughter that going forward there will be no secrets between us. She has promised to stand by my side through this ordeal. No matter the outcome. She is now aware of things I have chosen to keep from her in the past, but has asked that I not shield her any longer. I do, however, appreciate your concern." Eve stated proudly looking lovingly from her daughter to Joe.

Anne nodded at Joe with a small smile.

Joe reached for the recorder and informed the group he would make a brief introduction acknowledging who was being interviewed, the date, and those present.

Joe referred to his notes and began, "Mrs. Stockwell, what dates did you work at the Memorial County Hospital?"

"From 1960 to 1969."

"What department did you work in while employed at this hospital?" Joe asked jotting her answer to the previous question on his yellow legal pad.

"My primary department was obstetrics, but it was a small hospital so I did float to other departments as well."

"On the date of September 15, 1969, were you working in obstetrics?" Joe asked. He knew the date exactly as it was his birthday.

"It has been 30 years." Eve stated, cocking her head to the side, "but if you are referring to the date of your birth, yes I was."

"Can you describe in your own words what happened that day?" Joe asked very professionally. His years of experience keeping his emotions in check when discussing cases with clients helped him sound outwardly detached even though inwardly, he could feel his heart beating in his ears.

"The doctor had given your mother medication to anesthetize her as he knew he would have to use forceps for the delivery. As he delivered you, the baby, he noticed a bulge on the back which indicated strongly that the baby suffered from Spina Bifida, a disabling ailment which in most cases meant that the child would be wheelchair bound. He made a decision that the child should not be saved." Eve's head turned toward the window. She couldn't look at Joe as she finished her statement. "He asked me to get one of the boxes kept in the equipment room, boxes kept there for this type of case."

"Could not or should not be saved?" Joe asked looking at his yellow pad for reference.

"Should not. He, as well as other medical professionals at that time, believed they were saving the parents from a lifetime of caring for a disabled child." Eve stated remembering the words Dr. Jefferson so often uttered to explain his actions.

"Type of case?" Joe asked, "Could you clarify your meaning, and also you stated the doctor, which doctor are you referring to?"

"The doctor is Clayton Jefferson. The type of case is referring to what Dr. Jefferson referred to as 'hopeless'".

Her words took the breath out of Joe's chest as if someone had pounded on it. He had just been referred to as 'hopeless' at birth and told he should not be saved.

Eve saw Joe's face and softened her words, "Obviously, he was wrong in your case."

"Continue please," Joe said, the words coming out raspy. He reached for the water Anne had thoughtfully placed in front of him when he arrived, grateful now for her thoughtful hospitality.

"I didn't want to do it. I saw the horror on Carolyn's face as I brought the box in the room and realized that I, too, should be horrified at what Dr. Jefferson was doing. But he had done it too many times over the years for me to be shocked anymore."

Eve looked down at her lap and smoothed the blanket covering her legs.

"So, you felt what he was doing was right." Joe asked, hiding his disgust.

"No…. No… I didn't think it was right. It saddened me but I had other emotions that got in the way of doing anything about it. Luckily Carolyn, the other nurse attending the birth, didn't have that problem. After Dr. Jefferson put the tape over the baby's mouth and sealed the box marking it 'Baby B' he had me put it back in the equipment room. He usually returned in a couple of hours to pronounce the baby dead and it was then removed to the morgue." Eve reached down for the water in front of her. This revelation was difficult for her. Her hand was shaking as she grasped the water and some of it spilled on the floor. Anne rushed to get a towel to soak it up.

Eve looked down at Anne on the floor, their eyes locked, and Eve said with a tear escaping, "I'm sorry."

"It's ok, Mom. It's just water." Anne said with a small smile.

"No, I'm sorry for all of this." She said with a slight nod of her head, indicating the room, the interview.

Joe and James watched this exchange, both realizing that this was a highly emotional topic for them.

Joe stood up and asked Anne where the bathroom was located. She graciously led him down the hall and indicated a door with her hand. As he turned toward the door she touched his arm, "Mr. Steffan,"

"Please, call me Joe." He said, feeling a jolt of electricity where her hand rested on his arm.

"Joe, my mother is a good woman. She isn't perfect, but none of us are. We make choices and sometimes they are the wrong choices, and then we live with them. Thank you for helping her come to terms with her past. You are a good man." With that Anne turned and returned to her mother's side.

Joe stood for a moment admiring this young woman. She is hearing some very difficult things about her mother, and about how she was conceived, but yet is showing grace and mercy.

When Joe returned, he felt much better. He had needed some time to come to terms with what he was hearing, but was ready to continue.

Joe noted Eve was beginning to show signs of tiring, "Are you able to continue?" He asked solicitously.

Eve nodded her head and gave a weak smile. Now that she broke her silence, she wanted it all out there, once and for all.

Joe pressed the record button on the cassette recorder and continued. "You mentioned other emotions that got in the way. Could you please explain?" Joe asked, knowing that this was one of the things in her past she had tried to shelter Anne from knowing.

"I had been having a long-standing affair with Dr. Jefferson. I was already pregnant with his child at the time of this event. He was strongly pressuring me to have an abortion that he would perform to 'keep everything quiet'. I refused. I wanted my child even if he didn't." Joe noted that Eve reached down to hold her daughter's hand and Anne turned to give her mother a reassuring smile.

"Getting back to the events of that day. What happened after you placed the child in the equipment room, presumably to die." Joe asked flatly.

"Carolyn Steffan stopped me in the hallway afterwards. She grabbed my arm. She had a wild look in her eyes. She asked me what I had done with you, ...with the child. She asked if this had ever happened before." Eve took a breath.

"What did you tell her?" Joe asked, already knowing the answer.

"That it had happened many times." Eve stated emotionless. "Several minutes later I opened the door to the equipment closet and saw Carolyn standing there with you in her arms. Tears flowing down her cheeks. My heart broke for her remembering what she had recently gone through. I closed the door without saying a word."

Joe was curious. Why didn't she report her or try to stop her? "Did you know she was going to try to save me?" Joe gave up the pretense of 'the baby,' everyone present knew Eve was describing Joe's birth.

"I had my suspicion. I even tried to help as best I could by keeping Dr. Jefferson occupied with other things. I felt I owed her that much." Eve stated looking oddly at Joe.

"Owed her?" Joe felt uneasy. He wasn't sure what Eve was getting at, but the hair on his neck started to stand on end.

"Carolyn's still-birth that year. It wasn't a still-birth." Eve stated matter of fact. "I warned you that if I opened up this festering lie you would get more than you bargained for." Eve paused for a second, but quickly continued. "Dr. Jefferson attended that birth as well. It was a difficult delivery. Her doctor was busy with another emergency and couldn't get there in time. Dr. Jefferson used forceps. The baby was turned the wrong way and when he got the child out, he realized that he had blinded the child in one eye and caused some disfigurement on his face due to the forceps. The child was alive, but Dr. Jefferson didn't like to admit to making mistakes. I realized then that he had a god complex, many physicians did back then. We, as a society, gave it to them. He decided quickly to put tape over that boy's mouth as well and brought him to the closet himself as I wasn't going to do it. That was wrong. Carolyn would have wanted her child no matter the disfigurement. I knew that. I wanted no part in his decision.

I went to the closet as soon as I could get away to do just what Carolyn had done for you. But the child had died. It broke my heart holding him. I saw that same pain in Carolyn's face when I opened the door and saw you in her arms that day. There was nothing more I could do for her child. He was dead. I was wearing an angel necklace around my neck. My mother had given it to me when I graduated nursing school. I took it off and placed it around his neck and removed the tape from his mouth. I wrapped him in a blanket and put him back in the box. It was all I could do for him…" Eve's voice trailed off as she looked out the window. Averting her eyes as she dabbed her eyes with the edge of the shawl.

Joe was stunned. This revelation was shocking and heartbreaking. How was he going to tell his mother? Her child had lived. Maybe she had been right. Maybe he should have left things as they were. The last thing he wanted to do was cause her heartbreak after she had saved him and loved him unconditionally throughout his life.

They quickly wrapped up the interview. Eve was visibly exhausted. The day had brought many surprises.

Joe was putting away the recorder in his brief case when Anne came back out from her mother's bedroom. James had excused himself to start the car.

"I'm sorry. I hope this hasn't been too upsetting for your mother." Joe offered, truly concerned for Eve's well-being.

"She's tired but I think relieved that all of these secrets are finally out of her head." Anne said quietly.

"Yes, out of hers and into mine." Joe said with a small laugh as he picked up his coat. The metal crutch fell to the floor, knocking a glass over on the way. Joe and Anne both reached for it at the same time. "I'm sorry. I didn't mean to do that." Joe said, mesmerized by Anne's eyes.

"It's not your fault, Joe." Anne replied using his first name. "What's the saying, no harm, no foul." She laughed easily.

"I'm sorry," she said suddenly serious.

"For what?" Joe asked incredulous. She's the one person here who really had nothing to be sorry about.

"I'm sorry about this, all of this, and about your brother. It's obvious you didn't know." Anne reached out quickly without thinking and spontaneously hugged Joe, and although it should have felt awkward, it didn't. It felt good, and he found himself hugging her back, probably for a few seconds longer than necessary.

Joe was quiet during the long drive back. James knew Joe was a consummate professional, but it couldn't have been easy to hear that the doctor who delivered you didn't think that you deserved a chance at life. This case exploded with the opportunity to now add a charge of murder.

Joe, obviously reading James' thoughts, broke the silence. "How do we tie him to the murder without a body?"

"It is still her word against his. Hearsay. Unless….. how did they dispose of the bodies?" James asked curiously.

Since Joe wasn't driving, he was able to refer back to his notes, "Mrs. Stockwell stated that Dr. Jefferson had instructed the custodian, who was in charge of the hospital incinerator, to incinerate the boxes as he did with body parts or organs that had been removed for pathology purposes."

"Are we able to contact that custodian?" James asked.

"I'll check on it tomorrow." Joe stated making a mental note. His mind was on his parents and what Eve's revelation was going to do to them. He had set a pebble in motion and it had grown into a boulder, threatening everyone in its path.

"Where shall I drop you, your place or your parents?" James asked.

"My place. It's late and I've got some work to do tonight." Joe answered. The truth was he needed to figure out how to tell his parents that their son had been murdered.

The next morning the day was dreary and a mix of snow and rain precipitation hit the windshield as he was driving in to work. He was more determined than before to see this case through. But he was haunted by the stories Gramma Jo had told him and his sisters about his mother's depression after she lost her first baby. She wouldn't eat, couldn't sleep. She became a ghost of herself. Gramma Jo said she feared their marriage would collapse. The more Tom tried to comfort her the more she pushed him away. Her arms ached to hold her child. Gramma Jo use to tell Joe that he was the angel she had prayed would come to help her. Joe prayed another angel would come to help him as he broke the news to his mother. He turned his car around and grimly headed out to his parent's house. No use in putting off the inevitable.

As Joe came in the door he could hear his parents' voices in the kitchen. It was still fairly early and he caught the faint scent of bacon in the air. His parents hadn't heard the door open and close and didn't realize he had arrived until he poked his head into the kitchen.

"Any leftovers for me?" Joe asked trying to act jovial even though he felt anything but.

"Joe! Isn't this a welcome surprise on a weekday!" Carolyn exclaimed, jumping up to get another cup of coffee. "Of course there's more. I made scrambled eggs this morning. Would you like some?"

"Sounds great Mom. Did you put cheese in them?" Joe answered taking a chair next to Tom.

"Of course." Carolyn answered with a smile as she dished him up a large portion. It wasn't often Joe came by in the morning before work. She tried to ignore the uneasy feeling that came over her.

"What brings you home this early in the morning?" Tom asked, sensing it wasn't totally a social call.

"Well, yesterday James and I took a drive down to Rochester to interview Mrs. Stockwell again, at her request this time. I think Mom may have been an important factor in that decision." Joe said, giving a small grin to his mother as she set a plate of food in front of him.

"Did it go better this time?" Carolyn asked the feeling of unease growing.

"If by better, you mean did we get the information we were hoping for, the answer would be yes. Perhaps more then we bargained for." Joe stated clearing his throat slightly.

Both his parents looked at him sensing his agitation.

Joe continued, "We have decided to pursue murder charges along with the attempted murder charge."

"You mean the other babies Eve indicated?" Carolyn asked with a sense of foreboding.

"The murder charge is that of your first born." Joe stated looking at his plate. He forced himself to look into his mother and fathers' faces to see the look of horror he had dreaded since he learned of his brother's fate.

Joe re-told the information Eve had passed on to them in the interview. He knew his parents had a right to know and that he was the best one to tell them. But he also knew that he was opening a wound that had almost killed his mother when it happened so long ago.

Carolyn leaned back in her chair and closed her eyes. A tear came down her cheek and suddenly a wail came from her so deep inside it seemed as if she would break in two. Joe caught a glimpse of what his gramma Jo had shared. Both Joe and Tom were at her side in a second. All three of them held each other trying to give Carolyn the strength she needed to face this.

When her sobbing subsided, they heard, "I knew it all along. I knew it. I felt it." She had never spoken the child's name. No one knew that Carolyn had named him in her heart. Back when it happened the professionals had encouraged her not to name the child, to think of him as a miscarriage. Their rationale was that he would be easier to forget, but in her heart, he was Phillip. "Phillip was alive and I couldn't help him. I never got to hold him. He was alive. My baby was alive locked in that room, in that box." Carolyn gripped the arms of Tom and Joe. When she finally stopped shaking, she took Joe's face in her hands and said "Promise me he will pay for killing my son." Joe saw the feral gleam in her eyes. She wanted blood, Dr. Jefferson's blood.

Joe embraced her until she calmed and kissed his mother's head, "I promise Mom." Joe and Tom looked at each other and both knew that this wouldn't be over until Dr. Jefferson paid for killing Phillip.

Joe and Tom brought Carolyn into the living room and started a fire. She felt ice cold, her body was in shock. It was as if she had lost Phillip all over again. As Tom got the fire going Joe wrapped her up in a beige blanket kept across the couch for snuggling on cold winter nights, and rubbed her hands trying to warm them. "I'm sorry Mom. Maybe you were right; maybe I shouldn't have started this."

It was Tom who surprised Joe after overhearing his comment, "No! Don't ever say that. Our first son is dead because of that man and you almost died. It sickens me to think that people in this town, hell, in this county think he is a saint. The man is a murderer who killed innocent babies in a horrific god-awful way." Tom ran his hand through his hair. It was so rare that Tom displayed anger that both Carolyn and Joe were shocked to see this display. "You finish this, put that son of a bitch away, make people see the real Dr. Jefferson. I'm proud of you son. Whatever it takes, you put him away!"

Joe looked from his father to his mother's tear streaked face. Carolyn nodded her head and squeezed the hand she still held.

Joe answered, "Okay, then. I've got some work to do."

CHAPTER 12

When Joe got to the office, he sought out James. As Joe entered the office, James could see that Joe was upset and a bit disheveled. Joe ran his hand through his hair much like his father had done earlier. James leaned back in his leather desk chair, "Rough morning?"

"I drove out to see my parents this morning. I didn't want to put it off." Joe answered sliding into the chair in front of James' desk.

"Nothing like ripping the bandage off in one big swipe, right?" James said trying to lift Joe's spirit.

"Something like that." Joe answered with a small smile.

"How did they take it?" James answered seriously.

"They were quite upset obviously. Perhaps they are even more on board with my pursuing this than when I started."

"I did ask my mom if she knew a custodian by the name of Juan. That's the only part of the name Eve could remember. Luckily my mom said a Juan Garcia retired just last year. He still lives in the area last she heard. She remembers him coming to the hospital Christmas party this past year with his wife. I'll try to get an address and phone number for him."

"Okay, good work." James said.

Joe got up to leave, "James, I want your word, I sit second chair on this case when it goes to trial."

James looked surprised. He had always assumed Joe would be with him at trial, "Yes, of course."

Joe didn't leave. He had one more thing to ask, "And if the defense puts Jefferson on the witness stand, I get to depose him."

James leaned back in his wooden chair thinking this over. He knew this was important to Joe, and after a brief silence James nodded, "Okay. You got it."

Joe turned to leave with a determined look on his face. James heard him say softly but with cold conviction, "That son of a bitch is going to pay."

Joe was able to get an address for Juan Garcia with some difficulty, and headed out to interview him personally. It turns out there were quite a few Juan Garcia's in the area. He found the small green house with white trim quite easily but had difficulty maneuvering the gravel driveway with his metal cane. There were many pot holes created from the harsh winter and his cane slipped down numerous times causing Joe to lose his balance more than once. Once reaching the door he took a moment to regain his balance and rang the bell. No one answered at first so he started knocking. He could hear voices from inside but it was several minutes before someone finally came to answer.

"Is this the home of Juan Garcia?" Joe asked showing his card.

The person who answered was a pretty, young woman holding an adorable little baby. She looked at him, leery of strangers coming to the door, especially those connected with the law. She finally answered in very good English but with an obvious Spanish accent, "Yes. What do you want?"

Joe smiled trying to put her at ease, "Mr. Garcia worked at the Memorial County Hospital for several years in the maintenance/custodial department, correct?"

"Yes, but not any longer. He is retired." She stated a little less skeptical thinking perhaps this man had the wrong person.

"Yes. I'm aware of that. My mother is a nurse up there, Carolyn Steffan. She remembered your father. Please, I have just a couple of questions. Is he at home?" Joe prodded.

Reluctantly she unlatched the door and held it open. "Yes. Come in. I'm his daughter, Lucia. I'll get him." She indicated he should sit in the front room. It was nicely furnished with a crucifix hanging over the couch. There were several pictures around the room of smiling children at various ages.

A few minutes later an older gentleman with salt and pepper hair and a slight limp came into the room with a worried look on his face. He looked to be in good health.

Joe rose to his feet and extended his hand, "Mr. Juan Garcia? My name is Joseph Steffan. You may know my mother. She's the Assistant Director of Nurses at the hospital, Carolyn Steffan."

At the mention of Carolyn Steffan, Mr. Garcia grinned from ear to ear and his body relaxed as he reached to shake Joe's hand. "Of course, I know your mother," he said with a thick Spanish accent. "She's good people. You met my daughter, Lucia. She helped bring Lucia's son into the world two months ago. Such a nice woman!"

Joe smiled. He often heard people exclaim wonderful attributes regarding the mention of his mother, but he never tired of hearing of them. Mr. Garcia was correct. She is a nice woman!

"Mr. Garcia, I'm a lawyer with the District Attorney's office and I'm investigating a case that occurred many years ago. First of all, I want you to know that I'm not looking to incriminate you in any actions that may have occurred back then. But you have information that could be vital to my case." Joe explained.

Mr. Garcia looked confused, but nodded his head in understanding. "Whatever I can do for you, please sit down and we talk."

Joe began, "It has come to my attention that 30 years ago there was a practice at the hospital that boxes were brought to the morgue and you were given instructions to burn them in the incinerator along with pathology specimens. Is that correct?" Joe asked, looking at Mr. Garcia for understanding.

Mr. Garcia appeared uncomfortable, but nodded his head slowly and looked down at the floor.

"Mr. Garcia, do you know what was in those boxes?" Joe asked. Mr. Garcia's body language indicated he was uncomfortable with this.

Silence.

"Mr. Garcia?" Joe prodded.

Finally, Mr. Garcia nodded with his eyes closed. "Yes. I know. It happened by accident. Dr. Jefferson had come to me to ask me to do this, to burn the boxes. I didn't think anything of it, part of my job. I was anxious to please, to do a good job. I said 'yes, Dr. Jefferson, no problem' but after the third box or so, one of the boxes slipped out of my hand and hit the floor...." Mr. Garcia was visibly upset but continued, "The tape popped off the box and a small arm showed. I couldn't help but look." His voice trembled with emotion, "It was a small newborn baby... I ....I..cried. I couldn't burn it...it was a baby...my God....a baby. I'm Catholic, my faith didn't allow me to burn babies!"

Joe was stunned... Mr. Garcia didn't burn them! "What did you do with the boxes then?" Joe asked quietly.

"I buried them. I found a small open spot next to the hospital garage and buried them... each one of them." Mr. Garcia admitted, finally relieved of the burden he had carried these many years.

"Could you show me where?" Joe asked incredulously.

Mr. Garcia nodded and went to retrieve his coat. The March thaw had begun and the puddles were growing. Mr. Garcia assisted Joe to his car and got in beside him in the passenger seat. As they headed to the hospital, Mr. Garcia, looking straight ahead finally asked, "Why were the babies dead?" He always suspected something was wrong with this practice.

Joe answered, also looking straight ahead, "Babies that were born with some kind of a defect were put in the boxes to die. After they died, they were brought down to the morgue and eventually given to you to dispose of the proof."

Mr. Garcia's eyes began to water, "My God, what did I do." His hands started clenching as if he were in pain.

Mr. Garcia directed Joe to drive next to the hospital garage. They walked without speaking towards the back of the building. Mr. Garcia pointed to an area next to a tree. "I thought the shade of the tree would be nice." Mr. Garcia said his voice waivered. "I planted flowers back here."

Joe nodded looking over the space. His heart lifted. He found them. They are here. Maybe their little souls can be at rest now.

Glancing at Mr. Garcia, Joe saw a deep concern in his furrowed brow. There was no mistaking his look of shame. "Mr. Garcia, you had no way of knowing how those babies died. You were following the direction of your supervisors. If anything, you gave them legitimacy, you gave them a burial." Joe said trying to alleviate Mr. Garcia's obvious pain.

"Do you have any idea how many babies are here?" Joe asked.

Mr. Garcia shrugged, "20 or 25 maybe." He answered softly feeling as if he was on hallowed ground.

Joe felt a lump in his throat. My God, how could this happen.

"Mr. Garcia, come. I'll take you home now."

"I want you to know I prayed over each one of them. I wanted them to go to heaven."

Joe nodded. He could say no words. Mr. Garcia was a good man. Dr. Jefferson was the monster.

When Joe got back to the office he went straight into James's office, "We've got bodies!" Joe exclaimed.

"What do you mean? How many?" James asked sitting bolt upright in his leather chair.

"Twenty, possibly more, buried behind the hospital garage." Joe answered pacing the floor his metal cane making clicking sounds against the linoleum.

James dropped his pencil and sat back in his chair letting air out of his chest. "Whoa, come again?"

"Mr. Garcia didn't burn the boxes with the bodies in them. He dropped one and found out they contained babies and he couldn't burn them. He created his own cemetery behind the garage." Joe explained.

"Wow, let's think about this for a second." James said, clicking the pen cap while rocking his chair, as if the repetitive motion would help him form a strategy. "Okay. We have bodies, now skeletons. Probably no way to tell a cause of death or get DNA samples at this point due to decomposition. His lawyer will say they were still births. There's no way to prove those babies took a breath."

Joe looked up at the ceiling. He was running his fingers through his hair. How do they prove which babies were stillbirths and which ones were murdered? Or even just one baby! Just one count of murder would do. Suddenly Eve's voice played in his head, "I took off my angel necklace and placed it over his head, wrapped him in a blanket and put him back in the box."

"Find Phillip!" Joe exclaimed.

"Who?" James asked bluntly, not knowing the name that Carolyn had given her first son.

"Phillip, my brother. Eve said that she put her angel necklace around his head, wrapped him in a blanket and put him back in the box." Joe explained. "If we find the necklace, she could identify it to corroborate his identity."

James rubbed his chin deep in thought, "That may work!"

"I'll call Mrs. Stockwell to see if she can identify the angel necklace if we find it. It would be even better is she had a picture of it for comparison." Joe said, excited that they may have a piece of hard evidence.

"I'll call to get a warrant to excavate the site and get the paperwork started to charge Dr. Clayton Jefferson with one count of attempted murder and another count of murder in the first degree." James stated.

Minutes later Joe came back, "Eve said not only could she identify the necklace, she was wearing it the day she graduated from nursing school and it's in the picture." Joe said excitedly.

"Let's go." James said quietly, but with determination.

This case could make or break their careers.

CHAPTER 13

Joe went with two officers into the hospital. He looked around at the well- kept lobby and updated furniture, but knew this hospital had been the site of so many murders. "If these walls could talk," he said to himself as they went up to the reception area.

"Is Dr. Clayton Jefferson on the premises?" Joe asked showing his Assistant District Attorney's badge.

The receptionist looked quite upset with the police standing in front of her desk. "I don't know. I'll have to page." She lifted the phone receiver and started to page for Dr. Jefferson.

"Please just page him to come to the reception area." Joe asked not wanting to tip his hand and have the good doctor slip out a side door.

Ten minutes had passed when Dr. Jefferson appeared in his white coat, tie, and suit pants, looking every bit the part of a white knight there to save patients.

Joe was thrilled to be able to finally say, "Dr. Clayton Jefferson, you are under arrest for one count of attempted murder and another count of murder in the first degree."

As doctor Jefferson was placed in hand cuffs in front of several horrified visitors, Carolyn came around the corner. She stopped dead in her tracks, watching as they read Dr. Jefferson his rights.

Dr. Jefferson was ashen and his persona seemed to deflate right in front of her. He saw her standing there and became enraged, "We had a deal. If I go down so do you. I'll see to it that you are fired!"

"Get this piece of trash out of here boys," Joe stated to the cops. As Dr. Jefferson was led outside Joe went to Carolyn who had dropped the folders she was carrying.

Joe wrapped his arms around her shaking body trying to calm her. "It's over?" she whispered.

"No." He answered, "We are in the eye of the storm. Now we have to prove the case. Can we go somewhere to talk?"

Carolyn nodded pointing to her office.

Joe wanted to explain what was happening back behind the garage, to prepare her for what they may find.

"Mom, Juan didn't burn the bodies as Jefferson had instructed him to do. He buried them when he found out the boxes contained babies. They are buried back behind the hospital garage. We have men back there now carefully digging them up." He stopped, allowing time for his mother to digest this information.

Carolyn's face turned white and she gripped her chair arms with both hands. Joe could see the white knuckles. She didn't say a word, just turned in her chair to look out the window. She could catch a glimpse of men in dark blue putting up yellow crime scene tape.

Joe continued, "We are looking for Phillip. He holds the key to the case."

Carolyn's face snapped back to look at Joe, "The key?"

"Eve stated that when she went back to the closet after Dr. Jefferson had placed him there in the box, she intended on saving him, much like you did for me, but that he was already dead. She wrapped him in a blanket and took the tape off his mouth and placed an angel necklace she had been wearing over his head. That necklace could tell us which body is Phillip."

Carolyn's eyes glazed over. She no longer saw her office surroundings. She was remembering the closet and picturing her baby lying in a box with tape over his mouth. She covered her eyes trying to shut out the image, but it was too vivid.

Joe could see his mother's suffering and went to stand next to her chair. His metal crutch clanging against the metal desk. He placed his hand on her shoulder. She needed to feel warmth and his touch. He knew how hard this was for her.

"What will you do with his remains when you do find him?" She asked in a whisper, her chin quivering and a lone tear escaping.

"They will be brought to the city morgue until after the trial. Then they can be released to the family." Joe answered quietly.

"We need to bury him next to family." Carolyn said, her voice breaking with emotion.

"Yes, Mom. Where ever you choose. Headstone and all." Joe answered his voice cracking.

He reached down to hug his mom and allowed her to vent all the emotion she had been holding back. Her body shook with her sobs. His shirt became damp from her tears, but he didn't care. His tears mingled with hers.

She was finally mourning her lost son.

CHAPTER 14

The next morning the March sun rose to a beautiful spring day. Joe drove straight out to the hospital garage wanting to know the progress from the night before. They had unearthed five bodies so far but found no necklace on any of them. Joe was beginning to feel uneasy. They could prosecute Dr. Jefferson without the necklace, but it really was a substantial piece of evidence that Joe felt would warrant a conviction.

The crew was already hard at work when Joe arrived. It was tedious, painstaking work to unearth a body, but retain as much evidence as possible. Luckily, Juan hadn't dug the graves deep. While Joe was talking with the site captain, one of the excavators excitedly called out, "I think I found something."

Joe yelled out, "Bring a camera and photograph everything."

While the excavator was using a fine brush, the tarnished metal in the shape of an angel appeared around a small clavicle bone. It was Phillip. The box had degraded in the wet soil but small pieces of fabric, possibly a blanket, were also mixed in with the bones. Joe ran his fingers through his hair swallowing hard. Looking up at the sky he took a deep breath. This would have been his fate if his mother hadn't ….. I'm sorry Phillip. You will never know the truly remarkable mother we have.

"Catalog everything. Take a 12 inch swath around the whole body. They can sort it out at the morgue. Be very gentle. This body is our case." And my brother, Joe thought.

When Joe reached his car to head to the office, he spotted Carolyn's car drive by. She looked shaken. Perhaps the excavation of the bodies was too much for her. He decided he needed to call her as soon as he reached his office.

The office was a buzz with energy. By now everyone had heard of the arrest and the excavation that was happening across town. Everyone wanted Joe to stop and give them an update on the progress, but he really wanted to get to his office to call his mother. Something wasn't right. He could feel it.

When James motioned him into his office however, he couldn't refuse.

"Well, how's the excavation going?" James asked.

"We found Phillip, and the necklace, even some fragments of a blanket," Joe answered. "Thank God for cold Minnesota winters. The cold slowed the decomposition down."

"We've got him!" James exclaimed, rubbing his hands together.

"Looks like it," Joe said absentmindedly. "I need to go make a phone call. Please excuse me."

"Sure." James said, surprised at Joe's coolness and lack of enthusiasm as it has been him pushing this case from the beginning.

Joe shut his office door and sat down. He was happy with the progress of the case but knew it didn't come without a cost to his family. He dialed the phone quickly.

"Mom, it's Joe. Everything okay? I saw you leave the hospital."

"Yes, fine." Carolyn answered but her tone belied her words. "Why?"

"I saw you drive by the excavation site. You looked upset. What happened? You're normally at work at this time." Joe delved.

"I...I've.. been put on extended Leave of Absence." Carolyn finally stated quietly her voice breaking.

Silence.

"Joe, it's okay. They said my presence at the hospital now is a distraction from everyone getting their work done. They didn't fire me. Hell, they even said they'd pay me to stay home. I think they are waiting to find out how the case is resolved." Carolyn said. "And then they'll fire me." She added laughing slightly to make light of the serious situation.

"Mom, I'm sorry." Joe said rubbing his forehead with the tips of his fingers. Now this case could cost her job.

"Don't be sorry. I don't even know if I want to go back, too much has happened. Don't worry about me. I'll be fine. I finally have time to spend getting ready for the wedding." She said with more resolve than she actually felt. "How is the case coming?" She finally asked.

"Good. How about I come out tonight for supper and give both you and Dad an update?" Joe asked. He didn't want to tell her over the phone about Phillip.

"Sure. I'll make a nice dinner. I have plenty of time to cook today!" Carolyn answered brightly.

When Joe hung up the phone, he felt a weight on his shoulders. Of course, the hospital wouldn't fire her. They are afraid of a wrongful death legal case. If the jury sides with them there would be legal precedence and strong grounds for the wrongful death case. If the jury sides with Dr. Jefferson it would be an uphill battle. Unfortunately, that means the hospital will be trying its best to see that Dr. Jefferson is acquitted. If he is, you can be damn sure Carolyn's Leave of Absence will be permanent. But they weren't going to lose he thought. This case is too strong, but there will be strong emotions riding high and that alone can affect outcomes of a case. He jotted a note on his legal pad to remind him to talk with James about asking for a jury outside of the area.

His next call was to Mrs. Stockwell. They needed the picture of the necklace as soon as possible. Anne answered the phone.

"Good morning, Anne. This is Joe Steffan," Joe said pleasantly, surprised to hear her voice.

"Good morning, Mr. Steffan. How are you?" Anne asked, extending pleasantries, also very happy to hear Joe's voice.

"Fine thanks. How are you and your mother?" Joe reciprocated.

"Mom's been a bit tired but otherwise we're fine. How's the case progressing?" Anne inquired.

"We've had some major breakthroughs." Joe answered excitedly. "Your mother said she had a picture with the necklace in it. We need that picture as soon as possible. We think we found the necklace." Joe stated.

Anne paused. Her mother was resting today after her chemotherapy appointment two days ago and wouldn't be up to making the drive. "How about if I drive it up? My mother isn't feeling up to a road trip today, but I have the day off and it's a beautiful day." Anne offered. She also wanted to see if the electricity they had shared was real. She had found herself thinking more and more about the handsome lawyer with the black curly hair and brown eyes that seemed to mesmerize her.

"That would be great!" Joe said emphatically. "I'll even buy you lunch for your trouble." He offered, surprising even himself.

"That would be very nice. I'll leave here in a half hour and should be there by 12:30. Where shall I meet you?" Anne asked.

"There's a nice restaurant across from the court house called, The Country Diner. How about we meet there?"

"I'll be there, Mr. Steffan." Anne answered trying to hide the excitement in her voice. Her fingers tapped the counter with excitement at the prospect of seeing Joe again.

"Great, and Anne, call me Joe. We are probably going to see a lot of each other the next few months."

Joe looked up at the clock on his wall. He was actually counting down the time until he saw her again.

Joe arrived five minutes early and waited by the door. Anne was right on time. Her hand held a manila envelope. Oh, yes, the picture Joe remembered. He had forgotten the reason for the lunch date, just started looking forward to seeing her again.

Anne was a beautiful woman with a warm easy smile. Her strawberry blonde hair had highlights of red that were brought out by the sun. Joe was surprised she was single.

As they sat down Anne passed the envelope over to Joe. "This is the picture I believe you were wanting."

Joe opened the envelope and found an 8x10 photo of a very beautiful Eve Stockwell. It was easy to see where Anne got her good looks. Around Eve's neck was the angel necklace. It looks to be the exact match of the one found this morning. They would have to enlarge the photo to be sure.

"Thank you, Anne. It is exactly what we needed. Don't worry, we'll return the photo unharmed after the trial." Joe said.

"Fine. I trust you." Anne said smiling.

The conversation flowed easily between them. He found out she had gone to college at Winona State University and started working at the hospital in Rochester shortly after graduation. He knew from the background they had found on Eve that Anne was an only child and her father had passed away a couple years ago.

The topic of the trial came up briefly. She asked why now and he told her of the revelation that occurred during the Thanksgiving holiday.

"It was as if I was meant to do this now." Joe replied.

"You know, I've been thinking, we have something in common," Anne said. "You and I are two babies that Dr. Jefferson wanted dead, and the only ones lucky enough to have our mothers save us from him."

"You are right." Joe said contemplating that revelation. Her statement seemed to bond them together.

"Are you upset about the possibility of a trial against the man who is your biological father?" Joe asked her quietly.

Anne was quick to answer, "No. He wasn't my father. My father is the man that raised me, who would stop after a long day in the field, covered with dirt, famished, tired to the bone, but when passing by the beautiful playhouse he built with his own two hands, was never too busy to have a pretend cup of tea with his daughter. That man is my father." She said proudly lifting her chin and looking in the distance as if her father were still there with her.

"It sounds like he was a wonderful father." Joe answered bringing her back to the present.

"He was. I miss him every day." Anne answered her voice husky with unshed tears as she placed her coffee cup back on the table.

"That's another thing we have in common." Joe answered softly. "We both had great fathers that were not our biological fathers."

Joe reached his warm hand over to cover hers and they sat there for several moments relishing the simple touch of understanding from someone who very much understood the other.

It was well after 2:00pm when Joe realized the time. "I need to let you get back on the road. I'm sorry for keeping you here so long. But I've really enjoyed talking with you." He was truly sorry the time was getting late.

"I've enjoyed myself as well," she said smiling. "I've been meaning to ask you, when this case comes to trial is there a hotel or motel around here for us to stay? I think it would be too tiresome for my mom to go back and forth to our home in Rochester."

"I have a better idea. Let me work on it. I'll let you know what I come up with." Joe said, thinking he could offer his place and he could stay with his parents. That way he can keep an eye on them through this ordeal as well.

When they got up to leave, Joe found his one leg locking up on him. He had been getting complacent on his exercises the past couple of weeks thinking he could get by. Now he was reminded why the exercises are so important. Anne saw his difficulty and reached down to help. Joe hated people feeling sorry for him and was embarrassed. "I can do it." Joe stated, harsher than he meant to say it. Then regretting it the moment he said it. "I'm sorry, that came out wrong."

"That's all right. I know you can do it," Anne said smiling brightly, not at all put off by his statement. "But it gives me an excuse to hold your arm."

Joe had never had someone offer help in such a way and it brought a chuckle out of him. Anne was like a ray of sunshine that Joe was wishing he had in his life.

As they left the restaurant, they found they had parked next to each other. Joe turned towards Anne and was surprised when she hugged him. "Joe, thank you for lunch. I've enjoyed our visit. I hope I didn't take you away from work too long."

"It's been my pleasure." Joe answered honestly. He couldn't remember when he had enjoyed talking to someone more. She captivated him. "My mother will be very happy. You gave me a great excuse to take a lunch break. She says I lose weight when on a trial case because I forget to eat, just like my father."

They stood gazing at each other, neither wanting to say good bye. This was very new for Joe. He normally could put any distractions aside when on a case, especially as important a case as this one, but now he found the case a distraction from what was happening in front of him.

Anne touched his arm and said earnestly, "Joe, I want to thank you for giving my mother this opportunity to do the right thing. I can tell she is already much more at peace. If there's anything I can do to help all you have to do is ask." And then she placed a light kiss on his cheek and turned towards her car.

Joe was stunned. All he could muster was, "Have a safe drive. Could you call me to let me know you got back okay?" The last statement was a reflex. It came from years of living with Carolyn Steffan and her protectiveness with her children when it came to driving.

Anne smiled and waved as she drove off. Joe found himself still standing stiffly next to his car door, transfixed by what just happened.

Joe was at his parent's door promptly at 6:00pm. Carolyn was slightly shocked. He was generally 30 minutes late due to losing track of time. Joe was surprised to see Gramma Jo sitting next to the fire, but it was a good surprise.

"Gramma Jo, it's great to see you." Joe said, wrapping his arms around her.

"I called Carolyn and heard you were coming out for supper and I needed a hug from my grandson." Gramma Jo said, which was only part of the truth. Gramma Jo had heard the hospital had requested Carolyn take a leave of absence and thought her daughter could use a little moral support.

"The roast has about 30 minutes to go before it's done." Carolyn said giving Joe a hug, (Joe was known for his 30 minutes of tardiness). "Why don't you come in here and join us for a glass of wine." Carolyn and Tom loved to sit next to the fire before supper while the kids were growing up. They would talk with the kids about their lives. They went from stories about classroom exploits and recess arguments to plans for their future, and now their independent lives.

Joe made his way to the sofa and sat back finally relaxing after a very long work week. He knew he had to tell his parents about the discovery of Phillip's remains but with everything his mother had been through the past few weeks he didn't want to add to her burden.

Carolyn and Tom could see Joe was troubled and knew it had something to do with the case but waited for him to initiate the conversation.

"How were the roads?" Tom asked sipping his drink. "Any refreeze going on with all this melting?" March often brought sunny melting days which put water on the roads. The cold nights brought with them refreeze and potential for black ice.

"No, they were fine. But Gramma Jo, you know you could have called for a ride. I would have been happy to swing by to pick you up." Joe said concerned about his elderly gramma driving past dark.

Joe decided to discuss his recent meeting with Anne before revealing the recent discovery. Joe cleared his throat after taking his first sip, "I had lunch with Anne Stockwell today. Eve Stockwell's daughter."

"Oh," Carolyn said with some surprise.

"Yes. I called her to see if we could get a picture of the angel necklace. She offered to drive it up as it was her day off." Joe explained. "We met for lunch. She's a very nice person. I think you'd like her."

"I'm sure we would." Carolyn offered sending a smiling glance at her mother. Gramma Jo and Carolyn had been trying to get Joe matched up for a couple of years. She thought Joe sounded a bit smitten by this girl.

"She seems a lot like you, Mom, a very caring person." Joe said remembering Anne's sweet smile as she waved good-bye.

"When I was visiting with Eve, I saw photos. She looks to be quite a beautiful young lady." Carolyn stated watching the small smile dance on Joe's lips.

"Why, yes I believe she is." Joe answered with a coy smile taking another sip, continuing to play the game.

"I was wondering. Would it be ok if I stay here at home through the trial and offer my house to Anne and her mother? It's quite a drive back and forth to Rochester and with Eve in such ill health, I thought it would be nice if they could feel comfortable." Joe asked hopefully.

"Joe, you know your old room is always here waiting for you. You don't need to ask." Tom stated, also sensing a bond forming between Joe and Anne.

"Of course!" Carolyn stated affirming Tom's invitation.

"I'd be happy to bring over some food for them, too. A person gets tired of restaurant food." Gramma Jo offered.

"Thanks. I was pretty sure it would be ok, but I didn't want you to think I was being presumptuous." Joe stated smiling, so thankful to be in this warming caring family.

"By the way, how is the case coming?" Tom asked, sensing there was more Joe had to say.

"Good." Joe said, hesitant to divulge today's news. Joe cleared his throat and they all looked at him expectantly. "I have something to tell you." Joe took a deep breath. His face took on his serious persona. He looked at his mother's face, knowing there was no way to prepare her for the news, "Phillip's remains were found this morning."

Carolyn and Tom sat in stunned silence and a small gasp could be heard from Gramma Jo.

Tom was the first to find his voice, "How can you be sure?"

"The angel necklace was found around his neck with partially decomposed pieces of a blue baby blanket. Anne brought a picture of Eve wearing the necklace for comparison. It's a match. It's Phillip." He ended taking another drink this time more of a gulp. It felt good to get this out in the open.

There, it was said. For a few seconds all you could hear was the soft ticking of the grandfather clock given to Tom and Carolyn for their fifth wedding anniversary.

Carolyn finally spoke. Her voice came out softly, but with no tears. "I want to see him." This was more of a command then a request.

"Mom, it's been 30 years. His remains are skeletal. Do you really want to see him like that?" Joe asked just as softly. He understood her desire as a mother to see him, but wanted to protect her from the grotesque sight.

"Yes. I need to see him. I never got to see him at his birth. That was taken away from me. I need to see him, to know that he was real and he was mine." Carolyn stated firmly looking into the fire.

Joe looked at his dad. Tom looked shocked, but he knew that Carolyn's mind was made up. Tom nodded his acquiescence to her request.

Joe nodded, "I'll set it up."

They sat for a few more minutes in silence alone with their thoughts before Carolyn got up from her chair, "I'm checking on dinner. It smells done. I've never burned a roast and I'm not about to now."

As she left the room Joe and Tom exchanged looks without talking, each worried about what the visit to the morgue would bring. Gramma Jo's face was lined with concern.

Carolyn's voice came from the kitchen. "We need to call the girls home. Sunday dinner here so we can tell them." Again, this was not a request.

Joe spent Saturday working on the case. There would be few days off until the trial but Sunday would be spent with the family telling his sisters their brother had been murdered. Joe was dreading this family gathering.

Monday morning Joe got a call from the coroner. The special forensic pathologist was finished with his examination of Phillip's body. There was some disfigurement in the bones of the face but it wasn't the cause of death. Joe notified them that his mother wanted to view the body. He set it up for later that afternoon and notified his parents.

At 4:30pm they were outside the morgue waiting for Joe. The day was overcast with a soft drizzle coming down. The hallway outside the morgue was poorly lit and empty, the walls painted a light yellow, perhaps an attempt at adding light to the dark space.

"Mom, Dad, I want you to understand what you will be viewing. The remains are bones now." Joe said, wanting to buffer the shock.

"Joe, I'm a nurse. I've seen horrific accidents." Carolyn said, trying to reassure him that she was going to be fine.

"Yes," he said slowly, "but none of them were your children." Joe said sincerely looking into her eyes wishing he could take away the shock and emotions which will be brought out by what they were about to see.

The three turned towards the door and each took a deep breath. Joe held the door open for his parents to pass before him into the well-lit sterile room, the brightness of the room contrasting with the corridor outside. The odor was of formaldehyde and chemicals and death.

One of the steel tables by the window had a white sheet covering a small skeleton.

Joe said solemnly, "Please remove the sheet. These are the parents."

The Coroner came on the other side of the table and wordlessly pulled the sheet down careful not to disturb the placement of the bones. After they had measured and cataloged the bones, they had reassembled them as they had been found in the dirt.

Tears came from Carolyn's eyes soundlessly flowing down her cheeks as her hand reached up to cover her mouth. She moved closer to the table, drawn to the remains of her baby. The coldness of the metal reached through her clothes. She reached out to touch the cheek bone of the skeleton, gently feeling the worn bone of her first child under her fingertip. Her tears now flowing on the bones creating wet droplets where they landed. Tom came behind her wrapping his arm around her to lend support.

They stood staring at the remains of their son for many minutes letting the realization of his death wash over them, finally mourning their loss. Tom reached out to touch the hand bones of the son he would never know. Tom's hand visibly shook as his fingers touched the smooth bones. Flesh of his flesh, bone of his bone. Suddenly overcome, he needed to leave the room. Rage filled his body at his son's senseless death.

Carolyn leaned down and kissed the forehead of the skull whispering a mother's message. "Rest in peace my angel. We will always love you." A sob escaped as she gripped the table for support. Joe reached over and put his arm around his mother's shaking shoulder lending her strength as he led her out of the room. She gratefully looked up into his eyes, hers brimming with tears, pain etched across her forehead. She didn't need to say a word. With one look Joe knew what she was asking.

"Dr. Jefferson will pay for this." Joe answered calmly but with steel resolve.

They found Tom leaning against the wall his body tensing trying to regain control. The three of them stood clutching each other for strength.

Chapter 15

The next several weeks were filled with legal strategy meetings, depositions, and writing filing motions for pre-trial hearings. Joe had thrown himself into this trial with all the energy in his body. His sisters were horrified by the details of Phillip's death and were now fully vested in the outcome of the trial, but it didn't consume their lives like it did Joe's. Luckily Carolyn had so many details to attend to for Cassie's wedding that it allowed her to reach exhaustion most nights so she could sleep.

It was a Friday in the last week of March when Joe was surprised by a visitor at 5pm. The receptionist buzzed his office saying there was a young lady there to meet him. Joe was confused as he didn't have anyone on his schedule, but told the receptionist to send her back.

Anne walked into his office with a picnic basket in hand.

Joe smiled and indicated the chair next to the table in his office.

"What brings you here?" Joe asked, pleasantly surprised.

"Well, you had mentioned that your mother was worried you were losing weight because you forget to eat when you are working hard on a case. You took me to lunch a few weeks back so

I thought I would return the favor. Although I guess it is more like an early supper by the looks of the clock." Anne answered easily.

"Have you eaten today?"

Joe laughed, "As a matter of fact, no, and whatever you have in the basket smells terrific."

"Have you even been out of your office?" She asked noting the stacks of books and papers on his desk.

"No, not really," Joe answered slowly shaking his head.

"Well, how about a picnic?" Anne suggested, thinking the change of scenery would do him a world of good.

"That would be great." Joe answered grinning from ear to ear. "Let me make one phone call. I'll meet you in the reception area."

"I'll be waiting." Anne replied with a smile.

When Anne was safely out of ear shot Joe called his mom, "I can't make supper tonight. Something came up. Yes, I'll be eating. I'll stop by tomorrow morning. Okay, for breakfast. Love you too."

When Joe came out to the reception area he found Anne conversing easily with the receptionist, Carol, a warm friendly woman in her 40's.

"Nice to see you leaving before me for a change." Carol stated, as she watched Joe guide Anne out the door. Carol often thought Joe worked much too hard and needed some fun in his life.

"I'll be back later." Joe stated out of habit.

To which Anne replied easily, "Not if I have anything to say about it!"

Carol's eyebrows raised and a quick smile crossed her lips. Perhaps this woman is just what Joe needed to make him stop and smell the roses.

"Good night, Joe." Carol called.

"Have a good weekend, Carol," Joe called back, suddenly not in such a hurry to return after all.

When the elevator reached the ground floor Joe suggested they go to his place. He rarely entertained at his home. It was his sanctuary, but he suddenly wanted to share it with Anne. Pulling up to the house she felt a warm inviting feeling. His house wasn't ostentatious, but it wasn't small. It was one level, which she had expected. The front porch was inviting with a couple of white rockers and a small table. The rockers took her by surprise, expecting the house to lack a woman's touch. As Joe unlocked the door, he followed Anne's gaze to the chairs and apparently read her mind, "A housewarming gift from my grandmother. They really are quite comfortable."

"How long have you lived here?" Anne asked, a bit surprised he chose to live outside the city limits.

"About three years. After growing up on a hobby farm, I found city living too confining. I missed the clean air and stillness out here." Joe answered.

"It is a beautiful setting." Anne answered looking out over the rolling hills. His yard had several older trees and with an unusually warm spring this year the sound of tractors in the fields gently broke the stillness in the air.

Suddenly remembering the picnic basket in her hands, she suggested they have their picnic in the rocking chairs on the porch.

"I haven't had a chance to clean them off yet this spring. How about we eat in the solarium?" Joe countered.

Anne's eyebrows raised, solarium ...hmmm that sounded nice.

Joe held the door for her to enter the house. The woodwork was amazing for a new house. She ran her hand down the oak chair rail.

"My dad does a lot of woodworking," Joe said, reading her mind once again. "When I was building the house, he offered to do quite a bit of the finishing work. I helped out doing what I could."

"So, you built this house." Anne confirmed, amazed at his abilities.

"Yes. I wanted a house that was beautiful, but functional to fit my unique challenges." Joe answered hinting at the ramps and extra wide door frames.

Anne caught sight of a wheelchair in the corner, but didn't say anything. Joe caught her glance and answered with a slight hesitation, "I use it when my legs get tired and unsteady. If I've been working a long day and haven't done my exercises, I sometimes need to rest them. I don't like to use the chair at work, but here, I do what is necessary." Joe didn't usually talk about his disability, wanting instead to focus on his achievements. He felt vulnerable talking about things he couldn't do and as much as he needed the chair at times, he felt it made him seem weak and that is not what he wanted to seem to Anne. As he stared at the chair in the corner his mouth got dry and he wondered if bringing her here was the best idea.

"Joe, it's ok. I think your home is wonderful....I think you are wonderful." Anne said touching his arm.

Joe turned towards her and suddenly the chair didn't matter anymore and he was glad she was here. As if driven by a force he couldn't control he reached down to hold her face in his hands. His lips found hers and at first the touch was gentle, like a butterfly fluttering on her lips for a moment before fully tasting the response she held inside. The kiss turned intense and the picnic basket dropped to the floor so Anne could reach her arms around and hold this man she was falling in love with, to show him he was safe in her arms. Time seemed to stand still as their mouths joined to show the other the feelings they could no longer deny.

When the kiss ended Joe had to catch his breath. He had been a master of guarding his feelings and holding himself in check. This was very new for him. "Anne…" he finally said catching his breath and placing a light kiss on her forehead… wanting to continue but still unsure of where this could all go. He had never allowed himself to get this far in a relationship, where his feelings were more in control then he was. He had never wanted to take the risk. Since he was 15 he had studied up on Spina Bifida and when he read that 50% of the cases could cause sexual dysfunction including impotence or erectile dysfunction he had never felt safe enough to explore his sexuality. At first, he was afraid of a teenage girl's reaction if he tried and couldn't, and then he just put up walls around himself so he would seem aloof to girls in college. He became so good at it that he hadn't had a real date in years. He had invited girls to banquets and business functions, but the dates rarely went beyond that. He could tell many wanted them to, but he wasn't willing to risk his reputation. He never wanted to feel vulnerable. "Anne, don't you think we should eat? I'm getting hungry."

Meanwhile Anne's head was spinning. She had never imagined that she could feel so swept up by the touch of someone's lips. "Yes… I think eating would be good." But neither of them wanted to separate, they were drawn to each other like magnets. Finally, after several more minutes Anne reached down to collect the basket. "I hope the food is ok. I dropped the basket." She said apologetically, slightly embarrassed by her reaction to the kiss.

"I'm sure it will taste the same." Joe said. "And it was worth it." He said smiling.

Joe ushered her into the kitchen, which was beautiful with vaulted ceilings and oak cabinets. The solarium was off the kitchen and had several vibrant plants growing. The furniture was comfortable and inviting. The view was spectacular. She thought the view from the front of the house was wonderful, but the view back here she could look at forever. As she looked out over the meadow, she gasped. The sunset took her breath away. Joe heard her gasp and smiled. He was glad she loved his house. Her presence seemed to make the house a home. "It is beautiful isn't it?" He asked, moving close behind her. He could smell the light scent of her hair and it took a great amount of willpower to keep from taking her in his arms again.

"Joe, it's magnificent." Anne replied sincerely, unconsciously reaching for his hand. The solarium's glass walls and ceiling made a person feel as if they were actually outside experiencing nature.

"I've never shared this with another woman, Anne." Joe said softly wanting her to know how special she truly was. She looked up at him, her eyes soft and moist. His words touched her greatly. Joe brought her hand up to his lips and he placed a light kiss on the back of her hand before releasing it to take a seat on the cushy sofa.

Anne opened the basket and fished out the food. She had cold chicken, potato salad, fruit, fresh baguette rolls and a bottle of chardonnay. "Oops, one of the wine glasses didn't survive the fall," she said with a gentle laugh.

"No worries," Joe answered starting to get up, "I have lots of wine glasses."

"No, no, my mistake dropping the basket, just tell me where to get it in this vast expanse of a kitchen." Anne said jumping to her feet.

"Should be some hanging to your left." Joe directed as he opened the wine. "And I wouldn't characterize our kiss as a mistake," he said pointedly while pouring the wine.

"No, I wouldn't either." Anne said breathlessly reliving the feeling of Joe's tongue touching hers and the feel of his full lips as they swept over hers.

He saw the fire burning in her eyes and he gently took the full wine glasses and set them on the table in front of them.

He reached over to take her in his arms to relive that moment for himself. Between the stolen kisses and eating, hours passed by in the blink of an eye it seemed.

Suddenly Anne realized that the sun was long set and the sky was lit up with thousands of stars. "Oh my, this is fantastic." She said indicating the sky with her hand.

"Yes, it is," Joe answered, only his eyes never left Anne's.

Laying her head on Joe's chest, Anne had never felt so alive and so at peace. It's like she was meant to be here all her life. She closed her eyes to savor the moment. They lay like this for an hour, not saying a word but letting their fingers gently explore the outline of each other's face and lips.

Suddenly Joe sat upright realizing that erectile dysfunction was not his problem, but that also didn't mean that there wouldn't be other issues. He wasn't quite ready to fully explore his sexuality tonight. He glanced at his watch and realized it was midnight and he was about to turn into a pumpkin. "Wow, it's getting late. It's almost midnight."

Anne realized that Joe had gotten a little uncomfortable and she was a bit embarrassed that she had gone this far. "Yes, I had better pack up and head home. It's almost a two-hour drive."

Joe helped her repack the now empty picnic basket. As he walked her to the door, he realized he didn't want her to leave... ever. "I have a spare bedroom. Could you stay the night?" Joe asked, not wanting to presume facts not in evidence.

"Thanks Joe, but my mom is expecting me back tonight, and she worries." Anne said reaching up to touch his lips one last time. Their lips were slightly bruised and swollen from all the kissing, but she couldn't get enough of his.

As she slowly withdrew Joe said without thinking, "Could you be my date for my sister's wedding? It's a small wedding out at my parent's farm next weekend."

A small smile crossed her lips and she blushed slightly, "Yes, I'd be happy to."

"There's a rehearsal dinner on Friday evening and then the wedding is on Saturday." He said giving her every opportunity to say no if she felt uncomfortable.

"I'd love to meet your family." Anne said warmly.

"You could stay here...with me..so you wouldn't have to drive back and forth." Joe offered; also thinking, because I want you to stay here with me.

"Yes. I'll plan on it." Anne reached up with her hand to touch his face one last time before turning towards the door.

"Drive safe. Please call when you get home." Joe called out.

"I don't think I have your number here," Anne called back, realizing his card had only his office number.

"Check your pocket." Joe called back smiling.

Anne reached into her coat pocket pulling out Joe's card and flipping it over she found he had written his home number with a smiley face. It made her laugh. That man is special she thought. Without thinking she turned to wave and as an afterthought blew a kiss.

Joe watched her leave his driveway. This time her picnic basket was empty, but she took his heart with her.

Joe couldn't sleep waiting for Anne's call so he tried to read but found his mind wandering to soft lips and bright blue eyes. Suddenly the phone ringing startled him at exactly 1 hour and 53 minutes after she left.

"Anne?" Joe answered, not even thinking it could be someone else.

"I made it." Anne answered a bit breathless. She had gone straight to the phone and dialed his number when she arrived.

"Thank you for the wonderful diversion tonight." Joe answered. The pretense of professional distance fully faded away.

"You're welcome." Anne answered with a smile he couldn't see. "I had a great time." The sound of his voice sending shivers through her.

"Me, too." Joe answered and meant it more then she would ever know.

"I'm looking forward to next weekend. Are you wearing a tux for the wedding?" She asked realizing she hadn't asked him how formal the wedding will be.

"Yes I am." Joe said smiling.

She imagined his beautiful shoulders in a tux. "Is a short cocktail dress appropriate?" Anne asked suddenly aware that she was going to meet his parents and wanted to make a good impression.

"That would be fine for the wedding, and Friday night is casual." Joe answered, hearing the nervousness in her voice. "I'll call you with the times tomorrow." Glad to have a reason to hear her voice.

"Okay. I work until 3pm tomorrow." Anne answered, already looking forward to his call.

Suddenly Joe wanted more than to hear her voice. "Anne, how about dinner tomorrow night? I could drive down and pick you up at 6?" Joe offered hopefully.

Anne smiled, "How about 5?"

"Perfect." Joe answered quickly. "Anne…"

"Yes, Joe?" Anne prodded sensing Joe's hesitation.

"Sweet dreams." He answered quietly, adding in his own mind, 'dream of me.'

"You too." She answered, smiling as she hung up the phone.

"You're getting back kind of late." Eve said gruffly, knowing her daughter had to get up for a morning shift.

"Time got away from us." Anne said quietly looking at the phone.

"So, you are seeing the lawyer?" Eve asked, already knowing the answer from overhearing their conversation.

"Yes." Anne answered sensing some disapproval in her mother's voice.

"I hope you know what you are getting yourself into." Eve replied. She had always been protective of Anne, not wanting her to make the same mistakes she had. She knew Joe was handsome and a lawyer. But he also had a disability. Eve had always wanted a perfect man for her perfect daughter. Joe just came up short.

"Mother, Joe is a wonderful man. He is handsome, intelligent, a world class gentleman, and I plan to continue to see him into the foreseeable future. He may even be the one." Anne said quite emphatically. The fact is she was already falling in love with him and knew in her heart that disability or no disability he was the one she wanted to spend her life with. She knew from the moment she opened the door at their first meeting. Some things just feel right.

Eve could see that her daughter was quite set on her decision and nothing she said was going to deter her. "It's your life." Eve said quietly retreating back to her bedroom. The truth was, every time Eve saw Joe, she saw her mistakes, her misjudgments; the part of her life she wished she could erase. He was a living reminder of the wrongs she had committed. It wasn't that she didn't think Joe was a decent guy. He was a guy that according to her and Dr. Jefferson's actions shouldn't have even been alive and now he was going to tell the world about her misdeeds.

The next morning Joe was up bright and early doing his exercises. He had furnished one of the bedrooms with all the exercise equipment he needed and promised himself that he wouldn't slack off again. He needed extra arm strength for when his legs tired and he needed to keep his legs strengthened or the muscles would shrink which could leave him in the wheel chair permanently and cause other bodily functions to stop working properly. He couldn't have that now.

Carolyn was surprised when Joe walked in the door at 8am. She had barely started the coffee and was getting out the mixing bowl when he came up behind her to give her a big hug. She could tell he was in a fantastic mood. After these many weeks of working on the case and so many emotional days she was surprised but happy with this turn of events.

"You seem extraordinarily happy today." Carolyn said smiling as she put the flour in the bowl.

"I am," Joe answered unashamedly. "What are you whipping up?"

"Belgian waffles. Jessica's favorite. She came home last night with her new 'friend' and put in the request." Carolyn said with a wink when she got to friend.

"Hmmm do you think I should go wake her up and surprise her like she does to me all the time??" Joe asked smiling devilishly.

"Joe, stop. I thought I heard voices in there as I walked by this morning." Carolyn said not wanting an awkward moment this morning.

"I'm up and I heard every word you two just said," Jessica answered entering the kitchen with a flushed look on her face.

"Where's your 'friend' Miss Jessica?" Joe asked teasing.

"Brian is taking a shower if you must know." Jessica answered popping a strawberry into her mouth.

"Hey, those are for the waffles." Carolyn said feigning a swat to her hand.

"Morning, Mom." Jessica said leaning over to kiss her cheek. "Where's Dad?"

"Morning, baby." Carolyn answered back. "He's out feeding everyone. Then I think he could use your help in getting the place ready for the entourage of people. Cassie and Jacob should also be here shortly, and Gramma Jo is coming to double check the last minute adjustments on the dress. Joe, I need to double check your measurements for the tux."

"Sure mom," Joe said quietly getting a cup of coffee. "By the way, is it all right if I bring a date?"

Both Carolyn and Jessica stopped mid-sentence and turned to look at Joe. He sat quietly looking at the paper on the table. They exchanged glances and then Carolyn slid into a chair next to Joe wanting desperately to know details.

"Sure, honey. You are always welcome to bring a date. You just hadn't mentioned it before."

"I just asked her last night." Joe answered, knowing that his mother wanted details but not willing to share too much of his evening with Anne.

"Could I have a name for the place card?" Carolyn asked slyly.

Joe laughed, she was good, his mother. "Okay, Okay. It's Anne Stockwell."

Carolyn smiled, she had been right, when Joe had mentioned Anne, there had been a spark of something. "Well, she's very welcome. I look forward to meeting her. Will she be here just for the wedding?"

"No, I asked her for the rehearsal dinner as well." Joe replied, now getting a little uncomfortable with sharing the details.

"Oh," Carolyn's eyes got slightly bigger as did Jessica's when their eyes met sharing a little disbelief.

"Well, don't forget there's brunch here on Sunday with the family to open gifts." Carolyn added getting up.

"Oh, that's right," Joe stated remembering. "Better plan on her for that as well."

Carolyn went back to the waffles, digesting this newest turn of events. She was thrilled Joe was bringing a date, but this was obviously more than a date if she was coming for the entire weekend.

Suddenly Jessica chimed in, "Does she need a place to stay? She is from out of town and it is quite a drive."

"She's staying with me." Joe stated getting up from the table. He suddenly needed some air and knew if he stayed in the kitchen with those two there would be more uncomfortable questions.

Carolyn and Jessica both stared after him wanting more information, but knowing that Joe would only divulge what he wanted them to know.

Cassie and Jacob arrived shortly after breakfast and everyone was given a list of tasks to do to prepare for next weekend's big event. Joe happily pitched in, but whispered in Carolyn's ear that he needed to leave by 2pm for an evening engagement. Carolyn nodded her agreement and wanted to ask desperately if it had anything to do with a pretty blonde woman named Anne, but held her tongue. Joe would talk in due time – or his sisters would.

Jessica was helping Joe wash the windows in the house and sweep down the porch area when she broached the subject again. "Joe, I'm glad you are bringing a date to the wedding. I hope she's someone you really like. You deserve to find happiness."

"Thanks Jessica." Joe answered, rubbing a particular window pane briskly, really not wanting to go down this road again. But he did have questions. He felt his body respond to Anne very strongly, but he worried about exploring further, damn this disability. "I hope the family will like her and make her feel welcome." Joe paused then added, "This is important to me." wanting Jessica to know that Anne was important to him, not just a date for a wedding.

"I'll make an extra special effort, big brother." Jessica said smiling.

Joe smiled back, Jessica and he always had a special connection. It felt good sharing his happiness.

Exactly at 2pm Joe yelled through the door to his mother who was cooking up a storm, "Mom, I'm leaving now. Call me if you need anything this week. Love you."

"Drive safe. Love you too. Say hello to Anne." Carolyn called back.

Joe stopped in his tracks. How did she know he was going to visit Anne? He almost turned around to ask, but then he shook it off knowing Carolyn had a sixth sense with all her children.

Joe arrived precisely at 5pm at Anne's house. He was always well dressed making sure to buy pants that covered the braces on his legs. He walked with one metal crutch and held a bouquet of tulips in his other hand.

Anne came to the door in a beautiful outfit with a light brown suede coat and excused herself to put the tulips in water. Eve was sitting on the couch with a warm throw over her lap. She masked her feelings well. Her face held neither disapproval nor approval.

Joe acknowledge her presence with a smile, "Good evening, Mrs. Stockwell."

"Please, if you are dating my daughter, I think you can call me Eve." She answered with a slight smile noting Joe's handsome appearance.

"Eve." He answered nodding.

"The tulips are beautiful, Joe." Anne acknowledged. "Thank you."

"They are my favorite spring flower," Joe answered. "Their beautiful colors reminded me of you yesterday." Joe added a bit embarrassed. Could it have been only yesterday since they last saw each other? The time apart seemed much longer.

"Thank you," Anne answered glowing.

"Mother, we are just going to dinner. It shouldn't be too late." Anne told Eve, taking Joe's free hand. Joe felt the softness of her hand and gave her fingers a quick squeeze.

"Try not to 'let the time get away from you' tonight honey. You have another early shift tomorrow." Eve answered with light concern.

"Yes, Eve, I'll see to it she's back early," Joe answered reassuringly.

"Thank you, Joe." Eve answered, noting he was the perfect gentleman her daughter had stated glowingly last evening.

Eve watched them through the window. Joe opened Anne's door and gave her a quick kiss as he helped her into the car. Eve now realized what an awful thing it would have been if he hadn't lived. She was now filled with regret for allowing her own moral compass to be dictated by a man consumed with his own power. "Joe, forgive me," she softly whispered.

True to his word Joe kept an eye on his watch which wasn't easy as he only had eyes for Anne. Conversation was so easy with her. They were interested in the same sports, they shared the same humor, and the sexual tension between them was exhilarating. Joe had made reservations at one of the best restaurants in Rochester. He had excellent taste in food and wine, which Anne appreciated.

"This is a lovely restaurant, Joe. I had heard it was nice, but really have never had the opportunity to eat here." Anne had also heard it was ridiculously expensive.

"I wanted a place with ambiance, which is what they advertised." Joe answered, sliding his hand over hers. The heat between them was palpable.

"The ambiance is beautiful," she acknowledged with the small waterfall in one corner and the large fireplace in the middle of the room. "But I don't think anything could top last night's ambiance." She said smiling, running her index finger along Joe's hand.

Joe coughed and said hoarsely, "Yes, that was quite nice."

When Joe noted the hour was getting late, he dutifully asked for the check. Walking Anne back to the car he realized for the first time in his life he wasn't self-conscious about his disability. He was focused on the beautiful woman by his side. Anne glanced up to see the amazement in his face.

"A penny for your thoughts?" she asked.

"Just that you are a very beautiful woman." Joe answered leaning down to meet her lips. "And you are here with me." Their lips met in agreement.

When Anne slid into her seat her head was spinning. This is all moving so fast, but yet seemed to be in slow motion. Time raced when they were together and when they were apart seemed to be an eternity.

Joe slid into the driver's seat and looked over at Anne. In the darkness he could see her silhouette, her blonde hair shimmering in the moonlight the red highlights sent shivers down his body. He was so drawn to her in every way. "Anne....Anne," he began again. "Why are you here with me?" Joe asked looking forward, afraid of her answer.

"Joe? What do you mean?" Anne asked, not sure of his question.

"Why me?" Joe clarified. "You could have anyone. You are beautiful, intelligent, sensitive. You could be with any number of men who don't have the physical issues I do." Joe finally said it, and she understood.

"Joe, I've been drawn to you since the moment we met. I'm attracted to you. The more I see you, the more I want to see you, *need* to see you. You have become like my air. Why you? May I ask, why NOT you? You are extremely handsome, articulate, intelligent, funny, and a true gentleman. I'm a very lucky girl to be sitting here next to you." Anne said reaching over to touch Joe's hand on the steering wheel. Their fingers intertwined and she lifted his hand to her lips and kissed the palm delicately. "This is where you have me, in the palm of your hand." She said breathlessly.

Joe reached up to her face tracing the outline of her chin and slipped his fingers through her hair bringing her face closer so that he could place a light kiss on her lips and when he felt the wetness of her lips the kiss deepened. What was happening to him? He had never felt such attraction before. It was as if his body had a mind of its own. He understood Anne perfectly when she said she needed him because he felt the same way, but he couldn't believe how lucky he was that she felt this same need, same desire.

It took all of Joe's will-power to pull away and start the car. "I promised your mother to have you home early." Joe said trying hard to catch his breath. "Now I wish I hadn't."

When they pulled into Anne's driveway, they both dreaded the eventual good bye. Eve had conveniently gone to her room to give them privacy when she saw the car approach.

Joe walked Anne to the door slowly relishing the feel of her hand in his, putting off his departure as long as possible. He reached down gently taking her in his arms, this time it was his turn to show her she was safe. This relationship, what had blossomed so quickly, was safe and secure.

When Joe looked into her eyes he saw concern, "What's wrong?" Joe asked, gently moving a stray strand of her hair, hoping she wasn't having second thoughts.

"Things aren't going to change between us because of the trial, will they?" Anne asked quietly.

"No, those things have nothing to do with you, or with us." Joe calmly reassured her.

"But my mother, my biological father... will you think differently about me?" Anne asked needing his reassurance.

Joe searched her face. He knew what she needed to hear but he had never said it to another woman other than his immediate family. This was so fast, but he also knew it was never more true. "Anne, I'm falling in love with you. Nothing that happens in that trial will change that." He took her suddenly in his arms and their lips met silencing any doubts she had.

When the kiss ended, she looked up into his handsome face and brown eyes and whispered, "I love you, too."

It took all the will-power he had left to pull himself away from her to drive home alone. He could still see her in his mind, standing in the doorway waving and hearing her suddenly yelling, "Drive safe, call me when you get there."

Friday was going to be an eternity to wait!

Chapter 16

Joe was frantically trying to tie up loose ends in his office before Anne's arrival. The week was a whirlwind of activity; briefs, summary judgements, and late hours, but when Joe lay in bed looking at the stars he felt the emptiness without Anne. They spoke each night and although hearing her voice was wonderful, when he hung up the phone he had an ache within him.

He was just finishing up his request to put before the judge on Monday when he glanced up to see Anne in front of him. He immediately swiveled his chair to get out of his seat to greet her when she gently pushed him back down and crawled into his lap. Joe glanced at the door to see she had conveniently closed it.

"I missed you." She said her lips dangerously close to his.

"I missed you more." He replied slipping his arm behind her back running his hand up her spine to her neck and running his finger over her jawbone to her lips. "I missed this most of all." He said giving her a welcome kiss that made her glad she was sitting down.

"Are you almost finished?" She asked after they drew apart, her heart pounding and breathing erratic.

"Trying to tie up loose ends." He answered unable to tear his gaze from her face. "Shouldn't be more than a half hour."

"Do you want me to wait?" Anne asked.

"No, you are too much of a distraction." Joe answered smiling. "Why don't you go to my place and get settled." He said reaching for the spare key he thought to bring this morning. "My mom would like us at the church by 5:30 and then it's back to my parents for a casual buffet supper."

"Great! I'm looking forward to meeting them." Anne said extricating herself from his lap. "My mother speaks very highly of your mother."

"Do you remember how to get out to my place." Joe asked, although he had already started to think of it as their place.

"Yes, no problem." Anne said smiling. She loved being out there and without Joe she could really examine the surroundings. He is also a distraction, when he's there she only has eyes for him.

She leaned down to give him one last kiss and whispered, "I'll be waiting."

Suddenly a knock came from the door and Anne jumped back guiltily.

A grinning Joe said, "Come in."

James came in quickly not expecting anyone but Joe to be in the room but stopped mid-sentence upon seeing a woman standing next to Joe. He noted her flushed face and the lipstick smudge on Joe's cheek and correctly determined he had indeed interrupted something,"Er..sorry, Joe, do you have the pictures from the hospital site?" Trying to be as delicate as possible, when suddenly he recognized the beautiful woman next to Joe's desk, "Oh, hello Miss Stockwell, nice to see you again." Turning to Joe he raised his eye brows and gave him a questioning look.

Anne suddenly felt awkward. "Hello, I was just leaving. Nice to see you again."

"I'll see you in a little bit, Joe." Anne said wishing she could give him another quick kiss but felt it inappropriate under the circumstance.

"I'll be there shortly, Anne." Joe answered also feeling her awkwardness.

As she left James and Joe both watched her go. One of them wondering what was going on and the other wishing he was walking next to her.

"So?" James said, wanting details.

"So, what?" Joe answered thinking James was as bad as his mother, actually worse because his mother had pretty good intuition and put things together without him actually having to say a word.

"So?? Is this serious?" James asked, thinking back over this past week and noting the smile on Joe's face for no apparent reason. "Scratch that. It is serious." James said noting the same look on Joe's face right now.

"James, you just said hello to the future Mrs. Joseph Steffan." Joe said quite seriously, still watching Anne as she exchanged pleasantries with the receptionist.

James nodded his understanding. Joe had it, Joe had it bad.

When Joe finished about 45 minutes later he couldn't wait to get back home. He caught himself speeding several times, hoping he wouldn't get a ticket. Pulling up in his driveway he felt a deep sense of exhilaration. He would get Anne for an entire weekend. Life suddenly didn't seem so grim and this case that had consumed him would not consume him this weekend. This weekend he felt every bit the young man in love.

As he came through the front door he called, "Anne, I'm home," and thought how wonderful that sounded.

"I'm in the solarium." She called back.

As he made his way to the solarium he saw her suitcase in the great room. Evidently she wasn't going to make the decision where she was to sleep without his direction.

As he entered the solarium her presence intoxicated his senses. Leaning his crutch against the couch, he wrapped both arms around her, breathing in her perfume and placing a light kiss on her neck.

His arms felt strong around her and she turned to loop her arms around his neck. When their lips met their kiss was as deep as the first time they kissed in this house. They both were breathless afterwards.

"I'm sorry I'm later than I expected." Joe said with his eyes closed. His heart seemed to race and he felt light-headed.

"You're here now." Anne answered.

"But looking at my watch we need to leave for the rehearsal in 20 minutes." Joe moaned. "Joe, we have all weekend together." Anne said consolingly, "But I don't want to be late the first time I'm meeting your parents and siblings."

"Okay, you're right. I need a quick shower." Joe said with a quick kiss to Anne's forehead before heading in the direction of his room.

"I'll be waiting." Anne called after him with a laugh.

"Unless you'd like to join me," Joe said jokingly. He was only half joking, but he was still quite nervous about approaching the act of sex.

"Rain check" Anne called back, sensing that Joe wasn't quite ready for bare intimacy…yet.

When Joe was getting dressed, he turned to find Anne standing in front of him in a beautiful black pants suit. She looked ravishing. Joe's voice caught in his throat when Anne suddenly turned. "Joe, could you finish my zipper please?"

Joe nervously reached for the zipper. He started to zip up the top and found his finger tracing her spine sending shivers up her back. When he completed the task, she turned to kiss him and whispered, "When we get back maybe you can help me in reverse."

Joe was finding very little trouble with erectile dysfunction whenever he was in Anne's proximity. She lit him on fire. It was all he could do to leave the house without taking her in his arms, but he still had never completed the act of having sex. In fact, it terrified him. He would be totally vulnerable and admitting to possible ineptness. What would Anne think of him if he was unable to satisfy her sexually?

On the way to the church he could see Anne was getting anxious. "What if your family doesn't like me?" she asked nervously biting her lower lip.

Joe couldn't image this and scrunched up his face in reply, "There's no doubt in my mind that they are going to love you, almost as much as I do." He said hoping his words would reassure her.

When they entered the church, Carolyn turned towards them and enveloped Anne in a heart-warming hug.

"Anne, I'm Carolyn, Joe's mother. I'm so glad you could join us. Your pictures don't do you justice! You are beautiful! How is your mother?" Carolyn asked sincerely,

"She's holding her own." Anne replied. "I have a friend checking in on her this weekend to make sure she's eating the meals I prepared ahead and to call me with any problems. But it is nice to get away." Anne answered truthfully.

Carolyn nodded knowingly. Being a nurse can be draining on both heart and soul.

Joe quickly changed the subject introducing the rest of the family, "Dad this is Anne. Anne, my father, Tom. That's Jessica and her friend Brian, and the bride is my sister, Cassie, and Jacob, the nervous groom." While his sisters took turns hugging Anne, Joe got handshakes from Brian and Jacob with small nods of approval.

Jacob leaned over to Joe whispering in his ear, "You dog, you hit the mother-load."

Joe smiled and nodded his agreement. He didn't have to be told. He already knew.

Jacob's parents were here, but were quiet in the background. Joe knew his family could be overwhelming and hoped they wouldn't be too much for Anne to absorb but when he looked at her, she was smiling from ear to ear and even her eyes were glistening. He whispered in her ear, "See, they love you."

She whispered back, "They are great. I love them already."

The rehearsal went off without a glitch, with such a small wedding party not much could go wrong. Soon they were off to the farm for a small supper which turned out to be a small feast Carolyn had prepared. Gramma Jo was tending the food when everyone arrived. She came running when Joe walked in with Anne. He hadn't warned Anne about Gramma Jo and as she enveloped Anne in a hug. Joe noted Anne appeared to be relishing the hug of a grandmother as she never knew hers. Eve's family disowned her when they realized she was pregnant and unwed. Anne's grandfather on her father's side had already died when her father married Eve and his mother was in poor health, living in another state. Most of Anne's life it had been just the three of them, but their home never seemed to be lacking in love.

Joe gave Anne a tour of the farm and introduced her to all the animals. Anne fell in love with the baby lambs. "Oh Joe, I see why you loved growing up here. Our farm had just cows and pigs and my father didn't allow me to make pets of them. I did have a dog, a black lab mix and a couple of kitties to keep down the population of mice in the barn. You have a menagerie of animals and they are all so wonderful." Just then one of the lambs decided Anne's finger seemed like the nipple on her bottle and started to suckle it. Anne's surprised laugh startled the donkey who went off braying.

Jessica came into the barn just then laughing. "Don't mind Mr. Ed, Anne, he gets annoyed easily."

"Joe, you're needed at the house to go over the program for tomorrow's reception. You know, 'Best man duties." Joe glanced down at Anne and Jessica quickly read his mind.

"Don't worry, I'll keep Anne company. Brian and Jacob are playing a game of pool and I've got lots of stories to tell." Jessica said laughing.

"Don't believe half of them." Joe directed to Anne and reflexively leaned down to give Anne a quick kiss before turning to leave. "I won't be long."

"I'm fine Joe. I love this place." Anne said reassuringly, blushing slightly at his sudden display of affection in front of his sister.

"And Jessica, behave." Joe flashed his sister a quick smile and was off to find his mom.

Actually, Jessica was happy for the free moment with Anne and knelt next to her in the hay. "It really is nice here isn't it!" Jessica stated acknowledging Anne's obvious delight.

"Are you kidding? How did your parents get you to leave?" Anne asked, half seriously.

"We love the animals, but they are work." Jessica countered. Suddenly Jessica turned serious, "My brother has obviously fallen for you…hard," she stated flatly looking in the direction of Joe's departure.

Anne looked at Jessica trying to read her reaction. Was she jealous? No, she didn't look jealous. Protective? Yes, that was the look of concern she saw.

"I'd say the feeling is quite mutual?" Anne offered, hoping to relieve the look of concern on Jessica's face. "I care very deeply for Joe. He's a very special man." Anne said quietly, but sincerely.

"Yes, he is." Jessica agreed. "I just wanted to tell you that you must also be very special because Joe has always kept relationships at arms' length, but with you, he is blatantly displaying affection and the look on his face is complete infatuation."

Anne watched Jessica while still holding the lamb. She didn't know what Jessica was after. Anne was the last person who would ever dream of hurting Joe. She, too, had never felt this way about anyone else. "Jessica, I would never hurt Joe. He means the world to me. We've had this instant connection, like we can read each other's thoughts."

Jessica met Anne's gaze, "Then you must realize that he's scared at the prospect of having sex."

Anne's eyes got a little bigger and she moved slightly on the hay bale showing her discomfort in discussing having sex with Joe with his younger sister.

"Anne, I'm not trying to be nosy or inappropriate." Jessica explained while reaching in the small refrigerator they kept in the barn to fish out a bottle made up for the lamb's dinner and slowly mixed the ingredients. "I'm a medical student and you are a nurse. Surely you understand that men with my brother's disability can have difficulty with sex. There's the possibility of erectile dysfunction, inability to ejaculate, problems with different sexual positions. I'm just trying to prepare you because my brother rarely allows himself to open himself to being vulnerable. He's lived his adult life protecting himself. Just be aware that when you two take that step, he's taking a huge leap of faith in you and in himself to open up, to be at his most vulnerable. I can tell he loves you and from the look of things I think you love him too. But don't take that leap unless you are willing to help him past his insecurities. All I want is to see my brother finally happy. I can see you make him happy and you have my undying gratitude for that." Jessica handed the prepared bottle to Anne so she could remove her finger from the lamb's mouth and feed him. "Perhaps you are the perfect person to lead him through the scariest part of human relationships."

Anne and Jessica watched the lamb quickly drain the bottle. After, Anne handed the bottle back to Jessica and set the lamb back in his pen, "Don't worry, Jessica. Joe and I are in this together."

The night lights were coming on in the yard when Anne found Joe on the porch sitting with his mother in the swing. His arm was gently around her shoulders as they discussed tomorrow's activities. Joe rose slowly when he saw Anne approaching. He smiled seeing the straw clinging to the back of her pants and the moonlight dancing off the red hues in her blonde hair. Joe's arm went instinctively around Anne's waist and her hand intertwined in his fingers.

Carolyn smiled at the two of them together. They were an obvious match in her mind. He was handsome and she beautiful. Their eyes lit up when they met the other's gaze. Carolyn loved seeing her son happy. The squeak from the screen door startled them as Tom joined them, taking Joe's spot on the porch swing. "Jacob and Cassie left to bring Jacob's parents back to the hotel. Jessica and Brian went for a walk in the moonlight, and I'm tired." Tom reached over to take Carolyn's hand smiling.

Tom also noted the intertwined fingers and the closeness Joe and Anne shared. "Anne, did you enjoy your tour of the barn and meeting the animals?" Tom asked.

"I love your place." Anne answered warmly. "Jessica let me feed the baby lamb a bottle. I can't believe your children voluntarily left this place?"

"Well, they really haven't left. Their rooms are still here and when they're home, it feels like they never left." Tom answered.

"I'm glad you were able to join Joe this weekend. I don't think I've ever seen such a big smile on his face." Tom joked at Joe's expense.

"Yes, well, thanks Dad for embarrassing me." Joe responded only slightly miffed, "But seriously, it's a big day tomorrow so I think Anne and I are going to head out. See you both tomorrow." He said giving them both a hug.

Anne hesitated but a split second before also giving hugs. "Thank you both for a wonderful evening."

Carolyn and Tom watched as Joe and Anne made their way down the ramp to Joe's car and heard their laughter as Joe brushed off the back of Anne's pants from the straw still clinging to her clothes. Tom and Carolyn looked at each other and hearing their son's laughter, silently asking the other the same question and both hoping for the same outcome.

As the car turned into the driveway of his home, they both felt a tingling in the touch of their fingers. It was late, but it felt as if the night was just beginning.

Coming through the door Joe was keenly aware of the decisions that lay ahead. He felt like his breath was coming out of his chest. Anne gently touched his arm and lightly said, "Joe, I'm going to change out of these clothes. I think I have straw scratching my back."

"Ok, how about a night cap?" he asked, postponing the inevitable decision.

"Sure, I'll be out in two minutes." Anne said heading into the bathroom softly closing the door behind her.

She came out few minutes later in a beautiful cream nightgown and robe. She sat down on the brushed leather couch in the great room listening to the music Joe had put on the stereo. Joe brought her a glass of Bailey's and cream and brought the same for himself. Sitting down next to her he felt her move closer, the silkiness of her robe lightly touching his fingers. His hands suddenly felt sweaty as nervousness started to overtake him. They sat next to each other listening to the music each wanting the other to make the next move. She, not wanting Joe to feel pressured. He, not wanting to show his lack of experience. Slowly, almost imperceptibly, Anne rested her head on his chest. Instinctively his arm wrapped around her. The sweet perfume from her hair filled his nostrils. His head started spinning. Could this really be happening? But what if he failed, would it end their relationship?

Joe suddenly cleared his throat and stood up and took a couple of steps towards his room. He suddenly stopped, unable to move forward or backward his words tumbled out, "Anne.... I don't know if I can do this.." he stated with his back to her, his frustration evident in his voice, his right hand sweeping through his thick dark hair while his left hand gripped the metal crutch, a constant reminder he was different. "I want to, but ... many guys with this disability have problems... I've never tried... I've never felt safe enough to try." His raw honesty finally laid it out there for her. Joe waited for her response. It seemed like an eternity, but in reality, only a few seconds.

Anne now knew how right Jessica was in her perception of her brother. She heard Joe's pain, his fear. She knew this moment was the turning point and there was no going back.

Anne went to him. Her hand gently touching his face feeling the stubble under her soft finger tips. Slowly she ran her fingers through his hair and gently pulled his face down to hers meeting his lips with an invitation of more.

As their faces separated but remained close, their eyes met, his shrouded in anxiety and hers with strength, certainty, and love. She quietly said, "Joe, we aren't going to have sex tonight."

His eyes got big, and he hoarsely replied, "We're not?" His disappointment quite evident.

"No, we are going to make love… together." Anne said softly, but firmly. "The act of sex is mechanics. When two people make love, they meet here." She said pressing her palm against his heart. She slowly took his hand and gently led him back to his bedroom with 'Send Me An Angel' by Real Life, 1989, starting to play in the background. Joe suddenly realized Anne was the angel that was sent just for him.

"Do you believe in heaven above….Do you believe in love…"
"Open fire on my burning heart…I've never been lucky in love."
"Send me an Angel right now… Right now…Right now."
"My defenses are down …I can't survive on my own…"
"Send me an Angel right now… Right now..Right now.."

When they were next to his bed, she slowly unbuttoned his shirt and slipped it off his shoulders gently plying sweet soft kisses across his chest. When she came to his nipple, she slowly circled it with her tongue until it formed a peak.

"My defenses are down …I can't survive on my own…"
"Send me an Angel right now… Right now..Right now.."

The intake of air she heard him take indicated that he was affected strongly by her ministrations. She also saw by the bulge in his pants, erectile dysfunction was not going to be a problem. Slowly she undid his belt and pants and helped pull them down. He tried to brush her aside so he could undo the braces himself. He felt the braces were a symbol of his weakness. There were times he hated them, but she forcefully sat him on the bed and laid a soft kiss on his lips while she slowly knelt in front of him slipping the straps of the braces off gently and removing the braces expertly. Once his legs were free, she placed soft kisses along his naked calf and knees making this all a part of her foreplay.

"Don't give up… You can be lucky in love…"
"Send me an Angel right now. … Right now….!"

Joe was mesmerized by her patience and also her command of the situation. He didn't know that she had done her research on his disability and was willing to meet him more than halfway if that is what it took. Anne felt Joe take her by her shoulders lifting her onto the bed in a single motion. Joe's legs may have been weaker but his upper body more than made up for it in strength. She felt his lips on hers as they stroked each other's body, the moonlight shining in from the skylight overhead the only light in the room. Joe's tongue made a river of delight circling her breast and then finding her mouth once more. The song played over in his thoughts and gave him courage to keep moving forward. The moment was suspended in time, their primal urges taking over.

Joe felt Anne's hands on his chest gently but firmly forcing him down in the bed and climbing on top of him, helping him find what he had been yearning for all these years. A closeness he had avoided, fearing. Their climax reached together. Joe held her tightly a single tear silently making a wet track out of his closed eyes unto the pillow. They had truly made love and their connection was now complete. He no longer felt vulnerable with her.

"Anne…. Anne…You are my angel," Joe said hoarsely, emotion taking over his ability to tell her all he was feeling.

Anne propped her head up on his shoulder and whispered in his ear. "Joe, I love you. All of you, just the way you are." She lifted her head above his, her blonde hair cascading down with flecks of light reflecting off them creating a waterfall around their faces. Her eyes held his as she gently lowered her lips to lightly touch his. His hands intertwined in the waterfall and the kiss deepened until the other couldn't tell where their mouth ended and the other's began.

No more words needed to be spoken. Their limbs intertwined holding each other as they drifted off to sleep knowing that their soul-mate lay beside them in blissful slumber.

CHAPTER 17

Joe felt bright sunlight streaming through the skylight and heard soft music playing in the great room as he finally opened his eyes. Wanting to the savor the memories from last night he pulled Anne's pillow closer to catch her now familiar scent. He was no longer a virgin, but the wait was worthwhile. The taste of her lips still present on his tongue. He closed his eyes to remember her caresses and the feel of her skin underneath his own finger tips. A slight weight appeared on the bed next to him and before he even opened his eyes, he reached out to caress a bare leg.

"Wake up sleepy head." Anne said softly in his ear.

He opened his eyes to see the bright blue of her eyes watching him. "You rocked my world last night. I wanted to stay asleep dreaming about it." He confessed honestly.

Anne ran her fingers through his hair and gently plied her lips on his. Soon the kiss deepened and at Joe's insistence, Anne joined him on the bed. This time Joe was on top and she assisted him in ridding her of her nightgown once again.

His lovemaking left her breathless, suddenly she sat up, "Joe, you made me forget. I have breakfast ready. I hope it isn't burned."

Anne said throwing on his shirt lying on the chair from the past night.

"Don't worry," he called after her. "It was so worth it." He said falling back on his pillow smiling.

"Joe, really, you need to get up. Remember the wedding..." She called from the kitchen. "It looks like the food is still edible, probably not up to your mother's cooking, but you'll survive." Anne said smiling, as Joe joined her in the kitchen. He had taken the time to put on the braces and pants, but his chest was still bare and she yearned to run her hands over it.

"If I had to choose between food this morning and making love to you, it isn't even a contest." He said kissing her firmly on the mouth and patting her gently on her rear.

Anne smiled her agreement. "But you don't have to choose, you can have both," she said putting the plate in front of him. "Any time you want," she added between kisses.

Joe looked at his watch realizing that time was short. "Do you want to take a shower first or should I?" Joe asked.

"We could save time and water if we took it together." Anne said innocently taking a sip of coffee.

Joe almost choked on his piece of bacon. He thought for a moment how to phrase his response. He would love to run his fingers over her wet body, but where most men stand in the shower, he had to sit to reduce the chance of falls. He couldn't wear his braces where it was wet and he was much less steady on his feet without them and his crutch.

Anne felt the hesitancy in Joe's response and realized when she went into the bathroom last night after they made love that the beautiful stone shower had a shower chair in it. Anne placed her hand over his, "Joe, don't worry. I'll use the guest bathroom."

Joe slowly nodded, angry at himself for not being able to share everything with her, but thankful for her understanding.

He slowly stood up and took a last sip of coffee before making his way back to his room and laid the pieces of the tuxedo on the bed. As he entered the shower, he felt again the anger of being different, taking over a piece of him that made him feel less of a man. Anne went into the guest bathroom, but realized before climbing into the shower that her toiletries were in Joe's bathroom. Wrapping herself in a bath towel, intending to slip into his bathroom quickly and retrieve it without Joe realizing she was there. Joe's bathroom was huge, Anne cautiously came around the door, stealing a glance in his direction while reaching for her toiletry bag. His hand was against the wall and his eyes downcast. He felt eyes on him. He turned towards Anne and their eyes locked. He quickly looked away in embarrassment. She read frustration and disappointment in his eyes. She reflexively dropped her towel and picked up the sponge and soap. Gently, she started scrubbing his shoulders and back while massaging his neck. His eyes closed as he enjoyed her soft touch. He felt her lips laying soft kisses after the sponge stopped. He no longer thought about this being 'abnormal," this was normal. This was intimate. She turned her attentions to his chest and arms and suddenly he felt her weight in his lap. She gently plied his chest and face with kisses creating small streams across his body. His arms closed around her, reveling in the soft wetness of her body. Anne showed him that all expressions of love were normal and sometimes the adjustments they had to make because of his disability made lovemaking even more of an adventure. Today he was damn glad for the shower chair. When their bodies were spent Anne picked up his shower gel and gently washed his black curls gently massaging his scalp as he stole quick kisses. He couldn't get enough of her.

When their lengthy shower was complete, they realized they had to quickly finish dressing preparations. Anne helped Joe decipher the different parts of the tuxedo and Joe helped her pull up the zipper on her yellow spring dress. Both stealing kisses as they went.

When they were getting into the car, Joe leaned down to help her get the seatbelt adjusted. His deep brown eyes met her blue ones and he said gently, "Anne, you are the most beautiful woman I have ever known both inside and out." He placed a gentle kiss on her forehead. She was stunned and humbled by his remark. She suddenly remembered what her mother had said about 'knowing what she was getting into' and inwardly laughed thinking, 'Mother, if you only knew the total love I feel for this man and how special he makes me feel.'

They rode over to the church listening to music both lost in their own thoughts about the other, their fingers caressing the others on the center console.

CHAPTER 18

The church was already bustling with activity when Joe and Anne arrived. The florist was placing flowers and the photographer was snapping photos of Cassie and Jacob. Gramma Jo brought Joe a boutonniere of a red rose and baby's-breath with a cream ribbon. Gramma Jo started to pin it on Joe's lapel when suddenly she turned to Anne and asked, "Could you do this my dear, I'll get Tom's on him."

Anne smiled, "I'd be happy to, Gramma Jo."

"There's a wrist corsage in the box for you also." Gramma Jo said smiling.

Anne's face registered shock. She just met these people and they were including her as a guest of honor with a corsage. As she turned to Joe to pin on the beautiful flower, he lifted her chin with his finger and met her questioning gaze. "My mother asked me if it would be ok if she ordered the corsage. I said yes, because you are going to be an important member of this family from this day forward."

Anne finished pinning Joe's boutonniere on the satin lapel of his black tuxedo and reached up to place a light kiss on Joe's waiting lips.

"Whoa, you two, plenty of time left for that later today. We need to get photos taken." Gramma Jo said as she gently nudged both of them into the church, smiling at their backs so happy for her grandson to find such a wonderful woman. As they were staging photos Anne found an inconspicuous place to sit and watch as Joe was in snapshot after snapshot. His eyes always found hers between photos and the photographer had to tell him before each photo to look towards him. Exasperated after the 10th photo the photographer turned to where Joe was looking to see what the distraction was. He saw Anne with the sun gleaming off her hair and immediately knew why Joe was distracted.

"Ok, one last photo of the family together." The photographer said staging the photo.

Suddenly Carolyn saw Anne sitting there alone and knew she belonged in this photo, "Anne, come here please."

Anne stepped to the front of the church thinking Carolyn needed her to do something.

"Where would you like her to stand?" Carolyn asked the photographer. The family was surprised, but happy, and no one voiced any objections. Brian was also asked to join this photo. The family seemed complete with these additions.

"Who does she go with?" the photographer asked.

The group pointed to Joe as he raised his hand. Anne blushed slightly as the photographer placed her next to Joe's side and had her rest her hand on his arm. Brian was placed next to Jessica. The photographer stepped back to look at this group and noted the big smiles on the faces and said, "We should have done this one first. It is by far the best smiles of the day."

When the photos were complete the wedding party, laughing and joking, headed for the basement, awaiting the church to fill up. Jessica suddenly came down the stairs with her face colorless.

Something was wrong. She went immediately to Cassie and her face dropped as well.

Anne and Joe sensed something was wrong and went closer to the sisters.

Joe asked, "What's going on? Both of you look like you've seen a ghost."

Jessica glanced quickly at Anne and then back at Joe. "One of Cassie's high school friends brought Adam Jefferson as her date for today."

"Who's Adam Jefferson?" Joe asked. Realizing as he said the name, this man must somehow be related to Dr. Jefferson to illicit this reaction from his sisters.

"He's the youngest son of Dr. Jefferson." Cassie replied quietly. "Lee Ann replied on her RSVP card one guest, but didn't put down his name. I even wrote out the place card for the reception 'Lee Ann's guest' because I didn't know who she was bringing."

Carolyn had made her way over to her children's circle as she saw the faces and the heated whispering. She heard the last exchange and surmised the rest.

"Cassie, Jessica, it's okay. Adam Jefferson has done nothing wrong himself and for us to judge him based on his father's actions is wrong." Carolyn said firmly. "He is welcome as our guest."

The girls nodded their understanding. Joe was lost in thought as this Adam Jefferson was actually, by blood, Anne's half-brother. Anne had also made this connection.

Joe took Anne by the hand and moved her several feet away to privately ask her, "Are you okay with this?"

Anne slowly nodded, "Technically he's my half-brother. I get it. But we don't know each other, its fine." Changing the subject, Anne asked, "Where would you like me to sit during the ceremony?"

"Up front, where I can keep an eye on you." Joe answered, placing a kiss on the back of Anne's hand.

"Okay, I'll sit in the second pew behind your parents." She said reaching up to give him a parting kiss and headed up to the sanctuary.

The family was watching this loving exchange and surmised that last night had been a success. Joe watched her leave and as he turned his attention back to those still in the room, realized that all eyes were on him. He made his way over to where the groom and Brian and Tom were exchanging sports stories.

"Looks like you better start planning for another wedding, Tom." Jacob said smiling.

Joe just smiled and took a sip of water. His silence and flushed face gave the answer they needed.

The short ceremony went off without a glitch. Before they knew it Jacob and Cassie were running outside to jump in the horse drawn carriage and were off to the farm.

Anne got a glimpse of the large white tent from the road. It sat on an area to the east of the house where deluxe portable bathrooms lined the gravel parking area. Anne gasped when they stepped inside the tent. The round tables were adorned with beautiful centerpieces and the flowers from the church were now gracing the head table. She was surprised at how comfortable she was as it was April in Minnesota, but the tent heaters worked wonders and the day was beautifully sunny.

Joe found his chair at the head table and helped Anne find hers nearby at the table with his parents and Gramma Jo. As he was pulling out the chair for Anne, he saw Cassie's friend, Lee Ann come in with a very handsome man that had a strong resemblance to Anne. He correctly assumed this was Dr. Jefferson's son. He saw them find their table and was glad it was toward the back of the tent. Joe made his way over to the bar area and ordered champagne for Anne. He was unable to carry both drinks back as he was using his metal crutch, worried that the ground would have uneven footing in the tent. Jessica saw the dilemma and grabbed his glass for him. Joe smiled his thanks.

Soon the tent was full and everyone was enjoying a wonderful meal. Joe stood up to make his best man speech. Anne admired what a fine-looking man he is in his black tux. The white shirt off set his darker complexion and black curly locks.

"Could I have your attention please, everyone. For those of you who don't know, I'm Joseph Steffan, Cassie's older brother and Jacob's best man. I'd like to make a toast to the happy couple. You know when Cassie first brought Jacob home, I was leary of him – would he be good to my baby sister and treat her right. That was my job as a big brother, to love and protect her by chasing off all boyfriends that came around, because no one was going to be good enough for my sister. Jacob tolerated my overt overtures to run him off, but it didn't deter him. The more I got to know Jacob, the more I knew my job to protect her was over because Jacob would now take over. I saw in him a depth of love for my sister that at the time I truly didn't understand. Thankfully, I now know how deep that love can be." Joe looked squarely at Anne when he said the last sentence and his family's eyes followed his. Anne took a deep breath. Joe's words were beautiful and what's more she believed him. She almost didn't hear the end of the toast and scrambled to grab her glass of champagne to lift as Joe's toast concluded, "To the bride and groom, I love you both, be happy."

After the toasts were concluded and the music started to play, Joe made his way over to Anne. He sat down next to her in the chair his father vacated to make the rounds tending to the guests as the father of the bride should. She reached over to touch his hand, and leaned close to whisper for his ears alone, "Joe, your toast was wonderful."

He leaned even closer and Anne felt his breath on her ear as he whispered back, "I meant every word."

They watched as Cassie and Jacob had their first dance and Tom had his father/daughter dance. The dance floor opened for all guests when Joe leaned forward, "I'm not a dancer, for obvious reasons. I'm sorry."

"I understand. Don't worry. It's not the highlight of my day." Anne answered making light of his statement and bringing their thoughts back to how they started the day.

"Do you think we could walk over to the barn and see how Mopsy is doing?" referring to the lamb she had bottle fed just last night.

"I don't see why not." Joe replied hoping for a quiet moment alone. Joe leaned closer to Anne's ear. She could feel his warm breath, "Perhaps there's a hay bale with our names on it." Joe said with a playful innuendo.

They extricated themselves from the noise of the tent and into the peaceful but cool night. The stars overhead seemed to multiply outside of city limits. Anne's slim hand slipped easily into Joe's free hand as they headed toward the barn.

They found the lamb curled up sleeping peacefully in his pen. "Oh, I don't want to wake him." Anne whispered as she turned to look at Joe. Taking his hand, they both felt the sexual tension increase. "Joe, do you think we are moving too fast?"

Joe understood what she was asking but his feelings for her were going 100 mph and there was no way he could slow them down even if he wanted to. To answer her, he took her in his arms and silenced any further doubts with his lips.

A little while later they slowly made their way out of the barn. The kissing had made it tempting to go further... but as Anne pointed out, anyone could come into the barn at any time. Heading back to the reception they met Jessica and Brian heading to the barn as well. Joe and Anne exchanged relieved looks for their exercise in control. Joe slid his suitcoat over Anne's shoulders as the chill in the night came out.

As they headed back to the reception tent they heard loud voices. Anne and Joe hurried toward the angry exchange and saw a group of Cassie's friends gathered in a circle. Drawing closer Joe noted Adam Jefferson was at the center of the squabble. Not wanting the party to be ruined by the actions of a few, and as Best Man, Joe stepped forward to break up the argument. Little did he know it was his actions that had caused it.

"What's the problem here?" Joe asked stepping between Adam and two guys who appeared to be arguing with him.

"I just heard you had my father arrested and are taking him to trial!" Adam spat angrily.

Joe's eyes got big. He didn't think anyone didn't know about this so Adam's surprise took him off guard. "Yes, but he's not in jail right now. He posted bond."

"Who do you think you are? My father's a great man; one of the most important men in this town, more important than you." Adam yelled heatedly shoving Joe backwards, "He saves lives. What did you charge him with?" Adam asked his voice at a high crescendo indicating an escalation of adrenaline.

Joe didn't like where this was heading. Adam obviously had too much alcohol in his system to be thinking clearly. "Adam, this is not the time or the place to have this discussion. I think it's time you leave before you do or say something you are going to regret." Joe said calmly and deliberately hoping to defuse the volatile situation. Joe saw that Anne had gone to get Tom and they were heading over to the group.

"I asked you what he's charged with. I want to know!" Adam said again this time with more agitation. Joe knew that telling him would only ignite what was left of his control.

Joe's hesitation seemed to frustrate Adam and he finally took a swing at Joe with his fist connecting right above Joe's left eye laying open skin and causing blood to flow down Joe's face. Anne screamed and ran to Joe's side attempting to shield his body from any further attack. This was unnecessary as Anne's screams brought Jacob, Tom, and Brian running towards them and Adam was subdued on the ground in seconds. Tom and Jacob helped Joe to his feet while Anne grabbed a napkin from a table and put some ice in it to hold on the now open wound. Blood still trickled down from his forehead.

Cassie came running around the corner with Carolyn as soon as they heard Anne's scream. They weren't prepared for what met them as the circle widened. Joe, blood gushing from around his eye, was being helped by Anne and Jessica, Adam on the ground with Brian standing over him. Carolyn yelled, "What is going on?!"

Jacob gave her a synopsis with Joe filling in the missing pieces.

"Adam Jefferson, get the hell off our property," Tom said vehemently, pulling Adam upright by the neck of his shirt thrusting him in the direction of the parked vehicles.

"Lee Ann, you brought this trash to my wedding, leave and take it with you." Cassie said angrily with tears coming down her cheeks.

"I'm…. I'm… sorry. I didn't know. We've been studying abroad. Neither of us knew. I'm sorry." Lee Ann said following Tom and Brian who were escorting the now subdued Adam away from the fray.

"Well, now you know." Cassie said snidely. "And for the record Adam Jefferson, your father is a murderer of babies, innocent little babies. He killed my brother and tried to kill my other brother. He's not a great man. He's not a man at all. Now leave and never come back."

Jessica and Anne helped Joe up to the house as Tom and Brian made sure Adam got into the car and left the premises.

Jacob tried to calm the other guests as Carolyn left to attend to her injured son. Opening the door to the house, she saw Joe at the table with Anne washing out the wound.

"I think he could use stitches. Perhaps we should take him to the hospital?" Anne said calmly.

"NO. No hospital." Joe said emphatically. "Just put a bandage on it."

"Here, let me see," Carolyn said looking at the 2 inch gash above his left eyebrow. "Anne's right, stitches would be best, otherwise, we could try to steri-strip it." Carolyn offered knowing how stubborn Joe could be."

Jacob came in to check on Joe and his injury. He agreed stitches would be best. "I have some suture kits in my bag upstairs in our room. I could do it here."

"I'll go get it," Jessica offered. "Jacob, go rejoin your party. I've got this."

"Got what??!" Joe said emphatically. "You are in medical school. Jacob, you are in charge. This is my face."

"Then maybe you should go to the hospital!" Jessica countered.

"I can't." Joe answered quietly. "I don't want this to be all over the newspapers and create more controversy."

"Joe, you didn't do anything wrong." Anne said, "You didn't even hit him back. If you ask me you showed great professional restraint."

"It wouldn't have helped. He was drunk, angry, and scared. His father's about to go away for a very long time and will no longer be the pillar of society that he was raised to think he was." Joe stated matter of fact.

"Let's get this over with. Jessica you can do it. You're right, this is Jacob's party and he should be enjoying it with his new wife." Joe said conceding to his younger sister.

"How about a compromise," Jacob offered, "I'll get you numb and the suturing started and she can finish up."

Joe nodded, happy with the compromise.

Anne sat down next to Joe and held his hand not even aware that Joe's blood was all over her dress and hands.

Jessica finished suturing and placed a dressing over the wound. Turning towards Anne she noticed the blood on Anne's arm and hands and that her dress was a mess. "Anne, why don't you go clean up and I'll help Joe to the car. I'm sure you'll watch him closely tonight for any signs of a concussion."

Anne nodded, suddenly very tired. This day has been filled with surprises.

When Anne got to the car, Jessica handed her the keys. "He wanted to drive, but I thought better of it. Doctor's orders." Jessica said smiling.

Carolyn watched from the porch. She was worried about her son, but knew he was in good hands. Carolyn was angry that she had let Adam Jefferson stay at the church. This could have been avoided.

Carolyn and Jessica walked slowly back to the tent not really feeling festive any longer but knew that this was Jacob and Cassie's day, and they should try to salvage the celebration.

Anne wasn't quite sure how to drive Joe's car. She didn't realize it was any different until she got in the driver's seat. The accelerator was up by the steering column which she had to figure out. The ride home was quiet. Anne, attempting to drive in a new way, Joe, exhausted from the day and altercation.

When Anne pulled into the driveway and stopped the car, she noticed for the first time how pale and exhausted Joe looked. "Joe, I'm going to get the wheelchair, okay?"

Joe nodded. For the first time since he met Anne he was going to use the chair he absolutely avoided at all cost, but he knew how tired he was and that he had lost a fair amount of blood tonight. Head wounds bleed profusely.

Anne quickly brought the chair out and Joe was able to get into it without assistance. When she brought him into the house, she took him straight back to the bedroom, no arguments – he was going to rest!

Anne helped him undress, but this time was not trying to arouse him knowing that he wouldn't have the strength to make love and really, she didn't either.

Joe's head was pounding when she finished getting him into bed. She asked him where he kept his medications. He indicated the bathroom so she got him some Tylenol with a glass of water and an ice pack for his head. He took them gratefully and rested his head. Anne changed into some flannel pajamas and scooted in next to him on the other side.

Joe smiled noting the pajamas, "What, no negligee tonight?" He said wincing as he chuckled.

"No, Joe. No extra encouragement tonight. Sleep is what you need." Anne said with a smile.

"Do you think you are less fetching in those pajamas than in the negligee?" Joe asked. "You are beautiful in anything, or nothing at all." He said reaching for her.

"Joe, I will sleep in the other room if you don't lie there and rest." Anne said firmly.

"Okay. Okay" Joe acquiesced. "Will you please just lay beside me. I'll sleep better."

"Yes, but no funny business mister." Anne joked. Within minutes they were both asleep.

Three hours later Anne awoke. She was worried about Joe and reached over to check the bandage. Just a little seepage from the wound, but it didn't look fresh. She noticed his eyes open just a little as she lifted the edges of the bandage to check around it. "Go back to sleep, Joe. I'm just checking your wound."

He smiled as he reached up to pull her head down next to his and gave her a deep kiss. "Now I can sleep." He said quietly as he closed his eyes with a smile on his lips.

Anne smiled too. As she lay with her head on his shoulder, she realized that this was her home now. Lying next to him put her at peace.

The next morning it was Joe's turn to be up with coffee in hand for her. "Good morning buttercup." He said smiling.

"Joe, what time is it?" Anne asked afraid she had overslept. They were due at his parents' house by 1pm.

"It's 8:30," Joe answered.

"You scared me. I thought I had overslept. What time did you wake up?" Anne asked sitting up and reaching for the coffee he offered.

"7:00," Joe answered. Not telling her that he needed more Tylenol for his head. He didn't want her to think that he was anything less than ready to go.

"7:00! Why so early? How are you feeling? Do you need something more for the pain?" Anne ask solicitously.

"I'm fine," he said sitting on the bed gently. "I want to thank you for taking such good care of me last night." He said leaning forward to kiss her.

Anne smiled and blushed. "Thank you for the coffee this morning. Just what a girl needed!" She said running her fingers up his arm. "I need a good shower this morning. I think I still have flecks of your blood on me. Boy, head wounds sure can bleed!"

"Do you think I'll have a scar?" Joe asked suddenly self-conscious about his laceration.

"Perhaps a small one. It'll make for a good story for our children one day." Anne said without thinking.

Joe eyed her quietly without saying anything and Anne suddenly realized what she had said.

"Oh my, Joe, I'm sorry, I didn't mean… I'm being presumptuous…. See I said we were moving too fast." Anne stammered blushing. She jumped out of bed, embarrassed and headed for the bathroom. When she came out a few minutes later she couldn't meet his eyes.

"Anne, come here." Joe said patting the bed next to him.

She slowly came back to the bed, still quite embarrassed. Joe swept her in his arms and kissed her deep and with full measure of his devotion. Slowly his hold released as he quietly, but firmly stated, "I love you. There is no one else I would want to have children with or to share this bed. Do not be embarrassed by voicing what I myself have thought a thousand times since I met you." Joe paused wondering if he should go farther, but looking into the deep blue eyes that mesmerized him he couldn't stop himself, "Will you marry me?"

Hearing the words out loud that she had thought of from their first kiss was shocking. Her eyes got big and her voice waivered as she found herself saying, "Yes…Yes…." They sealed their bond with a deep lasting kiss.

As they showered and changed for the day, they were both lost in thought. Driving over to his parents' house they both started to talk at the same time. "You go first," Joe said politely.

"Joe, I love you and I want to marry you very much, but I think we shouldn't tell anyone until after the trial. I don't want to distract anyone from the seriousness of this case."

"I agree," Joe stated, "As much as I want everyone to know, we can keep it our secret for now." He placed a kiss on the back of her hand. How lucky he was to have such an intelligent, caring woman with which to spend the rest of his life.

Upon arrival Carolyn immediately hugged them and checked out Joe's wound. He tolerated her poking and prodding with good humor. He was use to his mother's protectiveness. Finally convinced he was fine, she went back to setting out food for the family with the help of Anne, Gramma Jo, and Jessica. Cassie and Jacob sat in the living room with his parents reliving the day before. They talked of the beautiful wedding and how nice the service was, avoiding rehashing the altercation that threatened to take center stage. Joe joined Tom and Brian on the front porch discussing the Minnesota Twins prospect for a new season. Tom briefly asked Joe how he was feeling and how the night went. Joe had answered succinctly stating that he was fine and joked that the night hadn't gone exactly how he had pictured it would but it was also fine.

Jessica called out to them to come and eat. Jessica was feeling time constraints as she and Brian needed to get back to the University and Joe was starting to feel his time with Anne slipping away as well.

The ride back to Joe's house was quiet. Each dreading the final good bye, feeling that the weekend had just begun and now their rendezvous was ending and the world would once again impinge on their time together. Anne silently went to the room they had shared and gathered her clothes and toiletries. Her eyes glistened with unshed tears.

Joe came behind her holding her in his arms, feeling the need for closeness as time was slipping away. Once again, their lips joined in a passionate caress trying to block out the insane world. Slowly while still intertwined, they made their way to the bed peeling each other's clothes off desperately grasping for one last moment together before feeling the emptiness of separation.

Afterward, as they lay basking in each other's arms, they looked out the skylight looking forward to the day they could call this their home together.

Joe's voice broke the heavy silence, "I want you to put your house on the market."

"What… when?" Anne asked surprised.

"Now." Joe answered, "I want you here…with me."

"But my mother, my job?" Anne answered. "I need time to get things in order. We aren't even telling people yet."

"Ok." Joe answered knowing she was right. "As soon as you have a ring on your finger and we make the announcement you are selling your house and moving here. There are hospitals here for you to work in – if you even want to work, and there's room here for your mother as well."

Anne was touched by Joe's generosity. He was willing to take in her mother in her last stages of life.

"Joe, let's get past the trial first, then we'll talk specifics." Anne answered pragmatically.

"During the trial you and your mother can have the house. I'll stay at my parents to make things less awkward. Although I'd much rather be here with you." Joe said stealing a kiss.

"Okay, agreed. Although I'd much rather you be here with me, also. But you will probably be more focused if we're not together. Plus, you will have more of an incentive to keep things rolling along if I'm your pot of gold after the trial is over." Anne joked.

Joe swung his legs over the side of the bed and put his braces and pants back on. Anne picked up his shirt and handed it to him, "I think you'd better put this on as well," she said hoarsely.

Joe looked at her questioningly.

"I'll never get out of here if you are walking around without that shirt. You are too much of a temptation." Anne said only half joking.

"I'll remember that," Joe said with a half- smile.

Joe helped her carry her things to the car. The sun was setting and he wanted her home before it got too dark. Their last embrace was sweet, the last kiss divine. "Call when you get home." It wasn't a question, it was a command.

"Yes." Anne said with a smile. She loved that he worried about her. "When can we see each other again? I'm off on Wednesday." She said hopefully.

"Then Wednesday it shall be. Do you want me to drive down or would you rather come here and have me cook dinner?" Joe asked.

"Hmmm, how about a compromise. Since I'm off I'll drive down here and I'll cook dinner. That way I can start finding out where you put things and the food will be done by the time you get home. We can have the evening to ourselves, watching the stars from the solarium."

"Do you have your key to the house?" Joe asked. She had tried to give the spare key back to him when he returned home Friday night but Joe was firm and put it back in her purse. It was now her key.

"Yes, it's on my keychain now." She said smiling.

"It's a date!" Joe said, now counting the hours until Wednesday. One last quick kiss and she was off.

CHAPTER 19

Joe had a difficult time sleeping Sunday night. His bed suddenly seemed too big. He wandered through the house and noted how empty it was now that Anne had gone. When he started to play some music hoping it would relax him, "Send Me An Angel" came on and he replayed their first time over and over in his mind, thankful that someone had sent him Anne.

He realized that it wouldn't be long before the trial started so he made a list of purchases, wanting to see to Anne and Eves'comfort. Since he was spending so much time preparing for the case, and didn't want to spend time shopping, he would ask his housecleaner if she would mind running some of the errands for him. He knew he hadn't quite won over Eve yet, but he was determined to show her that he would be a great husband to Anne.

Since he was unable to sleep, he got into the office at 5am Monday and already had made it through several stacks of summary judgements and reviewed all the data from the hospital excavation of the mass grave. The pictures of the skeletons of the babies sickened Joe, but the thought of Dr. Jefferson wanting to incinerate the bodies of the babies infuriated him more. How could someone who was a father himself do that to innocent children? Then he thought of Adam Jefferson and his hand reached for the bandage that Anne had lovingly changed before she left. He was reminded of the anger that boy had at the thought that his father wasn't the saint he had been led to believe. He, no doubt, would need much convincing that his father should rot in hell. Perhaps knowing his father had a long-standing extra-marital affair resulting in a child would start to change his mind. But Joe was grateful, that affair had brought him his Anne.

Joe looked up to find James in his doorway. James noted the rolled-up sleeves and the pile of paperwork on Joe's desk and surmised he had been there awhile. As Joe looked up James saw the bandage above Joe's left eye, "Hey, what happened to your head? Did you walk into a door or did your lady friend cold cock you?" James joked.

"An altercation with a Jefferson kid." Joe answered shaking his head.

"What?" James said stepping into the office and sitting down at the table.

"Clayton Jefferson's youngest son, Adam, inadvertently was invited as a plus one, the date of one of Cassie's friends at the wedding. He had been studying abroad and just returned home. Evidently his parents didn't tell him about the charges or impending trial. Someone at the reception tipped him off. He had too much alcohol resulting in an altercation. Don't worry I didn't swing back, nor would I let them take me to the hospital. Jacob and Jessica stitched me up and Anne was my personal nurse through the night." Joe finished with a smile thinking about the kiss after she checked his wound at 3am.

James's eyebrows raised at the completion of the story. "So, quite the story to tell your kids." He said with a laugh.

"Funny, but Anne said much the same thing." Joe said quietly with a slight smile.

This admission had James's eyebrows really raised, noting that Joe seemed quite happy about it.

"Nice to have your own personal nurse, especially one so pretty." James said.

"Yes. Yes, it is." Joe said. "But in my family, you can't shake a stick without hitting a medical professional. My sister was quite happy using her new suturing skills."

"So, the verdict is you'll live?" James asked. "Pressing charges? You know you are well within your rights to do so."

"I'll live. But I do admit to one heck of a headache! And no to the charges. I told the boy that he got one free pass. Not that he'll appreciate the gesture." Joe answered wryly.

"Looks like you've been in since the crack of dawn." James noted indicating the stack of files on Joe's desk.

"I couldn't sleep. Anne left for Rochester last evening. House seemed too quiet." Joe answered.

James nodded knowingly. Yep, Joe had it bad.

"Well, we were notified the trial will be starting in eight weeks." James stated, "So looks like these early mornings will be happening for all of us."

"Eight weeks! I thought we had at least three months?" Joe said incredulously.

"Jefferson's lawyer is pushing it up, feels like the longer it drags out the more likely people are to see him as guilty. Also, he may lose the backing of the hospital if his patients find other doctors to suit their needs. Funny, in the past it's always been the defense that drags its feet." James answered.

"Well, that's okay, the sooner the better as far as I'm concerned." Joe stated convincingly, for many reasons, one of which was Anne. He suddenly realized he had to go ring shopping, and soon!

"Joe, this is the list of witnesses the defense intends to call. Could you review it and summarize what you know about each one and what you think they bring to the case. I'd like the summary by Thursday afternoon for our team meeting."

"Sure. No problem, it'll be ready." Joe answered.

Joe arrived at the office every morning that week by 5am, before anyone else, and stayed until 10 or 11pm, every day but Wednesday. He spent many hours researching the names on the witness list James gave him, but still found a few names that didn't make sense to him. He couldn't find their connection to Dr. Jefferson or why the defense would be calling them.

Wednesday afternoon at 5pm Joe left quietly letting James know he had some business to attend to. He had gone out on his lunch hour Tuesday to the jewelry store across from the court house and picked out a beautiful diamond ring with a matching wedding band. He was to pick it up today. He wasn't sure when he would give it to Anne, but it made it feel more real having it in his pocket. When he drove home that afternoon the sun was still shining. It felt good to see her car in the driveway, just like it was meant to be there.

The house smelled of homemade baked rolls and roasting meat. Anne was leaning over the open oven basting a chicken when he walked in. He was so happy to see her that his frustration over the witness list was forgotten for now.

"You are a sight for sore eyes, and dinner smells fantastic!" Joe said quietly with a smile growing.

"Joe, you're home early," Anne said coming over to greet him properly. When their lips touched it was if they were both starved for affection. He gently picked her up and set her on the counter, gently kissing her neck and her chest where her shirt buttons gave way easily allowing access to what lay beneath. "Joe, I've missed you." She said running her fingers through his black waves of thick hair.

"Anne, this house is so empty without you. It's like you are the heart of my home now and when you're gone it's just sticks and mortar." Joe said sincerely, his dark brooding eyes holding her blue eyes captive. He had enjoyed the past three years living here alone. It had been his sanctuary and now without her here, it seemed a prison.

"I'm here now," she said smiling, "and if you help me down, I'll get you a glass of wine and we can relax a bit before supper.

Joe complied reluctantly, and set her gently on the floor. The table was beautifully set and a fire was going in the solarium, taking away the late April chill. A bottle of Chardonnay and a plate of appetizers awaited them near their favorite spot in the solarium.

"Not to change the subject, but how's work going?" Anne asked.

"Good. I told you the trial was moved up. It's beginning in eight weeks. Are you going to be able to take time off of work?" Joe questioned.

"Yes, I'm taking an extended leave of absence. I thought that would be easiest since we don't know how long the trial will last and what comes after…" Anne said, referring to his request for her to put her house on the market.

"Are you ready for the trial to start that soon?" Anne asked.

"Actually, yes. I'm just trying to go through the defense's witness list and a few of them don't make sense to me. You always want to know why the defense is going to call someone so you don't get blindsided during trial. It's been a bit frustrating." Joe admitted.

"Why don't you call your mother? She would probably know who the people are and maybe even why they are on the list." Anne suggested.

"That's not a bad idea," Joe said, "I'm going to call her right now to see if she'd have time to review it tomorrow morning."

Joe returned announcing apologetically that she had to stop by now. She and Tom were going out of town tonight and wouldn't be back until Friday. "Don't worry it will only take a few minutes, okay?"

"No problem, this is important." Anne said with understanding, but also hoping her dinner wouldn't be ruined.

A few minutes later the doorbell rang and both Carolyn and Tom were at the door, both a bit surprised to see Anne again so soon.

"I had today off so Joe and I made a date for me to come up and cook dinner." Anne explained, feeling a bit uneasy about how his parents may perceive her presence. Knowing that their relationship could seem to someone else as moving quite fast, but to Joe and Anne it seemed not fast enough.

"It smells wonderful," Carolyn complimented, noting the wine glasses in the solarium and the beautifully set table. "We'll make this quick. I know what it's like to have a nice meal ruined by bad timing."

Joe brought out a folder from his briefcase. "Mom, could you look over this list, please – the two names on the bottom, I assume they are somehow related because the last names are the same. Do you know them and how they might be connected to Dr. Jefferson?"

Carolyn studied the list. Her face went pale and her hands shook knocking the papers on the floor. Joe suddenly appeared worried, the hair on the back of his neck stood up. "Mom, what's wrong," he asked guiding her to a chair.

"Honey, what is it?" Tom asked. "Anne, could you get a glass of water?"

Anne grabbed a glass from the cupboard and filled it. Carolyn took it gratefully.

Joe asked again gently, "Mom, who are those people a Mr. William Pilarski and a Mrs. Margaret Pilarski?"

"They are your birth parents." Carolyn answered in a whisper, unable to meet Joe's eyes.

The three of them stood with stunned looks on their faces. No one said a word for several minutes.

Anne finally asked, "Why would they be testifying for Dr. Jefferson? He's being accused of attempting to murder their son?"

For several minutes no one answered. Joe stepped slowly towards the windows facing the back yard his metal cane tapping against the hard, oak floor, the only sound in the room. Finally, Joe answered facing the window, his mouth dry and voice hoarse, "Because they agree with Dr. Jefferson. They wouldn't have wanted a disabled child. They wouldn't have wanted me to live," his voice trailing off softly.

Joe knew by Carolyn's silence that he spoke the truth. Carolyn hadn't gone to them at the time of Joe's birth because she had a strong suspicion that they wouldn't want a child with a disability. She was afraid that if she told them he was alive, they would have felt forced into saving him, only to send him off to an institution at the urging of Dr. Jefferson.

The hush of the room was deafening. Tom and Carolyn watched in silent agony as Joe processed this information. They saw the anger pulsating through the veins in his neck as he stared out at the beauty of his back yard. Carolyn noted the white knuckles on his left hand as he gripped the metal crutch. This information was the ultimate rejection. Anne took a couple of steps towards him when Carolyn waved her to stop.

Joe ran his index finger across the worn metal. He looked down at his constant companion, a reminder of his physical limitations, his visible imperfection, the reason for his rejection. Rage suddenly filled his body and in one fluid movement he sent the metal cane through the window, shattering the silence. His anguish over all the terrible truths found out in this investigation finally vented. The rage left as quickly as it appeared and Joe fell to his knees, defeated.

Carolyn went to him careful of the glass that now laid strewn about the floor. No words were needed as she knelt next to her son, wrapping her arms about his shoulders, and consoled him as she had done many times throughout the years. The possible rejection by his birth parents was what she had feared would hurt him deeply when this quest began. Joe clung to the only mother he had ever known and took solace in her strength. Carolyn held him until the storm had passed. Anne and Tom stood watching as Carolyn tried to heal her wounded son.

Carolyn and Joe both looked out through the broken window their thoughts on the trial and what other devastating surprises lie ahead.

Carolyn and Tom left after helping clean up the shards of glass. Tom covered the opening with some plywood. He would come back tomorrow to replace the window. They were both glad that Anne happened to be there when Joe called to see them. They could see that she was very good for him. They were also realizing that Anne had become a fixture in Joe's life and surmised it was only a matter of time before she was officially a member of the family. This filled them with relief. Joe had found someone who he obviously was deeply in love with and she appeared to return this love without reservation.

When Joe closed the door after his parents' departure, Anne quietly set the food on the table. Joe was in a brooding mood. He put some soft music on the stereo to listen to while they enjoyed the dinner Anne had prepared.

"This is really good Anne. Another one of your talents discovered." Joe said with a smile, attempting to be more upbeat after the revelation of his birth parents, ashamed of his outburst.

"Thank you, Joe. I'm sure from what I've tasted of your mother's meals, it probably doesn't even come close." Anne replied softly reaching for Joe's hand, needing him to know she wasn't going anywhere.

Suddenly Joe became serious, "Anne, was I wrong to start this investigation? Was I wrong to want to punish a man who killed over a dozen innocent babies and who tried to kill me? Does the fact that some of those parents may have agreed with him exonerate his wrong-doing?"

Anne could see the torment he was feeling from his own rejection and wondered how it would be for him in court to hear from them on the witness stand. The public rejection he would have to endure.

"No, don't question your motive. You are an officer of the court and duty bound to hold people accountable for their actions. A doctor is human just like you and I and should not be above the law, above what is right and wrong and moral. Can I ask you if that was your child would you want the doctor to be punished? Look at your parents, the choice was taken from them. Their child was murdered. Who will speak for the innocents whose lives were lost because of his horrific actions? We as a society are judged by how we treat those that are most vulnerable. Most doctors would agree with what you are doing. How do we find cures for disabling disabilities? It's not by ridding ourselves of the people unfortunate to have them, but by medical research and finding new cures and treatments. I love you and support what you are doing. Win or lose you are shining a light on injustice for those most vulnerable."

After she was done talking Anne brought her plate to the sink and let Joe think about her words. "I hear what you are saying, but if you had a child would you want to travel down that road. Wouldn't you rather have a healthy child?" Joe asked getting to the heart of what troubled him.

She sat down quietly next to him and took his hand. "Joe, everyone who has a child hopes for the best outcome, the best life for their child. That being said, I would never reject our child for imperfections it may have. We are human. Our bodies are imperfect. I would hope to follow in your parent's footsteps in providing the best opportunities, seeking the best medical care, and loving our child unconditionally. And if I had a boy, I would want him to be exactly like his father, kind, loving, compassionate, and handsome." Joe smiled as she said the last word.

"If we had a girl, I would want her to be just like her mother beautiful, compassionate, and wise beyond her years." Joe said kissing the back of Anne's hand.

Anne stood up and whispered that the solarium had seats waiting for the star show. Joe smiled.

When they got comfortable on the sofa lounger, it suddenly occurred to Joe that Anne may have to work tomorrow. "What time do you have to leave? He asked softly, dreading her departure, inhaling the sweet scent from her hair.

"Tomorrow morning," she answered smiling up at him. "I traded for an afternoon shift."

Chapter 20

The projected start of the trial had been pushed back two more weeks from the original eight weeks that they had been told initially, due to a sudden illness by Judge Hanson. It was nice to have a couple of weeks with normal hours before the anticipated frenzied pace of court. Joe and Anne continued to grow closer. Joe worked 12 hour days, except when Anne came up on her days off. He made her a priority. They went for picnics, walks along the river, or just laid together on the cozy sofa in the solarium watching the stars peek out one by one. Anne relished the time with Joe and getting to know his family. She identified strongly with Carolyn and saw what high esteem people held her in throughout the community. Carolyn felt strongly indebted to Anne as she gave Joe a strong purpose outside of his job. She suddenly saw Joe fully enjoy life, laughing and joking and with such happiness that Anne truly became one of the family.

The trial was set to start on Monday. Anne drove her mother up to Joe's house to get settled on Sunday. Joe had his weekly housekeeper prepare the rooms and stock the refrigerator on Friday. Joe heard their car pull into the driveway and hurried to assist Anne in getting Eve inside. Joe was both exhilarated and nervous

188 Justice for Baby B

knowing that he hadn't quite won over Eve and he wasn't sure how much Anne had shared regarding their intimacy. He watched as Anne assisted her mother out of the car and was surprised how frail she appeared. Eve wobbled taking a step and grabbed for Anne. Joe remembered the wheelchair that sat unused, and opened the door calling for Anne to wait a moment. Joe brought out the wheelchair which Eve gratefully accepted.

"Mom had her last chemo yesterday," Anne explained. "She's quite wiped out today."

"Eve, your bedroom is all set up. Perhaps you'd like to lie down for a rest." Joe offered.

"Yes, that would be nice," Eve answered, her voice barely a whisper.

"She was experiencing some retching on the drive." Anne said sympathetically.

"No problem. I'll get a bucket just in case." Joe replied.

Joe directed them to the second bedroom on the left. It had its own bathroom. Anne was surprised at how nice it was and the wonderful view of the backyard which was green and lush with the early spring. Eve also noted the wonderful surroundings, grateful for Joe's hospitality, realizing that they could be in a small dingy hotel room rather than this beautiful home.

When Anne wheeled Eve into her spacious room, Eve's eyes widened and she was speechless at the lovely décor. The bay wall had a window seat with deep red and yellow pillows. The queen size bed looked very inviting with a mini fridge nearby which Joe had thoughtfully stocked with 7-up, ginger ale, and water. Anne was helping Eve into the comfortable bed when Joe came in with a bucket and a cool wet wash cloth for Eve's forehead. Eve nodded her thanks and as she gazed into Joe's eyes, he saw gratitude. She touched his hand for a moment. Anne pulled the covers up asking her mother if she needed anything else before she left, pointing out the bell Joe had thoughtfully placed on the night stand. Eve shook her head no. Joe had thought of everything. Anne reached for the door handle to leave when she heard her mother's weak voice, "You have chosen well, Anne."

It was only a few words and to anyone else they wouldn't make sense, but they meant the world to Anne.

Anne found Joe quietly sitting in the solarium. Joining him their kiss spoke for itself, admiration and thanks from Anne, love and happiness from Joe.

"Welcome home." Joe said with a quiet smile.

"Thank you, this does feel like home now." Anne answered, running her hand slowly over Joe's chest. "Thank you for being so considerate of my mother's needs. She just told me as I left her room that I 'chose well'. I must admit, I agree." Anne said laying her head against Joe's heart, welcoming the sound of its gentle beating. This was the heart of a good man. A heart she would guard with her life.

Joe wrapped his arms around Anne. He felt at peace when she was in his arms. They sat there together for quite a while just listening to the birds and watching the rolling acres, enjoying the peaceful calm before the storm of the trial begins.

Anne slowly sat up realizing that she had fallen asleep lying on Joe's chest. He had slowly extracted himself and covered her with a warm throw sometime during her nap. She saw him at the table with papers in front on him and knew he was reviewing notes for the case. She quietly came up to him placing a gentle kiss on his neck, "What shall I make for supper?"

Joe reached around and gently took her arm pulling her to his lap where he had better access to her lips. "No need to cook. When I told my mom you were coming today she offered to bring supper, so I invited them to join us. She figured you and Eve would be tired from the trip and she wanted to help."

190 Justice for Baby B

"Your mom must be the most thoughtful person on the planet." Anne said, grateful for the night off.

"She is, and she raised her son to be just like her." Came a voice from down the hallway. Eve made her way into the great room slowly, but much steadier then on her arrival. Anne didn't move from Joe's lap. Eve would have to adjust to seeing their loving embraces because Anne would no longer hide from her the great love she felt for this man. Anne was a bit surprised that Eve seemed not only accepting, but mildly happy seeing her with Joe.

"Thank you, Joe for your hospitality. You have a beautiful home. I now understand why Anne feels so at home here." Eve said pointedly, her smile giving the approval that perhaps her words didn't.

"Thank you, Eve." Joe returned. "I hope you will be quite comfortable in your surroundings. Please help yourself to whatever is in the house. I'll be staying at my parent's house while you are here. Anne can have my room." Joe said with a twinkle in his eye.

Eve nodded. She had a strong suspicion that Anne had already spent nights in Joe's room and thought about doing away with the pretense of having Joe stay at his parents, but decided she didn't want to make things awkward. If the opportunity came to have a private word with Joe she would.

The awkward moment passed as the doorbell rang. In the past, Carolyn had usually just opened the door and yelled for Joe, but now that Anne was in the house, she felt the need to follow certain protocols. Joe made his way to the door with Anne following to see if help was needed.

"Hi Mom," Joe said leaning over to give Carolyn a kiss as she made her way inside with a basket of homemade goodies. Anne offered her assistance, but Carolyn declined, carrying the basket into the kitchen with Tom carrying a big box filled with dinner items.

"Hello Eve. I hope your drive up wasn't too taxing on you." Carolyn said greeting her on friendly terms. Carolyn and Tom had decided there were plenty of mistakes made in the past and at least Eve was taking responsibility for her fair share. It was in Joe's and Anne's best interest that they make a concerted effort to make Eve welcome. Joe had confided to Carolyn and Tom that he had every intention of proposing to Anne in the near future and that he wanted Anne to move in as soon as possible. While they were mildly surprised by this admission by Joe as to how fast things were moving between them, they both acknowledged from the moment they saw them together it seemed like fate had a hand in bringing them together. They had never seen Joe happier.

"I hope everyone likes lasagna." Carolyn said smiling. "I have garlic bread, salad, and of course dessert."

"I'll set the table," Anne offered.

"I'll open the wine," Tom said smiling.

Eve made her way over to Carolyn and Tom. "I don't know if you remember me, Tom. We met many years ago." Eve said smiling.

"I do remember." Tom returned. "We've gotten to know Anne so well. It's a pleasure to see you again." Tom remembered Joe saying Eve was avoiding handshakes due to her cancer treatments, so he nodded his greeting while popping the cork of the wine bottle. "Would you care for a glass?" Tom offered.

"Yes, but a small one." Eve returned smiling. She hadn't had wine in some time due to all the medications she was taking, but felt tonight was a special occasion. Knowing how Anne felt about Joe and the loving words she spoke about his parents Eve felt like she was glimpsing scenes into Anne's future. A future she knew would not include her. Eve use to feel panic stricken when thinking about Anne alone after Eve was gone. Seeing Anne comfortable in Joe's house with his lovely parents doting on them and, of course, Joe (with whom Eve was now fully accepting as Anne's future husband), was a calming balm. Eve now knew Anne's future was here with them and they would take good care of her only daughter.

Carolyn was busy tossing the salad and warming the bread and lasagna, laughing with Joe over some antics Sammy did that morning, carrying a baby bunny into the house alive and releasing it to show them her new playmate.

"Anne, do you like dogs?" Carolyn asked suddenly.

"Yes, I do." Anne replied, "and cats, and lambs, and all the assorted animals you have at your place."

"Perhaps you and Joe should consider getting a dog." Carolyn offered. Knowing their future was together, and as secluded as their house was, a dog was a pretty good idea, but Joe had always declined stating his long work hours wouldn't be fair to the animal.

Joe looked at Anne and she back at him before he answered, "Hmmm that's something we may consider in the future."

Carolyn's eyes widened. This was the first time Joe had ever even considered taking on a pet.

"How's supper coming along?" Tom asked changing the subject. "I'm starving after smelling it most of the afternoon."

"Coming out right now." Carolyn answered.

Dinner was extremely good with many compliments to Carolyn on her cooking talents. Joe tried to keep the conversation light-hearted and steered away from the start of the court-case. Eve added a comment here and there and smiled throughout the meal watching their good- hearted repartee seeing that Anne appeared an equal contributor in their conversation and life.

When the kitchen was cleaned up, Carolyn and Tom said their good byes knowing that they would see them both tomorrow at the court house. Carolyn gave Eve a hug before leaving and Eve whispered for her ears alone, "Thank you for your kindness and acceptance of my daughter. You are a wonderful woman." As they pulled apart Carolyn saw Eve's eyes glisten with unshed tears.

Carolyn answered quietly, "You have raised a wonderful woman. We have grown to love her as a daughter. She's been wonderful for Joe."

Walking out the door, Carolyn asked Joe if he was still planning on staying at their house. He nodded slowly. It would be hard to leave Anne here but he didn't want to start any controversy tonight.

Joe had packed a bag and had his suit hanging over a chair when Anne came out of her mother's room. She had helped her get into her nightgown and settled for the night.

"Joe, are you sure you want to go?" Anne asked giving him a long kiss.

"Want to??...No." He answered with a slight grin, "But I don't want your mother to feel uncomfortable. She's had a lot to adjust to the past few months and I don't think she's entirely ready to have me and you coming out of the same bedroom, at least not without a ring on this finger," he said, kissing the ring finger on her left hand.

Anne nodded, unfortunately agreeing with Joe's thoughtfulness.

One last embrace left them both weak in the knees and Joe was off to his parents, left only to dream of Anne in their bed alone.

Chapter 21

The Trial

Joe woke up around 5am to the sound of rain against the window. He lay there listening to the droplets pelt the glass, thinking how appropriate to start a murder trial with foul weather. He slept fitfully during the night, sometimes thinking he heard someone else awake in the house. Thoughts of the case began running through his mind. He was preparing for the day, bracing himself for the reporters outside the courthouse. It wasn't every day you put a doctor on trial for murder.

Joe finally swung his legs over the side of the bed. Sammy whimpered and nuzzled Joe's back with her wet nose. She was unhappy that her bed partner was leaving. "Thanks for the company Sammy. You weren't my Anne, but you provided a warm bed." Joe scratched Sammy's head, wondering how Anne was sleeping in their bed without him. He envisioned her hair across her pillow with her hand stretched out toward his empty side. He silently hoped the trial wouldn't take long and they could get on with living their lives – together.

Joe expertly slipped his braces on tightening the straps without thinking. They were a part of his routine, a daily reminder of the extra challenges he faced, but which did not define him as a person. He decided on a tailored dark suit for his court appearance, his white shirt showing crisp and clean at the wrists accenting his slightly darker skin tone. His sisters were jealous of his slightly darker complexion. He always looked like he had a tan, even in the middle of a Minnesota winter.

Entering the kitchen Joe found the light on and his mother already up having coffee at the kitchen table.

"Good morning, Joe." Carolyn said over her cup.

"Good morning, Mom," Joe said giving her shoulders a quick squeeze and a planting a quick kiss on her head. "How long have you been up?"

"Most of the night I'm afraid." She answered quietly. "I've never testified in court before. I know I've waited a long time for Dr. Jefferson to be prosecuted for his crimes, but it will still be hard to face him from the witness stand." And harder still to face Joe's biological parents she thought silently. She had taken their son and he was now a successful lawyer. Who wouldn't want to claim him as theirs?

"You'll do fine, Mom." Joe replied calmly. "Thank you for supporting me throughout this fight. I know you and Dad were hesitant in the beginning, but I truly couldn't have done it without you." He said while taking a seat across from her at the table.

"We wouldn't be very good parents if we hadn't." Carolyn answered grimly. "You have also given us a chance to grieve the death of our other son. That was a gift to us. I pray you will never endure the pain a parent feels when losing a child, especially under suspicious circumstance."

"After this is over and they release Phillip's remains, we'll have a proper burial." Joe answered squeezing Carolyn's hand.

Carolyn nodded. She knew she had to keep it together during the trial and she was trying to exert a strong appearance, even though inside her gut was churning.

A few minutes later Tom joined them, surprised to find them both up in the kitchen and Joe already in his suit. He saw the grim looks on their faces and said a quiet, "good morning," as he retrieved some coffee. "I'm going to feed the animals."

"I'll have breakfast ready when you get back inside." Carolyn acknowledged only then looking up from her cup.

Tom leaned down to plant a kiss on her head. She reached up to touch his hand as his hand gently rested on her shoulder, each giving the other a quiet moment of support.

Joe called Anne before leaving for the courthouse to see how Eve was feeling and if they needed anything. Anne said they were fine and would see him at the court house. Their conversation was a bit stilted this morning, but before Anne hung up she whispered, "I missed you last night. I love you."

Joe smiled on his end, "Not half as much as I missed you although Sammy did try to fill your side of the bed. I love you too. See you later." Joe said quietly although he was sure his parents already knew what a loving relationship he already had with Anne.

The bustle of the courthouse was evident by the lack of parking. Joe had given Anne his parking space pass so that she and Eve could park close to the building knowing that Eve would need all her strength to testify. Eve was surprised by his solicitude, but Anne wasn't. Joe had always been more concerned about her welfare than his own.

Joe found himself parking two blocks away. As he set the emergency brake, he glanced in the mirror and saw that Dr. Jefferson's wife and three of their seven adult children were getting out of their car a short distance away. She was a pretty woman in her 60's with well-manicured nails and expensive makeup. Her hair was dark with hints of grey, but in a stylish French roll. Standing in the street their eyes met, her's dark with daggers, aimed straight at him.

This was the man who was taking everything from them, the money they had to spend on a defense attorney, the reputation and prestige they had enjoyed in the community. She had tolerated much in her married life. Her husband's career had been demanding, his marital infidelities (which he thought were well hidden), but nothing prepared her for this.

Joe began walking towards the courthouse, going as fast as he could with his braces and metal crutch aiding him, but he heard the snide remarks, the insults meant to be loud enough for his ears, "Look at the scared cripple go, Mom."

"Cripple is not an appropriate word, Adam." Joe heard Mrs. Jefferson say half-heartedly correcting her son. She always wanted to appear politically correct.

"I'd like to kick out that crutch and see how far he gets with those gimpy legs." Adam said again.

Suddenly Joe turned to face them. He wasn't going to take the bullying any longer. "Adam, you got one free punch. I understood your anger. But you touch me or my family EVER again and I'll see to it you join your murdering father in the cell right next to him. Got it." He stood staring into each of their faces touching each of them with his promise.

Mrs. Jefferson grabbed her son's arm to cool Adam down. His fuse had been lit, but his mother refused to let go. She couldn't afford another one of her family facing charges, nor did she think it would do her husband's case any favors.

Joe saw that they realized he meant business and Mrs. Jefferson gave a slight nod of her head to indicate her understanding. Joe turned and continued on his way at a steady, but not particularly hurried pace. Mrs. Jefferson stood watching him go and thought it best to allow some distance between them.

As Joe entered the court house he saw that Anne and Eve were already there seated on a bench outside the court room assigned to their case. Anne greeted him with a nervous smile. Joe leaned over to whisper in her ear, "You look beautiful." She blushed slightly, but rewarded him with a beautiful smile and a quick hand squeeze.

"You look quite handsome yourself counselor," she whispered back for his ears alone.

Joe leaned forward to greet Eve and explain the proceedings for the day. Anne wasn't a witness so she could take a seat in the gallery, but both Eve and Carolyn would need to be outside the courtroom until their testimony had been entered into evidence. Joe pointed to a conference room with a reserved sign he had one of their staff people place early this morning where they could wait more comfortably. He had his staff put a carafe of coffee and a few pastries in there as well to help quell their nervous stomachs. The District Attorney, James, would be questioning both Carolyn and Eve on the stands. Then Joe would question Dr. Bruce Paul, Juan Garcia, and the experts being called regarding the excavation of the bodies and the post mortem examinations. Carolyn and Tom had joined them by the time they talked about the order of questioning.

"I can't be in the court room?" Carolyn asked anxiously.

"No, not at the beginning. We will do our opening statements and the prosecution goes first to present our case. You will be the first witness so you will be able to join the gallery after your testimony." Joe answered his voice and tone very professional. A slight squeeze to his mother's hand was the only visible sign of his support. "Don't worry, Mom, we've got this." He added confidently for her ears alone.

With Eve comfortably settled in the conference room, Anne solicitously by her side, Joe headed into the courtroom. He noted his dad had found his seat in the first row of the gallery behind the prosecutor's table and his sisters were at his side. He was shocked to see Jessica as it was awfully tough to get the day off from medical school. He nodded at them both and they replied with tremulous smiles, both nervous for their brother and their mother. The chair on the other side of Tom was vacant with a coat on it, no doubt being saved for Carolyn after her testimony. Jessica also had a coat on the chair next to her. Joe wondered if Anne had asked her to save that seat as well. The gallery seats were filling fast, probably reporters from the Twin Cities, after all it wasn't every day a doctor went on trial for killing newborns.

James was at the prosecutor's table already with papers in piles in front of him. Joe sat down with his brief case and also began to prepare for the testimony he would present. They conversed between themselves strategizing quietly. Joe confirmed his mother was outside the door ready to be called as the first witness and Eve and Anne were in the conference room with Jose Garcia. Joe glanced over and saw Dr. Clayton Jefferson at the defendant's table with his lawyer, Michael Drew. His lawyer was from Minneapolis and specialized in criminal cases. Dr. Jefferson's family was seated behind him in the first row of the gallery. Dr. Jefferson wore a very expensive blue suit. His now silver hair was meticulously brushed. He was still quite a handsome man even after thirty years.

Joe had briefly met Mr. Drew during the bail hearing when Dr. Jefferson had entered a plea of 'not guilty', which had been expected by the prosecution. They had also waived the request for moving the trial. Mr. Drew was counting on Dr. Jefferson's community standing and those residents who loved their doctor and who couldn't dream of him making a mistake. The prosecution did win out on their request to bring in a jury from outside the county for impartiality.

As the large clock over the court room gallery wall struck 9am precisely, the court deputy stood and ordered, "All rise," in a booming authoritative voice. Everyone in the courtroom did as instructed and an older gentleman with a receding hairline dressed in a long dark robe entered and took his seat in the wooden structure which was elevated high enough to oversee all proceedings in that room.

Judge George Hanson, gavel in hand, hit the wooden circle signaling with a loud bang that made half the people jump. The deputy stated "You may be seated."

The judge's booming voice did not need a microphone, the acoustics were very pronounced in that room, but he had one none the less. "Deputy, bring in the jury. The deputy went over to the ante room where the jury had been instructed to wait and opened the door directing them to take their seats. They were seated closest in proximity to the prosecutor's table. Joe watched their faces as they came in trying to pick out the jurors who would be the leaders in the deliberation.

The Judge announced the case, "The state versus Dr. Clayton Jefferson." Both the prosecutors and the defense attorney and defendant stood. "Who will be representing the state in this case?" The Judge asked so that the record would reflect their names.

"James Kiehl, District Attorney and Joseph Steffan, Assistant District Attorney, Your Honor." James answered.

"Who will be representing the defendant?" The judge asked, turning his attention to the defendant's table.

"Michael Drew representing the defendant, Dr. Clayton Jefferson, Your Honor."

"Very well, the jury has been instructed on its duties and seated without reservation. Let us proceed with opening statements. Mr. Kiehl proceed."

"Your Honor, ladies and gentlemen of the jury, we intend to prove beyond a reasonable doubt that Dr. Clayton Jefferson during the course of his medical practice did intentionally attempt to kill the baby known as 'Baby B" and did in fact murder the baby known as Phillip Steffan. These crimes were committed 29 years ago, however, there is no statute of limitations on murder. These crimes are particularly egregious noting that they were committed against vulnerable newborns. Dr. Clayton Jefferson took an oath when graduating from medical school that first and foremost he would, 'do no harm' when practicing medicine. We will prove that not only did Dr. Jefferson take it upon himself to practice as god when deciding which child deserved to live or to die, he did so with malice towards the most vulnerable of human beings. When our evidence is presented and our case rested, I am sure that you will understand the depth and breadth of his inhumanity to man and will agree that Dr. Jefferson needs to be punished for his actions, which caused the death of at least one child and the attempted murder of another." James then sat down waiting quietly while the defense was allowed to present their opening argument, but rather then open their case at this time Mr. Drew opted to wait until the defense's case was presented.

Joe knew that the defense could possibly defer their opening statement but was rather surprised they did so in this case.

"Mr. Kiehl, present your first witness." The judge directed.

James stood and announced, "The prosecution calls Carolyn Steffan to the stand." The deputy stationed nearest the door opened it and directed Carolyn to come into the courtroom. Carolyn wore a black dress with a beautiful scarf with vibrant colors. Carolyn was in her 50's but still looked remarkable. Joe always knew that Carolyn was pretty in jeans and a flannel shirt, but realized that his mother was stunning when she dressed up.

Carolyn nervously pushed her hair behind her ear as she took the witness stand and was asked to give her oath to tell the truth. The deputy asked her, "Please state your name for the record."

"Carolyn Steffan," came her nervous reply.

"Mrs. Steffan, can you please tell me what happened on the date of October 24th, 1968?" James asked.

"Yes, I went into labor with my first child." Carolyn answered.

"Was it a normal labor?" James asked.

"It was a difficult labor, but most are," she stated quietly.

"The doctor felt something was wrong when I was fully dilated. I was having difficulty with the delivery. He decided it would be best if I was given some anesthesia and he would use tools such as forceps to get the baby out. Sometime after I was under anesthesia my doctor got an emergency call for another patient and unknown to me until recently, Dr. Jefferson was called in to complete my delivery." Carolyn looked over at the defense table for the first time and saw him sitting there very smugly in his pinstriped suit with his arms crossed in front of him.

"May I enter into evidence a copy of Mrs. Steffan's maternity chart for the event in question." James stated picking up the copied chart.

"So entered." Stated Judge Hanson. motioning the court deputy to take the folder into evidence.

"Do you remember anything from the delivery?" James asked, knowing the answer already.

"No, I was under anesthesia and didn't come out of it until I was back in my room. I remember asking for my baby and the nurse telling me that the doctor was working on him. Later I was told my son was stillborn." Carolyn wiped away a tear thinking about Phillip. "I asked to see him, to hold him, but back then when a baby was stillborn the school of thought was to tell the mother it was best to think of it as a miscarriage, not to bond with the dead child." Carolyn's voice cracked and she fought back tears, "I never got to hold my child or say good bye. I was informed just recently, however, that he was born alive." Carolyn looked directly at Dr. Jefferson with contempt in her eyes.

"Objection." Mr. Drew stated loudly, "Heresay. She didn't actually see the child alive. She's stating that she heard it was alive."

"Sustained." Judge Hanson ruled.

James had expected that the objection would stand, but also knew that the jury heard it and, although informed to disregard the last statement, it is hard to unring a bell.

"Now I would like you to turn your attention over to September of 1969, almost a year later. Please state for the court your occupation and where you were working." James directed.

"I am a Registered Nurse and was and am still employed by Memorial County Hospital." Carolyn answered.

"On the date in question did you assist with a delivery at that hospital." James asked, starting to question her about Joe's birth.

"Yes, I did, a beautiful baby boy." Carolyn answered glancing at Joe.

"Was this child born alive?" James asked.

"Yes," Carolyn answered.

"Was Dr. Jefferson the doctor delivering this child?" James asked.

"Yes, he was." Carolyn answered. The questioning seemed to be so stilted, but she understood the necessity. Everything must be put into the court record.

"Was this child born with a defect? A disability if you will?" James asked trying not to feel uncomfortable knowing he was speaking of his colleague.

Carolyn felt Joe's eyes on her as well and she tried to focus her gaze on James so as to not get emotional about what was to

204 Justice for Baby B

come. "Yes, the baby boy had a bulge on his back, which is known to be diagnostic for Spina Bifida, a defect in which the baby's spinal cord fails to develop properly. There are different levels of disability a person with spina bifida can experience."

"Was Dr. Jefferson actively trying to assist this child after his birth." James asked.

"Objection." Mr. Drew stated. "This nurse has no way of telling whether Dr. Jefferson was actively trying to assist this child."

"Your Honor, she is a trained medical professional as well and competent to testify. Also, I have another nurse willing to testify to this same question." James stated adamantly. This information was most important in pursuit of this case and the Judge's ruling quite important.

"Over-ruled." Judge Hanson stated, his eyes looking over his reading glasses. "Nurses are highly trained individuals and quite capable of determining whether a person is being tended to medically." Neither Mr. Drew nor the prosecutors knew that Judge Hanson's mother and grandmother had been nurses and he highly respected their input. "You may answer." The judge directed to Carolyn.

"No, Dr. Jefferson was not assisting the child. He directed me to get 'the box'. I thought he meant an incubator and when I started rolling it in to the room he snapped at me and said, not that. When I didn't know what he was requesting, he looked at Eve, the other nurse attending the birth. She hesitated a moment and then went to the equipment room and retrieved a box. I had never seen those boxes before." Her voice got soft and her fingers rubbed her thighs nervously.

"Is this the box he was referring to?" asked James, picking up the box that had been hidden for so many years in the basement of Carolyn's house.

"Yes." Carolyn answered almost inaudibly.

"Please speak up so the jury can hear you." James directed politely.

"Yes." Carolyn said this time much louder.

"What did Dr. Jefferson proceed to do?" James asked.

"He placed a piece of medical tape over the baby's mouth so that the nurses wouldn't hear the baby's cry and then placed the baby in the box and directed Eve to put the box back in the equipment closet." Carolyn said her voice wavering as she made eye contact with the jurors. The raw emotion evident in her eyes as she remembered Joe's face with the tape over his mouth. The jurors saw the tears she fought to restrain.

"Had you ever seen this happen before that day?" James asked.

"No, I had never seen it done before that day." Carolyn answered.

"What did you do?" James asked.

"I tried to go after Eve. I felt as if I was suffocating and not the baby." Carolyn said, a small tear escaping, "But Dr. Jefferson wouldn't let me. He said I needed to tend to the mother. After the mother was returned to her room, I went to find Eve and asked her where she put the baby. She told me the equipment closet. She said that the babies that Dr. Jefferson delivered that showed an obvious defect like this one, were brought to the equipment closet to die without food or medical attention, in boxes like those, or should I say coffins. After they died, he pronounced them dead and they were taken to the morgue, discarded like garbage, not flesh and blood."

Mr. Drew wanted to place an objection, but saw the jurors' faces and knew that she had struck a cord with this statement and any objection he might make would seem cold and calculating. He let it pass hoping that the prosecutor would move on quickly.

"After learning the fate of this child, did you go find him?" James asked.

"Yes," Carolyn answered loudly this time. "I had lost a baby earlier that year and couldn't stand by and watch an innocent baby die for lack of care. I found the baby in the box. He was turning blue and his chest was retracting due to his airway not being cleared after birth. Many babies need to be suctioned after birth and warmed after they are delivered. I took off the tape that had covered his mouth and grabbed some blankets to wipe off the newborn vernix. I suctioned him and grabbed oxygen tubing. I turned on the emergency oxygen tank and held the oxygen tubing by his nose. He pinkened up almost immediately. I wrapped him in blankets and held him. He was a beautiful baby." Carolyn said proudly looking at her son.

"Objection. The last statement is not fact but a judgement." Mr. Drew stated.

"No, it's a fact. See this picture. He was a beautiful baby." Carolyn said digging out a picture from her purse.

James was delighted. He reached for the picture and smiled. "Yes, I believe he was. Mr. Drew would you like to see? He really was a beautiful baby." Just then Judge Hanson reached for the photo.

"Why, yes he was. Would you like to present this as an exhibit for the jury?" Judge Hanson asked looking over the picture.

"I object your honor. We have no way of knowing that this is the baby in question." Mr. Drew stated emphatically, not wanting in any way the jury to look into Joe's big brown eyes.

"Eve can corroborate that this is indeed the baby I saved." Carolyn stated.

"It will be allowed." Stated Judge Hanson. Joe's baby picture was then entered into evidence. Joe was busy making notes on his yellow pad, his ears slightly red from embarrassment after his mother brought out his baby picture. But Joe and James both knew that this happened to be a brilliant move on Carolyn's part. It may have happened accidentally, but they couldn't have planned it any better.

"Getting back to the box. Is this the box the baby was placed in?" James asked, retrieving the box from the exhibit table.

"Yes," Carolyn answered without hesitation.

"Objection." Mr. Drew stated, "How could she know this was the exact box?"

"Because I cut a hole in the corner to feed the oxygen tubing through." Carolyn answered, pointing at the rough hole she had cut with her bandage scissors.

"Over-ruled," Judge Hanson stated.

James opened the box for the jury to see and the baby blankets were still inside.

"What is this?" James asked picking up a very old worn piece of tape.

"That is the tape I took off the baby's mouth." Carolyn stated quietly, but still loud enough for the courtroom to hear. She tried not to say Joe's name, to keep it factual to keep her emotions in check.

"Did anyone else see you go into the equipment closet?" James asked.

"Yes, Eve, the other nurse, she opened the door when I was holding the baby and administering oxygen." Carolyn answered.

"What did you do with the baby after you resuscitated him?" James asked not going into detail on her visit to the morgue or her leaving the hospital, knowing that Mr. Drew will be hammering her on this upon his cross-examination.

"I took him home. He is my son. My husband and I adopted him." Carolyn stated.

"You left the hospital with a baby that had been born to someone else." James clarified.

"Yes. A baby whose doctor left him to die in an equipment closet. That doctor signed a death certificate on this baby." Carolyn said pointing at Dr. Jefferson.

"After you saved Baby B did Dr. Jefferson continue with the practice of putting disabled babies in boxes to die?" James asked, moving back towards the prosecution desk.

"No, not to my knowledge. We had an understanding. He wouldn't say anything about the baby I saved and I wouldn't tell authorities about the babies he killed, but I also added the condition that the practice of putting babies in boxes must stop. I took an administrative position at the hospital as Assistant Director of Nursing so that I could make sure he followed through. All boxes were removed by me from the closet. I checked regularly to make sure there weren't any to be found." Carolyn stated calmly, ashamed that she had made a pact with the devil, but at the time it was all she could do.

"No further questions at this time." James stated nodding his approval at Carolyn.

"You may start your cross-examination." Judge Hanson directed to Mr. Drew.

"You stated that you adopted this baby." Mr. Drew stated upon standing. "But you and I both know that the adoption wasn't legal as his parents hadn't signed off on the relinquishment of their baby. You took this baby without a legal right to take him isn't that correct?"

"I took him to save his life." Carolyn stated adamantly. "I knew that if I went to the parents that Dr. Jefferson could quite possibly get them to agree that it would be best if the child didn't live. At that time not as much was known about his defect and some doctors believed they were saving the parents from having to raise a child who wasn't what they believed was 'normal'. If I went to the parents, I was going to lose my job and career as a nurse and quite possibly the baby could still die. I didn't want to take that chance. Nurses were taught not to second guess doctors back then." Carolyn answered truthfully.

"But you did." Mr. Drew stated flatly.

"I had to! I would not let that baby die that day or any other day." Carolyn answered defiantly, her eyes were like daggers causing Mr. Drew to take a step back.

"So, you believed yourself above the law; that you could kidnap a child and get away with it. Is it not true that you made a deal with the prosecution, that for your testimony you were given immunity from prosecution for your actions?" Mr. Drew pressed.

"It wasn't me who believed I was above the law. It was Dr. Jefferson. As I recall murder trumps kidnapping." Carolyn answered.

"So… you do admit to kidnapping?" Mr. Drew asked trickily.

"No… I believe you can't kidnap a corpse." Carolyn answered. "And by the letter of the law, that is what I did. There was a death certificate signed by Dr. Jefferson on this baby. Why would you sign a death certificate on a baby that was born alive? Why would you tell a mother that her child had died when it was alive lying in a box in an equipment closet with medical tape over its little mouth?" Carolyn spat back, her eyes locked on Dr. Jefferson.

Mr. Drew was losing ground and he knew it. This nurse was a hero in the jury's mind. He needed to choose a different tack.

"Didn't this child require extensive medical care? Surgery? Physical therapy?" Mr. Drew asked.

"Yes, my son had surgery and physical therapy, but he grew up as any normal child does." Carolyn answered.

"Didn't your husband renovate your home to be more accessible for this child?" Mr. Drew asked, careful not to use the pronoun 'your' when referring to the child.

"Yes. My husband is very handy with tools. It was a labor of love. Joe has been a blessing to us." Carolyn answered. She didn't like that Mr. Drew was making it sound like taking care of Joe was a burden. They never thought of him as a burden. He and his sisters were the light of their lives.

"Isn't it true that taking care of a child with disabilities could be very expensive, possibly bankrupting people?" Mr. Drew asked.

"I don't know. I'm not an expert on other people's children, only my own." Carolyn evaded.

"You are a nurse, correct." Mr. Drew stated.

"Yes."

"Are you aware that in 1969 when this occurred, many disabled children were placed up for adoption because their parents felt they couldn't provide for them? Many more were placed in institutions and lived out their lives there as wards of the state." Mr. Drew asked.

Carolyn looked at Joe. She couldn't imagine her life without him and her heart ached for the children who grew up without parents to love them.

"Yes. I was aware of those institutions. Many of the parents who placed children there did so at the urging of their doctors. Instead of helping those parents understand the needs of their children and how to overcome obstacles, these doctors, most of them men, urged parents to put their children in warehouses. That was wrong!" Carolyn stated fiercely. He had touched a nerve in her when discussing society's behavior towards those that carried some type of disability.

"Could it be considered more humane to let these children die a natural death than to live in such institutions, burdens of the state?" Mr. Drew asked.

Now Carolyn understood his tactic. He wanted her to say it would be better if they had never been born.

"Putting babies in closets with tape over their mouths until they died isn't humane Mr. Drew. It's murder. Even if a child were born with a defect that would take their life, didn't they deserve to die in their mother's arms feeling loved and cared for even if their life be but one hour? If they are born alive, don't they have the rights of everyone else who is alive?" Carolyn reached forward to crab the wooden oak railing gripping it emphatically, "No one has the right to play God with these children. No one!" Carolyn stated adamantly.

Mr. Drew could see that he wouldn't get Carolyn to budge on her beliefs and he was actually losing ground, best to get her off the stand quickly. "No more questions Your Honor."

Carolyn was dismissed. Exhausted, but not defeated, she climbed down from the witness stand.

Judge Hanson could see the emotions that were elicited from Carolyn's testimony had taken a toll on everyone and called for a 30 minute recess. People filed out of the courtroom quietly. Dr. Jefferson's wife glared across the aisle at Carolyn, knowing that she caused all this chaos in their life. Joe leaned over the dividing bannister to whisper in Carolyn's ear what a great job she had done. Carolyn smiled back at him her eyes glistening.

Dr. Jefferson leaned over and asked Mr. Drew, "Why didn't you keep her on the stand longer to try to trip her up?"

"Are you joking??" Mr. Drew snarled, dabbing the sweat on his balding forehead. "Didn't you see the jurors' faces? According to them that woman is a saint, and you, Dr. Jefferson, are the devil incarnate. She lit the flames and started fanning them. I'm going to have to try to extinguish what I can. If this had been tried in 1969 you would have had a much better chance of winning. Now, even though the passage of time has erased the most damning evidence, nurses are thought of as highly trained professionals and very trustworthy. They are now worthy adversaries and there are more of them willing to step forward to tell the truth than there are doctors willing to admit to killing babies, even if it was done almost thirty years ago." Mr. Drew snapped his folder shut and stuffed it back in his briefcase. "We'll have a much better chance with the next nurse. She's more flawed." Mr. Drew stated, drawing out Eve's folder and silently crossing his fingers that his assessment was correct.

When the court was called back in session it was Eve's turn to testify. Eve used a cane to steady herself as she entered the courtroom. Anne now sat in the gallery next to Jessica. James assisted Eve to the witness stand. Eve had chosen a brown pants suit with a multi-colored scarf to cover her bald head today. She chose not to take any pain meds this morning so her mind would be clear to give testimony, but the extra energy needed to come to court today was taking its toll.

After she gave her oath James asked her to state her name for the record.

"Eve Stockwell." She stated clearly.

"Did you work as a Registered Nurse at Memorial County Hospital in 1969?" James asked.

"Yes, I did. Mainly in the Obstetrics department, but I did float to others as well." Eve answered trying to keep her eyes on James.

"Did you assist Dr. Jefferson with many deliveries?" James asked.

"Yes. Since that was my primary assignment." Eve answered.

"We just heard testimony from Carolyn Steffan regarding a delivery in September 1969, a baby boy born with spina bifida. Do you remember this delivery?"

"Yes. Carolyn didn't normally work obstetrics, but we were short-handed so she was called back to assist." Eve stated flatly.

"This didn't turn out to be a normal delivery did it?" James asked.

"Objection." Mr. Drew stated. He was going to try to get as much of this testimony stricken as he could. "Leading the witness."

"Sustained." Judge Hanson stated.

"Please tell us about the delivery." James directed this time.

"The baby boy was found to have an opening on his back which indicated a defect called spina bifida. Dr. Jefferson was upset. He called for 'a box' and Carolyn didn't know what that was. We had boxes that were kept on a top shelf in the equipment closet. Dr. Jefferson and another doctor used them when they delivered a baby with a defect. The doctor would put tape over the baby's mouth and put the baby in the box. The box was then left in the equipment closet until the baby died and then it was brought down to the morgue. Dr. Jefferson had directed the custodian who disposed of pathology specimens in the incinerator to dispose of the babies' bodies as well." Eve answered very matter-of-factly.

"Did this happen once or twice?" James asked.

"No, at least a dozen times over my nine years at the hospital. Dr. Jefferson stated many times that he was saving the parents from a lifetime of dealing with a crippled child who would be a burden on society." Eve answered.

"Did you agree with his assessment, that these children would be a burden to their parents and would be better off dead?" James asked

"At first I did see his point of view. Institutions were full and they were gruesome places for a child to be placed." Eve reluctantly admitted. "But seeing what Carolyn and her family have done and the wonderful job they did raising their very successful, physically challenged son I have to say that their model is the model we as a society should aspire to. Instead of doctors telling parents their child will be a burden, medical professionals should encourage them to help their child reach the potential they have available to them." Eve said astutely. "I have come to believe that there's no telling what they may accomplish in life." Eve looked pointedly at Joe, trying to convey to him through her statement the esteem to which she now held him.

"What kinds of defects did the babies have that Dr. Jefferson deemed incompatible with life?" James asked.

"Several. Spina bifida was one of them, Down's syndrome, microcephaly, several. I can't name them all." Eve stated flatly.

"So, basically any physical defect?" James asked.

"Yes, a visual defect that couldn't be easily corrected." Eve answered.

"Getting back to the delivery in September of 1969, Dr. Jefferson decided that the baby boy should die?" James asked matter of fact, hiding his discomfort at asking these questions with Joe sitting ten feet away.

"Yes." Eve answered, also feeling discomfort at having to say these things in front of Joe and Anne.

"And you got the box for him since Carolyn didn't know what he was talking about." James clarified.

"Yes." Eve answered glancing down at her hands, now feeling the shame that she should have felt 29 years before.

"Did you think twice about this? Did you ever think, 'this is wrong, I should stop him'?" James asked.

"Yes, when I first started working at the hospital, but nurses were taught not to question doctors. Doctors were put on pedestals. They even had what we nurses' called 'god complexes'. We as a society did that. We gave them that power." Eve answered calmly.

"Had you worked with Dr. Jefferson often?" James asked, getting to the more personal questions.

"Yes." Eve answered, knowing that their private relationship was about to be revealed.

"Did you also have a relationship outside of work with Dr. Jefferson?" James asked delicately.

"Yes." Eve answered, looking at Dr. Jefferson for the first time. "We had an affair that lasted six years."

"Were you married?" James asked.

"No, but he was." Eve answered, seeing the look of horror on Dr. Jefferson's wife's face. She was aware of her husband's infidelity, but was angry that it was now on public record.

"Carolyn testified that you opened the door to the equipment closet when she was holding the baby boy in her arms. You must have known or at least had thoughts that she may try to save this baby?" James asked.

"Yes. I saw the tears on her face. I thought for a second of alerting Dr. Jefferson but I felt I owed it to her to keep my mouth shut." Eve stated keeping her focus on James.

"Why do you say you owed her?" James asked.

"The previous fall, I believe in October, Carolyn gave birth to a baby boy. She had been told it was a still birth, but it wasn't. Her baby boy was born alive." Eve said.

"Did that boy have a defect?" James asked.

"Not a birth defect per se. Carolyn's doctor had been called out of the delivery room due to an emergency. Dr. Jefferson stepped in to finish the delivery. Carolyn was under the effects of anesthesia. Dr. Jefferson used forceps to pull the baby out because he seemed to be stuck. The baby had turned the wrong way in the birth canal and the forceps went over the side of the baby's face causing the baby to be blinded in one eye, also causing some bone breakage in his face. Dr. Jefferson didn't like to admit mistakes. He felt if he let the baby die like the others, he wouldn't have to answer to the mistake and there would be no lawsuit." Eve stated trying to hide her emotions.

"Did you get a box for Dr. Jefferson for that baby as well?"
James clarified.

"No, not this time. I refused." Eve stated adamantly. "I knew
Carolyn wanted her baby and she would accept him no matter
what his condition. Dr. Jefferson got angry and stormed to the
closet himself and put the baby in the box with the tape over his
mouth and brought it back to the closet himself. I knew it was
wrong. I tried to do for her baby what Carolyn did for Joe, but
I got there too late. The baby had died. I saw a syringe with blood
on it next to the box. I think Dr. Jefferson had injected something
into the baby's vein to speed up the death." Eve said quickly.

Joe could hear his mother crying behind him and knew that
this news was more than she could bear. Dr. Jefferson had not
passively sat by until her son died. He actively participated in
his death. Tom quietly assisted her out of the court room while
Mr. Drew was voicing his objection, "Objection Your Honor,
speculation."

Judge Hanson sat quietly for a moment. He knew he needed
to sustain the objection but he also knew that Eve was telling the
truth and dreaded saying the inevitable, "Sustained."

"Let me fully understand. You felt you owed her a child?"
James asked a bit incredulous. "Do you feel partly responsible for
the death of her child?" James asked.

"I felt responsible for not stopping Dr. Jefferson. I was in
love with the man. He was very charismatic and handsome and
charming. I'm not excusing my actions just explaining them. Over
time I have come to feel his actions were morally wrong, but I was
a nurse and nurses didn't question doctors back then. They just
didn't. I felt helpless holding Carolyn's deceased son. I wrapped
him in a blue blanket and placed the necklace of an angel that
I was wearing over his head to watch over him, and placed him
back in the box," a tear escaped down her cheek but her voice

remained strong. "Dr. Jefferson was signing the death certificate when I came out of the equipment closet. I remember walking past him and saying, 'He's dead.'" Eve's voice broke with emotion.

"When you were first asked to testify in court for this trial you refused." James stated, "Why?"

"I left Memorial County Hospital right after the incident with Carolyn's son – the second son." Eve clarified. "I saw how strong she was and how much she was willing to risk for a child she hadn't even given birth. She gave me the strength to leave." (Eve paused) "I left to save my child, mine and Dr. Jefferson's." She paused to look him in the face as an audible gasp was heard from Mrs. Jefferson. "You see, when I told Clayton that I was pregnant with our child I thought he would happily leave his wife so we could raise our child together. Instead he was furious. He slept with me for six years, telling me that he loved me, but when I became pregnant, he wanted to perform an abortion on me to keep it quiet. He expected that we could continue our affair afterwards. I left to give our child a life. I wanted her even if he didn't. My daughter didn't know who her biological father was. I met and married a good man and he adopted my daughter as his own and he was an exceptionally good father. I didn't feel the need to tell my daughter how stupid I had been to fall in love with a married doctor and especially didn't want her to know the monster he turned out to be."

"Objection to the word monster Your Honor and objection Your Honor to the line of questioning regarding a supposed child - we don't even know if a child exists or if Dr. Jefferson is the biological father." Mr. Drew said strongly.

"Anne is right there, she exists, she's beautiful and she looks just like her father." Eve stated defiantly. The courtroom turned every eye on Anne, and, even though she was embarrassed, she kept a proud look on her face.

When Mr. Drew saw Anne it was his turn to gasp, because the resemblance to Dr. Jefferson was very strong.

Judge Hanson saw it as well, "Objection overruled."

"No more questions at this time Your Honor." James smiled. This last objection will leave an impression on the jury that Eve is telling the truth and that the defense is trying to cover up their sins….their many sins.

"Since it is time for lunch, I believe we will recess until 1:30pm when you can start your cross-examination. Court is adjourned until then." Judge Hanson proclaimed as his gavel hit the wooden block.

Eve looked visibly tired as James assisted her down from the witness stand. Joe suggested they go back to the conference room so she could rest and sent an assistant across the street to bring back some food for lunch. James agreed.

As they left the courtroom, they found Carolyn and Tom on a bench in the hall. Carolyn had gained her composure again, but looked quite tired. Joe reached down to assist his mother up and gave her a quick hug, "Mom, I'm sorry. I never wanted you to be hurt, but knowing what has been brought out in this trial, I'm really sorry." Joe said sincerely.

"No, Joe, you were right. Phillip is owed this. It may be hard to hear, but it is good to know the truth and be able to put his memory at peace." Carolyn said to her second son, straightening his lapel. She was right. This may be hard for her to hear, but the truth eased her mind and knowing the circumstances of Philip's life and death allows them to celebrate his short life on this earth; and finally mourn his death.

The assistant came back with an arm full of lunches and they all went into the conference room. Jessica had to say her good byes. She had a test that afternoon. After a quick hug for everyone, she was off. Her mother calling after her, "Call to let us know you arrived safely," Her sister, brother, and father felt, rather than saw, her eyes roll.

Joe pulled Anne out of ear shot of everyone else, "How do you think your mother is holding up?"

"Pretty good so far. Although I can see she is getting very tired," Anne replied with concern.

"Immediately after she finishes her testimony take her back to the house and have her lay down. I'll come by after we finish, but I think I'll have to come back to the office tonight to review the witness line up and questions for tomorrow." Joe said with regret.

Joe wanted to kiss her, but resisted to keep a professional image as several people were milling about in the corridor.

Anne's hand grazed his as they stood close together and his index finger slid over her thumb in a wordless caress.

Judge Hanson brought the courtroom to order at precisely 1:30 pm with the oak gavel hitting the wood underneath. Eve resumed her seat on the witness stand and was reminded she was still under oath.

"Mrs. Stockwell," Mr. Drew began, "You stated under oath that you brought the box with the baby boy into the equipment closet."

"Yes sir, under the direction of Dr. Jefferson." Eve replied, ill at ease with where he was going with this line of questioning.

"But Dr. Jefferson wasn't holding a gun to your head." Mr. Drew said for effect. "You could have stopped at any time. You could have carried the box out the door for that matter, but you didn't." Mr. Drew stated.

"No. I didn't. As I said before, he was a doctor. I was only the nurse." Eve replied haltingly.

"Perhaps you should be at this table instead of Dr. Jefferson." Mr. Drew challenged. "But I wager that you were given immunity as well, for your testimony."

"Objection, Your Honor. Counselor is testifying instead of the witness. Is there a question in the future for the actual witness?" James stated emphatically.

"Sustained." Judge Hanson ruled immediately and cautioned, "Mr. Drew stop grandstanding and question the witness."

"You stated there were 'many' babies that Dr. Jefferson had done this to over the years." Mr. Drew stated, referring to his notes.

"Yes, at least a dozen." Eve answered.

"But yet he is only charged with one count of murder. Isn't that odd?" Mr. Drew replied.

"Why is that?" Mr. Drew asked again.

"I wouldn't know – perhaps you need to ask the district attorneys. I'm not one of them." Eve answered a bit irritated.

"Objection, Your Honor. He is asking the witness to testify to things that she is not privy to." James stated – knowing what he was trying to get at, but at Eve's expense.

"Sustained. Counselor, don't make me warn you again." Judge Hanson answered piqued.

"Sorry Your Honor. Mrs. Stockwell, what is done with babies that are born dead, a still birth I believe is the term." Mr. Drew asked finally.

"We send them to the morgue." Eve answered.

"How?"

"We put them in the boxes and send them to the morgue." Eve finally answered.

"The same boxes as the one entered into evidence?" Mr. Drew asked.

"Yes."

"So how would we know which babies were still born and which were not?" Mr. Drew asked innocently, which was the same problem identified by James and Joe. How were they to tell if the baby took a breath?

"I saw them breathe, cry, move." Eve answered adamantly.

"You saw, but you are the only one testifying to this, except for the one baby that *you* say lived and was kidnapped by Carolyn Steffan." Mr. Drew stated, emphasizing the you, singling her out, but also damning Carolyn Steffan, portraying her as a criminal.

"Objection! Your Honor, counselor is testifying. This isn't closing arguments." James stated jumping to his feet.

"Sustained. Mr. Drew you have been warned to keep your opinions to a minimum and remember Carolyn Steffan has not been charged with a crime here. The jury is to strike the last statement and disregard." Judge Hanson ruled, looking over his reading glasses at Mr. Drew and the jury.

Mr. Drew knew he was pushing the limits of Judge Hanson's patience and bid a hasty retreat, "No further questions at this time."

"Rebuttal Mr. Kuehl?" Judge Hanson directed.

"Yes, Your Honor." James stated standing up.

"Mrs. Stockwell, you stated that Carolyn Steffan's first son was born alive, but had injuries to his face. In your opinion would those injuries have been life threatening?" James asked.

"No," Eve answered emphatically.

"You stated that you put a necklace over Philip's head when you saw he was deceased. Could you identify that necklace." James asked.

"Yes, it was given to me by my mother when I graduated nursing school. I wore it that day. It's in my nursing school graduation photo." Eve stated.

"Please note, states exhibit A – a blow up of your nursing school photo is that correct?" James asked.

"Yes, that is the necklace." Eve said examining the photo.

"Note, states exhibit B – this necklace was around the skeletal remains of a baby unearthed on the hospital grounds. Would you

state these necklaces are the same?" James asked handing her the
necklace and photo.

"Yes, and one of a kind. My mother had it made for me prior
to my nursing graduation." Eve replied seriously.

The necklace and photo were passed around the jurors' box
and many nodded their agreement to his comparison.

"The skeletal remains also had bits of a blue blanket found
scattered amongst the area of the skeleton. These are marked
Exhibit C." James stated. "Note the photo of the unearthed remains
as they lay in the ground before being removed." James passed
around the photos of the skeletal remains of Phillip as he was
found in the burial plots Juan had made. The jurors' expressions
told James he had struck a nerve with them.

Mr. Drew would have liked to object to this evidence as it
was presented, but knew it would have been overruled and just
serve to prolong the evidence in the jurors' hands. This was very
damning evidence. He knew in the jurors' mind there was no
doubt that this indeed was Phillip Steffan and this nurse was
testifying that he was born alive. He also knew that under oath
this baby's parents would never agree that his death was preferable
to raising a child with a disability. Yes, this testimony was a BIG
problem for their case.

"Thank you, Mrs. Stockwell, no more questions." James said,
then noticing her struggle in getting off the witness stand, rushed
to her aid.

Judge Hanson also noted her exhaustion and called for
a 15 minute recess, allowing her time to leave the court room
without feeling the gawking stares of the courtroom at her
back. Mrs. Jefferson scowled as Eve passed by, but she no longer
felt threatened by Eve's presence as she may have once felt in
their younger years. Eve was now noticeably in ill health while
Mrs. Jefferson looked amazingly well preserved in her expensive

dress and make up. Mrs. Jefferson and her husband, while still married, ceased to care about marital relations and each other on a personal basis, but would never divorce. Their image was too important to each of them.

Anne rushed to meet her mother and offer assistance. Joe saw the worried look on her face and he motioned for one of the office assistants to bring in the wheelchair he had standing by. Eve gratefully accepted the offered assistive device. As Anne wheeled her mother out of the court room, she wondered how she would get her back into the house and into her room alone. Joe needed to stay as he was the prosecutor presenting the next pieces of evidence. Joe turned to Tom and asked if he could possibly help Anne.

Cassie spoke up quickly, "No, you stay with Mom, Dad. I'll go help." Joe was surprised at this turn of events as Cassie hadn't been as friendly and inviting as Jessica, perhaps because she was a bit self-absorbed in her own world during the wedding.

"Thanks Cassie." Joe said gratefully.

In turn Cassie gave Joe a quick hug and whispered, "Well, she's almost family now, right?" Joe gave an almost imperceptible nod to those around him, but Cassie saw it plain and clear. Joe was in love and Cassie was thrilled for him.

As Cassie left to lend assistance, the rest of them took their seats again as the gavel came down. Joe was now center stage. He loved the court room. He had a magical gift of knowledge of law. He could remember the smallest of details and use it to his advantage in the prosecution of a case.

Judge Hanson called the room to order with the gavel sounding. "Call your next witness," he directed to the prosecution.

Joe called Dr. Bruce Paul, his pediatrician. Dr. Paul came into the courtroom in a smart Navy suit with a conservative blue and yellow striped tie. His salt and pepper hair combed back with a hint of gel. Joe smiled looking at the tie Dr. Paul chose to wear for this occasion. Dr. Paul was known in his office to wear ties that kids would like, palm trees, Dr. Seuss, puppies, kitties, anything to illicit a smile from an ailing child and give the parents a chuckle. Dr. Paul and Carolyn had become great collaborators on spina bifida. He kept her abreast of the newest treatment modalities and remedies. She shared her personal triumphs and real-life solutions. Dr. Paul had been trying to get Carolyn to join his practice for years and now, finding out she was on leave from her other position, again extended an offer, which she was seriously considering.

"Dr. Paul, two nurses before you testified regarding the medical treatment of some disabled children at birth in the 1960's. Were you practicing medicine at that time?" Joe asked directly.

"Yes, I was in residency until 1965 and was a practicing pediatrician from 1966 and still am." Dr. Paul stated confidently.

"Were you aware of different medical practices with regards to the treatment of some disabled children by those physicians delivering them back in the 1960s and 70s?" Joe asked.

"Yes, there were differences of opinion with regards to children born with disabilities. My practice was to provide care to the best of my ability to each and every patient without regard to disability. There were children born with terminal diagnoses, but even those babies should have been treated with comfort care and given to their parents to share their brief moments of life. As a new physician at that time, I knew the most up-to-date medical treatment for several disabilities. Unfortunately, there were older physicians who felt they had the right to withhold medical treatment from these children. They thought treating them was a waste of time and resources. Luckily, no one at the hospital where I practiced felt this way, at least to my knowledge. I have made it a priority in my practice to change some of those antiquated ideals." Dr. Paul answered.

"So, it was known in medical circles that there were physicians who would not provide even the most minimal care to babies born with disabling diagnoses. That they went so far as to put them in boxes without air, placed tape over their mouths, and put those boxes in closets for those children to die." Joe said heatedly.

"Unfortunately, yes, even more barbaric were doctors who actually took a baby's life by putting their thumbs on the posterior fontanels of the skull and pressing it in, ending the baby's life." Dr. Paul stated matter of fact. This last statement caused gasps from many of the jurors and people in the gallery. Joe looked at his mother with wide eyes and she returned the look with shock and horror on her face.

"Do you feel doctors who indiscriminately chose to withhold medical treatment from babies or who killed them outright committed murder?" Joe asked directly.

"Objection, Your Honor, witness is being asked to give an opinion not stating fact." Mr. Drew stated quickly.

"Your Honor, the witness is a practicing physician who has direct knowledge of the dates in question and medical practice at the time of the crimes. He is an expert in the field." Joe defended.

Judge Hanson stated firmly, "Overruled, the witness may answer."

Dr. Paul looked at Dr. Jefferson and answered with one word, "Yes."

"You were the pediatrician on call the night Baby B was brought in to the emergency room on the day of his birth were you not?" Joe asked more calmly then he felt.

"Yes, I was." Dr. Paul stated, grateful to get to a more factual part of his testimony rather than opinion based.

"Do you feel that medical treatment should have been withheld at the time of this child's birth?" Joe asked calmly.

"No, the baby in question suffered from Spina Bifida and there are varying degrees of disability. Even those doctors who believed in withholding treatment should have recognized this, but sadly there probably were many babies who died that should not have." Dr. Paul stated frowning.

"What did you tell Carolyn Steffan when asking her to foster this baby?" Joe asked, remembering Carolyn's mantra.

"I told her to focus on the child's possibilities, not his disability." Dr. Paul stated smiling, remembering the many times Joe repeated this back to him at his doctor appointments.

"Now that you've been told the true circumstance of Baby B's birth and Carolyn Steffan's role in raising Baby B, what is your opinion of her actions?" Joe asked, hoping to solidify her role in a positive way.

"I was shocked to hear how she came in possession of the baby. Without a doubt I believe she saved that baby's life." Dr. Paul answered sincerely.

"Do you think her actions were criminal as the defense would have us believe?" Joe asked softly.

"No, quite the contrary. It took quite a bit of bravery to do what she did and in my professional opinion she and her husband did an outstanding job of parenting Baby B and his success is partly due to their unwavering support." Dr. Paul said, smiling at Carolyn and Tom.

"No more questions at this time." Joe stated.

"No questions at this time, Your Honor." Mr. Drew stated. He knew he would not be able to discredit Dr. Paul. His medical reputation was above reproach. Better to get him off the stand and hopefully his own medical professionals would do as well.

Judge Hanson excused Dr. Paul and directed Joe to call his next witness.

Joe called Juan Garcia to the stand. Mr. Garcia approached the stand dressed in a nice suit with a tie. The suit showed some age and, in truth, he bought it 35 years ago when he took the oath of citizenship. He was very proud to be an American. Mr. Garcia placed his hands on the Bible to be sworn in. Those watching could tell his hands were a bit gnarled due to age and hard work. He told his wife and children they were the hands of a man who didn't mind hard work to provide for his family. As the questioning began, he rubbed his hands together nervously. He had prided himself on his work ethic and always doing what was asked of him from his supervisors. Now he felt betrayed by these same people. He knew he was offered immunity from legal prosecution, but worried about the ramifications of eternal damnation for what he had done in accordance with his own Catholic faith. He felt he betrayed those babies and their families by not questioning this practice sooner.

"Mr. Garcia, you were the custodian/maintenance engineer at the Memorial County Hospital in the year 1969 were you not?" Joe asked, beginning the deposition.

"Yes sir, until I retired this past January." Mr. Garcia answered haltingly.

"Are you familiar with these boxes?" Joe asked holding up the box that held him as a baby.

Mr. Garcia nodded.

"Please answer verbally for the record, Mr. Garcia." Joe directed.

"Ye..s.. s...ir," Mr. Garcia answered, perspiration dotting his forehead.

"What were you directed to do with these boxes?" Joe asked, already knowing these answers.

"I was told to burn them along with the pathology specimens that came downstairs when the lab was through with them. We had a special incinerator that got hot enough to burn anything we put in it." Mr. Garcia answered.

"Did you know what was inside of the boxes?" Joe asked.

"Not at first. But as I was about to put the third box into the incinerator, I dropped it. When I picked it up, I saw a small arm.

I had to open it up to put it back inside and I saw it was a little baby." Mr. Garcia was visibly shaken when he got to the end of his statement.

"Did you then continue to burn the boxes?" Joe asked quietly after allowing Mr. Garcia time to compose himself.

"No, I couldn't. My faith would not allow me to burn babies. I found some ground by the hospital garage and buried the boxes there. I planted flowers around and tried to make it pretty. I always said a prayer before putting them into the ground. I'm sorry. I didn't know anything was wrong. I just knew I couldn't burn the babies." Mr. Garcia said shaking his head while looking at his hands, as if he still saw the black dirt from their graves on them.

"When did the boxes stop coming down?" Joe asked.

"1969, early 70s I guess. I don't remember exactly." Mr. Garcia answered truthfully. It had been a long time ago.

"But wouldn't there have been still births even after the killing stopped?" Joe asked knowing there would be an objection.

"Objection, Your Honor, to the word killing – this has not been established." Mr. Drew stated loudly knowing the word 'killing' would be very detrimental to his case.

"Sustained. Please rephrase Mr. Steffan." Judge Hanson directed.

"Why weren't there boxes after that period of times?" Joe asked.

"At first I didn't know. When I questioned one of the staff, they said that the new Assistant Director of Nursing had made a policy that any child that was born dead, the parents now got to hold and if they chose, bury. I guess they all decided to bury their babies after that." Mr. Garcia answered.

"Who was the new Assistant Director of Nursing at the time?" Joe asked.

"Carolyn Steffan. She still is." Mr. Garcia stated pointing a finger in the direction of Carolyn.

"So, just as Eve Stockwell and Carolyn Steffan testified, the boxes of dead babies stopped just after the birth of Baby B, now known as Carolyn Steffan's son; after Carolyn Steffan testified that she gave Dr. Jefferson an ultimatum requiring him to stop killing children with disabilities in November of 1969." Joe stated.

"Objection Your Honor." Mr. Drew stated, hoping to get this last statement stricken.

"Overruled. The last statement will stand." Judge Hanson ruled.

"Yes, the time frame is correct. I remember because I was grateful not to have to bury more babies." Mr. Garcia stated.

"No more questions." Joe stated sitting back down.

Mr. Drew was directed to start his cross-examination.

"Mr. Garcia, you never saw one of those babies alive, did you?" Mr. Drew asked.

"No, sir." Mr. Garcia answered.

"No. You have no idea what caused the death of those babies?" Mr. Drew asked the same question in a different way hoping to drive home this point.

"Objection, Your Honor. This man is not qualified to answer questions regarding cause of death." Joe stated emphatically.

"Objection sustained." Judge Hanson stated. "The witness will disregard this question.

"Thank you. No more questions at this time." Mr. Drew stated, trying to get him off the stand as quickly as possible. Mr. Garcia did have first-hand knowledge of the boxes with dead babies but he could not corroborate how they died or if any of them had at one time been alive after birth. That was favorable for them.

Judge Hanson looked at the large clock over the door and saw the time was approaching 4pm. "We will adjourn for today and meet again tomorrow morning at 9am." The large wooden gavel came down with a bang signaling the end of a long emotional day.

Joe and James stood while the judge left and then filed papers into manila folders and put them in their briefcases. James headed back to the office and Joe planned on meeting him shortly.

Joe turned toward his parents who sat directly behind the banister separating the inner courtroom from the gallery. "Mom, Dad, how are you holding up?"

Tom nodded, "Okay, glad the day is over though."

Carolyn didn't say anything, but offered a weak smile for her son. She was exhausted and couldn't wait to get home to rest.

"Will you be staying at the house tonight?" Tom asked.

"I'm going to go over tomorrow's scheduled witnesses with James and then I'm going to head to the house to see how Anne and Eve are doing." Joe answered. "Perhaps I'll pick up some dinner for them."

"No need," Carolyn stated. "Gramma Jo was bringing over a hot dish for us tonight and she said she was going to make a second one and drop it by for Anne and Eve."

"This family is something else." Joe said smiling.

Carolyn suddenly reached over the banister and hugged her son and whispered in his ear, "Yes we are, and you are one of us. Don't forget it. I love you."

"I love you, too, Mom." Joe answered sincerely. His arms tightened around this woman he loved so much.

"We'll leave the door unlocked for you, but we'll understand if your plans change." Tom stated quietly as he gave his son a quick hug.

The courtroom had long since emptied by this point. The jury had been dismissed to their hotel rooms and the defendant retreated with his family and lawyer to a conference room to review the day's testimony and the damage done to their case.

Joe walked with them out to the lobby, watching them leave the courthouse. He then retreated to the group of offices upstairs.

James was in the conference room with his papers already laid out and coffee on the table. "Good work today, Joe."

"You, too." Joe answered. The case really had progressed quite well. The important element was the judge allowing the nurses to testify as experts. Thirty years ago that would not have been allowed. He realized his mother had been correct. Had she gone to the authorities back when this crime was committed, she wouldn't have stood a chance. Her actions, now looking back, were the only plausible chance to save him.

James and Joe spent two hours outlining the last witnesses they would call in the case: the expert testimony from the forensic coroner from Hennepin County, the coroner from their municipality, and the lead investigator who unearthed the little bodies.

"The only major problem I can foresee is that Eve is the only one who can testify to the fact that Phillip was born alive." James stated grimly. Carolyn's medical chart had been reviewed thoroughly. The only other nurse with initials or mentioned in the narrative at the birth had died in a car accident ten years ago. They were not aware of any other hospital personnel that could be subpoenaed to corroborate her testimony.

"We'll have to rely on the other testimonies and evidence." Joe stated, also knowing that Eve's testimony would, in all probability, differ from Dr. Jefferson's. Joe was looking forward to looking the defendant in the eye, hoping his mere presence would unnerve Dr. Jefferson, taking him off guard. Perhaps even tripping him up on his practiced testimony.

James looked up at the clock and saw it was already 7:30pm.

"Geez, Joe. Time to go home, relax, get a good night's sleep and be ready to rock and roll tomorrow morning." James said slapping Joe on the back.

"Okay. Say hello to Tina for me, and the kids." Joe replied as he gathered up their notes and folders.

"After this is all said and done you need to find yourself a wife and settle down, raise a family." James replied as a friend. "You deserve to be happy."

"That's my plan." Joe replied seriously looking James directly in the eye. "And I wouldn't mind a family either, if it happens." Joe stated glancing away. He still worried that might be a problem, but no matter what, he and Anne would face it together.

"Well then, go home and see Anne. She seems like a beautiful, smart girl. Why are you still here??" James asked prodding Joe out the door.

"I'm going. I'm going!" Joe answered with a smile.

CHAPTER 22

Joe pulled into the driveway and saw the light beaming through the skylight of the great room and kitchen. He walked in to the sound of soft music and thought, it seems warm and inviting in here now, sure beats a dark, quiet house. Dropping his keys in the key bowl on his side desk, he smiled, noting Anne's keys lay in there as well.

"Anne, I'm home." Joe called, not wanting her to be startled by his presence.

A door down the hall opened and closed. Anne had been in her mother's room helping her get ready for bed. Hearing Joe's voice she excused herself, but Eve surprised her by asking if Joe could come to her room before she fell asleep.

Anne slipped her arms around Joe's waist giving him a warm hug and inviting kiss. "Welcome home, honey. I've been missing you." Anne said truthfully. Even though the house was exquisitely built, it wasn't a home without Joe.

Joe smiled, returning her hug, feeling loved and wanted. His thoughts went back to a few short months ago when he hadn't thought this would be possible for himself.

"How's your mother?" Joe asked solicitously, concerned the emotion packed day may have pushed Eve beyond her endurance.

"Good, but very tired. She slept for three hours when we got back. Gramma Jo came by with supper, such a sweet lady! I just helped Mom into her night clothes. She's about to fall asleep, but when she heard you come through the door, she asked if she could see you before she does." Anne answered, wondering what her mother wanted to say to Joe.

"Sure. I'll go see her now." Joe answered picking up his metal crutch. "Is there any leftover supper?" Joe asked as he went down the hall.

"I made a plate for you. I'll heat it back up." Anne answered. She was sure he would forget to eat and wanted to make sure he kept his strength up during the trial.

Joe smiled. Anne has many of the traits he loved about his mother. He realized that perhaps that is why he loves her so much.

Joe knocked gently on the door making sure he heard an answering voice before entering. The bedside lamp was still on and Eve had a book lying across her chest. She was trying to stay awake until she talked with Joe.

"Eve, Anne said you wanted to see me?" Joe questioned softly.

"Yes, come, sit next to me." Eve stated softly patting the bed.

Joe carefully sat down next to her slight frame.

Eve nodded her approval and a slight smile was on her lips. "I wanted to thank you for today."

Joe's eyebrows went up and surprise was evident on his face. He had never been thanked by a witness before.

"You gave me an opportunity to do the right thing; to face my demons, try to right some of the wrongs in my life, for that, I am truly grateful. I've tried to do the right things with my Anne, but I have many things that I've done in my life of which I'm not proud." Eve paused for a moment, glancing down at the pretty new comforter that she was sure Joe had purchased with her comfort in mind, trying to gain the courage to be totally honest.

"I didn't care for you at first. You are certainly handsome and successful, but you also represented the sins of my past. Looking at you reminded me of the things I've lived to regret. I've been watching you with Anne the last couple of months. You are the best thing that's happened to her in a long time. She said you are quite the gentleman and she was totally correct." Eve paused and looked directly into Joe's big brown eyes, "You know she's in love with you." Eve noted Joe's expression soften and a subtle quiet nod. She noted the quiet nod and sincere smile on his face.

Joe answered her unspoken question, "And I am in love with her."

"I thought as much. I just wanted to hear it," Eve acknowledged, relaxing a bit back into the pillow. "We both know that I don't have much time left on this Earth. I don't want things to be left unsaid. You have my blessing, if you want it. I would be honored to have you as a son in law. I know that you will love her almost as much as I do." Eve placed her hand over Joe's and gave it a squeeze, "Now I think I need to get a good night's sleep," she said letting him know that she said what she felt she needed to say, closing up her book and putting it on the nightstand.

Joe stood up to leave and looked down at this lovely woman whose body has been ravaged by disease. He gently leaned down to place a kiss on her forehead. "Thank you, Eve. There's only one thing I want you to know. I love her more than anyone will ever know, and I intend to be a good husband. Sleep well."

Turning towards the door, his hand reaching for the knob, Joe heard Eve say quietly, "No need to go to your parent's tonight. Your place is here with Anne. I'll see you in the morning. Sleep well."

Joe closed the door quietly behind him smiling.

Joe walked towards the wonderful smell of Gramma Jo's specialty. He realized how hungry he really was. Anne was just pouring a glass of water and setting it next to his plate. As he sat down to eat Anne joined him, sipping a glass of wine. "Anything wrong?" She asked curiously.

"Why no, what could be wrong?" Joe answered, smiling. Knowing Anne was very curious about what was said in Eve's room.

"What did my mother want to talk about?" Anne asked prodding, hoping her mother had behaved herself.

Joe smiled, putting the first bite of food in his mouth. "She thanked me for making her testify." He answered laughing just a bit, "That's a first for me." He said shaking his head a little in disbelief.

Anne just sat in stunned disbelief. That's what her mother wanted to say?? Then Joe leaned over and covered her hand with his, gently saying, "Then she gave me her blessing, saying she would be proud to have me as a son in law."

Anne was even more surprised at that admission. She knew her mother's stance had softened quite a bit towards Joe over the past several weeks, but she was stunned that her mother went as far as giving Joe her blessing without first asking Anne.

Joe went on, "She told me you were in love with me." His eyes twinkled as he gazed into her blue eyes which were now wide with surprise. He leaned forward to kiss her stunned lips.

"She did, did she?" Anne answered as his lips were almost on top of hers.

"Yes, she did." Joe answered quietly.

"And what did you say?" Anne replied, her blue eyes now smoldering.

"I said I was also in love with you." Joe answered, quickly kissing away any further discussion.

When they separated Anne pointed out that his dinner was getting cold and it was getting late. Weren't his parents going to be worried about him.

Joe went to work finishing his food as he was now very anxious to get to bed. "My dad said they would understand if my plans changed." Joe said smiling.

Anne smiled back but nodded towards the hall, "What about my mother?"

"I forgot. That was the last thing your mother said, 'no need to go to your parent's tonight, my place was here with you.'" Joe said getting up from the table and walking over to where Anne now stood in the kitchen, her eyes wide with anticipation. He put his plate in the sink and turned to embrace her with one arm, the other resting on the crutch. He softly said, "I think it's time for bed? Don't you?" His words sent shivers of expectation down her body.

Anne just nodded her head, relishing the feelings this man generated inside her.

Resting in each other's arms, Anne smiled. Her mother was asleep in the next room but this never felt right. Eve was correct. This is where Joe belonged. Anne leaned on her elbow looking down at Joe's face in the light from the skylight, "You know my mother was right. I do love you." Anne said before brushing her lips against his.

"Your mother is a wise woman." Joe stated factually. "I only corrected her on one thing."

"What was that?" Anne asked with concern, her antennae raised.

"She said that she knew I would love you almost as much as she did." Joe answered, brushing Anne's hair behind her ear. His eyes locked in a gaze with hers as he slowly but firmly stated, "I told her that no one will ever know just how much I love you and that I intend to be a good husband." As he finished his statement, he reached over to the bedside table and took out the box he had been wanting to open since he purchased it. His fingers reached for Anne's hand and placed the ring on Anne's finger. "Will you do me the honor of becoming my wife?"

Anne was overcome with emotion. Tears of happiness rolled down her cheeks as she threw her arms around Joe's neck and whispered in his ear, "Yes,….., yes," was all she could say. Their commitment sealed with a kiss of passion.

Joe had never been happier. As they drifted off to sleep both dreamed of a future together.

CHAPTER 23

Joe awoke at precisely 5am without an alarm. When an important case was being tried, it was as if his body had an inner alarm. He slowly eased out of bed so he would not wake Anne. He looked down at his future wife's face relaxed in slumber and the perfectly shaped lips puckered in sleep. This was a picture he had longed for and would now be etched in his memory. His dark blue suit was laid out the night before knowing he would rise early to prepare for court. He quietly went in to shower, but found the bed empty when he came out 20 minutes later. A light was on in the great room and the smell of bacon wafted through the open door. Anne was up.

Joe was dressed except for his tie when he entered the great room to find Anne busy at work in the kitchen, the table set, with orange juice poured. He came up behind her as she tended the eggs on the stove and smelled her soft scent as he nuzzled her neck laying kisses along the beautiful white skin.

"Good morning sweetheart. I didn't mean to wake you." He said softly in her ear trying not to wake Eve.

Anne turned around in his embrace giving him a morning kiss filled with future promises. "I wanted to send off my future husband with plenty of fuel for the day." She said smiling, no longer wanting to keep their engagement a secret.

Joe couldn't help grinning, "This is the best way to wake up, I swear. Well, second best," remembering the morning after their first intimate encounter.

"Perhaps the best way on a work day?" Anne countered, also remembering back to that morning.

"Breakfast is ready." Anne said, directing Joe to sit down.

"So, what is your plan for today?" Joe asked enjoying his big breakfast.

"I'm going to court, of course!" Anne answered, surprised at his question.

Joe registered a look of surprise on his face. "You and your mother can rest today. I know yesterday was quite taxing on her. I may need her in court when the defense starts its case, but that won't be today." Joe answered.

"You are right. My mother was quite tired after yesterday. She is going to stay home. I will get her breakfast and help her get ready for the day, then Gramma Jo is coming over to sit with her. She offered when she dropped off dinner last night." Anne said, bringing Joe up to speed on the arrangements.

"That doesn't surprise me," Joe said shaking his head, "Gramma Jo is the best." He said with a smile.

"I'm going to love having a grandmother," Anne said grinning.

"She already loves you." Joe said with a wink while picking up his plate to put it in the dishwasher.

"Joe, leave the dishes. I can do them." Anne said wanting to feel useful.

"Anne, I was raised with a mother who worked. Yes, she did a lot for us, but we were taught to tow our own weight. I don't expect you to be a wife who waits on me. You are my partner, my confidante, my lover, but most of all, my soul-mate." Joe said, lovingly embracing Anne and kissing her passionately.

"Bravo," came a voice from the darkened hallway. Eve slowly came into view to the couple still locked in each other's arms.

"Eve," Joe said slightly embarrassed by his statement meant only for Anne. "I'm sorry. Did we wake you?"

"No, I've been awake a little while." Eve answered, walking with her cane, steadier than last night. "And no need to be embarrassed. What you said to my daughter was beautiful!"

"Mom, we have news," Anne said smiling. Stepping closer to her mother. "We're engaged." She said holding out her left hand for Eve to see the ring.

"So now it's official," Eve said smiling. This time her full warmth and acceptance was evident in her voice. "Congratulations to both of you!" Eve slowly walked towards them giving first Anne a hug and then Joe. "You make a beautiful couple. I hope you will be very happy together."

Eve, in her happiness, gave Anne another tight hug and whispered in her ear, "You chose very well my darling."

Joe was still smiling when he walked into the office at 6:30 am. James was already in his office with the door open.

"Good morning, James, beautiful day." Joe said greeting him with a grin that looked like he had eaten a canary.

"What's up with you? We're trying a murder case, but you look like someone who just won the lottery." James asked suspiciously.

"I did. I asked Anne to marry me last night and she said yes." Joe answered grinning guiltily.

"That's fantastic!" James answered getting up to shake Joe's hand. "I like seeing you so happy, but, please, when we are in court today try not to look so god damn joyful."

"Don't worry," Joe said, "One look at Dr. Jefferson will put a frown on my face." Joe stated heading out the door to his office.

Joe got busy preparing and reviewing the questions outlined for the next two witnesses. He definitely could compartmentalize his feelings because when he went down the elevator to the lobby and headed to the courtroom the look on his face was all business. He was surprised to see Tom and Carolyn waiting to file in to the courtroom.

"Mom, Dad, I didn't know you were planning to come today." Joe stated while giving them both a hug, knowing how exhausted they must have been after yesterday.

"We'll be here every day until the end, Joe" Carolyn answered with determination. "It's something we have to do."

Joe nodded his understanding. He wished they would skip this day's testimony as the subject matter could be very upsetting to them.

Joe saw Anne coming down the hallway and went to meet her. Carolyn and Tom watched them with approval as they embraced. Joe looked at Anne's hand and noticed the ring was missing.

Anne saw Joe's gaze landing on her hand and whispered in his ear that she didn't want to take focus away from the trial today. She wondered if they could go out to eat with his parents later and they could tell them in happier surroundings.

Joe nodded solemnly. He was right. She was a very wise and thoughtful woman.

Joe indicated it was time to go into the courtroom. Tom and Carolyn took the same seats as they had yesterday and, today, Anne sat next to Carolyn. Carolyn asked about Eve. Anne explained that Gramma Jo was staying with her. Carolyn smiled just as Joe had earlier this morning.

The familiar gavel rang out with all court room personnel standing as Judge Hanson entered. Dr. Jefferson was at his familiar seat at the defense table with his lawyer next to him and his wife behind him with her face void of expression. Two sons sat next to her, one of them, Adam. Anne remembered him distinctly as the boy who had hit Joe at the wedding reception. Anne's jaw was tense with anger as her eyes locked with Adam's. He sneered back at her which angered her even more. That little piss ant wasn't worthy of tying Joe's shoes she thought. She remembered Joe's blood on her dress and how she felt seeing Adam's fist connect with Joe's head. She suddenly had to avert her eyes as she realized her own hands were making fists. She felt a hand resting on top of hers and glanced up to meet Carolyn's knowing glance. Carolyn leaned down and whispered in her ear, "He's not worth it." Anne nodded, embarrassed that Carolyn saw her anger.

Joe glanced back noticing Anne's agitation. He sent her a questioning gaze asking without words if she was okay. To put him at ease she answered with a small smile trying to steer her mind back to this morning and the wonderful things Joe had said to her.

Judge Hanson interrupted her thoughts as he instructed the prosecution to call their next witness. Joe was conducting this testimony and Anne listened intently to the exchange. The first witness was the field investigator who had conducted the excavation of the bodies from the hospital property. He meticulously gave a step by step account of how the bodies were unearthed, preserving 12 inches of dirt around each one. They spent much time on the site of Phillip's burial and pictures of every square inch given to the jury. Anne looked over at Carolyn and saw tears welling up in her eyes. She reached over to take Carolyn's hand and give it a comforting squeeze. Carolyn looked into Anne's eyes and saw compassion and empathy. Anne was indeed one of them already. Carolyn silently hoped Joe would propose soon, but thought perhaps he wasn't ready yet.

After the in-depth testimony, Judge Hanson noted it was 11:30 am and dismissed court proceedings until 1pm. As they got up to stretch, Anne felt a little woozy. She quickly sat back down and reached for a candy in her purse, thinking her blood sugar might be low. Joe hadn't yet turned around so he didn't notice, but Carolyn did. Noting that Anne was a little pale Caroline suggested that the four of them eat lunch across the street.

"I was going to run back to Joe's to check on my mother." Anne answered, but the rumbling of her stomach could be heard by all. "I ate with Joe this morning at 5 am. I think the food is running out." Anne said softly trying to divert attention.

Joe joined the three of them at that moment.

"Why don't you call to check on your mother instead, and we can get some food in you." Carolyn suggested out of concern for Anne.

"That's a great idea," Joe answered also noting Anne's pallor. "There's a phone in the conference room outside the courtroom."

Joe took Anne by the arm steading her as they went into the conference room to make the call. All was well with Eve and Gramma Jo. They had been playing cribbage and Gramma Jo was making lunch.

Joe and Anne joined Tom and Carolyn at the restaurant across the street, the same restaurant Anne and Joe had enjoyed their first lunch together. When the order had been placed, Joe leaned over and asked Anne to put the ring on. He was going to tell his parents there. Anne did as Joe requested.

"Mom, Dad, Anne and I want to tell you something important and although I know with everything that's been going on perhaps this isn't the best time. Anne has agreed to marry me." Joe said smiling.

Carolyn and Tom were smiling from ear to ear. "That's the best news we've had since Cassie's wedding! We knew you two were right for each other, but didn't know how long Joe would take to figure it out." Carolyn said getting up to give them both a hug. Tom followed suit.

Joe picked up Anne's left hand and proudly showed them the ring. They had never seen him so happy. The ring was beautiful.

"Was that on your hand this morning?" Carolyn asked shocked that she could have missed it.

"No," Anne said shyly. "Joe gave it to me last night, but I didn't want to tell you in the courtroom. Evidently Joe couldn't wait a moment longer."

"I can see why." Tom stated. "You two make a wonderful couple. We are so happy for you!"

"Any idea where and when you want to have the wedding?" Carolyn asked as the consummate wedding planner.

"No, we just want to get through the trial first." Joe said soberly.

"I know this is a rough time. It's emotional and feelings are on a roller coaster, but I'm so glad you didn't put off such a happy event. It helps to balance the rest of life." Carolyn stated as their lunch arrived.

As they ate their lunches, Carolyn and Anne talked about weddings and showers while Tom and Joe talked about sports and the animals. Joe's arm remained around Anne possessively and she found it a comforting safe haven. Anne did feel better after they ate. Perhaps it was just low blood sugar after all.

As they got up to go back to the courthouse, Joe realized that Dr. Jefferson's family was just three tables away. Walking out of the restaurant every one of their eyes bore into the back of Joe's head. Their animosity was palpable. He didn't mind their anger being directed at him, just not at his family or his future wife.

Joe assisted his parents and fiancée to their seats. It wasn't difficult to think of Anne as his future wife. To him they were already bonded, marriage would just affirm it to others. Before Judge Hanson's gavel brought the room into session Joe glanced quickly back at Anne to reassure himself that she was indeed truly okay. She noticed his glance and gave him a reassuring nod and smile.

The rest of the afternoon testimony was technical and verified that the skeletal remains were indeed that of a full-term infant. There was some disfigurement in the facial region, possibly due to trauma during delivery. Cause of death was indeterminant due to the amount of years that had gone by post mortem. Joe asked about the other infant remains that had been unearthed. The forensic pathologist stated almost all were calculated to be of the size of a full-term infant except for three, which would have been considered to be premature. They had unearthed 24 skeletons. Subtracting three premature infants would leave 21 full-term babies. Joe then asked of the 21, how many skeletons could be identified as having some type of birth defect. The pathologist answered definitively nine, but that not all defects could be identified with just skeletal remains. Carolyn and Tom's faces were glued to the testimony being presented. Their hands gripped together in solidarity. At the end of the day, the prosecution had finished presenting the case against Dr. Jefferson. Tomorrow the defense would begin.

As James was packing up his brief case, he leaned over to Joe and whispered, "That's quite a rock on Anne's hand. You may want an armed guard escorting her at all times." Joe reddened, but gave James a sheepish grin.

James stopped Anne in the court house lobby to congratulate her as well. "My wife and I would like to have you both over to dinner after the court case concludes to celebrate, hopefully a duo celebration." Referring to a case win and the engagement.

Anne smiled while shaking his hand, "We'd like that."

"Whooee, that sure is a nice rock." James stated again smiling and giving Joe a quick wink before leaving.

"Are you staying late again?" Anne asked trying to figure out dinner plans.

"No. Tonight, we go home and relax." He said smiling, looking forward to curling up next to her on the sofa.

"Sounds good to me." She whispered in his ear.

As Carolyn and Tom came back from the restroom, Anne could see how wearing this trial was on them.

"You two look beat. Is there anything I can do to help?" Anne asked sincerely.

Carolyn gave her a quick hug. "We'll be fine, honey. Going home to have a quiet evening with the animals."

Anne and Joe watched as Tom and Carolyn left arm in arm, marveling at their strength. Anne felt very lucky to be marrying into such a supportive and loving family.

CHAPTER 24

The next morning Joe was awake by 5:00 am, but had brought home what he wanted to review before court so he wasn't rushing to get dressed. Anne woke up at 5:30 am to find Joe at the kitchen table with files open on the table.

"Good morning sweetheart," Anne said as she bent to give Joe a kiss while tying the belt on her robe.

"Good morning." Joe said smiling, thinking this is exactly how he would like to wake up every morning. "I made coffee."

"Thanks, you are a good man!" Anne said laughing.

"Is that all it takes to be a good man?" Joe teased, relishing the sound of Anne's laughter in the morning.

"No. No it isn't." Anne replied seriously taking a seat next to Joe at the table.

Joe remained silent, but attentive as it seemed Anne had something she wanted to say.

"Joe, I was engaged three years ago. It lasted about a year." Anne started.

"Anne, what you did before me is of no concern to me. What matters is that we are together now." Joe stated firmly.

"No, I want you to know this. When my mother became ill, I went to stay with her when she started chemotherapy. I was the only person she had in this world. I needed to support her emotionally. Chad didn't like that I was away so long and gave me an ultimatum, basically choose between my sick mother or him. It didn't take me a split second to realize he wasn't the one I wanted to be with. You see my father always told me to look for a husband who would always care more about me than about himself, and if I cared more for him than myself our marriage would last. My father was a wise man." Anne said with glistening eyes.

"I knew you were the man for me when I met you. I have never experienced the passion, the undeniable attraction for anyone before I met you, but it was your loving care and consideration for me and my mother that absolutely told me you were the one I want to have a family with, the one I want to share the rest of my life." Anne said adamantly.

"Anne, I will always love and care for you, but about having a family. I would love to have children with you, but it may be more difficult for us to conceive due to my disability. I want to be honest with you so you know before committing yourself to me, in case it's a deal breaker for you." Joe said staring at his coffee cup. He had wanted to bring this up for week, but feared losing Anne. He realized it was selfish not to discuss this prior to asking her to marry him, but at least they could discuss it before the wedding.

Joe felt the warmth of Anne's touch on his arm, "Joe, the most important thing to me is being your wife, your partner. I would love to have kids but only because they would be an extension of our love for each other. You would be a phenomenal dad. Don't worry, we will see it through together."

Anne's words were such a relief to Joe. He leaned over to embrace her.

"Now, what can I get you for breakfast." Anne asked softly.

"It's my turn to make breakfast." Joe stated flatly, "You've been making it every morning."

"You can do it on Saturday." Anne stated firmly. "Right now, you need to concentrate on winning this case. How do omelets and toast sound?"

"Okay. It's a deal." Joe agreed. "And omelets sound great." Joe acknowledged, getting back to his review of the case.

Anne busied herself in the kitchen, but after a few sips of coffee felt a queasiness come over her. She swallowed hard and made a piece of toast for herself hoping that would settle her stomach.

"Is Gramma Jo coming over today to stay with Eve?" Joe asked without looking up.

"Yes, that's the plan." Anne said, her voice waivering a bit, but Joe didn't notice.

Anne handed Joe his plate and excused herself to the bathroom. Just as the door closed, she deposited the toast she had eaten and the rest of the contents of her stomach into the toilet. She sat on the floor wondering if this was the stomach flu and realized she wasn't running a temperature, and she hadn't had her period since she and Joe had started the intimate part of their relationship. She pulled herself off the floor and washed her face and brushed her teeth.

Looking into the mirror she knew she could no longer lie to herself. She was sure she was pregnant. The realization made her both upset and happy. She knew that she and Joe wanted kids, but she also wanted to be married first – well, that ship has sailed she thought. She also didn't want to say anything to Joe until it was confirmed. The last thing she wanted was to get his hopes up only to find out it was a false alarm.

Joe knocked on the door and asked if she was okay. She heard the concern in his voice and knew he needed reassurance.

"I'm fine, Joe. I'll be out in a minute." Anne said trying to make her voice sound normal when she felt anything but normal.

As she opened the door she put a reassuring smile on her face. Joe was standing there waiting with a very concerned look. "It's all yours," she said joking, trying to lighten the mood.

"Hey," he said reaching for her arm to bring her closer, "Are you really feeling okay? I know you've been pushing yourself, trying to take care of your mom and me and spending every day at court. Perhaps it's been too much. I should have stayed at my parents so you wouldn't be getting up at 5am to make breakfast."

"Don't be silly, Joe! Of course I want you here! It's not too much for me. I must have caught a little bug, so maybe you shouldn't kiss me right now." She said with a devilish glint in her eye, steering the subject away from her queasy stomach.

Joe wrapped his arms around her, "I'll take my chances," he said with a grin, kissing her passionately. "Now, I've got to take a shower and get ready. No time for fun and games this morning." He said, giving her another light kiss before heading into the bathroom.

Anne laid out his clothes. She wanted him looking his best in court. As she laid out his suit, she couldn't stop herself from running her fingers down the lapel imagining his chest beneath her finger tips. Yep, she had it bad. When she agreed to marry Chad it sometimes bothered her that they didn't seem to have the passion she had heard from others. When she brought her concerns to her mother, she had said that a good marriage isn't always based on passionate sex, but a companionship and mutual love and respect. Although disappointed, she had believed her mother and found Chad to be a suitable mate until he gave her the ultimatum. She immediately saw red flags and her initial misgivings became huge road blocks. She remembered giving him his ring back. She was never so sure about something in her life. Chad tried to change her mind, but she never wavered. It was over. It was more than over, and now she knew why. Chad was never right for her. With Joe she had it all, passion, love, mutual respect, caring. She still couldn't believe how lucky she was.

CHAPTER 25

Anne was able to get her queasiness under control with a few saltines and some sips of 7 up, just to be sure she tucked some crackers in a baggy inside her purse. Tom and Carolyn were already seated when Anne arrived, but they had saved her a seat next to them. She greeted both of them with a hug. They were already like family to her.

Joe was seated at the prosecution table, but noticed her arrival and greeted her with a smile. No sooner had she sat down when the court deputy ordered them all to rise.

Judge Hanson now directed the attorney for the defense, Mr. Drew, to make his opening statement since he had deferred this from the beginning of the trial.

Mr. Drew stood up and slowly approached the jury. He was a middle-aged man, with grey hair and balding. Joe had told Anne he was quite renowned in legal circles and even though his appearance was not sharp, his legal mind was.

"Ladies and gentlemen of the jury, the prosecution has laid out their case for you to judge, but you must not cast your opinion until you hear the full case. We have waited patiently while the prosecutors have cast allegations on my client, a well- known and well-regarded physician who has saved many lives during his long and distinguished career. We do not deny that there are skeletal remains of a baby, of several babies. But there is no corroborating evidence that those babies ever lived, that they ever took a breath outside the womb. You have the testimony of one nurse, who at that same time, was having an affair with the defendant and who by her own admission was pregnant with the defendant's child. Who better to have reason to defame Dr. Jefferson? I will admit my client showed poor judgement in his extra-marital affair, but who really was hurt? My client's wife, yes. My client's family, yes. The witness who made these allegations? She went on to have a beautiful child." (Anne could feel the entire courtrooms eyes on her.) "She went on to get married and have a good life. As for the child who was kidnapped due to an alleged attempt on his life, he went on to be a successful lawyer." (Now, for the first time, all eyes were on Joe.) "The prosecutors are digging up allegations from almost 30 years ago. Why now? Why not then? Those are questions you must answer before finding my client guilty." Mr. Drew finished confidently.

Joe glanced at Anne and she back at him. Joe was right, he was good, very good.

Mr. Drew began calling his first witness. Mr. Drew had a list of at least a dozen witnesses who would all testify that Dr. Jefferson had been their doctor and saved them all from various ailments. All thought he was a wonderful man who treated them with compassion and care. Anne was sick to her stomach, not because she was pregnant, but because of how these people talked about a man who she knew to be a baby killer.

Dr. Jefferson had a slight smile on his face as his friends and co-workers testified, nodding at them as they left the stand. It was like a retirement party without the cake. He sat back and accepted their accolades with pride. This is what he knew to be true. He had done nothing wrong in his own mind.

When the gavel sounded dismissing court at the end of the day, Anne, Tom, and Carolyn were exhausted. Joe gave them each a hug in the lobby as he headed off to his office for a strategy session with James on how to do damage control.

As Joe walked away headed to the elevators, Anne saw Adam Jefferson watching them from the corner. Hate in his eyes. Anne's senses went to high alert. Her hair follicles seemed to stand up straighter. She was afraid, but she couldn't quite say why. Was it the run in at the wedding or was it the look of distain and hate in his eyes now? She found herself increasing her pace while heading to her car, willing herself not to look back, fearing that he was following her. When she reached her car, she fumbled with the keys and then they dropped to the ground. Just as she stood, she felt a hand on her arm and inwardly screamed. She turned around and saw it was Tom. She almost fainted with relief.

"Anne, you left your sweater in the courthouse." Tom stated. "I saw you drop your keys and thought I would help you to your feet." He explained noting her relief. "I didn't mean to frighten you."

"No…No.. Thank you. I just saw Adam Jefferson looking at Joe and I, and I guess it unnerved me. I think he may still harbor some ill will after the wedding fight. I'm so happy it was you behind me." She said with relief and gave him an impromptu hug. "I'm fine now." she said nervously brushing her hair to the side.

Tom noted her paleness and shaking hands and realized that she really was frightened.

"Anne, go ahead and open your car and get in with me here. From now on we will walk you to your car at the end of the day. No need to be fearful." Tom said reassuringly.

"No... I'm fine now. I shouldn't have been scared, see, no one is around. I was just unnerved." Anne said glancing around, but she did quickly unlock her car and get inside. Tom stood waiting for her to back out and waved at her as she left. Tom made a mental note to talk with Joe about this. Perhaps there was something Anne should fear.

Near the exit of the parking lot Adam Jefferson sat in his car watching Anne leave. He was furious that she existed, but that she would date and now it would appear to be engaged to, the man accusing his father of murder. This murder trial had invaded his life. His parents told him he would have to drop out of his private college as they had to direct their monies to paying a defense attorney. He could attend a state college next fall, but Adam wasn't thinking about next fall, he was thinking about the here and now. The world as he knew it, had fallen apart at the hands of Joe Steffan.

Adam tapped his thumbs on the steering wheel of his car as he watched Anne drive away making note of the make and model of her car, license plate MLC 543. Revenge was all he could think of now. If the bitch was someone Joe Steffan cared about, maybe she was the weapon he needed.

The district attorney's office was still buzzing about the trial and employees milling about discussing the case and what the next step should be. As Joe and James walked by co-workers gave words of encouragement. They knew the basics of the case, but weren't privy to the inner workings.

James and Joe headed into the conference room between their offices and knew a long night was ahead of them.

"Well, we knew Drew was going to be tough," James stated rolling up his sleeves. "Dr. Jefferson has lived in the community a long time. People are going to rally around him. What did we expect?"

"Yes, but you can't get away with murder just because, hey, you've lived here awhile." Joe stated irritated by the presumption of Dr. Jefferson's innocence by these people.

"If you were accused of murder, wouldn't you want your friends to rally behind you?" James asked.

Joe didn't answer. He was already trying to get inside the jurors' heads.

Just as James was reaching for the coffee pot one of the office assistants knocked on the conference room door. "I have a nurse out here that says she has some information for you. It seems pretty important."

"Tell her to come in, by all means," James stated raising his eyebrows at Joe.

A plain looking woman in her later 50's came inside. She looked to be very shy, dressed in dark brown pants and a striped blouse.

Joe stood up and extended his hand, "Hello, I'm Joe Steffan, assistant district attorney, and this is James, district attorney. Please have a seat." Joe indicated an open chair.

"Hello. I'm Melinda Schultz. I'm a nurse at the Memorial County Hospital." Melinda stated, her voice waivering. Joe and James could tell how nervous she was by her flushed cheeks and the way her fingers intertwined constantly.

"I understand you have some information for us?" Joe stated with a smile, hoping to put her at ease.

"Yes, I don't know if it's important or not. I know your mother, Carolyn. She's a good woman, a good nurse. I felt really bad when she lost her first child. I wanted to say something at the time. You see, I saw Dr. Jefferson with the baby, her baby." Melinda said stumbling at times on the words.

Joe and James immediately sat up straight, listening intently.

"But your name wasn't anywhere in her hospital records. Did you help with the birth?" Joe asked.

"No, it wouldn't have been. I wasn't helping with her delivery. We were really busy that day. I was helping with the birth of the woman who would deliver right after your mother. I was opening the door to the delivery room to see if they were through so I could set up for the next delivery. I saw the baby on the table next to one of those god-awful boxes from the closet. They had already moved your mother out of the room. Dr. Jefferson was alone in there with the baby. It was fussing and moving when I saw Dr. Jefferson rip off a piece of tape and put it over the baby's mouth." Melinda's lower lip began to quiver, "I saw him do it before to other babies and … they never lived. I knew what he was going to do. It made me sick to my stomach. He told me to get out. But I saw that he had picked up a syringe and put it in the box, too. That I hadn't seen before." Melinda stopped and nervously looked at the table.

Joe asked, "You personally saw this, and would swear to this on a witness stand?"

Melinda nodded her head slowly. "Yes," she said softly but resolved in her decision.

"Why are you coming forward now?" James asked curiously.

"Twelve years before this happened, my mother gave birth at home to a baby who we would now say, had Down's Syndrome. If she had given birth in the hospital, Dr. Jefferson would have put her in that box and she would have died, or he would have told my parents to send my sister to an institution." The look of distain was unmistakable on Melinda's face. "My sister grew up and lived her life on our family's farm. She gave such happiness to my parents and to me. She never thought ill of anyone, always took great pleasure in the little things in life, a butterfly, the smell of a flower, the softness of a kitten. My sister is gone now, passed away due to a heart condition 15 years ago but I loved her so much. I am doing this for her and for all the other kids like her. She deserved a chance at life and so do the rest of them. They shouldn't be murdered just because they aren't physically perfect." Melinda wiped away the tear that escaped while she talked about her baby sister. Melinda dug in her black purse for a moment and pulled out a picture of a girl with down's syndrome smiling as she held a baby kitten. Melinda handed the picture to Joe, "She had such a kind heart." Melinda proudly stated. "She helped with house chores and fed the calves and helped in the garden. Her life was beautiful. She was wonderful. I miss her every day."

Joe and James were silent for a moment. Joe got up and walked over to Melinda and gently touched her shoulder in a show of support. "Thank you for coming forward Melinda, and I'm sorry about your sister."

Joe asked her to write down her name, address, and phone number for him and gave her his card. As she left and the door closed, James asked, "Well, now what do we do. She's a day late. We rested our case."

Joe walked back to his chair lost in thought. He suddenly turned towards James, "There might be a chance. The defense will have to open the door though. If they put Dr. Jefferson on the stand and I'm almost positive they will, I will ask him directly if Phillip was dead at birth. If he says yes, we have the chance to put Melinda on the stand as a rebuttal witness."

James nodded. It was a good plan, "The defense won't know about her and it will discredit Dr. Jefferson's whole testimony as a fraud. But what if they don't put him on the stand?"

"Oh, I can say with almost certainty that they will. He wants his day in court. He wants everyone to see what a cocky bastard he is." Joe said with disgust.

Both James and Joe felt good about the case after Melinda's surprise visit and left with heightened anticipation for the days ahead.

By the time Joe got home the house was dark. He and James had ordered in a pizza so Joe headed straight back to the bedroom. Anne was asleep in the bed and he relished the thought of crawling in next to her. Pulling off his tie while turning to shut the bedroom door, he heard a noise in Eve's bedroom. He quietly rapped on the door before opening it but couldn't hear a reply. Slowly he opened the door not wanting to bother Eve if she was sleeping. Looking towards the bed he saw that it was empty. Concerned he scanned the room and saw Eve lying on the floor surrounded by bed sheets and rushed to her side.

"I'm sorry Joe. I lost my balance." Eve explained in short gasps, short of breath from the exertion of trying to separate herself from the bedding.

"Are you ok? Shall I wake Anne?" Joe asked, concern evident in his voice as he surveyed her body for injury. A large bruise on her thigh had started to form but she was moving her arms and legs.

"No, please don't wake up Anne. She wasn't feeling so well this evening. I'm fine, I just need some help getting up." Eve stated, already trying without success to get up. "Would you mind helping me?"

"Not at all," Joe said removing his suit coat. How about I reach under your arms and lift you up?" Joe offered, successfully extricating the bed linens from around her.

"Let's try it." Eve answered, amazed at how helpful Joe was being.

Joe had her up in no time and actually assisted her back to bed, straightening the bed linens and comforter. "While I'm here, do you need anything? Some water? Food? Are you hungry?" Joe offered.

"No. No. I'm fine now. Joe, it's almost 1am. Are you still in your suit from work?" Eve asked realizing he hadn't been to bed yet.

"Yes, I just got home actually. Late night strategy meeting." Joe answered. As he turned to leave to return to his room, he realized Eve had said Anne wasn't feeling well tonight. "You said Anne wasn't feeling well, is everything alright? Should I be worried?" Joe asked.

"No, she said she was fine, just retired early, probably just exhausted from the emotions of the day." Eve said, although she had other ideas. She was keeping them to herself until Anne confirmed it.

"Okay. Good night Eve." And suddenly, as an afterthought, he stepped back and gave her a kiss on the forehead. "Thank you for raising a wonderful daughter." He then silently left the room shutting the door gently behind him.

Eve felt a warm spot where his lips had touched. He truly was a remarkable young man.

Joe undressed next to the bed with only the light of the moon peeking through the skylight. He looked down at Anne curled up so sweetly in slumber and gently slid under the covers curling up next to her with his arm over her slumbering body. She slightly roused enough to realize he was home and turned to rest her head against him. "Joe, you're finally home." Came her muffled greeting.

"Yes, now go back to sleep. Your mother said you weren't feeling well." Joe whispered.

"I'm okay." Anne sleepily reassured him. "Good night. I love …you…"Anne said as she drifted back to sleep.

Joe held her softly against his body, "I love you, too." He whispered back trailing off to sleep on the last word, exhaustion taking over.

Joe woke at 6:30 am. He sat up with a start, noticing Anne was already out of bed. He rushed to get dressed and joined her in the kitchen. "Anne, how long have you been up?" Joe asked pouring himself a cup of coffee.

"Just got up 20 minutes ago. You were sleeping so peacefully I didn't have the heart to wake you and since you got to bed so late, I thought you needed the sleep." Anne said scrambling eggs.

"It was a long evening." Joe said rubbing his forehead as he sat down at the table with his coffee.

"What do you think the defense will present today? More of the same?" Anne asked sympathetically.

"I hope not," Joe said gratefully taking the plate of eggs and toast from her. "I'm tired of hearing how great Dr. Jefferson is."

"It's too bad you can't parade around the disabled children he killed." Anne said offhandedly, taking a sip of tea, hoping it would settle her stomach better than the coffee.

"Now there's an idea," Joe said laughing. "Oh, I think I'm so tired I'm punchy." But then he suddenly stood up and went to his briefcase and jotted a couple of notes. As he came back to the table, he kissed the top of Anne's head, "You are a genius." He said grabbing the remaining slice of toast and headed to the bathroom to shower. Anne watched him go in bewilderment, wondering what she said that was so smart.

"Oh, and Anne, when I came home at 1am I found your mother on the floor in her room. I helped her back to bed. She appeared to have no injuries, but you may want to check her out today." Joe said around the corner before disappearing in their bedroom.

"Why didn't you wake me? You didn't need to deal with that!" Anne called out softly, following him into their room.

"Because I was awake and she appeared only to have a bruise on her thigh. I could handle it so I did. You haven't been feeling well." Joe said kissing her forehead.

"No temperature. That's a good thing." Joe said positively, "Perhaps you are over this bug."

Before she could correct him a wave of nausea hit her again, the herbal tea didn't work either. She made a dash for the bathroom and deposited the contents of her stomach once again, with Joe following close behind her.

"What's going on, Anne? I want you to see a doctor. Today." Joe said adamantly.

"Joe, I'm ok." Anne said quietly splashing water on her face and brushing her teeth.

"How can you be okay? You've thrown up two days in a row and your mom said you weren't feeling the best last night. Anne, I'm worried. Please, for me, see a doctor." Joe begged.

"I don't need to see a doctor, Joe," Anne said gently. "I know what's wrong, or at least what's causing this. Joe, we aren't going to have any problem starting a family. We've already started one." Anne finished, watching his face for understanding.

Joe's eyes got big and he sat on the bed, "You mean....you're pregnant!"

"I haven't gone to the doctor yet but I took a pregnancy test and it came out very positive. That's why I was up so early today," she paused, letting the enormity of the situation set in a bit. Anne took a deep breath, "I'm sorry Joe, I wish we were already married, that would be ideal. But now we know, we have no problem getting pregnant." Anne said hoping to smooth over the shock.

"Anne, I'm not upset. I'm happy. Today you've made me the happiest man on the planet." Joe said going over to Anne and embracing her tightly. "We are going to be parents!"

"Yes, perhaps we should discuss moving up the date of the wedding." Anne said hopefully.

"We can get married today if you want." Joe answered blissfully thinking about the future.

"I don't really think that's necessary, but perhaps in a month or two." Anne answered. "Maybe a small wedding in the backyard here?"

"Your wish is my command." Joe stated before he kissed her deeply. "Can we tell our families?"

"Not yet." Anne said firmly. "I want to make sure everything is okay before we make any big announcements."

"So.. all of this not feeling well is because of the pregnancy?" Joe asked, concerned again for her welfare.

"Yes, pretty much on schedule." Anne answered.

"How far along is the pregnancy?" Joe asked.

"I'm not sure. I haven't had my period since we were intimate the first time. But I've never been regular in my cycles. When I see a doctor, they can do an ultra-sound to check dates." Anne replied.

"Make that appointment," Joe said tipping her chin slightly upwards with his finger.

"With whom? I don't know any of the doctor's around here and I can't ask your mom without her figuring out why." Anne said flatly.

Joe thought for a moment. "I'll call my old pediatrician, Dr. Paul. He could give us a good recommendation on an OB/GYN. I have something else I want to ask him anyway."

Joe glanced down at his watch and realized it was getting quite late. "Unfortunately, I don't have much time to talk now, but I want to take you out to celebrate." He said embracing Anne for the last time and lightly kissing her before heading into the bathroom.

As the bathroom door closed, Anne heard the doorbell. Could Gramma Jo be here already? A godsend since the trial started, Gramma Jo enjoyed her visits with Eve. Gramma Jo's stories and wit serving as a great distraction for Eve thus allowing Anne to focus on Joe and the trial.

Gramma Jo carried in a crock pot with lunch for Eve and herself, and enough leftovers to feed an army. The aroma sent a flood of nausea over Anne, which caused her to step back and swallow a couple of times. Anne hoped she didn't arouse Gramma Jo's suspicion. Gramma Jo was getting set up in the kitchen and immediately went to work putting dishes in the dishwasher. Joe came around the corner with his shirt off towel drying his hair.

"Anne, did you want to ride with me this morning?" He asked, just as he spotted Gramma Jo. "Gramma Jo, you're here early today." He smiled giving Gramma Jo a hug, as he realized he was only half dressed and Anne was still in her pajamas and robe.

Gramma Jo didn't seem at all surprised to see them both together at this early hour in their state of undress.

"What did you ask?" Anne inquired, distracted by the nausea.

"If you wanted to ride together to the courthouse. I'm not planning on staying late tonight. I thought perhaps I could take you out to dinner afterwards. Could you stay a little later, Gramma Jo?" Joe asked.

"I don't need a babysitter" Eve said coming out of her bedroom. "You kids go out. I'll be fine."

"Mother, you're up already. Do you have any pain? Joe said you fell last night." Anne asked doing a quick visual inspection. Eve appeared to be walking without pain, using her cane and nothing was wrong with her talking.

It appeared to be more like Grand Central Station in the house this morning. "Why don't we drive separately." Anne said with a bit of irritation. She didn't feel great and all this chaos heightened her sense of nausea. "I can come home to check on things and then meet you back at the restaurant. That way if you and James want to talk about the case afterwards you can." Anne suggested, also thinking that perhaps she may want a nap before dinner.

Joe nodded his head in agreement, "That sounds good. I need to get going." Joe said heading back to the bedroom.

Eve turned to Anne, "Well, aren't you going to get dressed also?"

Anne, a bit self-conscious about going into the same bedroom to get dressed as Joe, started walking slowly down the hall. With relief Anne noted that both Gramma Jo and Eve went to the kitchen table with their coffee, already deep in conversation.

"Well, I guess the secret is out of the bag." Anne sighed.

"You mean about the baby?" Joe stated with surprise.

"No, that we are sharing the same bedroom. Gramma Jo must realize now that we've been sleeping together." Anne stated flatly.

"Anne, I think she'll know as soon as we tell everyone about the baby. Don't worry, everyone who matters will be very happy for us. I am." Joe said, taking Anne's hands in his and placing a kiss on each one before planting a kiss on her forehead and a hand on her stomach. "Now I have to go or I'll be late, and we can't have that. Are you going to be okay? If you aren't feeling up to coming to court, I understand." Joe said seriously.

"No, Joe, I want to come. I'll be fine. I'll just put some crackers in my purse." Anne said firmly.

"Okay, I'll see you there." Joe brushed his lips on hers before leaving the room. Leaving her would always be tough, but the thought of returning always put a smile on his face.

Anne sat down, the room suddenly spinning. "Wow, baby can you give your mommy a break. I have to go watch Daddy." Anne thought out loud, touching her belly with her palm. She suddenly leaned back against Joe's pillow and smelled his scent. "I love that man." Anne was still in awe at the prospect of bringing their child into this world.

Chapter 26

Joe glanced over to see Anne coming in to the courtroom and taking her familiar seat next to Carolyn. She appeared to feel better, just slightly pale. Joe was concerned, but needed to focus on the trial when he was in that room. He was still in amazement with her announcement this morning, but now when he added up all the evidence, he couldn't believe how dense he had been thinking she had the flu. It just never occurred to him that they could get pregnant so easily.

When the gavel landed firmly, Joe found his thoughts being brought back to the here and now. He glanced over at the defense table and saw Mr. Drew conversing with Dr. Jefferson, both seemed at ease with how the trial was progressing. Dr. Jefferson's wife, Delores, was again in a stunning silver suit with her hair coiffed beautifully sitting in her usual place behind him. Two of her sons sat next to her. He realized that Adam Jefferson hadn't missed a court day. He was their youngest son and attended a very prestigious college that must cost a fortune. He saw Adam glaring at someone and following his eyes, was unhappy to see the recipient was his Anne. He suddenly felt uneasy about the focus on his fiancée.

Mr. Drew called his first witness, and Joe sighed inwardly, more of the same. A colleague of Dr. Jefferson talking about how skilled he was as a doctor and his recent humanitarian of the year award. Joe scowled at the witness.

Toward the end of the morning Mr. Drew called Mr. William Pilarski to the stand. Joe's body turned stone cold. This was the man whose genes he shared. Mr. Pilarski ambled up the aisle toward the witness stand. He was a bit overweight with large hands that, when placed on the Bible and raised for the oath, showed they were stained from dirt and sweat and had callouses from years of lifting heavy machinery and feed for animals. His plaid shirt was clean and he wore his Sunday best pants. When he sat down his gaze rested on Dr. Jefferson as if he were avoiding looking at the son he had fathered, but now would not only disown, but swear to God that he would not have wanted to live.

Joe felt his parents' and Anne's eyes on him. He knew they were worried about his reaction to this testimony and he was bound and determined to make sure he didn't give Dr. Jefferson or his witness any reaction that would give them satisfaction.

The deputy was swearing in the witness. Joe focused on the witness's voice and heard him state his name, William Pilarski, for the record. Joe wondered briefly what his name would have been had he been raised a Pilarski. His stated occupation is farming. Joe already knew this because he had dealings with the Pilarskis' son and daughter, whom Joe realized now, were his biological siblings. Willard, their youngest son, had been sited for DWI twice and served 30 days in jail and Karen, who had been brought up on child endangerment charges, which were dropped due to insufficient evidence. Joe knew of a third sibling, Jeanne, who moved out of state. She had been an excellent student and was now a school teacher. Joe remembered upon learning this information, he had thought, good for her for getting away.

Mr. Drew was now getting background information from Mr. Pilarski, where they lived, how long they had lived there, and what encounters they had experienced with Dr. Jefferson.

"Mr. Pilarski, you say that Dr. Jefferson has been your family physician for over 30 years. Have you ever had cause to doubt him or the care given to your family?" Mr. Drew asked pointedly.

"No, Dr. Jefferson has always been good to us. Saved my life once or twice and my mother's." Mr. Pilarski stated with confidence.

"You are aware now of the circumstances of your first son's birth?" Mr. Drew asked.

"Yes, Dr. Jefferson told us that he was born with a defect. I believe he called it spina bifida." Mr. Pilarski said cautiously, scratching the back of his neck with his finger, not exactly knowing everything about the disability, but wanting to sound smarter.

"You had been told that the infant died at birth, but now are aware that the baby was taken by one of the nurses and adopted and raised as her own." Mr. Drew stated. It angered Joe that Mr. Drew twisted what happened to make it sound like his mother was the guilty party.

"Had you been told that the child was alive at birth, how would that have changed your life?" Mr. Drew asked.

"Well, me and the wife and kids, we work hard on the farm. Everyone has to pull their own weight. Wouldn't have had much time to devote to putting in all kinds of ramps or run to doctor's appointments and such. Dr. Jefferson told me that there are special institutions where these types of kids can go and they take care of them." Mr. Pilarski stated.

Joe, who had unknowingly been gripping his pencil forcefully, felt it snap inside his hand. Carolyn heard the noise, but couldn't see the pencil. She did see the muscle on the side of Joe's face pulsate with anger. Joe had always been very good in the courtroom, keeping a stoic demeanor, hiding frustration or anger at what was being said, even if it was a bald-faced lie. But that was before he heard the man who had sired him tell him and a court full of people that if they had been told about him, they would have institutionalized him rather than raise him.

"Let me get this straight, Mr. Pilarski. Are you okay with Dr. Jefferson's action regarding the birth of your son who had a defect?" Mr. Drew asked, this time looking at the jury and resting his gaze on each face.

"Yes sir, it was the best thing." Mr. Pilarski stated. "Dr. Jefferson delivered my other three children and everything came out fine."

"No further questions Your Honor." Mr. Drew concluded.

"Cross examination?" Judge Hanson stated looking at James and Joe.

"Yes, Your Honor." James stated. It had been decided that James would do the cross examination due to the fact that the testimony directly involved Joe. James was in a better position to put personal feelings aside this time.

"First of all, I'd like to say sorry for your loss." James stated sincerely.

"What loss?" Mr. Pilarski stated.

"Why, the loss of your son, of course." James answered.

"I didn't really feel any loss, sir. I have another son." Mr. Pilarski stated flatly.

"So, you really didn't feel a sense of loss when Dr. Jefferson told you your son was born dead?" James continued, thinking this man was cold, very cold. Joe was lucky he was taken by Carolyn. "He did come out of the delivery room and tell you the son your wife just delivered was dead, did he not?"

Mr. Pilarski squirmed a little. "Yes, I guess he did."

"You guess or you know?" James persisted.

"Yes, he was the one who told me." Mr. Pilarski stated, sweat now covering his brow. He was unaccustomed to court and certainly not use to answering questions under oath. He wiped his forehead with his forearm using the arm of his plaid shirt.

"So, Dr. Jefferson told you the son your wife had delivered was dead, but now we find out he is miraculously alive? Hallejuiah! Wouldn't you say?" James stated emphatically.

"Objection, Your Honor. Counselor is badgering the witness." Mr. Drew stated.

"Withdrawn Your Honor. I'll hold my Hallelujahs for church." James stated smiling, eliciting a small chuckle from the gallery.

"So now you find out your son was in fact alive and raised by someone else. Do you hold ill will against the nurse, Carolyn Steffan?" James asked. Joe thought this was a bold line of questioning since it could back fire, but James was on a roll.

"No, I guess not. Looks like she did a good job." Mr. Pilarski admitted begrudgingly.

"A job you and your wife would not have wanted to attempt, correct." James asked.

Mr. Pilarski looked at the floor but nodded his head.

"For the record please answer verbally." Judge Hanson directed.

"Yes, we couldn't have done for him what she did." Mr. Pilarski said ashamedly.

"You stated you are a farmer, Mr. Pilarski. In your line of work, you raise animals correct?" James asked.

"Yes sir, pigs, cows, chickens." Mr. Pilarski answered, not sure what this lawyer was getting at.

"If one of your animals gave birth to an animal with a defect what would you do?" James asked.

"Kill it." Mr. Pilarski answered quietly.

"So, you think we as human beings should be treated like animals, Mr. Pilarski?"

Mr. Pilarski looked at him with big round eyes. He had never had it put to him like that. He was dumbfounded as to how he should answer.

"If a child is born with a defect (to use the word you and the defense like to use) should the child be killed?" James asked pointedly, this time looking at the jury as Mr. Drew had.

"I don't know, when you put it like that." Mr. Pilarski stated, confused.

"What other way is there to put it?" James asked. "If a doctor puts a piece of tape over a child's mouth and puts it in a box without air holes, and puts the box in a closet, is it expected the child will live or die?" James said holding the box in the exhibit area up for emphasis.

"What defects warrant death in your mind Mr. Pilarski? A club foot? Spina bifida? Down's syndrome? Blindness? What disability should we allow or do we all as humans have to be perfect to be allowed to live, to deserve to live?" James stated, his voice getting louder with each statement.

"Objection, badgering the witness." Mr. Drew stated, but from looking at the jury he knew that James had more than swayed a few who now looked at Dr. Jefferson with stares of disdain.

"No more questions Your Honor." James stated with disgust.

"The witness is excused." Judge Hanson stated. "In looking at the clock it is now ten minutes to 12. We will recess until 1:30."

Joe reached out his hand to shake James's hand on that perfectly executed cross. "You were perfection, James." Joe said with a smile.

"You deserved nothing less." James answered seriously, placing his hand on Joe's shoulder as a sign of support and friendship.

They stood to leave when Anne suddenly got woozy and reached out to grab the banister to steady herself. Joe saw this and hurried to her side.

"Are you okay, Anne?" Joe asked with concern etched across his face.

"Just a little faint. I didn't keep any breakfast down." Anne whispered her pallor very evident.

"The room feels a little warm. Can you help me outside?" Anne said reaching for Joe's arm.

"Are you sure you can walk? I can carry you." Joe stated, worried she was going to end up on the floor at any moment.

"Here's some water." James stated, handing her a glass from the pitcher on the prosecution table.

Anne sat down to drink it and Joe looked at James who looked back knowingly at Joe. James' wife had just delivered their second child and he knowingly put two and two together. James leaned closer with a smile whispered just for Joe's ears, "Looks like we'll have three things to celebrate."

Tom poked his head around the door, "Are you two coming to lunch?"

"Be right there, Dad." Joe replied.

"Feeling any better?" Joe asked solitiously of Anne, concern etched across his forehead.

She nodded her head as she handed the glass back to James. "Thank you."

Joe put Anne's hand firmly in the crook of his arm and assisted her to what had become their routine lunch restaurant.

After the food arrived it was evident to everyone that Anne was starving. She ate voraciously. Joe leaned over and whispered to her, "Slow down honey or you may get sick. The baby can't handle all this food at once."

Anne dropped her fork on her plate and pinkened just a little. In an effort to steer the attention away from her plate, she stated, "I thought James did a great job on cross-examination this morning."

"Yes, I thought it was an excellent job." Carolyn answered, wondering what was going on with Anne. If she didn't know any better, she would swear she was pregnant.

"How are you holding up, Joe?" Carolyn asked with a furrowed brow, remembering some of the hurtful things Joe just heard.

"Okay, considering." Joe replied as he finished his last bite. "I now know how much I need to thank you. Had you not taken me, I would have been dead or in an institution." He said motioning for the check. "In all seriousness, Mom, you were spot on in your assessment that fateful day. I will never question your actions again. Thank you, from the bottom of my heart." Joe said as he squeezed Carolyn's hand.

Carolyn was a bit overcome by Joe's admission, but managed a weak smile.

As Joe paid the bill, he noticed Dr. Jefferson's wife and sons at a nearby table. Adam Jefferson was unabashedly glaring at Joe and Anne. Tom glanced in that direction to see what precipitated the scowl on Joe's face and saw Adam.

Anne and Carolyn were discussing Eve's midnight fall as they headed back to court when Tom pulled Joe aside for a quick word, relaying Anne's fearfulness of Adam. Joe's neck hairs stood up and although he didn't show outward signs of anger the muscle in his cheek again began to flex. Tom suggested that one of them walk Anne to her car after court was dismissed today. Joe nodded stating he would take care of it. Joe glared back at Adam putting him on notice.

Returning to the courthouse, Anne excused herself to the bathroom while the rest of them found their seats. Leaving the restroom, she was startled by Adam Jefferson, who was leaning against the wall causing her to nearly run into him. Jumping backwards she hit the door with her elbow allowing Adam time to grab her arm and whisper, "You and your boyfriend ruined my life. I'd watch your back."

"Get your hands off me." Anne stated angrily.

Joe saw Adam with his hand wrapped around Anne's arm and called to a deputy to follow him. As they were approaching, Adam released her arm.

"Keep your hands off of her," Joe said in a firm low voice. His eyes throwing a look of daggers at Adam as he protectively slid his arm around Anne's waist.

"Are you okay?" Joe asked.

"Yes, I'm fine now." Anne answered, grateful for Joe's presence.

"I was just helping the lady up. She almost fell." Adam lied.

"You, stay away from her. I don't want you to so much as blink in her direction." Joe stated firmly to Adam. Then turning to the deputy standing nearby, "See that he keeps his distance from her and my parents."

Joe then escorted Anne back to her seat, and whispered in her ear, "Wait for me after court. I don't want you walking to your car alone."

Anne nodded her agreement. She was a bit shook up by the whole incident and wanted very much for the day to be over.

Carolyn turned to see court deputies escort Adam back to his seat just as Anne returned. Concerned, Carolyn leaned over to ask if everything was okay. Anne nodded her head, but her shaking hands and pale face told a different story.

They didn't have long to wait until the gavel once again brought the trial into session. Mr. Drew proceeded to call Mrs. Margaret Pilarski to the stand. Joe watched with rapt attention as the mother he never knew approached the witness stand. She had dark hair like his, but hers was now interspersed with grey. She was thin and wore a spring dress that was clean, but well worn. Her face was pleasant. He could tell that she had probably been quite fetching in her younger years, but years of hard work and money worries had put lines on her face. He glanced back at Carolyn who nervously figeted with her fingers. He knew she would have strong feelings as this witness gave her testimony.

"Margaret Pilarski, is it correct to say that you gave birth to a baby boy September 15, 1969?" Mr. Drew asked.

"I was told I did. I was under anesthesia for the delivery and never saw the baby." Margaret said quietly, glancing at the prosecution table and seeing for the first time the man she brought into this world. She noticed with pride he was quite handsome. Next to him on the side of the table stood the metal crutch, the only outward sign that belied the fact that he battled physical challenges every day.

"You were told at the time that the baby was stillborn, correct?" Mr. Drew asked.

"Yes," Mrs. Pilarski stated, turning her gaze back to Mr. Drew.

"But you recently found out that baby was indeed born alive, but with a defect called spina bifida and subsequently stolen by a nurse and raised as her own." Mr. Drew stated calmly.

"Yes." Mrs. Pilarski stated while nodding her head tentatively.

"Had the child not been stolen, and instead you had been told that your child had a disabling diagnosis which would require years of physical therapy, surgeries, and special accommodations, what would you have done?" Mr. Drew asked concisely.

"I don't know." Mrs. Pilarski answered honestly. "We didn't have much money. We were young, too young perhaps to be having babies. I think we would have done whatever our doctor told us to do."

Joe knew what Mr. Drew was trying to obtain. He wanted her to say that Dr. Jefferson would have had her blessing to put him in the box, to end his life before it really began.

As a mother, Margaret's heart couldn't bring herself to mouth the words that would have given her consent for Dr. Jefferson to end her son's life. Instead she tried to excuse her husband's and her reaction, "We really weren't prepared to raise a disabled child. My husband and I had just gotten married when I found out we were pregnant. We were happy but scared."

"Mrs. Pilarski, is it or is it not true that when you were told that you had given birth to a child with spina bifida, but the child was dead, your exact words were, 'It is for the best.' I can call witnesses to verify this." Mr. Drew stated, prodding her to answer.

There was dead silence in the courtroom when Mrs. Pilarski, her head hanging down, stated softly, "It's true".

"Please say again, so the courtroom can hear." Mr. Drew stated firmly.

"It's true. Lord help me, it's true." Mrs. Pilarski stated a tear coming down her cheek that she dabbed away with a Kleenex. She looked over at Joe who met her gaze before he quickly turned away with a look of distain. When he looked away, she knew she had been dismissed, from the witness stand and from his life.

James did the cross examination but Joe could not listen. His ears were ringing with the words, 'It's true'. His nerve endings were on fire. He wanted to run screaming from the room, but unfortunately, he could never run. Listening to this testimony was like hearing a eulogy on himself, but this time it wasn't what a great life he led. No, it was that his life shouldn't have existed at all.

It didn't matter to Joe that James got Mrs. Pilarski to state that she was happy to find out that the son she thought dead, was in fact alive, a very successful lawyer, and had been raised in a loving home with parents who adored him.

When the gavel hit, Joe jumped, bringing his thoughts back to what he had his staff prepare in anticipation of this testimony. Joe asked Tom and Carolyn in a low voice if they could sit with Anne for a few minutes. He had something he had to finish and then he would be able to walk her out to her car.

Joe quickly walked out of the courtroom into the lobby. He was a man on a mission. He saw Mr. and Mrs. Pilarski and two of their children and asked them for a moment of their time. They nodded, but with quizzical looks on their faces. Joe ushered them into the side conference room. Tom and Carolyn saw this just as the three of them came out of the courtroom. Carolyn looked at Tom asking the unspoken question with her eyes. What was Joe doing with those people. Tom's eyebrows raised, but he shrugged his shoulders in answer to her question. He had no idea. They found a nearby bench to wait for Joe. Anne excused herself to the bathroom again, but this time Tom and Carolyn were in plain view of the exit.

Approximately 15 minutes went by when Joe came out of the room. He didn't offer an explanation, but gave them both a hug before leaving the building with Anne. They were left to wonder what transpired between Joe and his birth family. But from his actions when he came out of the room, it was obvious that his feelings for them hadn't changed. Carolyn and Tom knew better then to pump him for information. He would tell them in his own time.

Joe held Anne's hand as he walked her to her car. This day had been long and exhausting. Joe's thoughts went back to the testimony that had been presented when Anne prodded him back to reality.

"Hey, we're at my car." She stated, putting her hands under his suitcoat, feeling his chest muscles rise and fall. "Thank you for walking me out, but really you don't have to worry so much about me."

"Yes, I do. It's my job as your future husband." Joe said smiling as he looked around for any suspicious behavior. His smile put her at ease, but he still felt a sense of unrest. He didn't trust Adam Jefferson. Joe did see him walk out of the courthouse with his mother just as he had gone into the conference room so he was less concerned at this moment, certain he had long since gone home. At this point he just wished the case was finished.

"Are you still up for dinner tonight?" Joe asked quietly.

"Would you be terribly disappointed if we postponed?" Anne asked quietly. She was quite exhausted and just wanted to crawl in bed for a nap.

"No, not at all." Joe didn't want Anne to think that he didn't want to celebrate this morning's surprise announcement, but after the day's testimony he wasn't in much of a celebratory mood and tomorrow he would have to cross-examine Dr. Jefferson and wanted to be at the top of his game. "Would it be ok if I drove out to my parent's house before heading home? There's something I need to give them." Joe asked, knowing they must have questions after seeing him in the conference room with Pilarskis.

"That's fine Joe. Will you be home for dinner?" Anne asked.

"Don't plan on me. I'll either catch something here with James or at my parent's. Just get some rest." Joe directed kissing her forehead. "Oh and by the way, here's that phone number I got from Dr. Paul. She's one of the best OB's on staff, comes highly recommended by Dr. Paul, who, by the way, is very happy for us." Joe said as he reached inside his suit jacket and brought out a neatly folded piece of paper with the name, Dr. Janice Allen, and a phone number. Joe didn't share with Anne he had voiced concerns to Dr. Paul about passing the spina bifida gene on to their child. Dr. Paul was very reassuring, stating that the chances of that were less than 4%. Even though 4% was miniscule to

Dr. Paul, Joe wouldn't be entirely relieved until they had an ultrasound to verify this.

Anne gave him a weak smile taking the paper and putting it on the seat next to her as she climbed into her car.

Joe protectively stood watch as Anne's car drove away before turning and heading to the offices upstairs to check in with James, bringing him up to speed on Adam Jefferson's behavior to see if he had any suggestions, and discuss the impending cross-examination expected tomorrow.

CHAPTER 27

Joe rubbed his forehead as he headed his vehicle toward his parent's hobby farm. He was accustomed to being tired during normal trials, but he was pushing himself to exhaustion during this one. He didn't want to admit it, but he was actually relieved when Anne nixed the dinner out tonight. As happy as Joe was about the pregnancy and wanting to spend every moment he could with Anne, there was so much on his mind that he couldn't have done justice to a dinner out. Joe felt his stomach clench and growl as he pulled into his parent's driveway. He had forgotten to eat again.

He was glad to see a light in the front room. It was only 8 o'clock, but with the emotion packed days they had experienced, he half expected them to have gone to bed early. He was surprised to see Tom and Carolyn sitting at the table eating a late supper.

"What a nice surprise!" Carolyn exclaimed. They hadn't seen much of Joe outside of the days in the courtroom, but knew he was busy with Anne and Eve at his home. "Come join us. Did you eat yet?" she asked, but already getting up to get a plate full of hotdish and home-baked bread.

"Thanks, Mom." Joe answered, sheepishly shaking his head, "I just left the office and we didn't stop to order supper. My stomach gives you its thanks!"

"To what do we owe this unexpected visit?" Tom asked, curious as to what would bring him out here this late.

"I just missed you guys." Joe said chuckling.

Tom smiled, "Okay, good to hear," But silently wondered what Joe had to tell them.

Joe reached into his coat pocket and brought out a folded document. "You probably were wondering why I went into the conference room with the Pilarskis."

Carolyn set the plate down in front of Joe, a look of curious concern on her face.

"It's none of our business." Carolyn stated softly, looking at her own plate of half-eaten food.

"Unless you want it to be our business." Tom said looking from Carolyn back to Joe.

"Mom…Dad… you know that you are the only two parents I have. I love you and nothing will ever change that and certainly nothing we heard in court today would lead me to believe otherwise. But I wanted something in writing signed by them relinquishing any rights to me or my property. I also included a clause stating that they give up any rights to a civil suit against you for taking me thirty years ago." Joe stated seriously, flattening the document with his hand before handing it first to Carolyn who looked it over and then passed it to Tom for his perusal.

"I wanted to tell you both, but I didn't want it to be in the lobby of the court house. If it had been up to me, I would have had someone else do this as I didn't enjoy being in a room with those people, but I felt my displeased presence would be intimidating enough to get them to sign and do it quickly, and I was correct." Joe remembered Mr. Pilarski wringing his hands while sitting at the table, his grim frown staring at him. Mrs. Pilarski was a bit more emotional realizing that the son she never got to raise now wanted absolutely nothing to do with them partly due to their own testimony in support of a doctor who tried to kill him. She had tried to refuse to testify, but Mr. Drew had backed her into a corner by stating she would be subpoenaed anyway. Unfortunately, words stated many years ago came back to haunt her. She had stood up when Joe turned to leave with the document in his possession. She awkwardly reached her arms out and asked if she could hug him. He coldly stated no. He didn't hug strangers and especially those who supported the man who tried to kill him. He walked out the door and never looked back.

Joe reached over with his hands and took a hand of each of his parents, "I owe you both everything. You loved me and believed in all that I could become. There are no words…."

Carolyn started to cry and reached over to hug the son she had protected since his birth. Joe also welled up with tears, the emotions of the day spilling over. He hugged the mother who saved him, the only mother he ever wanted to know. The hurtful rejection of his birth family now forever in their past.

As Carolyn wiped her tears away, she pointed to Joe's plate, "There's more where that came from, eat up. I have a feeling that you have skipped many meals this past week."

Joe pulled his plate closer and started to devour its contents. "Mom, Anne is just like you, worrying about my not eating, so I can't actually say I've missed many meals since the trial started. Maybe that's one of the reasons I love her so much. She reminds me of you."

"It's quite evident that you love her, and she you. I'm so happy you found each other!" Carolyn said, genuine joy in her voice.

"Yes, but there's some concern about Adam Jefferson. He grabbed her arm outside the bathroom today and he's been glaring at her every chance he gets. He's made us both uneasy. I talked with James about it this evening, but he said unless Adam makes an actual threat against one of us or you two, he can't authorize a protection detail. So, I want that door locked at all times until this thing is totally over and things settle down!" Joe said protectively, emphatically pointing to the front door.

The shrill ring of the phone made them all jump, then nervously laugh. Carolyn went to answer it while Joe finished the last bites on his plate, now anxious to get back home to see how Anne was doing.

"Joe," Carolyn called from the other room, "Did Anne go straight back to your house from court?"

"Yes. Why?" Joe said getting up and moving closer to the kitchen.

"Gramma Jo's on the phone. She said she was getting concerned because neither of you were home yet and wondered if you were over here or maybe had gone out." Carolyn's eyes now darted between Tom and Joe who were both in the doorway of the kitchen.

Joe quickly turned toward the front door. Tom was close behind.

"Call James and tell him Anne's missing, Mom. Ask him to notify the Sheriff's office and tell them to cover every inch from town to my place." Joe said opening the door.

"I'm going with Joe," Tom stated adamantly.

"I'm going to head over to Joe's house. Call there with any updates," Carolyn stated as the door closed.

The sun was setting as they headed out. Tom insisted on driving as Joe knew Anne's car the best, and he was really concerned that Joe may not be in the best shape to drive. Both sets of eyes were darting from one side of the road to the other, Joe's anxiety growing by the second.

"Dad there's something I have to tell you," Joe said, his voice notably anxious. "Anne is pregnant with our baby."

Tom suddenly swerved with this news, but quickly corrected. "Well, that explains a lot of things," Tom said with a short laugh. "Don't worry Joe, we'll find her."

Tom tried to lighten the mood, but now more than ever he was as worried as Joe. Tom caught sight of a pair of tire marks going into the ditch next to the swampy marsh, from their angle it was a pretty steep drop below and couldn't be seen from the road. Tom pulled his truck to the side and put the flashers on as Joe jumped out, even before the truck stopped completely. Joe and Tom stood at the edge of the road and looked down into the swamp. Joe caught sight of the back end of Anne's Ford. The front end was midway into the swamp. It looked like Anne's car got caught between two trees which thankfully had stopped the car from submerging into the swampy waters. "JESUS," Joe said, his eyes wide with fright.

"Joe stay right here. I'm going to phone this in." Tom said heading to his truck, but thankfully a sheriff's deputy was coming down the road presumably looking for Anne as well. Tom flagged him down and told him the situation. Meanwhile Joe was heading into the swampy area. It was only up to his knees as he made his way to the car through the murky water, but quickly got up to his waist before he reached the tree that her car was lodged up against. He was able to hang onto the tree and get a footing next to the car. The car window was shattered from a branch which Joe was able to break off to reach Anne and assess her condition.

"Jesus," Joe said under his breath as he looked into the driver's window. "Anne, I'm here… Anne…Anne…" Joe yelled, each word getting louder as Anne sat unconscious in her seat, the seat belt still holding her tight against the seat. The air bag smeared with blood. Joe reached his trembling hand next to her throat feeling for a pulse. He sighed with relief.

"DAD, SHE'S ALIVE." Joe yelled up to Tom. "BUT SHE'S UNCONSCIOUS."

The Deputy ran back to his squad car to relay this information on, requesting the jaws of life and some chainsaws along with an ambulance.

"Joe, ...Joe...,"Anne moaned as she was coming to.

"Anne, sit still, don't move anything." Joe said calmly.

"Joe...It hurts.." Anne said

"What hurts?" Joe asked with dread.

"My wrist and nose, I think they're broken." Anne said quietly starting to cry. "Did we lose the baby?" Her eyes were glassy and Joe knew she was in shock.

"Honey, everything is going to be fine. We don't know about the baby. Keep thinking positive thoughts." Joe replied, anxiety welling up inside him. Where are the rescue vehicles?? Off in the distance he heard sirens. Relief flooded over him. He touched Anne's left hand, the one that wasn't broken. It felt cold and sticky from the blood. Please God let her be okay! Joe prayed over and over in his head.

"Anne, what happened?" Joe asked quietly, already picturing the accident in his mind.

"I don't know ... I remember a large vehicle, I think it was black, but the sun glared off the hood. It came from behind very fast and hit the back of my car." Anne said tears coming down her face. "I tried to speed up to get away. It went on the shoulder and hit my car on the side. I don't remember anything after that." Anne said her words getting hard to understand as she was overcome by emotion. Fresh blood starting to flow again from her nose which now looked a little like an 's' shape. Her breathing sounded labored as she fought to breathe through the blood and now loose cartilage in her nasal passage.

"Shh..shhh.. it's okay. I'm here and I'm not going to let anything happen to you." Joe said softly trying to soothe Anne. He moved a strand of blonde hair caked in dried blood out of her eyes. He noticed a gash on her forehead that had apparently clotted off thankfully.

Rescue workers were bringing a chainsaw down and crowbars.

"Sir, we need you to come down now. We'll get her out." A confident rescue worker said reaching his arm up to assist Joe down.

"Anne, they are here to get you out. I have to go up to the road now." Joe said quietly.

"Joe, no, don't leave!!! Joe…!!" Anne cried, she was overwhelmed by her senses, her sticky blood streaked hand desperately tried to claw at him, fear overcame her, "JOE, JOE.." her voice trailing into sobs.

"Anne, I'm not leaving!! I'll be with you in the ambulance. Please..They have to get you out!! Think of the baby!! Stay strong for just a few more minutes than they will need a crow bar to get us apart!! I love you." Joe leaned into the car making sure none of his weight was on the car and kissed her lovingly on the forehead. Before his resolve wavered, he made his way back into the cold, black swampy water giving the rescue workers space to work. He found his metal crutch lying next to the edge of the murky water and used it to climb back up the steep slope to the shoulder of the road.

Tom came down to help Joe gain the last few steps up. His dad was shocked to see Joe walking in the murky water without his crutch and even more shocked when he saw him climb the tree. Love does strange things.

"How is she son?" Tom asked as Joe dried off with a towel the ambulance drivers offered.

"She's alive. That's all I know for sure at this moment." Joe answered visibly shaken at the thought that he could have lost her.

"Did she say what happened? Could she remember anything?" Deputy Sheriff Jackson asked stepping closer with a small notepad and pen.

"She said a large vehicle, possibly dark in color, came speeding up behind her, but instead of passing her, he rammed her from behind. She tried to speed up to get away, but then he passed her on the right shoulder and hit her car causing it to go across the lane and over the edge." Joe relayed matter-of-factly.

"You kept saying he when you referred to the car, did she say it was a man driving the car?" the deputy probed.

"She didn't have to say. I know who did this." Joe said with distain. "It was Adam Jefferson. I know it was."

"How do you know?" the deputy asked.

"We've had a few run-ins with him since the start of his father's trial." Joe explained."

"But no eye witness account of the accident." Deputy Jackson tried to confirm.

"This was no accident." Joe heatedly replied. "Eye witnesses?? Look around deputy, this road is fairly deserted, a perfect place to stage an attack. This wasn't an accident. This was pre-meditated attempted murder."

Joe walked back to the edge of the road, catching a glimpse of them lifting Anne carefully into the rescue basket. Her neck had been braced and in the dimming light Joe saw her dress was full of blood in her pelvic region. His heart sank as he was now sure they had lost the baby. A lump grew in his throat as he fought back tears. The rescue workers carried her quickly to the edge of the swamp where other rescue workers waited to lift her to safety. Joe was at her side in a moment.

"I'm here, Anne." Joe said as her eyes darted around trying to find him. She lifted the non-injured hand trying to reach for him. He grabbed her hand and she squeezed, trying to tell him without speaking that she needed him. "Don't worry, honey I'm not going anywhere." Joe said leaning close to her ear. He saw a tear trickle down sideways from her eye. He brushed it away with his dirty thumb, smearing dirt over the wetness. He could hardly breathe from the heaviness in his chest. His whole world was crashing down around him. The paramedics carefully lifted her unto their cart and did a preliminary assessment of her injuries. It was obvious that her right wrist was broken and they attempted to immobilize it. Her nose was also broken causing her chest to retract, but the paramedics didn't feel her breathing was compromised to the point of needing intubation. They taped a large gauze pad under her nose to prevent her from swallowing the blood now coming out of her bruised nostrils. Her legs had large bruises over both thighs probably from the impact of the steering wheel. They would x-ray them in the emergency room. They lifted the blanket to see the large area of blood on her dress indicating possible internal injuries.

Joe hoarsely stated, "She's pregnant with our child." His eyes quickly turning away to fight back the tears that threatened to fall, a queasy feeling in his stomach as he was sure with this amount of blood the pregnancy would not be viable any longer.

"Don't lose faith, just because there's blood doesn't mean the pregnancy is gone." The short paramedic who had a Spanish accent stated calmly as he placed his hand on Joe's shoulder reassuringly.

Anne heard those words and began to cling to hope once more. The other paramedic, a tall, thin man with glasses, heard her whisper, "Please God, let our baby be alive."

Joe also heard her words and squeezed her hand to let her know he heard, his throat too choked up to speak words.

"Okay, let's get her loaded." The tall paramedic stated.

It occurred to Joe at that moment that they would be headed to Memorial County Hospital where Dr. Jefferson was on staff. Joe stated loudly, "We are going to Prairie View Hospital not Memorial County."

The paramedics looked at each other, "But Memorial County is three miles closer." The shorter paramedic explained, protocol would have them going to the closest hospital.

"The guy who did this has a father on staff at Memorial County. We are NOT going there." Joe said adamantly.

The paramedics exchanged glances and nodded their agreement.

"Anne, I'm going to tell my dad where to meet us. I'll be right back." Joe said next to her ear. Then to the paramedics, "I'm riding with her." Joe stated firmly.

Tom was a few feet away watching as they extricated Anne's vehicle from the swamp.

"Dad, they are loading Anne now. I'm having her taken to Prairie View Hospital. I'm riding in the ambulance. Please call Mom at my house and tell her and Eve to meet us there." Joe stated hurriedly, trying to get back to Anne.

"Sure thing." Tom said giving Joe an impromptu hug. "Tell her we love her." Tom whispered. Joe nodded, unable to get words out to convey his feelings.

CHAPTER 28

The ambulance bay doors opened up and a team of doctors and nurses took over. Anne's eyes stayed on Joe and her hand gripped his like a vice. They shouted questions over the noise in the garage as doctors barked orders that only the nurses understood.

Joe answered the questions as best he could. The paramedics had an IV going in her left arm. He didn't know about any medications, but hadn't seen her take any. She confirmed this with a barely audible, "No." Joe listed his place as her address. She had been residing there off and on for several weeks and her place was all but sold. Her purse had been recovered from the vehicle and they retrieved her insurance information from the card inside. They also brought along the now dirty and half shredded piece of paper with Dr. Janice Allen's name on it. The paramedics had called that ahead and Dr. Allen met them in ER as they brought her into the trauma bay. The nurses tried to get Joe to let go of her hand, but Anne's grip was so tight Joe refused, knowing at that moment she needed him.

Anne's clothes were removed and a gown placed over her naked body. Joe saw the bruises covering her torso and thighs and ached to hold her close to keep the outside world from hurting her further.

Dr. Allen ordered an ultrasound machine to be brought into the bay. She frowned when she saw the blood in the pelvic region. They needed to know if the baby was still viable before proceeding to x-ray for assessing other injuries. Dr. Allen ordered everyone out as she prepared Anne and Joe. "It is possible that the fetus is still viable, but I want to prepare you for the possibility that it may not be."

Dr. Allen inserted the transvaginal ultrasound into Anne's vaginal canal. Joe looked at Anne's abdomen trying to give his baby strength as well. Suddenly the monitor came alive, and there it was, a small white blip and they could see the blip pulsate before them. Joe looked at Dr. Allen's face and saw a smile indicating positive results. "You see the pulsation on the monitor. That's your baby's heartbeat. It appears strong."

Anne and Joe burst out with wide grins and tears of happiness as Joe reached over to touch Anne's face with his other hand and kissed her gently on her dry lips. Anne started to cry, but this time with tears of happiness.

Dr. Allen smiled noting how happy this couple was to be pregnant. Dr. Paul saw a very concerned, disheveled Joe come into the emergency room holding the hand of someone on the stretcher. Dr. Paul waited until he overheard good news before joining them. "Did I hear I will soon have another patient?" Dr. Paul asked smiling.

"Yes…Yes you will!" Joe answered with relief, the lump in his throat finally getting a bit smaller.

"Looks to be about 9 or 10 weeks," Dr. Allen noted.

"But, all the blood, what was that from?" Joe asked quietly.

"Could have been a subchorionic hemorrhage precipitated by the blunt force of the steering wheel. Thankfully the airbag deployed. They will check her out for other possible internal injuries and from the looks of all the bruises she will be sore for quite a while. The wrist and possibly her nose will need surgery and I want her on bedrest for a few days to make sure there isn't continued bleeding. You are a very lucky young woman." Dr. Allen said smiling.

"Thank you, Doctor." Anne and Joe said in unison and then smiled.

Anne released Joe's hand and reached up to touch his face, "Our baby's alive." She said trying to comprehend this wonderful news. "Everything's going to be okay now." She said trying to reassure Joe, believing finally that it truly would be okay. "Joe, go tell your parents and my mom. I'll be fine now."

"Okay, but say the word and I'm right back by your side." Joe said kissing her forehead before heading to the waiting room.

Eve was in a wheel chair sitting next to Carolyn, and Tom was seated next to her holding her hand, their grim faces watching the door for answers. All eyes were on Joe as he pushed through the doors with a smile on his face putting them at ease. "Anne's doing okay. They are surveying the rest of her injuries, but her vitals are good. She will need surgery for a broken wrist and nose. She has some very nasty bruises but is otherwise doing well."

"What about the baby?" Eve asked.

Joe was surprised that Eve knew, but answered, "Thankfully the baby appears to be fine, a good strong heartbeat." Then added, "You knew?"

Carolyn's face registered vague surprise as she hadn't been told about the baby but not shock as she had suspected something from the symptoms Anne had been experiencing.

"No, I suspected." Eve said with a smile. "Congratulations."

"Oh, my goodness," Carolyn said standing up and hugging Joe as she realized that she was going to be a grandmother. "Why didn't you tell me??" She admonished him.

"Anne wanted to see the doctor first, but the doctor met us in the ER!" Joe explained. "She wasn't sure how far along she was. Dr. Allen just did an ultrasound and estimates the pregnancy is about 9 or 10 weeks along."

Joe sat down, suddenly feeling exhausted from the ordeal. "There was a lot of bleeding from the accident and we were really afraid we had lost the baby." Joe said softly, finally voicing the fears he and Anne had experienced for the last several hours.

Joe looked up to see one of the ER doctors coming toward them. He stood up quickly, "I'm Dr. Peterson. Anne asked me to come out and update everyone. You are Joe, the fiancé, correct?" Dr. Peterson asked extending his hand. Joe nodded shaking his hand and proceeded to introduce everyone else.

"How is my daughter?" Eve asked impatiently, wanting to do away with the social pleasantries.

"She's going to be fine, Mrs. Stockwell. She will need surgery on her right wrist and nose which we will do in the morning. She also has a bruised liver which we are going to keep an eye on in case there is a laceration hiding. Dr. Allen updated Joe and Anne on the status of the pregnancy. She will need to take it easy for the next several weeks or so. She'll have some soft tissue damage which takes time to heal. There's a cut on her head which we've stitched but she'll need to be watched for a concussion. All in all, could have been much worse. From the pictures of the accident and what the paramedics told us, she's very lucky."

"Can I go back in to be with her?" Joe asked.

"They are going to be moving her to ICU shortly." Dr. Peterson stated, then when seeing Joe's alarming look added, "Just a precaution for overnight due to the bruised liver and subchorianic hemorrhage. You can join her there. It's on the 2nd floor."

"Joe, perhaps you would like to change first." Carolyn said lifting the small bag in the corner. "Dad told me you went into the swamp and climbed a tree in your suit!" She said sounding astonished. "I grabbed some clothes from your room thinking you may need to change. From the looks of your clothes, I was right." Carolyn said, tiredness creeping into her voice.

"Thanks Mom," Joe said, gratefully accepting the bag. She had also included some toiletries for both him and Anne.

"Could I see her before leaving?" Eve asked. She looked exhausted, but Joe knew she would sleep better after seeing Anne.

"Sure," Joe answered. "Why don't we all go up and you can say good night. I'm staying here tonight." Tom and Carolyn nodded knowing there would be no dissuading him from his decision. Although they knew he would probably not sleep much, if at all.

Joe changed into his sweats in the bathroom. The entourage then proceeded quietly up the elevator heading for the ICU. The sign on the door stated visitors were to be kept to two per patient. Tom and Carolyn said they would wait in the waiting room while Joe brought Eve to the bedside of her daughter.

Joe pushed the wheelchair next to Anne's bed and heard an audible gasp from the normally quite stoic Eve. She quickly recovered her composure so as not to alarm Anne, but her hand trembled as she reached for Anne's laying on top of the white sheet. Anne's head turned toward her mother, her neck now free of the collar they had placed on her before taking her out of the car. Purple bruises were evident over most of her face due to the broken nose.

"Mom, you should be in bed." Anne said, always the caregiver, noting her mother's pallor and weak hand grip.

"Well, I had to see that you were all right before I let them take me home." Eve said her lower lip trembling slightly at seeing her only child with bandages on her head and wrist and her bottom lip cracked and bruised. A hematoma was growing on her forehead and Eve knew from experience that tomorrow she would look worse.

"I'll be all right." Anne said, trying to reassure her mother with a weak smile.

"Congratulations on the baby," Eve whispered softly, tears welling up in her eyes. "You will both be great parents."

"Thanks Mom," Anne said a tear gently sliding down the side of Anne's face. Joe reached out to blot it with his now clean thumb. Eve noted the expression on each of their faces. They only had eyes for each other.

"Joe, you can take me back out to the waiting room and let Tom and Carolyn say their goodnights." Eve reached out to kiss Anne's hand. "I love you my darling." She said, before Joe wheeled her out. Anne saw Joe touch Eve softly on her shoulder trying to comfort her as they left.

Tom and Carolyn came in to say a quick good night and congratulations on the baby. They could see that Anne was exhausted and knew Eve was reaching the end of her body's tolerance as well. It was decided that Carolyn would stay the night at Joe's with Eve since Joe would be at the hospital and Tom would pick them up in the morning.

"Thank you for everything, Mom." Joe said hugging Carolyn tightly before they left.

"Of course, honey. We will always be here for you and Anne," Carolyn said and as an afterthought, "and of course, my grandbaby!"

Joe chuckled. He knew his parents would be loving, doting grandparents from the moment they heard.

"Dad, thanks for coming with me to find Anne. Appreciate it." Joe said hugging his dad, feeling a bit overcome with emotion as he thought back to the moment he saw the car caught in the trees of the swampy marshland.

"Joe, it's going to be all right." Tom said softly for Joe's ears alone.

After his parents left, Joe sat next to Anne, not needing to talk, just needing to watch her breathe. The soft rise and fall of her chest reassured him that everything was okay.

"Joe, you need to get some sleep." Anne said raising her hand to cup his face as he drew closer to hear her. "You have court tomorrow."

"No, he doesn't." said a voice near the door. James stepped closer in the light. "I'll take care of that." James said firmly. "With all that's happened tonight, I would guarantee a continuance at least until Monday."

"Thanks James." Joe hadn't even thought about leaving Anne's side let alone about being in court in the morning. It was already midnight and Joe's body was aching from the physicality of the day and also the emotional roller coaster.

"No problem. Anne, get better. Joe, can we talk out here for a moment so we don't disturb Anne." James asked, clearly having some things on his mind.

Joe followed James into the waiting room outside the ICU unit and took the coffee James poured from the complimentary pot that was kept hot 24 hours a day for the unit that never slept.

"I was notified of the accident four hours ago. I've been going over what Anne said happened and comparing it to the damage on the car. It correlates. This was no accident." James concluded, verifying what Joe had already pieced together.

Joe nodded, his anger under control at the moment, no need to spout off at James. He already understood the severity of the case.

James went on to elaborate, "Adam Jefferson is our main suspect, really our only suspect at this time. There's a catch. His mother is covering for him. We sent out investigators immediately to question him and his mother swears he was at home the entire time. Of course, I don't believe her, but without an eye witness I can't charge him. We've gotten warrants for each of the vehicles registered to immediate family members of the Jefferson's, but have yet to find the black vehicle that matches the paint found on Anne's car."

"We can't let that son of a bitch walk, not now. He almost killed my Anne and my baby." Joe said vehemently.

"No, we won't. This is the top priority of the DA's office now. He went after one of our own. I feel partly to blame. You brought your concerns to me and I didn't act on them. Who would have known the bastard would be so stupid. But that's all going to change. From now on there's going to be protection for you, Anne, and your parents, 24 hours a day, until we get that lunatic locked up." James said shaking his head, "That bastard's going to pay."

"Thanks James," Joe said standing up. He was itching to get back to Anne's bedside.

"No problem. Keep me up to date on Anne's condition." James said knowing Joe was anxious to get back to Anne. "And Joe, I'm glad to hear the baby's okay."

"Thanks, me too!" Joe smiled as he headed back to where his world lay sleeping.

Around 2am the nurse came in to check on Anne noting Joe sleeping with his head on the bed, his hand resting protectively on Anne's. Anne woke up as the nurse was doing her neuro exam. Joe started to stir.

"Honey, you need to find a bed. You look exhausted," Anne said to Joe as he rubbed his blurry eyes with the heel of his hand.

"I'm fine." He answered with a yawn. "You just worry about getting better." He said stretching. As he stood up his leg locked up and he grabbed for his crutch. He proceeded to walk around the nurses station trying to get his leg muscles and nerves to work together. He heard the whirr of the respirators and alarms on the IV pumps and the alerts on the telemetry machines as they pierced the air. It was a wonder anyone could sleep here. He bent his knees and tried to stretch muscles that had never been pushed to such extremes before tonight. Perhaps the tree climbing was a little much for his legs, but he would do it again tomorrow if that's what it took to get to Anne.

Entering her glass room he saw the nurse had replaced the normal chair with a chair that folded out into a recliner and even put a pillow and blanket there for him. He smiled his thanks at the nurse, as she gave him a wink.

"Can't have you getting sick on us. Now get some rest. She's doing fine." Nurse Laura stated, leaving the room and shutting the glass sliding door.

Leaning over Anne's bed, he saw she was back sleeping peacefully. He gently applied Vaseline to her cracked and bruised lips and brushed her hair to the side.

Joe gratefully took off his shoes and braces, which, due to their dampness from the swamp, were causing abrasions on his calves. The chair, although uncomfortable to some, felt like heaven to Joe as he closed his eyes in exhaustion.

Joe woke up with a start. The overhead light was on and they were prepping Anne for surgery.

"Good morning sunshine," Nurse Laura said with a smile.

"Good morning. Is everything okay?" Joe asked with concern.

"Yes, she had a good night. We are just getting her ready for surgery on that wrist." Nurse Laura replied.

"Hey, guys, I'm right here." Anne said, annoyed that they were talking around her.

"Sorry, Anne." Joe said standing next to her bed, reflexively taking her hand in his. "How are you feeling this morning?"

"Sore, like perhaps I was run off the road and landed in some trees." She answered glibly.

"Any more bleeding?" he asked anxiously, looking from nurse to Anne. They both knew he was talking about the baby.

"So far so good," Anne said squeezing his hand.

"Dr. Allen will be up shortly to do rounds and she's requested we have the ultra sound machine here." Nurse Laura answered.

"Did I hear my name?" Dr. Allen said smiling as she joined them in the glass enclosure. She looked stunning in a red dress with a long white lab coat with her name embroidered on it.

Joe and Anne smiled as Dr. Allen rolled the ultra sound machine next to the bed and proceeded to access Anne's abdomen.

"How did you sleep?" Dr. Allen asked spreading the sticky gel once again all over Anne's stomach noting the bruising that was apparent now from the trauma she had experienced.

"Off and on." Anne answered. "Having some pain from the wrist, but tried to use pain medication sparingly."

"Good girl." Dr. Allen said. "Although please take it if you need to. I'm sure after surgery you'll need some for a couple of days."

Just as Dr. Allen finished talking, the fast beating swoosh, swoosh, could be heard and Dr. Allen found the little white blob on the monitor. "Just as I expected. All is well this morning. We'll keep a close eye on you for the next 48 hours. If all goes well, you could leave some time over the weekend I'd imagine. I'll have you follow up with me in the clinic next week and we'll get prenatal vitamins going after surgery. If it's convenient we'll get you on the schedule next week for your prenatal workup."

Joe and Anne both nodded and were extremely thrilled with the news that the pregnancy was going to be okay. As soon as Dr. Allen left, Dr. Peterson and his associate, Dr. Roma, the Orthopedic specialist entered in scrub attire. They reviewed the proposed procedure and asked if they had any questions. Nurses followed administering medications and proceeded to take Anne down for surgery. As they prepared to wheel Anne out of the room, Joe leaned over to give Anne a quick kiss. His eyes showing her the full measure of his devotion. The stretcher moved down the corridor carrying his whole world. Tom and Carolyn came off the elevator pushing Eve in the wheelchair just in time to give Anne a quick greeting and kiss before they took her down for surgery.

Joe gathered their belongings as he was told she would go to recovery and then to a regular room after surgery. She would be in the pre-op area for at least an hour, then surgery and post op, so Carolyn suggested they go to the cafeteria to grab some breakfast.

The day was filled with waiting, which was harder than running a marathon. Carolyn had called Joe's sisters and both were anxiously awaiting word on her condition. Jessica would swing by and pick up Gramma Jo and be at the hospital by late afternoon to visit. Cassie and Jacob would come tomorrow. James stopped by shortly after the surgery was completed. No new word on Adam Jefferson or the investigation.

The exhaustion on Eve's features was quite evident, but she refused to rest. Her only concern today was making sure Anne was okay. Eve had been kept in the dark about the exact cause of the accident until James's visit when a question came up about how the trial was proceeding. James replied honestly that due to the questionable circumstance of Anne's accident possibly involving a family member of Dr. Jefferson the Judge offered a continuance until Tuesday, a day longer than expected.

"What do you mean, involving a family member of Dr. Jefferson?" Eve asked.

"Well, we suspect one of his sons ran Anne off the road. The investigation verified that from the damage to Anne's vehicle this wasn't an accident. This was something that someone purposefully did to her." James clarified.

Eve hung her head. Joe knew she was wondering if this trial was worth the cost. Joe was starting to wonder the same thing. If Anne had died, he knew the answer would be no. Joe went to Eve and sat down next to her.

"Eve, I'm sorry. I wish I could go back in time and change things but I can't. At least Anne is alive and will fully recover, and we will prosecute to the fullest extent of the law the individual who did this." Joe said locking eyes with James so he knew that Joe would never rest until this was finished.

"He's right. The entire department is following up on leads. We think we know the individual. We just have to find the car, the proverbial, 'smoking gun' so to speak." James stated matter-of-factly.

Anne was wheeled into the room, interrupting the conversation. Everyone moved to the hallway except Joe. He took her hand and leaned over to kiss her forehead. Her eyes fluttered open with the touch of his lips on her skin.

"Good afternoon sleeping beauty." Joe said softly.

"Hello, my prince," she replied jokingly, groggy from the anesthesia.

"Did everything go as planned?" Joe anxiously asked the nurses who brought her back.

"Yes, she did great." A hospital worker named Naomi dressed in scrubs from the OR answered. Two nurses walked in and asked Joe to step out for just a moment so they could get her into bed and give report.

Joe stepped reluctantly into the hallway. Jessica and Gramma Jo walked quickly towards the group with a big bouquet of flowers for Anne. Jessica hugged Joe, her brow furrowed with concern for Anne.

"She just got back from surgery," Joe informed them. "Everything appears to have gone fine."

"Thank God," Gramma Jo interjected relief flooding over her features.

Dr. Roma, chief of orthopedics, and Dr. Kemple, ear, nose, and throat specialist, came behind them and confirmed Joe's assessment. "Everything does appear to be fine. Her wrist will have some healing to do. No writing for a few weeks. We've put a pin in place to stabilize it allowing it to heal." Dr. Roma updated.

"The rhinoplasty will probably cause some more bruising, although the accident already caused plenty. Better to get things set in place now so it can heal correctly. The bandage below her nose will need to be changed when it's saturated, but once the bleeding resolves, can be taken off. The baby tolerated the procedure fine." Dr. Kemple interjected, not realizing that not everyone knew that they were engaged, let alone expecting a baby.

"A baby," Jessica said loudly, shocked but overjoyed for Joe and Anne.

"Yes, a baby," Joe said smiling, "and by the way, we're engaged."

Jessica, thrilled, gave Joe a big hug and Gramma Jo grinned from ear to ear.

When the nurses were through settling her in and giving report the entourage entered her room. Thankfully Anne had a private room, requested by Joe and the police department, easier to identify visitors and provide security protection.

Eve was happy simply to sit and hold Anne's hand and now that the surgery was over was flooded with relief.

A sheriff's deputy entered the room alerting them he was on duty. Jessica and Gramma Jo were confused until Joe explained to them the circumstances of the accident and the need for police protection until they arrest the person who did this.

Anne dozed intermittently. Joe and Eve looked notably exhausted so Jessica offered to drive them home. Carolyn offered to sit with Anne while Joe went home to shower, shave, and nap. Jessica offered to stay with Eve for the night so Joe could stay with Anne. Joe was grateful for his family's support and followed Jessica back to his house where they were met with yet another sheriff's deputy. The presence of the deputies was both reassuring, and unsettling. Their peaceful existence shattered by the possibility of lurking danger.

Joe returned to the hospital three hours later, clean clothes, a shave, and an hour nap had him feeling at the top of his game. He brought some testimony to review while Anne was sleeping, but found himself restless and pacing the floor. He wanted this trial over. Joe found himself staring out the hospital window now covered with rain drops wondering if this time, justice was worth the cost. His mind drifting back to the time spent with Anne, her laughter at dinner when he made a joke, their first real kiss in his entry-way with the picnic basket, the touch of her tongue against his, sitting in the solarium surrounded by nature, the stars clearly visible overhead, enjoying the crackling of the fireplace. She's made him come alive as a man since she walked into his life....

Anne was stirring in the hospital bed, "Joe," came her soft voice, tinged with discomfort.

"I'm here Anne," Joe replied coming quickly to sit next to her on the bed, "What do you need?" His heart ached seeing her casted right arm propped on the pillow, her fingers swollen and bruised. Her left hand was gripping the bed covers tightly in a fist, knuckles turning white. He knew she was fighting the pain, "Honey, you need a pain pill."

"No, I'm trying not to for our baby's health." Anne replied gritting her teeth.

"It's not good for you to be in pain either. I'm willing to take the chance – take the pill." Joe stated firmly, unable to bear watching this.

"Joe, lay next to me. Just feeling you close may help." Anne begged.

"I don't want to hurt you," he said dubiously.

"You won't." Anne said with confidence.

Joe climbed carefully next to her putting his arm under her head, feeling her nestle her head under his chin. He softly stroked her left arm with his finger-tips in a soothing rhythm. It wasn't long before her fingers relaxed and her breathing took on a rhythmic pattern telling him she had fallen asleep. He smiled feeling gratified that his touch could soothe her and soon his breathing joined her in the comforting blanket of slumber.

It was dark when they woke, first Joe, then Anne. He felt her body stirring as she attempted to turn towards him in the bed. A moan escaped her lips.

"Anne, can I help?" Joe quietly asked.

"Joe, I want to turn. I want to see you." Anne said in the darkness.

"Anne, I'm right here," He helped adjust the pillow under her arm so she could face him. He felt her swollen finger tips against his cheek.

"Joe, I want to be home, in our bed." Anne said softly with emotion. Joe felt a spot of wetness on the pillow and knew a tear had slipped from her eye.

"I'll bring you home tomorrow." Joe promised, his voice choking with emotion. His arms enveloped her and their child protectively.

It had taken some convincing, but with the help of Carolyn and Jessica, Joe was able to convince the doctors that Anne would be extremely well cared for at home. As the car approached the house, Jessica was already bringing the wheelchair out to the car. Joe carefully extricated Anne from the front seat. The leg bruises made it extremely painful for Anne to move but Joe was very patient. He meticulously placed her arm on a pillow and secured her sling before Jessica started to bring her inside, leaving Joe and Carolyn to get the items and menagerie of flowers and potted plants that had arrived during Anne's stay, many from Joe's co-workers.

Joe found Anne being carefully tucked into their bed with freshly laundered bedding and several pillows surrounding her. Carolyn and Jessica left the room with smiles after they both gave Joe a hug.

Approaching Anne's side of the bed Joe gingerly sat on the edge, taking her hand and leaning down to give her the first real kiss since before the accident. They both savored the connection, igniting a need in both that they knew would have to be denied for the time being.

"Looks like there won't be room for both of us in this bed." Joe joked, indicating the piles of pillows surrounding her.

"The pillows can be replaced." Anne said with veiled heat as she threw one to the floor, "You can't," she said jokingly, pulling him towards her with her non-injured hand, placing a light kiss on his lips.

Joe felt a stirring he knew he must keep in check. Clearing his throat, he announced, "Sleep is the next order of business. I promised the doctors that you would get excellent care. I intend to keep that promise…." He said, planting a quick kiss on Anne's forehead. Then looking into her blue eyes and placing a hand gently on her abdomen, adding one word, "forever!"

CHAPTER 29

Joe felt surprisingly energized at the prosecution table waiting for James's arrival. The last few days had flown by taking care of Anne. He could see that Eve's health had started to deteriorate, but she was trying to do for herself so he could concentrate on Anne's needs. Joe was surprised when Cassie showed up on Monday evening saying she had taken a week's vacation to help take care of Anne and Eve so Joe could concentrate on the trial. Anne was surprised and moved by his family's sacrifice for her and her mother's well-being. Cassie had brushed it off saying, 'This is what families do.' Although not as surprised, Joe, too, was touched by the care and attention his family showered on them.

Joe looked back to the courtroom gallery to see his mom and dad enter the courtroom and take their normal seats. The seat next to his mother would remain empty as Anne was in no shape to sit through hours of testimony. Today was the day the defense was expected to put Dr. Jefferson on the witness stand. Carolyn wouldn't miss it for anything. Dr. Jefferson entered from a side door with Mr. Drew. They must have been conferring in the defense side room. Mrs. Jefferson came breezing into the courtroom with three of her kids. Adam was the last to enter. He walked with the posture of someone who thought he was getting away with something. Joe had seen that same posture with several criminals, until they found out they weren't as smart as they thought. He immediately locked eyes with Joe and gave him a snide smile.

James came in with his overfilled briefcase at his side. He shook Joe's hand and touched his shoulder in support.

"Joe, are you ready for this?" James asked, more out of consideration for what Joe had been through then actual concern for his preparedness.

"I was ready for this the day we started this trial." Joe said calmly but with a glint in his eye that told James that he was ready to put Dr. Jefferson away.

"Let's do it," James said nodding his approval.

The deputy called the court to stand and Judge Hanson took his customary seat hitting the gavel calling court to order.

"Is everyone ready to proceed?" Judge Hanson asked the prosecution and defense. Both acknowledged they were prepared.

"Then proceed with the defense calling its next witness." Judge Hanson directed.

"The defense calls, Dr. Clayton Jefferson," Mr. Drew stated buttoning his suit coat.

Dr. Jefferson took the oath and proceeded to the witness box.

"Please state your name for the record," Mr. Drew directed.

"Dr. Clayton Jefferson," he acknowledged.

"Dr. Jefferson, how long have you been a practicing physician at Memorial County Hospital?" Mr. Drew asked.

"I've been there since 1962, 36 years total, 23 years as the Medical Director." Dr. Jefferson said smugly.

"In those years, how many babies do you think you've delivered?" Mr. Drew asked.

"I don't know an exact number. I would imagine the number to be in the hundreds though." Dr. Jefferson answered.

"In your tenure at Memorial County Hospital did you ever deliberately kill a baby?" Mr. Drew asked directly. The question startled many people in the gallery as well as the jury.

"As is with every doctor we do lose patients and there were, sadly, several babies during that time that did not make it. But it was not by any deliberate action I took." Dr. Jefferson answered evasively.

"Did you kill babies with disabilities?" Mr. Drew continued.

"I did not. I did have conversations with my pregnant patients and their spouses regarding their babies. I asked them if their baby were to be born with a debilitating disability, which would not allow them to grow up as a normal functioning member of society, would they want me to perform heroic measures to save it. Most of those babies, if saved, would end up in institutions or costing their parents money they didn't have to provide for them for the rest of their lives." Dr. Jefferson stated firmly. "Therefore, if a baby were born with that kind of disability, we did the humane thing and put it in a box and allowed it to die of natural causes." Dr. Jefferson stated without emotion or remorse.

"The parents agreed ahead of time to this procedure?" Mr. Drew asked.

"Yes, they didn't know exactly the procedure, but they agreed to the outcome." Dr. Jefferson stated adamantly.

"No more questions." Mr. Drew stated sitting down.

"Cross examination," Judge Hanson directed.

Joe stood up and approached the witness stand using his metal crutch, its metallic sound ringing out with each step. Dr. Jefferson leaned back in his chair, his face taking on a pale undertone. He appeared surprised that Joe would be cross-examining him and not James.

"Dr. Jefferson, you spoke in generalities a moment ago, 'delivered hundreds of babies', 'children with disabilities,' killed 'babies' not baby. I'm not interested in your generalities although putting babies in boxes and waiting for them to die is not how I would define humane treatment. I am going to speak in specifics. You are charged with the murder of one baby in particular and the attempted murder of another. The baby murdered was Phillip Steffan. You stated in your testimony that you had the consent of parents when you allowed a child to die. Did you have that written or implied consent from Mr. and Mrs. Steffan?" Joe asked pointedly.

Dr. Jefferson shifted uncomfortably in his seat, "She hadn't been my patient prior to delivery. She was seeing Dr. Erickson for her prenatal visits. But that child was stillborn to my recollection." Dr. Jefferson stated.

"We have the testimony of a nurse assisting with the delivery that you put that baby in a box and then placed the box in the equipment room. She found the baby in the box in the equipment room with a bloody syringe next to the box. Are you stating this is inaccurate?" Joe asked very specifically. If he was going to call Melinda as a rebuttal witness, he needed Dr. Jefferson to go on record as stating Eve was lying.

"Yes. I don't know what that nurse was talking about. It is her word against mine. She is a bitter woman who is hoping for some sort of revenge when I ended our affair and chose my family over her." Dr. Jefferson stated smugly.

"Tell you what, we'll get back to that in a moment." Joe stated professionally. "The attempted murder charge is regarding a different baby."

"Yes, but you heard the parents of that child. They agreed that if that baby was disabled, they would rather it not survive, perhaps even relieved when told it hadn't survived." Dr. Jefferson stated hoping to draw Joe off his game. Joe stared back at him emotionless causing Dr. Jefferson to squirm. Dr. Jefferson was now a bit worried as he knew that baby was standing in front of him, a more then capable adversary, and he was out for blood, his blood.

"What did you say constituted your criteria for killing a baby?" Joe asked pointedly.

"Objection Your Honor to the word killing. My client stated he did not kill a baby. He allowed it to die of natural causes." Mr. Drew stated loudly, knowing the word killing constituted an active participation.

"I'll rephrase Your Honor." Joe stated conciliatorily. "What criteria did you use to decide which babies did not have the right to live?" Joe asked seriously. He rephrased his question, but it still carried a heavy negative connotation, but there was nothing Mr. Drew could object to.

There was a pregnant pause.

"I can remind you if you'd like," Joe stated, and then proceeded without waiting for his consent, "I believe it was 'debilitating disability which would not allow them to grow up as a normal functioning member of society' was it not? I can have the court reporter read it back if you like." Joe offered.

"No, that won't be necessary." Dr. Jefferson stated. "Yes, those were my words."

"So, again, I ask you, how did you decide, in the moments after a child's birth what constituted 'debilitating disability'?" Joe prodded, knowing Dr. Jefferson was trying to dig himself out of a hole. His attorney had been foolish enough to put this man on the witness stand, but he couldn't protect him from this cross-examination. Little beads of sweat were forming on Dr. Jefferson's forehead. He took out a handkerchief to wipe them off.

"You seem to be having a difficult time defining this, but from what we've been told you made pretty quick decisions when a baby was born. It seemed to only take moments from the testimony we heard from two nurses." Joe continued. "Did you think a child with say, downs syndrome, a cleft palate, or spina bifida should be put in the box?"

Jefferson's eyes darted from his defense attorney to his wife.

"This is a simple question Dr. Jefferson." Joe prodded.

"Yes, yes I did. Allowing the child to die rather than sending it off to an institution to live out its days was much more humane." Dr. Jefferson stated proudly. He was tired of dodging these questions.

"Why did you think they had to go to an institution at all?" Joe asked curiously. "Why couldn't they just have gone home with their parents and grow up as a member of their family?"

"You don't understand. It was a different era. Parents didn't have the money to pay for specialists. There weren't programs for such children." Dr. Jefferson stated trying to make the jury understand that he wasn't a bad man.

"Getting back to your criteria for using the box. You do realize I am that baby that you attempted to murder. Your intention was for me to die in that box, asphyxiated. Gasping out my last breaths alone, in a closet." Joe stated, briefly feeling a lump in his throat. Joe locked eyes with each juror's face. He could see the picture he painted had affected each of them. Turning back to Dr. Jefferson, Joe continued with measured tones, "You deemed me to have a debilitating disability which would prevent me from being a productive member of society, did you not?"

Dr. Jefferson stared at Joe. What was he to say?

"Did you not?" Joe asked this time louder and more forceful.

"I guess...at the time..." Dr. Jefferson stuttered an answer.

"At the time?... You were putting a baby in a box to die ... permanently... not ...at the time.... Look at me. The child you deemed not fit to live. I have a job. I'm well educated. I pay taxes. I'm engaged to be married. Am I not fit to live?" Joe asked loudly.

Mr. Drew stood up and loudly objected, "Your Honor, badgering the witness."

Judge Hanson was intently watching this interaction, and without taking his eyes off Joe and Dr. Jefferson, he stated, "Overruled. The witness will answer the question."

Seeing that the judge was not going to end this exchange, Dr. Jefferson finally threw up his arms, "Obviously I made a mistake in your case."

"In my case?" Joe asked cocking his head to the side. "How did you know that any one of the other children you chose to kill would not have led the same life if given a chance? You took that away from them, from their family, from society. You played god, doctor," Joe placed his hand on the wooden banister separating the jury from the rest of the court room, "and your medical license does not give you that right."

Joe turned and walked calmly back to the prosecution table.

"No more questions at this time, your honor but we request the right to recall the witness."

"The witness is excused." Judge Hanson stated.

Mr. Drew stood up. "The defense has no more witnesses your honor."

"The prosecution requests to call a rebuttal witness, Your Honor." Joe stated.

"Very well, proceed." Judge Hanson stated.

"The prosecution calls, Melinda Schultz, RN to the stand."

Melinda came to the front of the courtroom. She had purchased a nice blue dress and had her hair tied back away from her face. After she took the oath and sat down in the witness stand, she fidgeted slightly with her glasses. Her body language indicated she was quite uncomfortable in these surroundings.

"Miss Schultz, please state your name and occupation for the record." Joe instructed softly trying to put her at ease.

"Melinda Schultz, Registered Nurse at Memorial County Hospital for 36 years." Melinda stated gaining confidence as she answered the questions.

"On the day Phillip Steffan, the son of Carolyn and Tom Steffan was born, were you working in the obstetrics area?" Joe asked concisely.

"Yes, I was." Melinda answered. She was doing great at only answering the question put before her, just as Joe had instructed her to do.

"It is my understanding that you did not assist with that birth and that is why we did not know about your involvement until now. Is that correct?" Joe asked.

"Yes," Melinda replied.

"Objection, Your Honor, this witness was called as a rebuttal witness not to introduce new evidence." Mr. Drew stated.

"Your Honor, Miss Schultz will verify that Eve Stockwell's testimony was true and accurate as Dr. Jefferson gave conflicting testimony." Joe explained.

"You may proceed counselor but please keep your questions sequestered to that area." Judge Hanson cautioned.

"Yes, Your Honor." Joe acknowledged.

"Miss Schultz, did you see the baby now known as Phillip Steffan alive in the presence of Dr. Jefferson?" Joe asked.

"Yes, I did. I opened the door to the delivery room and saw the baby on the table with the medical equipment used during delivery. Dr. Jefferson was standing over the baby tearing off a piece of medical tape. I saw one of those god-awful boxes they put babies in when they didn't want them to live, sitting next to the baby." Melinda answered strongly, her distain quite evident in her voice.

"Was the baby alive?" Joe asked.

"Yes, it was moving its legs and crying. I could tell it had an injury to its head. Dr. Jefferson was upset that I opened the door. He hurriedly put the tape over the baby's mouth and put it in the box," Melinda's voice broke then as she remembered the sound of the muffled cries after the tape was put over the mouth, a shudder went through her body. "Then he threw a syringe in the box and carried it to the closet himself, pushing me out of the way."

"Thank you, Miss Schultz. No more questions." Joe finished, confident that everyone in the jury now knew who was telling the truth.

Mr. Drew stood up to do his cross-examination, although it seemed as if he was taken aback by this new witness. As a rebuttal witness, she didn't need to be on the witness list prior to the start of the trial.

"Miss Schultz, are you sure it was Dr. Jefferson who was in that delivery room and not another doctor. You are all in scrub uniforms, correct." Mr. Drew asked, deciding to try to leave some level of doubt that he was in fact the doctor in that room.

"It was Dr. Jefferson. His mask was down. His dirty blonde hair was sticking out from the top and he spoke to me. I knew it was definitely him. His voice is very distinctive." Melinda stated adamantly.

"Well, how did you know it was the Steffan baby that was on the table?" Mr. Drew asked, trying a different angle.

"I was just outside the door when they wheeled Carolyn out of the room. She was still sedated, but I knew Carolyn and I recognized her on the gurney. I later heard her baby had died, but I knew what really happened to the baby." Melinda said, now very confident with her answers.

"But you never said anything to Carolyn Steffan or anyone else before now?" Mr. Drew asked.

"No," Melinda said softly looking ashamed. "Telling Carolyn would only have served to hurt her more, nothing could bring her baby back, and I couldn't prove what I saw. As for the other nurses, they knew what went on, but no one could stand up to the doctors. No one until Carolyn that is. She's the reason that no more boxes were sent down to the morgue. I've admired her for years."

Mr. Drew had drawn close to the witness stand and saw Melinda was holding on to what looked like a sheet of paper. He wondered if she was reciting rehearsed answers so he asked what she had in her hands.

"It's a picture of my sister. She's gone now. She was the light of my life and her memory gave me the strength to come forward. I'm holding it to give me strength today." Melinda said with a waiver in her voice. She lifted the picture so Mr. Drew could see, but the jury also saw, a picture of a beautiful, smiling 12 year old, with down syndrome, lovingly holding a kitten.

Mr. Drew was absolutely floored. If Melinda had closed the coffin with her testimony, her sister's beautiful picture had put the nails in it, and Joe had nothing to do with it.

Joe and James looked at each other smiling. They had nothing to do with what just happened, but Melinda was a star witness.

Mr. Drew quickly withdrew to his seat stating, "No more questions."

Judge Hanson dismissed the witness.

The defense rested its case.

Judge Hanson stated closing arguments would be heard tomorrow at 9am. It was possible that this case could wrap up by the weekend.

When the gavel hit, dismissing them, Joe turned toward his parents. For the first time since the trial started, he had forgotten they were there. He realized that this new testimony was difficult for them. They now had independent corroboration that Phillip had lived. They still didn't know how Dr. Jefferson had used the syringe to hasten Phillip's death; did he inject something into his tiny body or just an air embolism. Either way, they were absolutely certain he did something…and Phillip was dead.

Chapter 30

Joe lay awake gingerly holding Anne in the crook of his arm. The closing argument he would be presenting the next morning, running through his thoughts. This was perhaps one of the most pivotal moments in his career, from both a public and private stand-point. Anne wanted to attend, but Joe was adamant she needed to rest. He wanted to keep her as far away as possible from Adam Jefferson. His sneer that morning as he glanced at her empty chair spoke volumes to Joe. He knew Adam had run Anne off the road, but no solid proof had been found so far. So the bastard was free, free to disrupt Joe's thoughts and more importantly free to hurt those Joe loved.

Joe glanced over at the clock on his nightstand. The red letters read 1:13am. Joe leaned back into his pillows. The night was going to drag by slowly he thought to himself running his right hand through his thick black hair. He felt Anne stir next to him and gently pulled the covers up over her shoulders in case she was cold. Her injured arm had slowly drifted low on the pillow so Joe carefully repositioned it and then placed a light kiss on the top of her head. He could smell her light scent in her hair. The only light in the room was provided by the moon through the skylight and the reflection through the windows that faced the bottom of the bed.

The shadow of the outline of the trees in the distance was visible through the windows. He realized he had forgotten to close the blinds. Using care to not wake Anne, Joe slid out of bed and using his metal crutch, made his way to the trio of large windows facing west. Pulling the cord to lower the designer blinds, he caught the glimpse of a black shadow rounding the corner of the house. Joe immediately pulled the blind back up thinking it was a wild animal or maybe just a shadow, but an inner voice told him this was no animal. The form was on two legs and dressed all in black. Someone was on his property. Joe quickly lowered the blinds once again and headed straight for his closet. He had a safe in the back of the long walk in closet lined with suits and shirts. He quickly dialed the combination fumbling once and having to start over. He pulled out a revolver that he kept inside for the past three years at the urging of James. After Anne was run off the road, Joe loaded it as extra protection, prepared for just such an emergency. He knew he physically could never out run an assailant so he had learned to shoot a gun when he was in law school after reading several news stories of lawyers and judges being singled out for revenge by defendants or their family members.

Joe's blood ran cold as he headed past the windows making sure they were securely locked from the inside. He grabbed a key from his night stand and slipped out the bedroom door locking Anne safely inside. He didn't want to wake her, scaring her out of much needed slumber if his conclusion was wrong, but the hair on his neck standing on end told him he wasn't wrong.

Joe headed quietly to the front door to find the deputy on protection duty. Joe slowly opened the front door noting the deputy was not in the chair as he had been when they went to sleep. Joe was trying to decide if he should chance going out to the police cruiser to see if the deputy was inside when a shadow came around the side of the house. Joe's hand was on the light switch and he flipped the light on quickly. Relief flooded his body as the police patch on the deputy's arm came into view.

"Mr. Steffan?" the deputy asked, his hand on his revolver.

"Yes, it's me." Joe said with relief. "I thought I saw the shadow of a man on the west side of the house when I was shutting the blinds a few minutes ago."

"I thought I heard something myself, so I made a perimeter check. I didn't find anything though." The deputy replied, a bit concerned that both of them thought there was something out of the ordinary.

"I made sure the windows were secure in my bedroom," Joe stated.

"I'll make perimeter checks every 15 minutes for the next few hours." The deputy confirmed, trying to put Joe at ease, even though he, himself, was a bit nervous by this exchange.

Joe nodded and retreated back inside. His senses continued to be on heightened alert.

Joe was unlocking the bedroom door when he heard a noise from Eve's room. It sounded like she took another fall. Joe quickly went to the door and knocked before opening. Not wanting to alarm Eve he hid the gun in his robe pocket when opening the door. Her room was dark. Joe reached down to turn on the lamp on her nightstand.

Eve's bed was empty. He scanned the room expecting to see her on the floor, but instead she was standing by the bathroom with a black gloved hand over her mouth. Joe's stomach sank. Eve's eyes were large with obvious fright.

The blinds were making an eerie sound waving in front of an open window. Joe knew immediately why the deputy didn't see anyone. He was already in the house.

The man in black moved Eve closer. By the soft light of the bedside lamp Joe could see a gun to Eve's head. Joe's blood ran cold. Although the intruder wore a black mask and black clothes, Joe knew it had to be Adam.

"What do you want, Adam?" Joe asked calmly keeping his hands in plain sight, but itching to get the gun from his robe pocket.

Joe could see surprise in the eyes looking out from the black mask. The intruder quickly lifted his mask showing the glowering eyes Joe had come to recognize in the court room.

"You were expecting me?" Adam asked.

"I knew it was you who ran Anne off the road." Joe said trying to stay unemotional even though he could feel heat rising in his face from anger.

"I don't know anything about that." Adam sneered. He knew what had happened, but he wasn't going to give the man who had ruined his family any information.

"No need to lie now, Adam. We know you did it and as soon as we have the evidence, you'll be charged. Put the gun down. Don't make matters worse for yourself." Joe stated simply, trying to make sense out of Adam's senseless acts of violence.

"You took everything from me. I was the youngest child of my father. When you arrested him, everything changed in my life. My mother said I had to drop out of the college of my dreams. My whole family went there. Mom said Dad's lawyer's fees were high and if he was found guilty, he may have to go to prison. She's never worked. She doesn't know how to work." Adam said working himself up into a frenzy, his eyes wild with hate. "You took from me everything, and after tomorrow you will take my father as well."

"Adam, no one knows how the trial is going to turn out, but it's not my fault your father did what he did." Joe stated trying to keep his voice calm to see if that would stabilize the situation, but as the moments passed Adam seemed to get more unstable.

He started to move the gun about wildly around Eve's head. He had taken his hand from her mouth, but she remained quiet not wanting to draw attention to herself.

"Adam, why don't you let Eve leave the room. Let's settle this between you and me. Your fight is with me, no one else." Joe stated slowly and distinctly.

"Don't tell me what to do." Adam answered loudly.

Joe could hear the bedroom door open down the hall and prayed that Anne wouldn't follow his voice to her mother's room. He heard soft faint steps down the hall and the front door opening. Relief flooded his features.

Adam could tell something was different. He threw Eve to the floor and Joe lunged forward trying to break her fall but now Adam had two hands on the gun and Joe was forced to freeze. *Shit.* Joe thought, I should have grabbed the gun. He could feel the barrel against his leg.

What was taking the deputy so long? He was probably calling in for back up. Keep him talking, Joe thought. "Adam, where'd you get the black car?" Joe asked. Usually when criminals have already admitted to a crime, they enjoyed putting the pieces together, showing off their intelligence and Adam was no different.

"I don't know what you're talking about." Adam stated coldly. "I didn't do anything to your bitch…yet."

A rustling noise came from outside the window.

"You bastard, she went to get the cops didn't she." Adam said as he was pulling the trigger. At that moment Eve threw her cane up at Adam's arm knocking it towards the ceiling. The shot missed its mark just grazing Joe's shoulder. Anne screamed as she saw Joe reel backwards, drops of blood flying on the hallway wall. Joe knew that Adam would be coming for Anne if he didn't get him first. Joe reached into his robe pocket just as the deputy came through the window. The deputy and Joe both got off a round hitting Adam in the chest. Joe's shot hit the right side of Adam's chest and the deputy's shot was on the left severing the aorta causing massive bleeding. Adam died instantly.

Sirens were coming up the driveway quickly, but Anne sat on the floor holding pressure to Joe's wound. Eve was assisted to the bed by the deputy who grabbed a throw blanket from the end of the bed and laid it over Adam's body. Suddenly everyone came through the door. Guns were quickly holstered as the situation was assessed as under control, the threat neutralized. Joe and Anne were led out to the waiting ambulance where her wad of bloody tissue was replaced by a pressure bandage. Joe fought the idea of going in to the emergency room, but Anne was insistent this time.

The deputy called Carolyn and Tom to come to get Eve who thankfully did not sustain any injuries other than a few bruises and the coroner was called to take away the body of Adam Jefferson.

Joe's wound was cleansed, stitched, and dressed. He was signing the discharge paperwork when James came through the double doors.

"Looks like you'd do anything to get one more day to work on your closing argument." James stated.

"Almost anything." Joe stated laughing.

"I'll give you and Anne a lift home." James said holding open the door.

"I don't think we need a protection detail any longer." Joe stated as they went by the deputy standing at the door.

"Humor me. Dr. Jefferson has three more sons." James stated laughing.

"Something bothers me though," Joe stated trying to make sense of Adam's denial of the car attack. "Adam flatly denied having anything to do with Anne's car accident. Do you think there could be someone else behind that?"

"Well, we'll keep the case file active in case some other evidence presents itself. Meanwhile, how about you two just lay low for a little while, at least until we get this case finished." James stated adamantly.

Chapter 31

Joe was ready for the closing arguments. His shoulder was still sore. He had been told to immobilize it for a week, but he refused to do so while in court. Tom , Carolyn, Cassie, Jacob, Jessica, Anne, and Eve were all in the courtroom today as Joe faced his demon for the last time.

Just before the gavel hit, Dr. Paul came in with two mothers who were each carrying beautiful children with challenges. One mother, nicely dressed in pants and a blouse, held a beautiful little girl with Down Syndrome who wore her hair in pig tails and had on a spring outfit with duckies on the front and black shiny shoes. Her smile lit up the court room and Joe couldn't hold back smiling at her. She smiled back as she held out a rattle toward him. The other mother's child had legs that were braced, but he was a very beautiful little boy with black hair in curls. The little boy reached up to lay a hand on his mother's face giving her a smile. Dr. Paul smiled and waved, giving him a thumbs up for good luck.

After the procedure for calling the court to order and seating the jury, Joe was told to start his closing arguments.

Joe stood up and moved to face the jury box. Anne had carefully picked Joe's dark suit, white shirt, and yellow tie to offset

326 Justice for Baby B

Joe's dark good looks. Joe acknowledged the jury, "Ladies and gentlemen of the jury, it is soon to be your job to decide whether we have presented enough evidence to convict Dr. Jefferson of attempted murder and murder in the first degree. Many of you may be asking 'why now?' He did these acts nearly 30 years ago. Is it really that important to try this case? But I would ask you to think about the families that have lived without their child for the past 29 years. We were able to bring evidence pertaining to one child but many more were left to be buried in unknown graves, no stones to mark their passing."

"What Dr. Jefferson did was wrong, morally and ethically, and he knew it. When a child was born with an imperfection, he took it upon himself to choose which babies he would treat and which mouths he would cover with medical tape and place in a box without so much as wrapping them in a blanket. No one could hear their cries then, but you can answer their cries today. Clayton Jefferson treated them as animals, not as human children. He readily admitted this fact. He may claim he had the parents' best interest in mind and verbal permission, but we know in the case of Phillip Steffan, he did not. In this case, Dr. Jefferson was covering up a mistake and he got away with it for almost 30 years. There is no statute of limitations on murder, ladies and gentlemen, because there is no end to the grief. Carolyn and Tom Steffan never got to hold their son, never got to watch him play ball, and will never hold Phillip's children, their grandchildren, in their arms."

"We had three different nurses give corroborating testimony to Dr. Jefferson's actions. A custodian testified as to how the bodies were ordered to be destroyed by the defendant, but were buried instead. An unmistakable identifying marker, an angel necklace, placed over Phillip Steffan's tiny head, unknowingly, would provide irrefutable identification years later. As for me, the child he attempted to murder, this is the box that was to be my coffin." Joe said holding up the old disheveled box that Carolyn had kept hidden all these years. "This is the tape that had been placed over my mouth to smother my cries. He may have had the parents who birthed me state they agreed with the killing of their disabled child, but that was never their right. Federal law states that when a child takes a breath outside of its mother's body, it is now a separate individual and deserves all the rights of a human being. They may not have supported my right to live, but they had no right to *deny* me the right to live."

"A medical degree does not give anyone the right to decide which baby should die at birth. He had the responsibility as a doctor to do everything in his power to save those children, to save me. He deemed those children unworthy, too expensive, a burden to their parents. Well I ask you, does it appear I am unworthy to live? I am well educated, I have a good career, I pay taxes, I am soon to be a husband and father, and I walk with a limp. Truth be told if each of us had to pass a test on worthiness perhaps there is something about each of us that would make us unworthy in someone's eyes; but we are not supposed to pass a test. We are supposed to be born and put into the arms of our parents and be brought home to live, not in an institution, but in a home with our family. Think of your own children. How much would you sacrifice to see them healthy and happy?"

"It was Dr. Jefferson's job to encourage parents to accept a child with or without disabilities, but he didn't. Instead, he encouraged parents to give him permission to destroy their child if it was born imperfect, to give permission even before it took a breath of air." Joe carefully walked toward the gallery and stood looking at the children of the parents Dr. Paul had contacted to be in court that day. The little girl was smiling and clapping her chubby hands together. When Joe turned suddenly toward the jury, he saw all their eyes on this sweet little girl.

Joe walked over to the evidence table and picked up the angel necklace. "This necklace was found around Phillip Steffan's remains. We know he was born alive. Two nurses independently corroborated the evidence. Dr. Jefferson made a mistake during delivery, a mistake that, rather than taking responsibility, he decided to bury by burying Phillip. That is the problem when we give too much power to an individual. We give them a God complex. We tell them that they are above the law. It's a slippery slope. We as a society made Dr. Jefferson who he is, but now we must send a message to him and to others like him that they will be held accountable for their actions, even if it takes 30 years. Send that message with a guilty verdict."

Joe slowly walked back to the prosecutor's table and sat down, relief flooding over him.

"Mr. Drew, you may begin your closing argument," Judge Hanson directed.

Mr. Drew stood slowly and buttoned his grey pinstriped suitcoat before approaching the juror's box. "Ladies and gentlemen, we are trying a case that should have been tried in the 1960s, if at all. The prosecution brought this case now, based primarily on testimony that could have been presented back in 1969. Why now? This is a different era of time with different moral viewpoints. Back in the 1960s we didn't have the American's with Disabilities Act, nor did parents have resources as they do today, to access assistance and specialists not available in the 1960s to parents with disabled children. Dr. Jefferson did what he thought best at the time and with the resources available then, not now. If the parents of the child he is accused of attempting to murder did not fault him, how can you."

"As for the murder case, you don't have a definitive cause of death for that child so how can you say it was murdered. The case against my client is weak. This is a doctor who has spent his entire medical career helping the people of this community. Do not repay his dedication and hard work with a guilty verdict. Thank you."

Judge Hanson looked back to the prosecution table. They hadn't prepared a rebuttal closing argument, but Joe felt compelled to stand, "Your Honor, we have a rebuttal statement." James looked at Joe wondering what he was going to say.

"Ladies and gentlemen of the jury, the defense would like you to believe that the rules of society have changed in 30 years, but it has been my experience that the rule, 'Thou Shalt Not Kill' has been in effect for the past 1900 plus years and shows no sign of changing. As for the resources available to parents, look at me. I grew up in that era, my parents raised me without special resources, and in several cases my mother was a great advocate not only for me, but for other students needing special considerations in school and in the community. Truth be told, there wouldn't be an 'American's with Disabilities Act' without people like her to advocate for change." Joe looked over at his mother, realizing once again what a special person she was.

"The defense states that my 'parents' agreed with Dr. Jefferson, but I have here a signed termination of parental rights post-dated back to my date of birth signed by Mr. and Mrs. Pilarski." Mr. Drew tried to hide his shocked look. "Since they have no parental rights, I would disagree with the defense, and since I am of age to speak for myself, I state unequivocally that I do not give Dr. Jefferson the right to terminate me."

"And lastly, we may not have a definitive cause of death, but we know that Phillip Steffan's death can be directly attributed to be at the hands of Dr. Jefferson. He made no attempt to save that child and we have two eye witnesses that state he carried the death box to the closet himself shortly after Phillip's birth. As for Dr. Jefferson's career in the medical field I would ask how many good deeds outweigh murder?" Joe asked making eye contact with each juror for the last time before deliberations.

Judge Hanson proceeded to give the jury instruction before they started their deliberation, they solemnly filed out of the room to decide Dr. Jefferson's fate. Judge Hanson's gavel sounded, dismissing the court. The waiting began. It was now 11am. Joe's supportive entourage slowly left the courthouse and headed back to Joe's house. The court clerk would call his pager when the verdict was reached.

Joe packed up his briefcase with James' help and he headed out of the courtroom, briefly stopping in the lobby to acknowledge the reporters camped outside. There would be no statement until the jury returns. Heading to his car in the courthouse garage, he saw Dr. Jefferson's wife sitting in a black SUV. She must feel her world crashing down around her he thought. His car was two down from where she was sitting and he felt a bit uneasy walking by. He heard a window go down.

She called to him, not an angry voice but rather a resigned tone, "Counselor, may I have a word?"

Joe hesitated, then turned, perhaps she needed closure, he felt he owed her that. "I'm late. I'm meeting people." He stated a bit impatiently, trying to expedite his exit.

"I just wanted to say I'm sorry." Mrs. Jefferson said, no longer looking the debutante, town aristocrat.

"Excuse me?" Joe stated, not sure he heard her correctly.

"I'm sorry," she said again louder. "I know what my son did and I'm sorry that he hurt you and your girlfriend."

"My fiancée." Joe corrected.

"Yes, well, I'm glad this will soon all be over." She stated flatly. Her eyes held resignation. She knew that no matter what the verdict, her life as she knew it was over.

"I'm sorry for your loss," Joe said quietly. He meant for the loss of her son, but the narcissistic personality she had, felt the loss much more personally, the loss of status, the loss of wealth… the loss of a son was not her top priority.

"You know, I hated you for disrupting our life," she said emotionless. "You may despise my husband for what he did, but perhaps you should thank him. If he hadn't killed Phillip Steffan, would you really be where you are today? Do you think that Carolyn would have taken you home? She would have had her own son to love. You would have been in the ground in his place, or your birth parents would have hidden you away in some institution. Think about it, you should be thanking my husband." Joe felt like she had thrown ice water in his face. She couldn't have hurt him more if she had hit him with her vehicle. Joe stood stunned by her words while she pulled her vehicle out and drove away, not giving Joe a backward glance.

Joe had to jump back to avoid actually being hit and that's when he saw the silver paint against the black scuffed left front bumper. Up close you could see a nonprofessional had tried to paint over the scuff mark, but the recent paint wasn't adhering well and Joe's briefcase brushing hard against it easily removed the paint. Joe quickly looked at the license plate and jotted it down in his car. Picking up the recently purchased car phone, he dialed James' number.

"This is Joe. Run plates 'NPL 369' and put out a warrant for the vehicle. Mrs. Jefferson is driving it and it has front end damage with silver paint on the left front bumper. She tried to paint over it, but did a sloppy job. Catch her before she tries to cover it up again."

Joe started his car. Her words ran over and over in his head. He knew she was just trying to hurt him, but the nagging question wouldn't leave the back of his mind.

Joe's family had gathered at his house. Carolyn and his sisters had put out food for lunch. His mother tried to give him a plate but he wasn't interested in food at the moment. Anne had already laid down to rest. His family rallied around him congratulating him on a great closing speech and rebuttal. His dad hugged him and told him how proud he was. Joe smiled, but deep inside him was a pit. Was Mrs. Jefferson right?

Joe walked out to the patio area off the solarium alone. It was a cool windy June day, even the sky seemed to take on Joe's overcast demeanor. Joe sat alone with his thoughts until he felt an arm around his shoulders. Without even looking he knew it was his mother.

"What's wrong, Joe?" Carolyn asked.

"Nothing, just thinking." Joe lied.

"Joe, I've been your mother for a lot of years. I know when you aren't telling the truth," Carolyn said with a grim smile on her face. Pulling a patio chair next to him, Carolyn waited for Joe to answer.

"Mom, if Phillip had lived, would I still be your son today?" Joe asked, quietly looking out at the rolling hills thinking about how different his life might have been, or if he'd have had a life at all.

Carolyn was quiet for a moment. This was a defining moment for Joe and she knew it. "Joe, our lives all have a purpose I believe. Some purposes are greater than others and some have more pain and suffering associated with it, but we are all meant to live out that purpose as best we can. I believe that I was never meant to parent Phillip. He was a soul gifted to us, but for a moment and you were given to us to fulfill Phillip's purpose, to give all those murdered souls a voice. When you started this case, I didn't want you to do it. I felt in the end it would hurt you, and as your mother, I never want to see you hurt. Now I feel it was your destiny and in fulfilling that purpose you were able to fulfill Phillip's and eventually you were able to find the happiness with Anne that you so much deserve." Carolyn took Joe's face in her hands and looked into his eyes, "Joe, you were my gift. I was always meant to be your mother, and will always *BE* your mother." Carolyn placed a kiss on Joe's forehead and walked back into the house.

Joe dismissed the words of Mrs. Jefferson. This is where he was meant to be and they are his family. One thing was for certain, he felt sad for Phillip, that he would never know the beautiful family he was born into.

The pager went off at precisely 4:25. Joe's fingers were shaking as he dialed the number to the courthouse.

Joe turned toward the family gathered around, "The judge is reconvening court at 5:00pm. He said he wants this case done today." Joe said with trepidation in his voice.

Driving back into town he worried. What if the jury finds Dr. Jefferson not guilty? This case caused pain and suffering on both sides. His mother would most probably lose her job. His career could be hurt. James's career could be shattered, and most of all, Phillip would have died in vain. Will justice have been served?

James joined him at the prosecution table. Joe's family decided they would wait for him back at the house. Anne was still resting and Eve was exhausted from the morning. Carolyn hugged him as he walked out the door and whispered in his ear, "No matter what happens, I love you and we couldn't be more proud of you. He heard the emotion in her voice and squeezed her just a little harder to let her know he understood.

"What, no entourage?" James asked as they waited for the gavel to sound.

"No, they decided to wait at the house." Joe answered, worry etched on his forehead.

"Don't frown so much." James said trying to lighten the situation, "I have confidence in that great summation and rebuttal you gave. You need to have the same confidence. "James pointed to the empty chair of Mrs. Jefferson. "They caught her just as she was pulling into her garage. She's in custody now. Didn't put up much of a fight. I think she was expecting us. They found the black paint in her garage. House paint, can you believe that!! Her finger prints on the brush."

Joe nodded, grateful that this case was concluding.

Just then the gavel sounded, startling them both.

CHAPTER 32

Joe's Epilogue

Carolyn was putting the finishing touches on Anne's hair. Part of her hair was up and laced with baby roses with the rest trailing down her back. Gramma Jo had made a beautiful tea length ivory dress. Anne nervously waited to walk down the aisle. She gazed out at the backyard. Chairs now faced a rose adorned arched garden trellis. The late July day was beautiful with a light breeze.

Anne and Joe wanted to keep the celebration simple with just close friends and family attending the late afternoon ceremony with a light supper afterwards. The twenty or so people had found their way to their seats in anticipation of the bride's appearance. Joe, James, Tom, and Jacob were in the solarium discussing where would be the perfect place to build the jungle gym.

Jacob smiled slightly and said off-handedly to Tom that he needed to keep the blue prints as they were going to need a second one soon. All the guys exchanged handshakes and claps of congratulations on Jacob's news. Carolyn came around the corner and said they were ready to start any time. Joe offered his arm to Carolyn and escorted her up the small aisle to the playing of the soft trio of a violin, cello, and harp. Joe hugged Carolyn and placed a light kiss on her cheek, whispering, "Thank you" to his mom. It seemed like such a small gesture compared to everything she had done for him. He saw that she wore the necklace he had given to her the night before, a mother's necklace with a heart lined with the birthstones of all four of her children. Carolyn's eyes glistened with tears of happiness.

Joe then turned to Eve, who was already seated in a wheelchair across the aisle, and hugged her as well. He noted that Eve wore the angel necklace he had ordered hand-made for her, a replica of the one she had placed on Phillip. After the trial had concluded and the guilty verdicts read, the necklace had been returned to Eve, but she gave it to Carolyn saying it was a gift to her son, Phillip. Carolyn had placed it in Phillip's coffin right before it was lowered into the ground next to her father in a small graveside ceremony two weeks after Dr. Jefferson was sentenced to 20 years in prison. She later told Joe that the necklace belonged with Phillip, it had been protecting him since birth.

The music changed and all stood waiting for Anne to make her breathtaking appearance. Tom was honored to be asked to walk her down the aisle. Joe watched in happy anticipation as Anne drew closer. Anne's arm had healed and she was the picture of health as she approached her soon to be husband.

Joe repeated the vows they had written without faltering, "Anne, I promise to love and cherish you and our children all the days of my life. Thank you for choosing me as your husband. You bring out the best in me." Joe concluded by kissing Anne's hand.

Anne was overcome by emotion. This was the man she had always hoped that she would find. "Joe, I promise to love and cherish you and our children all the days of my life. Thank you for coming into my life and giving me purpose. You bring out the best in me." Anne reached over and kissed Joe's cheek.

They exchanged rings, and as they turned toward their guests, the pastor declared, "For the first time, Mr. and Mrs. Joseph Steffan."

It had been a magical day. The honeymoon had been postponed as Eve's health was deteriorating quickly and within eight weeks she was gone. Although expected, Eve's death was difficult for Anne, losing her one remaining parent opened a void in her world. She had hoped that her mother would have been able to see her first grandchild.

Anne remembered the night she had to say good bye. Joe had stayed by Eve's side most of the night so Anne could sleep. Around 4am Anne was drawn to Eve's room and saw her mother watching her in the low light. As she sat next to her on the bed Eve placed a hand over Anne's growing abdomen and felt the baby move. "She's strong, she will be beautiful like her parents." Eve then closed her eyes and drifted off to eternal sleep with a serene smile on her face. Eve, with Joe's help, had been able to address the regrets of her life and now felt free of her demons.

Anne and Joe didn't know the sex of the child. When they came into the hospital, Anne was already in very active labor. Joe wouldn't leave her side throughout the delivery.

Anne's forehead was perspiring from the work of bringing their child into this world. Dr. Allen was calmly in charge giving orders to the nurses and directing Anne when to push. Joe wasn't listening to any of it. His focus was all on Anne. He suddenly heard Dr. Allen tell Anne that she had to stop. The cord was around the baby's neck. It was as if ice water had been put in Joe's veins. Something was wrong. Anne saw the wild look in Joe's eyes and calmly touched his face.

"Joe, look at me." Anne said. "Joe look at me." The second time louder and more forceful. "It's going to be fine."

Then Dr. Allen directed, "One more big push and we'll have a baby."

Anne bore down with all the strength she had left.

Dr. Allen held up a very messy little baby that was already crying. "You have a very loud daughter, Joe and Anne." Dr. Allen placed their daughter on Anne's stomach while a nurse was wiping her off. Joe and Anne were both crying.

"She's okay, doctor?" Joe asked.

"She's perfect, Joe." Dr. Allen said with glistening eyes. Dr. Allen was usually all business and very professional, the top in her field, but this couple was very special to her.

Dr. Allen was busy finishing the delivery and directing Anne to push to deliver the placenta. A nurse wrapped the baby in a pink blanket and placed her in her daddy's arm. Joe was overcome by happiness as he proudly carried their daughter to Anne. "She is perfect, Joe." Anne said counting fingers and toes.

Joe lifted up the blanket to look at her back. "It's perfect," he said running his finger down her spinal column, fighting back tears. Even though the ultrasounds had all shown the baby's spinal column to be intact, he still had a fear that their child would be born with his disability. He would love their child no matter the challenges presented, but he wanted their child to be able to run and play and do everything that he wished he could do.

Dr. Allen finished stitching Anne and reached for the baby wanting to check her out. "Have you finished picking out a name for this little beauty?" Dr. Allen asked as she listened to the baby's heart and the nurses measured the baby's vital statistics.

Joe and Anne looked at each other and as tears formed in Anne's eyes, Joe took her hand, "Evelyn, after both of our mothers." Anne said, a tear trickling down her face. Joe squeezed her hand, knowing she wished Eve was here to share in her joy.

Her mother would not be here to see Evelyn grow up but she had a special gift for her granddaughter. Joe reached into his pocket and handed Anne a small package. She looked at Joe with questioning eyes.

"It's a gift from your mother." Joe said.

Anne opened the box to find the replica angel necklace Joe had given Eve. A note scribbled in her mother's handwriting read, 'For my grandchild. I'll be watching from above, love you, Gramma Eve.' Tears flooded down Anne's face as she clutched the necklace and Joe.

Carolyn and Tom came rushing into the room as soon as the nurses gave the all clear, followed closely by Jessica, Brian, Cassie, and Jacob.

Carolyn couldn't wait to hold her first grandchild. As she beamed with delight they asked in unison, "What's her name?"

Joe answered, "Evelyn after both of her amazing grandmothers." Carolyn was speechless as she looked into the little face of perfection.

Carolyn noticed a gold chain around Evelyn's neck and saw the guardian angel on top of the pink blanket. "Both your grammas love you little one, and one of them is your angel."

Carolyn's Epilogue

Carolyn wiped her forehead with her sleeve, leaving a dirt smudge on her cheek as she noticed the blue sky, all clear except for a small white cloud passing by. It had been four years since they re-buried Phillip in this quiet corner of the cemetery next to her father. Every spring since then Carolyn came out here to plant flowers on both of their graves. These were quiet moments of meditation as her hands met the earth of the graves that held two of her loved ones. Reflections of the past year of memories rambled in her mind.

Jessica was now a doctor, doing her pediatric residency with Dr. Paul as her mentor. A man who has always had Carolyn's respect, even more so now as she worked side by side with him doing research projects on disabling diseases of children. Carolyn made a mental note that she needed to finish the last-minute touches to Jessica's wedding gown tonight before she and Brian came for the weekend.

Cassie and Jacob were expecting their second child any day. They had miscarried their first child in the fourth month. Cassie had been heartbroken, but her strong family ties had helped her through the mourning. Carolyn knew only too well the grief Cassie would carry with her.

Carolyn's wistful reminiscence was interrupted by the sounds of a child's laughter in the distance moving towards her. She recognized the voice of her oldest grandchild. Standing to greet them she saw Joe coming hand in hand with the little fire-ball. Evelyn carried a stuffed teddy bear in one hand and gripped her daddy's hand tightly with the other. Carolyn couldn't help but smile at the antics of her grand-daughter when she caught sight of Carolyn waiting patiently in the distance. She heard the delighted high squeal, "Gramma!" Joe let go of her hand so she could run quickly into Carolyn's waiting arms.

Joe smiled approaching the grave of his brother, leaning down to embrace two of the loves of his life. "Hi, Mom. Dad said you'd be here. Nice flowers." Joe acknowledged as he knelt down to look at the angel on the gravestone.

"Here, Gramma. This is for baby Phillip." Evelyn said handing the bear to Carolyn.

"Now isn't that sweet of you." Carolyn answered giving her grand-daughter a kiss on the forehead. "Why don't you put it up by the angel, honey." She said setting Evelyn on the ground next to Joe.

They watched as Evelyn went up to the headstone and sat the bear down next to the angel etched into the marble. Her tiny fingers proceeded to trace the angel figure.

Her tiny voice asked innocently, "Baby Phillip's our angel baby isn't he Gramma?"

"Yes, darling, he is." Carolyn answered as she knelt down next to the grave so Evelyn could climb into her lap.

"Daddy, look, Gramma planted pretty flowers." Evelyn said pointing with her chubby fingers.

"Yes, love, she did. Do you want to smell?" Joe asked, helping Evelyn reach the flowers.

Evelyn came back to Carolyn's lap and unceremoniously sat down. Her chubby hands reaching for her gramma's cheeks. "Gramma, Daddy said you are angel baby's mommy, too."

"Yes, honey I am. I'm also your daddy's mommy, and Aunt Jessica's, and Aunt Cassie's."

"Gramma, do you love all of them?" Evelyn asked somberly. Her little blue eyes innocently searched for answers that all children wonder.

"Yes, I love them all very much! I also love you very much, my very precious grandbaby!" Carolyn said with a squeeze.

"How are you?" Joe asked, always concerned that these cemetery visits would upset her.

"I'm good," Carolyn answered with a soft smile as Evelyn ran in circles trying to catch a butterfly. "It's peaceful out here. I'm alone with my thoughts. But don't worry, they are good thoughts." She said taking Joe's hand.

"Anne asked me to extend an invitation to have supper with us tonight." Joe said with the hint of a smile. "We have some news for you and Dad. I've already invited Dad. He'll pick up Gramma Jo and head over after work."

Carolyn smiled, already surmising correctly the news was a new sibling for Evelyn. "I'll be there with bells on!" Carolyn said standing up and twirling Evelyn until she ended up on her hip.

"I'll carry the spade and planting supplies back to the car for you." Joe offered, gathering the planting tools. "Looks like you have your hands full."

"Yes, they are, full of bunches of love." Carolyn said giving Evelyn a big hug as she headed back to the car.

They walked in solitude, only the voice of an excited child breaking the silence.

Carolyn watched as Joe lifted Evelyn, placing her in her car seat with a quick kiss on her head. Joe was a wonderful dad. Carolyn knew he would be.

When Joe turned toward his mom, she embraced him tightly, "Joe, I'm so proud of the man you've become."

"I am who I am because of you, Mom. Thank you for giving me the chance to live." Joe answered solemnly, now fully comprehending the depth of truth in that statement. Looking out over the graves covering the rolling acre, he realized his fate had it not been for the actions of this woman. "I owe you my life."

BOOK CLUB DISCUSSION GUIDE

A little background on how this story formulated in my mind. My mother was also a nurse (for over 50 years of her life!) and in the 1960s she did witness the horror of the actual delivery scene portrayed in this novel. Unfortunately, that baby did not live, but she never forgot it and I think it haunted her until her death. Toward the end of her life she talked in greater detail about that incident and even told me the disability was spina bifida which is why my main character was given that disability. The last time we spoke about what she had witnessed I felt goose bumps on my arms and something inside of me told me this was a story that needed to be told. The questions that haunted me were, what if the baby had lived? What life could he have had? We will never know.

When talking about my novel I share what my mother witnessed and most are stunned to learn that this was accepted medical practice in our country in the not so distant past. This reinforced my need to continue to move forward with the telling of this story. So, while this story and its characters are fiction, the premise of the story did happen to not one baby, but many babies. The protections offered with the Americans with Disabilities Act were not available before 1974.

Questions to generate discussion:

1. What were your first impressions from the book? Did the story hook you immediately or did it take a while?
2. Do you think the book was plot-based or character driven?
3. Who was your favorite female character? Why?
4. What was your favorite passage or chapter?
5. What themes played out in the novel?
6. Do you feel Carolyn should have been punished for the kidnapping?
7. If Phillip had lived do you think Joe would have died?
8. Did your opinion of any of the characters change as the story evolved?
9. Which character did you relate to the most?
10. Did you like the ending? What did you like most? What did you like least?
11. If this novel were made into a movie who would you like to see play the roles?

If you would like to include the author in your book club discussion either in person or by Zoom, or have written questions you would like me to address via email contact me at merrileakylloauthor@gmail.com.

You can also check out the author's website at merrileakylloauthor.com.